Praise for #1 *New York Times* bestselling author Debbie Macomber

"[Debbie] Macomber is known for her honest portrayals of ordinary women in small-town America. [She is] an icon of the genre."
—*Publishers Weekly*

"Macomber is one of the most reliable, versatile romance authors around. Whether she's writing light-hearted romps or more serious relationship books, her novels are always engaging stories that accurately capture the foibles of real-life men and women with warmth and humor."
—*Milwaukee Journal Sentinel*

"Debbie Macomber shows why she is one of the most powerful, highly regarded authors on the stage today."
—*Midwest Book Review*

Praise for *New York Times* bestselling author Tanya Michaels

"[Tanya] Michaels' characters are wonderful and really reach out to the reader from the first page to the last."
—*RT Book Reviews* on *Rescued by a Ranger*

"Michaels makes it easy to sympathize with both the hero and the heroine in this fantastic book…. It's truly enjoyable to watch their relationship develop and love win the day once again."
—*RT Book Reviews* on *Her Secret, His Baby*

DEBBIE MACOMBER

is a number one *New York Times* and *USA TODAY* bestselling author. Her books include *1225 Christmas Tree Lane, 1105 Yakima Street, A Turn in the Road, Hannah's List* and *Debbie Macomber's Christmas Cookbook*, as well as *Twenty Wishes, Summer on Blossom Street* and *Call Me Mrs. Miracle*. She has become a leading voice in women's fiction worldwide and her work has appeared on every major bestseller list, including those of the *New York Times, USA TODAY, Publishers Weekly* and *Entertainment Weekly*. She is a multiple award winner, and won the 2005 Quill Award for Best Romance. There are more than one hundred million copies of her books in print. Two of her Harlequin MIRA Christmas titles have been made into Hallmark Channel Original Movies, and the Hallmark Channel has launched a series based on her bestselling Cedar Cove stories.

For more information on Debbie and her books, visit her website, www.debbiemacomber.com.

TANYA MICHAELS

New York Times bestselling author and three-time RITA® Award nominee Tanya Michaels writes about what she knows—community, family and lasting love! Her books, praised for their poignancy and humor, have received honors such as a Booksellers' Best Bet Award, a Maggie Award of Excellence and multiple readers' choice awards. She was also a 2010 *RT Book Reviews* nominee for Career Achievement in Category Romance. Tanya is an active member of Romance Writers of America and a frequent public speaker, presenting workshops to educate and encourage aspiring writers. She lives outside Atlanta with her very supportive husband, two highly imaginative children and a household of quirky pets, including a cat who thinks she's a dog and a bichon frise who thinks she's the center of the universe.

Visit her website for more information on Tanya and her books: www.tanyamichaels.net.

#1 *New York Times* Bestselling Author

DEBBIE MACOMBER

Ready for Romance

HARLEQUIN® BESTSELLING AUTHOR COLLECTION

Recycling programs
for this product may
not exist in your area.

ISBN-13: 978-0-373-18086-8

READY FOR ROMANCE
Copyright © 2014 by Harlequin Books S.A.

The publisher acknowledges the copyright
holders of the individual works as follows:

READY FOR ROMANCE
Copyright © 1993 by Debbie Macomber

MOTHER TO BE
Copyright © 2009 by Tanya Michna

Printed in U.S.A.

CONTENTS

READY FOR ROMANCE 7
Debbie Macomber

MOTHER TO BE 205
Tanya Michaels

Dear Friends,

A universal question for writers is "Where do you get your story ideas?" The answer is as varied as the stories themselves. Some of my ideas have been inspired by old movies. Who *wouldn't* fall in love with heroes like Humphrey Bogart? Other than *The African Queen,* my favorite Bogart movie is *Sabrina,* starring Bogart, Audrey Hepburn and William Holden. (The film was remade some years back with Harrison Ford in the Bogart role.) Not only did Humphrey Bogart inspire two books—*Ready for Romance* and *Ready for Love*—but we named our dog Bogie after him!

I loved the idea of two brothers—one of them dedicated to his career while life passes him by. A man so completely out of balance that he wouldn't recognize love if it stared him in the face. Meet Damian Dryden in *Ready for Romance,* my version of the Humphrey Bogart character. It takes a woman falling in love with his *brother* to wake him up to what's really important in life.

Then there's his brother, Evan—who got his own story in a later book, *Ready for Marriage.*

Just think, a bowl of popcorn and a rented DVD of a fifty-year-old movie (fifty at the time, anyway!) inspired me to write two books. Not a bad way to spend a Friday night, is it? One night soon, when you're "ready for romance," curl up with a bowl of popcorn and this book. Enjoy both stories—*Ready for Romance* and *Mother To Be* by the talented Tanya Michaels.

I love to hear from readers. You can reach me through my website, www.debbiemacomber.com, or through Facebook. You can also write me at: P.O. Box 1458, Port Orchard, WA 98366.

Debbie Macomber

READY FOR ROMANCE
Debbie Macomber

Judy Habner for her kind and generous heart

Prologue

Jessica Kellerman looked both ways, then slipped around the corner of the Dryden four-car garage. She flattened her body against the wall and moved cautiously, one infinitesimal step at a time. It was vital no one see her.

Evan's vehicle, a fancy sports car, was parked just outside the garage—and in direct view of the house. She needed to be quick.

Squatting down by the side mirror, she withdrew a bright red tube of lipstick from her pocket, opened it and heavily outlined her lips. Taking a soft white rag from the pocket of her jeans, she wiped his mirror clean and then kissed it several times. The imprint of her mouth was left in bold red.

Jessica sighed with satisfaction as she carefully

opened the door on the driver's side and crawled into the front seat. The mirror over the dash was next. Her heart was pounding hard and fast, but it wasn't entirely due to her fear of being discovered. Her heart rate tended to accelerate whenever she thought about Evan.

There wasn't a man in all of Boston who could compete with Evan Dryden. To think she'd lived next door to him all these years and hadn't noticed until recently what a gorgeous hunk he was! As far as Jessica was concerned, he was the handsomest man in the universe.

She remembered the exact moment she had realized her destiny. She hadn't been the same since. The Dryden estate, Whispering Willows, was next to her own family's, and she'd often spent time in the huge oak tree spying on the two brothers. Damian was in law school now and Evan in college. Being an only child, Jessica was left to invent her own amusement, and spying on the Dryden brothers had always been great fun.

Jessica had been sitting in the tree one day when Evan had walked to the pond and stood on the footbridge tossing rocks into the water. His back was to her and she held her breath, wondering if he'd seen her hiding in the thick foliage.

She must have made a sound, because he turned abruptly and stared into the tree.

"Jessica?"

She didn't dare move or even breathe.

He stared upward and the sun cut across his shoulder, highlighting his handsome features. It was then that she realized Evan wasn't just an ordinary boy. He was an Adonis. Perfect in every way.

After that she started having dreams about him. Wonderful dreams about him falling in love with her. Dreams about them marrying and having a family. It seemed so...so right. It came to her about a week later that fate had thrown them together. They were meant for each other. The only problem was that Evan had yet to make this discovery for himself.

Jessica had recently turned fourteen and Evan was much older. Six whole years, but it might have been a hundred for all the notice he gave her.

That was when Jessica decided she had to take matters into her own hands. She was a woman of the world, and when a woman knew what she wanted, she went after it. It, in this case, was Evan Dryden.

Jessica soon discovered she wasn't nearly as dauntless as she would have liked. She must have phoned him ten times or more, and each time he answered, she lacked the courage to so much as speak, much less tell him about her undying love. Each call had ended with her replacing the receiver and stewing in frustration.

She'd always been better at expressing herself with the written word, so she'd taken to writing him love notes, pouring out her devotion. She let her best friend read one such note, and the girl claimed it was the most beautiful love letter she'd ever seen. Unfortunately, Jessica hadn't found the courage to sign her name.

This latest trick, planting kisses on his rearview mirror, was sure to accomplish what nothing else had. He'd know it was Jessica and he'd finally come for her, and together they'd ride into the sunset in his sports car.

Outlining her lips with a fresh coat of brilliant red, Jessica was about to kiss the interior mirror when the car door was flung open.

"So it *is* you."

Her heart sank all the way to her knees. Slowly she looked over and her eyes connected with Damian Dryden's. He was taller than his younger brother, dark and handsome in his own way. She was certain the day would come when some girl would feel as strongly about him as she did about Evan.

"Hello," she said, pretending it wasn't the least bit out of the ordinary for her to be sitting in his brother's car kissing the mirrors.

"You're the one, I bet, who's been phoning at all hours of the night."

"I've never called past ten," she denied heatedly, then realized her mistake. It probably would have been best to pretend she didn't know what he was talking about.

"The notes on Evan's windshield have been from you, too, haven't they?"

She could have denied that, but it wouldn't have done any good. Feeling trapped in Evan's car, she swung her legs around and gingerly climbed out. "Are you going to tell him it was me?"

"I don't know," Damian said thoughtfully. "How old are you now?"

"Fourteen," she said proudly. "I know Evan's older, but I was hoping he'd be willing to wait for me to grow up so we could get married."

"Married!"

Damian made the word sound ludicrous and Jessica bristled. "Just wait until you fall in love," she challenged. "Then you'll know."

"You aren't in love with Evan," he said gently. "You're too young to know about things like that. You're infatuated with him because he's older and—"

"I most certainly do love Evan," she flared, stuffing the lipstick tube in her pocket. She wasn't about to stand there and let him ridicule her. She might only be fourteen, but she had the heart of a mature woman and she'd made her decision. Someday she would marry Evan Dryden, and nothing Damian could say or do would stand in her way.

"I'm sure my brother's flattered by your devotion."

"He should be. The man who marries me will see himself as the luckiest man in the world." Her words were fed by pure bravado.

Damian laughed.

Jessica had been willing to overlook his earlier statements, but this was unforgivable. Hands braced against her hips, she glared at him with all the indignation she could muster, which at the moment was considerable.

"You might be older than Evan, but you don't know a thing about love, do you?"

Her question appeared to amuse him, and that only served to irritate her further.

"When a woman makes up her mind about a man, nothing can change the way she feels. I've decided to marry your brother, and not a thing you say or do will have the least effect, so save your breath. Evan is my destiny."

"You're sure about this?"

At least he had the courtesy to wipe the grin off his face.

"Of course," she said confidently. "Mark my words, Damian Dryden. Time will prove me right."

"Does my brother have a say in this?"

"Naturally."

"What if he decides to marry someone else?"

"I...I don't know." Damian had zeroed in on her worst fear—that Evan would get married before she had a chance to prove herself.

"There's something else you haven't considered," Damian said.

"What's that?"

He grinned. "I just might want to marry you myself."

Chapter 1

Jessica Kellerman's time of reckoning had arrived. For the first time in eight years she was about to face the Dryden brothers. Evan didn't concern her. She suspected he wouldn't even remember what a nuisance she'd made of herself. Then again, he just might. But Damian was the brother who worried her most. He was the one who'd caught her red-handed. He was the one who'd mocked her and suggested her devotion to his brother was a passing fancy. Now she was forced to face him and admit he'd been right. She sincerely hoped Damian would have the good grace not to drag up the past.

Swallowing her dread, Jessica walked into the high-rise office building in the most prestigious part of downtown Boston. The building was new, with a glistening black-mirrored exterior that towered thirty stories above the ground. The Dryden law firm was one of the most distinguished in town, and in Boston that was saying something.

Jessica's footsteps made tapping sounds against the marble floor in the lobby. Although she'd been in this part of town often—the university wasn't far from the business section—this was the first time she'd been inside the impressive building.

She was nervous, and rightly so. The last time she'd spent any time with either of the Dryden brothers she'd been caught kissing rearview mirrors.

Looking back, she knew she'd been a constant source of amusement to the brothers and their respective sets of parents, as well. Young love, however, refused to be denied. Risking her family's censure, Jessica had diligently sought Evan's heart all through high school. It wasn't until Benny Wilcox asked her to the graduation dance that she'd realized there were other fish in the sea. Sweet, attentive, good-looking ones, too. Yes, Evan had been the man of her dreams, the one who'd awakened her to womanhood. She held her love for him in a special place in her heart, but was more than willing to forget the way she'd embarrassed herself over him, praying he did, too.

Although Jessica had let her infatuation with Evan die gracefully, neither set of parents had. Particularly, Lois and Walter Dryden. They thought the way Jessica felt about Evan was "cute," and they mentioned it every now and again, renewing her embarrassment.

When Walter Dryden heard that Jessica had recently graduated from business college with a certificate as a legal assistant, he'd insisted she apply with the family firm. In the beginning Jessica had balked, but jobs were few and far between just then, and after a fruitless search on her own, she'd decided to swallow her pride and face the two brothers.

She was warmly greeted by the receptionist, who gave her a wide smile. Jessica smiled back, hoping she looked composed and mature. "I have an appointment with Damian Dryden," she said.

The woman, who appeared to be in her early thirties, with large blue eyes and a smooth complexion, glanced at the appointment book. "Ms. Kellerman?"

"That's right."

"Please have a seat and I'll let Mr. Dryden know you're here."

"Thank you." Jessica sat in one of the richly upholstered chairs and reached for a *People* magazine. She'd dressed carefully for this interview, choosing a soft dove gray suit with a double-breasted jacket. The silver-dollar-size buttons were made from mother-of-pearl with flashes of deep blue and white. She wore high heels, hoping to seem not only professional, but sophisticated. Her glossy brown hair was sophisticated, too, cut in a flattering pageboy. She'd grown up, and it was important Damian know that.

Jessica hadn't even scanned the magazine's contents page when the elder Dryden brother appeared. She'd seen Damian often, from a distance, but this was the first time they'd spoken in months, possibly years. She'd forgotten how tall he was, with broad shoulders that tapered to slim hips. She remembered how much he enjoyed football as a teenager, and how good he was at tackling the opponent. From what she remembered about Damian, he preferred to tackle problems head-on, too. She knew him to be aggressive, hardworking and ambitious. He'd taken over the leadership of the law firm upon Walter Dryden's retirement three years earlier, and the firm, which specialized in corporate law, had thrived under his leadership.

"Hello, Jessica. It's good to see you again," Damian said, stepping forward.

"It's good to see you, too." She stood and offered him her hand.

He clasped it with both of his own. He wasn't an especially large man, and at five-eight she wasn't especially small, but her hand was dwarfed in his. His grip was solid and strong, like the man himself.

"I've come to talk to you about a position as a legal assistant," she said. The direct approach would work best with Damian, she felt.

"Great. Let's go to my office, shall we?"

She was struck by the rugged timbre of his voice. It exuded confidence, sounding deep and firm. Little wonder Damian was one of the most sought-after corporate attorneys in Boston.

He motioned her to be seated, then walked around behind the deep mahogany desk and claimed the black leather chair. He tilted it back slightly, conveying ease and relaxation.

Jessica wasn't fooled. She sincerely doubted that

Damian knew how to relax. His mother, Lois, had often voiced her concern about her elder son, complaining that Damian worked too many hours.

"Thank you for seeing me on such short notice," Jessica said, crossing her legs.

"It's my pleasure." He rolled a pen between his palms. "I understand you recently graduated from college."

She nodded. "I have a degree in early American history."

The motion of the pen between his palms froze and a frown creased his brow. "Unfortunately we don't have much call for historians here at the firm."

"I realize that," she said quickly. "About halfway through my senior year, I realized that although I love history, I wasn't exactly sure what I planned to do with my degree. I toyed with the idea of teaching, then changed my mind."

"And you want to be a legal assistant now?"

"Yes. I was dating a law student and I discovered how much I enjoyed law. You see, we often did our homework together. But rather than register for law school and invest all that time and effort, I decided to work as a legal assistant—sort of get my feet wet and then decide if becoming an attorney is what I want to do. So I went to business college and got a certificate." She said all this in an eager rush. "Your father suggested I come and talk to you," she added, winding down. She opened her purse and produced her certificate for his inspection.

"I see." The pen was in motion again.

"I'm a hard worker."

Damian smiled fleetingly. "I don't doubt that."

"I'll work any hours you wish, even weekends. You can put me on probation if you want." She hadn't meant to reveal how much she wanted the position, but despite her resolve, she couldn't keep the anxiety out of her voice.

"This job means a great deal to you, doesn't it?"

Jessica nodded.

"I think," Damian said casually, "you're still infatuated with my brother."

He spoke as if it had been only a few days since she'd all but thrown herself at Evan. Heat radiated from her cheeks. "I…I don't believe that's a fair statement."

Damian smiled shrewdly. "You've had a crush on Evan for years."

"Perhaps, but that has nothing to do with my applying for a position here." She closed her mouth and collected her composure as best she could. She should have known Damian wouldn't conveniently forget their encounter all those years ago.

"It's true, though, isn't it?" Damian seemed to take delight in teasing her, which infuriated Jessica. She clamped her mouth shut, rather than argue with the man she hoped would employ her. "I was there the day you put kisses all over his rearview mirror, remember?"

Not trusting herself to speak, she nodded.

"I watched you look at him with those big worshipful eyes. I've seen plenty of other women do the same thing since, all gazing at my younger brother as though he were an Adonis."

Jessica's eyes widened at the use of the term. That was exactly the way she'd viewed Evan. A Greek god.

"It's true isn't it, or are you going to deny it?"

Jessica's mouth refused to work. She opened and closed it a number of embarrassing times, not knowing how to respond, or if she should even try.

Cathy Hudson, her best friend, had claimed it wasn't a good idea to apply for work with a family who knew her so well. Jessica was about to concede that Cath was right.

"I did have a schoolgirl crush on your brother at one time," she confessed, "but that was years ago. I haven't seen Evan in...heavens, I don't remember. Certainly not any more often than I've seen you. If you believe my past feelings for Evan would hinder my performance as a legal assistant, then there isn't anything more I can say—other than to thank you for your time."

Damian's smile was slightly off-kilter, his eyes bemused as if, despite himself, he'd admired her little speech. Slowly a look of sadness crossed his face. "Evan's changed, you know. He isn't the man you once knew."

"I'd heard from my mother that he's been unhappy recently." She didn't know the details and hoped Damian would fill in the blanks.

"Do you know why?"

"No."

Damian gave a soft regretful sigh. "I might as well

tell you, since you'll find out soon enough yourself. He was in love possibly for the first time in his life, and it didn't work out. I don't know what caused the rift, and neither does anyone else, not that it matters. Unfortunately, though, Evan can't seem to snap out of his depression."

"He must have loved her very much," she whispered, watching Damian. He was genuinely concerned about Evan.

"I'm sure he did." Damian frowned, apparently at a loss as to how to help his brother, then shook his head. "We've ventured far from the subject of your employment, haven't we?"

She straightened and folded her hands in her lap, wondering if Damian would take a chance and hire her. She was a risk, too, fresh out of school, with no job experience.

"You're sure you want to work here?" he asked, studying her with a discerning eye.

"Very much."

Damian didn't immediately respond. His silence made her uncomfortable enough to want to fill it with something, even useless chatter. "I know what you're thinking," she said breathlessly. "In your eyes I'm a love-struck fourteen-year-old, convinced your brother and I are meant for each other." She shook her head. "I don't know what to say to convince you I've grown up, and that nonsense is all behind me, but I have."

"I can see that for myself." A glint of appreciation sparked in his eyes. "As it happens, Jessica, you're in luck, because the firm could use another legal assistant. If you want the job, it's yours."

Jessica resisted vaulting out of the chair and throwing her arms around Damian's neck to thank him. Instead she promised, "I won't let you down."

"You'll be working directly with Evan," he replied, still studying her closely.

"With Evan?"

"Is that a problem?"

"No... No, of course not."

"Just remember one thing. It doesn't matter how many years our parents have been friends. If you don't do your job and do it well, we don't have room for you here."

"I wouldn't expect you to keep me on if I didn't pull my weight," she said, trying hard not to sound defensive.

"Good." He reached for the intercom and glanced at her. "When would you like to start?"

"Now, if you want."

"Perfect. I'll ring Mrs. Sterling. She's Evan's secretary, and she'll show you the ropes."

Jessica stood and extended her hand. "You won't be sorry, I promise you." She pumped his hand enthusiastically until she realized she was overdoing it.

Grinning, Damian walked around to the front of his desk. "If there's anything I can help you with, let me know."

"I will. Thank you, Damian."

She hadn't meant to call him by his first name. Theirs was a professional relationship now, but it *was* difficult to think of him as her boss. A personal bond existed between them, but until this interview Jessica hadn't realized it was there. To her surprise she found she had no such problem regarding Evan.

She and Damian walked out of the office together and down the corridor to a door with Evan's name engraved on a gold plaque.

Damian opened the door for her and allowed her to precede him. Jessica's gaze fell on Evan's secretary. The woman was middle-aged, with sharp, but not unattractive, features. She seemed to breathe efficiency. One look and Jessica was confident this woman could manage Evan's office and the entire law firm if necessary.

"Mrs. Sterling," Damian said, "this is Jessica Kellerman, Evan's new legal assistant. Would you show her around and make her feel at home?"

"Of course."

Damian turned to Jessica. "As I said earlier, come to me if you have any problems."

"Thank you."

"No, Jessica," he said cryptically on his way out, "thank *you*." The door made a small clicking sound as it shut.

Mrs. Sterling rose from her chair. She was a small woman, barely five feet, a stark contrast to tall and slender Jessica. Her salt-and-pepper hair was cropped short, and she wore a no-nonsense straight skirt and light sweater.

"I'll show you where the law library is," Mrs. Sterling said. Jessica glanced toward the closed door, wondering if Evan was in. Apparently not, otherwise Damian would have made a point of letting his brother know Jessica would be working for him.

The secretary led the way out of the office and down the hall. The library was huge, with row upon row of thick dusty volumes. Long narrow tables with a number of chairs were scattered about the room. Jessica knew she'd be spending the majority of her research time here and was pleased by how pleasant it was. She noticed the faint scent of lemon oil and smiled as she saw various types of potted plants set here and there, including a speckled broad-leaved ivy that stretched across the top of one large bookcase.

"This is very nice."

"Mr. Dryden has worked hard to make sure our work environment is pleasing to the eye," the woman remarked primly.

"Damian's like that," Jessica murmured.

"I was speaking about the younger Mr. Dryden," came the surprised response.

"Oh, of course," Jessica said quickly.

By the end of the first day, Jessica felt as though she'd put in a forty-hour week. She'd been assigned a small desk in the corner of the room and her own phone. Mrs. Sterling seemed to feel it was her duty to keep Jessica occupied with a multitude of tasks which included taking lunch orders, organizing file cabinets and hand-delivering messages throughout the office.

Just when she was about to think she wouldn't even lay eyes on Evan her first day, he breezed into the office, stopping abruptly when he saw her. He was as tall as Damian, at least six-two, with chestnut hair and dark soulful eyes. To Jessica's way of thinking, it wasn't fair that any one man should be so breathtakingly handsome.

"Julia," he whispered, as though he'd stumbled upon a treasure chest. His eyes suffused with delight. "What are you doing here?"

"It's Jessica," she corrected him, refusing to be offended by his failure to remember her name. "I'm here because I'm working for you now."

"Your brother hired Ms. Kellerman as your new legal assistant," Mrs. Sterling explained.

Evan stepped forward, gripping Jessica's hand in his own. "This must be Christmas in July! Why else would Damian present me with such a rare gift?"

"Christmas in July," Jessica repeated, having a difficult time not laughing. What she'd heard about Evan was true, she decided. He was a flirt, but such a pleasant lighthearted one that it didn't seem to matter. She knew he wasn't serious.

"There are several matters here that need your attention," Mrs. Sterling said stiffly from behind Evan.

"I'll be with you in a few minutes," he said.

"I know you will," Mrs. Sterling said. "Just don't leave before these letters are signed, and while we're at it, there are a few items we need to discuss—when you have the time."

"I promise to get to the letters first thing," he said as if he had no interest beyond studying the young woman who stood before him. "Just put everything on my desk and I'll look through it before I leave."

"You won't forget?"

Evan chuckled. "My, my, how you love to mother me."

"Someone has to look after you," his secretary said, her eyes crinkling above a bright smile.

Jessica watched in amazement as Evan charmed the older woman. Mrs. Sterling had been the picture of cool efficiency until Evan walked in the door. The minute he did she turned into a clucking mother hen. Before Jessica had a chance to analyze this reaction, Evan grinned. "You love me, Mary, and you know it."

"It's just that you've been a bit forgetful of late," Mrs. Sterling said with a concerned frown. She reached for a stack of letters and leafed through them. "It doesn't hurt to offer you a little reminder now and then, does it?"

"I suppose not," Evan said and, taking the letters with him, walked into his office as if he hadn't a care in the world.

"Have you been working on the brief for the Porter Corporation?" Mrs. Sterling asked, following on his heels.

"The Porter Corporation," Evan repeated as if he'd never heard the name before. "It's not due anytime soon, is it?"

"Yes, it is," the secretary said, and Jessica heard a hint of panic in her voice. "First thing Friday morning."

"I'll have it ready by then. What day is this, anyway?"

"Mr. Dryden, you've got to start coming into the office before closing time!"

"Don't you fret. I'll have everything ready the way I always do," he said as he ushered his secretary out the door. He paused when his gaze fell on Jessica and he winked. Then the door closed and Evan disappeared.

Mrs. Sterling shook her head and glanced toward Jessica. "Mr Dryden's been going through some rough times lately," she explained.

"How long has he been without a legal assistant?"

"Quite a while now. He didn't seem to think he'd need one. Damian's cut his workload and, well, things just haven't been the same around here for quite a while."

Jessica was leaving for the day when she happened upon Damian. Looking dignified and businesslike, he was talking to his secretary. A few silver hairs at his temple added a distinguished air. He made a striking figure, and she wondered briefly why he hadn't married. Tagged onto that thought came another. One that took her by surprise. She realized she was *happy* Damian hadn't married.

He must have seen her in his peripheral vision, because he straightened, smiled and walked toward her. "Well, Jessica, how'd your first day go?"

"Really well."

"Mary isn't working you too hard, is she?"

"Oh, no, she's great."

"Mary's one of the best secretaries I've ever worked with. She may be a bit abrupt, but you'll get used to that." He was walking with Jessica now, their steps matching, his hands clasped behind his back. Mary was abrupt perhaps, Jessica mused, but not with Evan.

"I'll always be grateful to you for being willing to take a chance on me," she said conversationally.

Damian's smile was rueful. "You may not be thanking me later. My brother can be a handful, but if there was ever someone who could get him back on the straight and narrow, it's you."

"Me?" she asked, not understanding.

Damian broke eye contact and looked away. "Everybody needs to be looked at with wide worshipful eyes now and then, don't you think?"

"Ah…" Jessica didn't know how to respond. One thing was becoming abundantly clear. Damian hadn't hired her because of her high test scores at business college.

Chapter 2

"You actually got the job?" Cathy Hudson said over the telephone line, her voice raised with astonishment. "You were hired, just like that, by one of the city's most prestigious law firms?"

"It helps to have friends in high places." Jessica was excited about this job, but she felt mildly guilty knowing the only reason she'd been hired was that their families were such good friends. However, Damian had made it plain she'd need to pull her own weight. Jessica was determined to prove herself; she'd be the best legal assistant the firm had ever hired. It was a matter of pride.

"Why is it everything comes so easy for you?" Cathy lamented. "You set your sights on something that would give Norman Vincent Peale second thoughts and—"

"Me? You're the one trying out for a lead in *Guys and Dolls*. Talk about setting your sights high."

"All right, all right," Cathy said with a dramatic sigh, "you've made your point."

"So how did the tryouts go today?"

"I...don't know. It's so hard to tell. I would kill for the part of Adelaide, but then I watch the others, and they're all so good. I came away today thinking it's just a pipe dream. David, the director, is wonderful. Working with him would be one of the highlights of my career, but I don't dare hope I'll get the part."

"I have faith in you. You're a natural, Cath." It was true, her friend had a knack for the dramatic, and that had always made their friendship so interesting.

Cathy laughed softly. "How can I fail, when both you and my mother are convinced I'm destined for stardom? Now, before we get off the subject, how did the interview with Damian go?"

"Really well, I think." Damian had dominated her thoughts all afternoon. He'd changed, she decided, or perhaps she was the one who was different. Whichever, she found herself enthralled by the man. The thought of working with him excited her.

"What about the younger brother?"

"Actually I'll be working directly for Evan."

Cathy must have noticed the hesitation in her voice because she asked, "Does that worry you? What's the matter? Do you think you're going to make an idiot of yourself over him—again?"

So much for Jessica's delicate ego. "No way. I was fourteen years old, for heaven's sake."

After she'd hung up, Jessica slipped a CD into the player, choosing an invigorating medley of jazz hits, and set about fixing her dinner. She whipped together a hot chicken-and-spinach salad and stood barefoot in her kitchen, humming along to the music, her heart singing its own melody.

Later that evening, she relaxed with the paper. Despite her best efforts, her thoughts drifted to Damian. The last thing she wanted was to make a fool of herself over another Dryden.

To the best of her knowledge, the source of which was her mother, Damian wasn't currently involved in a relationship. Joyce Kellerman said that Lois Dryden had complained that her elder son didn't take enough time for fun in his life. What Damian needed, Jessica decided now, was to fall in love with a woman who would take his mind off his work. Someone fun. Someone who would make him laugh and enjoy life. Someone who appreciated him.

An hour later, as she was getting ready for bed, Jessica realized she'd spent most of the evening thinking about Damian. Well, quite understandable, she rationalized. After all, he was head of the firm she was working for.

The following day, Evan didn't show up at the office until well after eleven. As she had previously, Mrs. Sterling fussed over him as though he were the prodigal son the moment he waltzed in the door.

"Good morning, Mr. Dryden." Mrs. Sterling gushed, nearly leaping from her chair. "It's a beautiful day, isn't it?"

Evan seemed to need time to think about this. "I hadn't noticed, but you're right, it is a gorgeous day," he said as he reached for his mail and leafed through the envelopes.

He was on his way into his office when he noticed Jessica sitting at her desk. She felt his scrutiny and was pleased that she'd dressed carefully, choosing a smart-looking flowered silk dress with a blue jacket. In her heels, she was nearly as tall as he was.

"Good morning, Mr. Dryden," she offered.

"Evan," he insisted. "You can call Damian Mr. Dryden if you insist, but I'm Evan."

"All right. Good morning, Evan,"

"It is a good morning, isn't it?" he asked, giving her a roguish grin. Jessica couldn't help but respond with a smile of her own. She hadn't noticed it so much the day before, but there were definite changes in the Evan she remembered. He was thinner and his smiles didn't quite reach his eyes. Another thing she couldn't help noticing was the way everyone walked on eggshells around him. Mrs. Sterling had made a point of letting her know Evan's work load had recently been cut, and Damian had said Evan hadn't yet recovered from a broken relationship. It must have been pretty serious, she mused.

"It's been a long time since we've had a chance to talk, hasn't it?" Evan asked, walking over and sitting on the edge of Jessica's desk.

"A very long time," she agreed, praying with all her heart he wouldn't resurrect her girlish antics. It'd been embarrassing enough to have Damian do it.

"I think we should make up for lost opportunities, don't you? Tell you what—I'll treat you to lunch." He checked his watch and seemed surprised at the time. "We'll leave in half an hour. That'll give me enough time to clear whatever's on my desk."

"You want to take me to lunch?" Jessica asked. "Today?"

"It's the least I can do," Evan said with a shrug. "I'll have Mary make reservations."

"But—"

"That's an excellent idea," Mrs. Sterling interjected, clearly pleased.

"I...I've only just started work," Jessica said. "I'd enjoy lunch, perhaps in a week or so, after I've settled into the job." The last thing she wanted was to give Damian the impression she was already slacking in her duties.

Evan pressed his thumb to her chin and gazed deeply into her eyes. "No buts, and no arguments. We're going to lunch and you can fill me in on what you've been doing for the last five or six years."

Mrs. Sterling followed Evan into his office, looking inordinately pleased with the turn of events. She returned a few minutes later, casting a delighted look in Jessica's direction as she picked up her phone and called the restaurant to make reservations. Evan chose Henri's, one of Boston's finest, well-known for its elegant dining. It also happened to be a good fifteen-minute drive from the office, which meant they were going to be out for lunch much longer than usual.

"I doubt we'll be back in an hour if we have lunch at Henri's," Jessica felt obliged to say.

"Don't worry about it. You'll make it up another time, I'm sure."

"But this is only my second day. I don't want to give the wrong impression."

"My dear, Mr. Dryden is your boss. If he wants to take a leisurely lunch with you, don't argue. You should be counting your blessings, instead."

"I know but—"

"From what I understand, you two are old family friends," Mrs. Sterling interrupted. "It's only natural for him to want to personally welcome you into the firm."

It seemed the reservation had barely been made when Evan reappeared. "Are you ready?"

Jessica blinked back her surprise. "Yes, of course, if you'll give me just a moment." She finished typing her notes into the computer, stored the information and pushed back her chair.

Evan took her elbow and told his secretary, "We'll be back in a couple of hours."

They were on their way through the corridor leading to the front of the office when Damian appeared. His gaze shifted from Evan to Jessica.

"Jessica and I are on our way out to lunch," Evan explained. "Do you need me for anything?"

"No. You two go on ahead. I'll talk to you later."

Damian nodded, and it was all Jessica could do not

to blurt out that this lunch date hadn't been her idea, but there wasn't the opportunity and she doubted it was necessary anyway. Damian must have known she hadn't invited herself out to lunch. Nevertheless, she didn't want him to think ill of her.

"We'll probably be late getting back," Evan said to his brother, guiding Jessica out of the office.

They arrived at the restaurant by taxi and were seated immediately. The ambience was formal, with soft chamber music playing unobtrusively in the background. The waiters, who dressed like diplomats, were attentive, the tables were well spaced, and the meal was served with a good deal of ceremony.

Evan seemed disinclined to talk about himself, asking her a series of questions about school, her friends and activities. He appeared attentive, but she suspected his thoughts were far removed from her and their lunch. At least he didn't dredge up the past and her infatuation with him. She could have kissed him for that.

After their dishes were cleared away, Evan took out a pad and pen. "I'm going to be working on a civil suit that'll demand a fair amount of research," he told Jessica. His eyes were bright with an enthusiasm she hadn't seen before. "The case involves Earl Kress— you might remember reading about him."

"Of course." The unusual details of the case had filled the local news for weeks. The twenty-year-old former athlete was suing the Spring Valley School District for his education.

Jessica wished she'd brought along a pad and pen

herself. She listened, enthralled, as Evan explained the details of the suit. It seemed Earl was a gifted athlete and the key figure in three of the school's biggest sports—football, basketball and track. In order for him to participate in these sports he had to maintain a C average. Unfortunately Earl had a learning disability and had never mastered reading skills. Although he'd graduated from high school and been awarded a full scholarship, he was functionally illiterate.

Evan explained that the school district had pressured Earl's teachers, and they'd been forced to give him passing grades. After he graduated from high school, he went on to college, but a severe knee injury suffered during football training camp effectively ended his career. And within the first two months of school, Earl flunked out.

"That's so unfair," Jessica said when Evan finished. If Damian was concerned about his brother, she thought, then offering Evan this groundbreaking case was sure to take his mind off other things. It would give Evan purpose, a reason to come to work in the morning, the necessary incentive to look past his personal problems.

"There've been a number of similar suits filed in other parts of the country," Evan continued. "I'm going to need you to do extensive research on the outcome of the cases previously tried."

"I'll be happy to help in any way I can."

Evan grinned his appreciation. "I knew I could count on you."

So this was the real reason for their lunch. The

case clearly meant a good deal to Evan, and consequently to Jessica. She was grateful for the opportunity to prove herself.

By the time they returned to the office, their lunch hour had stretched to three. It seemed everyone in the office was staring at them, and Jessica felt decidedly uncomfortable.

She walked directly to her desk, keeping her face averted when she passed Damian's office. His door was open, and when he saw her walk by he stood up, called her name and then glanced pointedly at his watch. It was all Jessica could do not to tell him it had been a *business* lunch.

Damian had made it painfully clear that he expected her to do her job. He wasn't paying her to romance his brother during three-hour lunches, and Jessica didn't want him to have that impression. She longed to explain, but she'd look ridiculous doing so in front of Evan. The only thing she could do was stay late that evening in an effort to make up for the time spent over lunch.

Although it was after seven when she started out of the office, a number of others were still there. With her sweater draped over her arm, she was on her way down the long corridor when Damian stopped her.

"Jessica."

"Hello, Damian," she said. He was standing just outside his office.

He relaxed, crossed his arms and asked, "How'd your lunch go with my brother?"

"Very well, but…"

"Yes?" he prompted when she didn't immediately finish.

"I want you to know it was a working lunch," she said, rushing the words in her eagerness to explain. "We discussed the Earl Kress case. I didn't want you to think we'd spent three hours socializing."

"It wouldn't have mattered."

"But it does!" she insisted fervently. "The lawsuit was the reason Evan asked me out. He wasn't interested in renewing an old friendship."

Damian's frown was thoughtful. "Did he seem pleased with the assignment?"

"Very much so," Jessica recalled Mrs. Sterling's saying that "things just haven't been the same around here for quite a while," implying *Evan* hadn't been the same. She wondered if Damian realized the extent of his brother's unhappiness.

Damian grinned; Jessica had the feeling he didn't do that often, which was a shame. The grooves in his cheeks and the sparkle in his gray eyes were very attractive. "I thought he might need a change of pace. Did you two have a chance to talk about old times?"

This was a casual way of asking if she'd noticed the changes in his brother, Jessica guessed. "A little. Evan really was hurt, wasn't he?"

Damian nodded. "Generally he disguises it, but I wondered if you'd detect the changes in him."

"I couldn't help noticing." She'd seen it almost from the first moment. Even though she hadn't seen Evan for years she could see how hard he was struggling to hide his misery. No wonder his parents and brother were so concerned.

Damian glanced at his watch and arched his brows. "It's late. We'll talk again some other time. Good night, Jessica."

"Good night, Damian."

As she waited for a train in the subway station, Jessica at last understood what Damian had meant when he'd told her that everyone needed to be looked at with wide worshipful eyes sometimes. It made perfect sense now that she thought about it. Damian still viewed her as that teenage girl infatuated with his younger brother. If ever there was a time that Evan needed a woman to idolize him, it was now. She'd been hired, not for her legal skills, but to help his brother forget the woman he'd loved and lost. Damian was looking to her to heal Evan's pain.

The following morning around ten, Evan, his smile bright enough to rival the sun, breezed into the office and presented Jessica with a bouquet of a dozen bloodred roses. Their perfume filled the room.

Jessica was speechless. "For me?" The flowers took her completely by surprise. Mrs. Sterling, too, from the look the secretary cast her.

"I need a favor," Evan said, leaning against the edge of her desk, his face scant inches from her own.

"Of course." She was holding the flowers against her like a beauty queen, inhaling their heavenly scent.

Evan reached into his jacket pocket and withdrew

a folded sheet of yellow paper. "I need you to do some last-minute research for me."

"Certainly."

"There're some statutes I need you to look up and report back to me on as soon as possible. This stuff is as dry as old bones—I'm sorry about that."

"Don't worry about it." Jessica looked at the items Evan wanted her to research and her heart sank at the number. "How soon do you need this?"

"Yesterday," was his frank reply.

Mrs. Sterling made a small tsk-tsk sound in the background, which made Jessica smile. Evan's eyes twinkled and he whispered, "There's nothing worse than a woman who can't let 'I told you so' pass. Remember that, Jessica."

"I will," she said with a small laugh. "I'd best get started. I'll have the information for you before I leave tonight."

"Good girl."

Mrs. Sterling produced a vase for the roses, and after setting them on the edge of her desk Jessica got down to work. She ensconced herself in the library and kept at her research straight through the lunch hour. She didn't notice the time until it was after three, when her stomach rumbled in protest. Even then she didn't take the time to sit down to eat, but grabbed an apple and munched on it while she continued to search for the required data.

The next time she looked up, the clock on the wall said seven forty-five. She'd heard the others leave, but that seemed like only minutes ago. She stood up and, placing her hand at the base of her spine, arched her stiff back and breathed in deeply.

Her eyes felt tired and her back sore as she carried her paperwork into the office. She stopped, surprised to find the room dark. She flicked on the lights and looked around, certain Evan had left a note for her.

He hadn't.

Picking up one of the roses, she held it to her nose and closed her eyes as she tried to battle down the weariness—and the disappointment.

"Jessica, what are you doing here?"

"Damian." She could ask the same question of him.

"It's nearly eight o'clock."

"I know." She rotated her overworked shoulders. "I guess time got away from me."

"So I see. I had some reading I was catching up on, but I assumed I was here alone. There was no reason for you to stay this late."

She glanced toward Evan's office. "What time did Evan leave?" she asked casually, not wanting him to know how abused she felt.

"A couple of hours ago. Why?"

"He said he needed this information right away." She'd been in a frenzy attempting to finish the task as quickly as possible. She'd assumed he would wait until she'd collected the data he seemed to need so desperately.

"I believe he had a dinner engagement," Damian explained.

"I see," she muttered. In other words, he'd cheerfully abandoned her.

"You sound angry," Damian said.

"I am. I worked through my lunch hour getting this stuff for him." And dinner hour, too, she thought, feeling even angrier. She realized too late that she probably also sounded jealous.

"I'm sorry, Jessica."

Evan's thoughtlessness wasn't Damian's fault and she said so, then asked bluntly, "Is there anything to eat around here?" She blinked back unexpected tears. Hunger always had a strange effect on her emotions, but it was embarrassing, and she tried not to let Damian see.

"You mean you haven't eaten since lunch?"

"Not since breakfast, unless you count an apple, and if I don't eat soon I'm going to cry and you really wouldn't want to witness that." The words rushed out and she felt a sniffle coming on. "Never mind," she muttered, turning away from him. She wiped her nose with her forearm and returned to the library. Several ponderous law volumes were spread open across the tables. She closed them and began lugging them back to the shelves.

"I found a package of soda crackers," Damian said, coming into the room.

"Thanks," she said, ripping away the clear plastic wrapper and sniffling again. "I'm sorry, I don't mean to act like this." She ate a cracker quickly and managed to hold back a sob. "Don't look so concerned. I just needed to eat."

"Let me take you to dinner." Damian lifted a couple of the volumes and replaced them for her.

"That isn't necessary." A second cracker had made its way into her mouth and she was beginning to feel more like herself.

"We owe you that much," Damian countered. "Besides, I'm half-starved myself."

"The least he could have done was waited," Jessica fumed.

Ignoring her comment Damian suggested a popular seafood restaurant nearby.

"He made it sound like it was a matter of life and death, and then he doesn't even bother to tell me he's leaving," she continued to fume. "You're right," she said as Damian cupped her elbow and led her out the door. "Evan *has* changed."

Damian didn't respond to this comment either.

They walked the three blocks to the restaurant. It wasn't too crowded, and they were given immediate seating at a wooden table near one of the windows. Even better, the waitress brought hot bread and chowder no more than a minute after it was ordered. Damian must be a regular here to get such service, Jessica thought, her good mood restored now that her stomach had something warm and filling.

"This is excellent," she said. "Thank you." She sighed in contentment as she spooned up the last of her chowder.

Grinning, he finished his own soup, then reached for another piece of bread.

"What's so funny?" she demanded. How like a man to keep something humorous to himself and then feel superior about it.

"I think I might just have averted a lawsuit. Can't you hear it? 'Woman Sues Boss over Lost Meals.'"

"I'd get a huge settlement." The corners of her mouth twitched with a smile. Her eyes met Damian's and soon their amusement had blossomed into full-blown grins.

He had very nice eyes, Jessica mused. They were a dark gray and revealed his keen intelligence, his sharp insight. She wanted to clear away any lingering misconception he had about her and Evan, but she couldn't think of a way to do it without sounding as if she was jealous of whatever person Evan spent his personal time with.

Jessica wondered what Damian saw when he looked at her. Did he see the woman she'd become, or did he view her as the pesky kid next door who'd adamantly declared that his younger brother was her destiny?

The waitress arrived then with their main courses. Damian had ordered oysters and Jessica baked cod, which was delicious. By the time they'd finished, she felt completely restored.

"I said some things I shouldn't have back at the office," Jessica began, feeling self-conscious now but eager to explain. "You see—"

"You'd worked far longer than necessary and were starving to boot," he interrupted. "Don't worry about it."

"I just wanted to be sure I hadn't provoked you into firing me."

"It'll take more than a demand for food to do that," he assured her, hardly disguising his amusement.

The June sky was dark and overcast and the temperature cooler as they came down the stairs and into the street. "It looks like rain," Damian said. No sooner had he spoken when fat raindrops began to fall. Taking Jessica by the elbow, he raced across the street. Neither had thought to bring an umbrella.

"Here," Damian said, running toward an alcove in front of a bookstore. The business had closed hours earlier, but the covered entrance was a good place to wait out the cloudburst. Jessica was breathless by the time they stopped. A chill raced over her and she rubbed her arms vigorously.

Damian's much larger hands replaced hers, then he stopped and peeled off his jacket, draping it over her shoulders.

"Damian, I'm fine," she protested, fearing he'd catch a chill himself.

"You're shivering."

The warmth of his coat was more welcome than she cared to admit. No doubt about it, Damian was a gentleman to the very core.

The downpour lasted a good ten minutes. Jessica was surprised at how quickly the time passed. When the storm dwindled to a drizzle and eventually stopped, Jessica discovered she was almost sorry. She was talking books with Damian and discovered they both shared an interest in murder mysteries. Damian was as well-read as she was, and they tossed titles and authors' names back and forth without a pause.

"Did you drive to work this morning?" he asked. She shook her head. She'd taken the subway.

"I'll give you a lift home, then."

"Really, Damian, that isn't necessary. I don't mind using public transit."

"*I* mind," he said in a voice that brooked no argument. "It's too late for you to be out on the streets alone."

How sweet of him to worry about her, she thought. "But I already have enough to thank you for."

"What do you mean?"

"I was just thinking—I seem to be continually in your debt. You've got a heart of gold."

He chuckled. "Hardly, little Jessica."

"You hired me without any real job experience, then you fed me dinner, and now you're driving me home."

"It's the least I can do."

They returned to the office building, walking directly to the underground parking garage. Damian opened the car door for her and she nestled back in the leather seat.

One thing she'd learned during their time together was the fact that Damian was protective of his younger brother, though she doubted Evan appreciated that.

"You're worried about him, aren't you?" she asked, without clarifying her question. Damian knew who she was talking about.

"Yeah," he admitted.

"Evan's the real reason you hired me, isn't he? You

think I might be able to help him through this…difficult time." It wasn't a responsibility she welcomed or wanted. She was about to explain that when she noticed the way his mouth quirked into an amused smile.

Instead, she told him sharply, "I'm not a silly fourteen-year-old infatuated with an older man. What I felt for your brother was just a crush. It was over years ago." That was the simple truth.

His shrug was noncommittal.

"Nevertheless," she forged on, "you hired me because of Evan?"

It took Damian a long time to answer. "Sometimes I wonder," he finally said. "Sometimes I wonder."

Chapter 3

Jessica arrived early the following morning, hoping to have an opportunity to thank Damian again for dinner and more importantly to let him know how much she'd enjoyed the time they'd shared. But when she passed his office, the door was closed and his secretary was searching urgently through a file drawer. It didn't look like the time to pop in unannounced.

Not surprisingly, Evan was nowhere to be seen. Mrs. Sterling arrived ten minutes after Jessica, greeting her with a small approving smile, and set about sorting through the mail.

Jessica spent the first part of the morning organizing the material she'd researched the day before and typing up her notes. That way, Evan wouldn't be forced to waste time deciphering her hasty scrawl.

She'd just completed printing out the results when a breathless Evan entered the office. From the look of him, he'd raced all the way up from the parking garage. Briefcase in hand, he marched up to her desk.

"Do you have those notes ready?" he asked, reaching for the file before Jessica had a chance to present it. She stood up, intending to discuss a number of points with him, but he brushed past her and hurried into his office without a word. She would have followed him, but he closed the door.

Jessica was taken aback; unsure of what to do, she looked at Mrs. Sterling. The secretary sighed and shrugged. "Working for Mr. Dryden can be a real trial," she muttered, then grinned and added, "No pun intended."

No sooner had Mrs. Sterling finished chuckling over her own little joke than Evan reappeared, looking composed and confident. He'd removed his raincoat and was leafing casually through the file. He looked over at Jessica and his face relaxed into a broad smile.

"You're an angel," he said, kissing her cheek as he walked past. Jessica had seen him kiss Mrs. Sterling in the same affectionate way.

"I'll be in a meeting with Damian this morning," Evan announced on his way out the door.

As the morning progressed, Jessica found herself wondering exactly what her role in the office was. Although Evan had recently been assigned the Earl Kress case, his workload had been light in the past few months. Now that she'd finished the research project, there was barely enough to keep her busy.

From various bits and pieces, Jessica had learned that Evan's interest in corporate law had waned recently. Surely Damian hadn't hired her expecting miracles! Since he was so closemouthed about Evan's troubles, Jessica wondered if Mrs. Sterling could fill in some details. She didn't want to be obvious about asking, which could prove tricky since the woman was so clearly devoted to her employer.

"That Evan's a real charmer, isn't he?" Jessica began conversationally.

"He always could charm the birds right out the trees," Mrs. Sterling answered proudly.

"He's different now from the way I remember him. More...intense."

Evan's secretary nodded and muttered, "I'd like to shoot that woman."

Jessica's heart leapt with excitement. "What woman?" she asked, hoping to hide her eagerness. She was about to learn what had happened to change Evan so drastically from the man she'd known.

Mrs. Sterling glanced up, as if surprised that Jessica had heard her mumbling. "Oh...it's nothing."

"But it *must* be something. Evan isn't anything like he was a few years back. Oh, he's charming and sweet, but there's an edge to him now. A sharpness, I guess. Something I can't put my finger on." She looked expectantly at the other woman.

"That's true enough," Mrs. Sterling reluctantly conceded.

"You say a woman's responsible for the changes in Evan?"

"Isn't it always a woman?"

"What happened?" Might as well try a more direct approach, Jessica thought. Tact wasn't getting her anywhere.

"It's a pity, a real pity."

"Yes, Evan just isn't the same," Jessica said, hoping to encourage the other woman to continue.

"It shouldn't come as any surprise, really. Yet it does, Mr. Dryden being the charmer he is. Plain and simple, he fell in love with someone who didn't feel the same way about him." Then she clamped her mouth closed as though she'd already said far more than she should—far more than was circumspect for a secretary to say about her boss.

But this much she already knew. What she was looking for were the particulars. Who was this woman who'd hurt Evan so badly? Her back stiffened at the thought of someone rejecting him. The man she'd worshiped from afar during her tumultuous teenage years. Whoever this woman was, Jessica decided, she was a fool.

About eleven Evan walked into the office. He smiled as he strolled past Mrs. Sterling's desk to hers. "The research you did was wonderful, Jessica. Thank you."

His appreciation caught her off guard. She wondered if Damian had said something to him and was momentarily speechless.

"I appreciate the effort that went into your report," he continued. "I'm very pleased by the quality of your work."

"I…I was happy to do it. That's my…my job." The words stumbled off the end of her tongue. Jessica was amazed that his praise could fluster her so. She was embarrassed now by the way she'd overreacted last night when she'd learned he'd left the office. It was her own fault for not taking time to eat lunch. Evan's disappearance wouldn't have bothered her in the least if she had….

"Damian said you were here till almost eight."

So Damian *had* mentioned that. "As I said earlier, I was only doing my job."

"Mom and Dad are having a barbecue this weekend," Evan continued, "Saturday, around four. I'd like you to attend it with me."

His invitation threw her. She wasn't sure what to say. Although she hadn't had a lot of work experience, she knew that dating the boss could lead to problems.

"This shouldn't be a difficult decision," Evan said, grinning.

His pride had already suffered one blow, and Jessica discovered she was unwilling to deliver a second, no matter how slight. "I'd enjoy that very much," she said. "Thank you for thinking of me."

He smiled affectionately. "You always were a sweet thing."

As a teenager, Jessica's daydreams had been filled with such scenarios. She'd close her eyes and pretend Evan had asked her out. Now her dream had come true, but Jessica was left wishing it had been Damian issuing the invitation, instead of his brother.

"I'll pick you up. You are living in the city, aren't you?"

Jessica nodded. "Wouldn't it be simpler if we met at the party? As it happens, I'm spending the weekend with my parents, and I can walk over with them."

Evan seemed a bit surprised by her suggestion. "You're sure?"

"Positive."

"Then that'll be fine. I'll look forward to seeing you there."

There'd been a time in her life when she would have gladly walked across a bed of hot coals to attend a party with Evan. Any party. Anywhere. Hadn't Damian been counting on that when he hired her—even if he claimed to know she was long over her crush?

"The festivity's in honor of some dignitary," Evan went on. "Mom's worked herself into a tizzy for the event. I can guarantee this will be the most elaborate barbecue Boston has ever seen. The last I heard, Mom hired a country-and-western band."

"It sounds like fun."

"Considering all the effort that's going into it, I'm sure it will be. You can do the two-step, can't you, sweet Jessica?"

"Of course." How easy it was to stretch the truth. In fact, she'd only done the two-step once or twice before. "Well, I'm pretty rusty," she amended.

"Me, too. We'll leave the fancy footwork to Damian."

Damian, she thought with a sigh. There was definitely something wrong with her, something psychological, something rooted deep in her childhood, she guessed, if she could agree to date one brother while longing for the other.

The hours flew by and before Jessica knew it, the workday had come to an end. Mrs. Sterling had just stepped out of the office when Damian strolled casually in.

"Evan's left for the day," Jessica said, a little flustered to find him standing in front of her desk. Especially since she'd again been thinking how much she'd have preferred to attend the family barbecue with *him*.

"I'm not here to see my brother."

"Mrs. Sterling will be right back."

"I came to see you," Damian explained, his eyes dark and intense as they settled on her.

Jessica tensed. Did he have some complaint with her work?

"Don't look so worried. I came to tell you my parents are holding a party this weekend. A barbecue."

"Yes, I know. Evan mentioned it earlier."

Jessica swore Damian's eyes brightened with interest. He crossed his arms and leaned against her desk. "What did he say about it?"

"Not much. Apparently it's in honor of some dignitary."

"I see." He hesitated as if he was unsure, which Jessica knew was completely out of character for Damian. "I was wondering..." he began, then straightened and buried his hands deep in his pants pockets. "Would you like to come to the party with me?"

Her shoulders sagged as she opened her mouth to explain that Evan had already invited her, but before she could respond, Damian added, "I realize it's short notice, but I didn't hear the details myself until this morning." A hint of a smile turned up the corners of his mouth. "Mother phoned, wanting to be sure I'd be there. She seems to be taking her duties very seriously."

"Ah…"

"There's a problem," he guessed.

She nodded glumly. "Evan's already invited me to the party—as his date." She wanted to tell Damian she'd much prefer to attend with him, but she couldn't. "I'm sorry," she added.

"He did?" Instead of looking displeased at this turn of events, Damian sounded positively delighted. "Don't be sorry."

His reaction annoyed her.

"It isn't like a real date," she said, wanting to make that clear. "At least, that wasn't the impression Evan gave me. The invitation was his way of thanking me for working so hard on the research project."

"My brother wouldn't invite you if he wasn't interested in your company," Damian insisted. "Besides, I wouldn't want my brother to think I was cutting in on his territory."

His territory.

Damian must have guessed her feelings, because he said, "Evan asked you first."

He was right about that, she thought, but little else.

Damian turned away, and it suddenly became important to Jessica to explain herself. "I don't think you should put much stock in Evan's invitation. It really *was* just a way of thanking me."

"It's a start, though, don't you think?" Damian said over his shoulder. "A good start, at that." He left her then before she could say anything more.

Jessica was upset, and it wasn't until she got home that she figured out why. Damian hadn't invited her to the party out of any real desire for her company. He'd assumed that Evan hadn't asked her—and he was looking for an opportunity to throw her and his brother together socially.

Jessica arrived at her parents' house early Saturday afternoon, after spending all morning shopping for the perfect outfit. Cathy had come along to offer encouragement and advice.

She might not be attending the barbecue with Damian, but when she showed up looking like a movie star, he'd wish she was. This was her mission, plain and simple.

Evan had casually mentioned the country-and-western band, but he'd also said the barbecue was in honor of some dignitary. These somewhat contradictory snippets of information served to confuse her about how to dress. Nothing in her closet seemed suitable, but then little in the shops did, either.

In one outfit she resembled Annie Oakley, and in another Jackie Kennedy. There didn't seem to be much of a middle ground—until she found a long denim skirt, a red shirt decorated with rain-bow-colored fringe sewn about the yoke and white cowboy boots. A white silk scarf tied around her neck lent a touch of elegance.

Her mother's eyes widened with approval when Jessica modeled the outfit. "I wish now I'd gone shopping, too, and bought something new myself. You look great."

"Thanks." Her mother's praise gave Jessica confidence. Cathy, who tended to dress like a character in a sci-fi movie, had also said she looked great, but Jessica wasn't sure she trusted her friend's fashion sense.

"It was so sweet of Evan to include you," Joyce Kellerman went on to say. "Not that I'm surprised, his being your boss and all. Life is certainly full of little twists and turns, isn't it?

"It sure is," Jessica said without elaborating.

"I'm thrilled that you're working with Evan."

"He's a nice person."

"He's *wonderful*. It's always been my dream, I know it's silly, but well, we're such good friends with the Drydens... I've hoped you'd grow up to marry one of Lois's boys."

"Whatever you do," Jessica said quickly, "don't say that in front of Damian or Evan."

"Why not, dear?"

"Mom, it'd embarrass me to death!"

"But you were so keen on Evan a few years back, and I thought... I hoped..."

"Mother, I was only fourteen!" Her old infatuation with Evan was turning into the proverbial albatross around her neck—thanks to Damian and her mother.

If it wasn't for them, the whole thing would have been forgotten by now.

"You'll make a beautiful bride," her mother said, adding the finishing touches to her own outfit. Suddenly she changed the subject. "Lois has worried herself sick over this silly barbecue."

"But why?" Mrs. Dryden had thrown a hundred parties more elaborate than this.

Her mother sat on the bed and leaned back on her hands. "I don't suppose there's any reason to keep it a secret. Walter's been approached about running for the Senate."

Walter Dryden had been active in community affairs for years. Although he'd never held public office, he'd often managed the successful campaigns of others. He'd taken an early retirement from the law firm, and, from what Jessica understood, had grown restless with inactivity. Running for office would doubtless come as a welcome challenge.

"Has he decided he's going to run?"

"Your father and I think so. He hasn't declared his candidacy yet, but we're confident he will. He's testing the waters with this barbecue tonight. Several people from the political arena will be present. This is probably the most important party of Lois's marriage. Little wonder she's a nervous wreck."

Even before Jessica and her parents arrived for the barbecue, the pungent smells of tomato sauce, spices and roasting meat mingled with the afternoon sunshine and drifted over the fence.

As they were greeted at the front door, Jessica

was reminded, by the way Lois hugged her mother, what very good friends the two women were. Their friendship had spanned twenty years, and they were like sisters. Jessica felt the same way about Cathy. They'd met in college, where they'd been roommates for three years.

When Jessica didn't immediately see Evan or Damian, she wandered outside. A series of round tables decorated in red-checked tablecloths were scattered across the lush expanse of lawn. The day was perfect, warm but not hot, and the sky was cloudless. A soft breeze ruffled the leaves of the large shade trees that lined the property. This was New England summer at its best. The smells of food were heavenly, too, reminding her how hungry she was. Shopping and preparing for the party hadn't left time for lunch.

Several dozen guests had arrived, and Jessica scanned the crowd. She spotted Evan standing next to a lovely blonde in a chic white fringed dress with a turquoise belt and silver buckle. Jessica didn't recognize the woman, and a few discreet inquiries got her nowhere. She became all the more curious. She attempted to make her way to Evan, since she was officially his date, but in actuality, she was seeking an introduction to the lovely blonde. Perhaps this was Evan's new romantic interest, she thought hopefully. But before she could reach Evan, she was waylaid by some family friends. Most of the Drydens' guests were older people, established names Jessica had known or heard all her life.

"Hello, Jessica," Damian said from behind her. She

turned to find him in the sort of suit he wore at the office. He'd made an attempt to dress to the theme with a black Stetson, which, Jessica thought, looked entirely out of place on his very Bostonian head.

His eyes glimmered with appreciation. "You look—" he hesitated as though he didn't know what to say "—good."

Jessica wagered that it wasn't often Damian was at a loss for words. It lifted her spirits considerably.

"I imagine you're wondering who that blonde is, the one draping herself all over Evan," he suggested casually.

Jessica pretended she was, although she couldn't help being grateful to this unknown woman for keeping Evan occupied. Otherwise he might feel obliged to pay attention to her, and she'd much rather spend her time with Damian.

"Who is she?" Jessica asked, playing his game.

"Do I detect a small hint of jealousy?"

"Of course not." The question irritated her.

"That's Romilda Sidonie."

"Who?"

"The European dignitary's daughter."

That explained it. Naturally Evan considered it his duty to make Romilda feel welcome. Jessica was pleased to see him apparently enjoying himself.

"Would you like me to introduce you?" Damian asked.

"No," Jessica said, noticing Evan and Romilda moving toward the dance area. "Evan's having a good time. I don't see any reason to interrupt him."

"You're his date."

"But only because you prompted him into asking me."

Damian's eyes narrowed. "What makes you say that?"

"I'm not completely naive, you know. I think the reason you came into my office to invite me was that you didn't think Evan had—you wanted to make sure the two of us were together in a social situation so you could see what happened. Am I right?"

He joined his hands behind his back and took two small steps away, then turned to face her again. She saw a hint of a smile in his eyes. "If you're right—though I'm not saying you are—I'd never admit it."

"You must wreak havoc on a jury."

"That's what my clients pay me for."

Jessica looked toward the dance area again and couldn't see Evan and the European woman. When she glanced over at the picnic area, she found the pair sitting at a table beneath a large elm tree munching on barbecue sandwiches.

"She's lovely," Jessica murmured, watching the couple. "No wonder Evan's forgotten me."

"Romilda may be lovely, but so are you," Damian returned quickly, then looked as if he regretted speaking.

"Thank you."

"I shouldn't have said that."

"Why not? That makes me think you didn't mean it."

"I shouldn't be the one saying such things to you," Damian replied. "You're Evan's date."

"He seems to have forgotten, which is just as well. I'd rather spend my time with you."

"With me?" Damian repeated, sounding appalled by the mere suggestion. "Have you eaten?" he asked hurriedly. They were standing next to the dessert table. It was laden with an enormous chocolate cake decorated with fresh strawberries, a lemon torte that would have tempted a saint and a fresh blueberry cobbler, which Jessica knew from years past was the caterer's specialty.

"I'm not hungry just yet," she said, thinking Damian might have used her desire to eat as an excuse to squire her away to one of the tables and conveniently leave her.

Damian eyed her speculatively. "You're sure about that? I'd hate to see a repeat of what happened the other night."

"Well, yes, I guess I will have a bite…but may I sit with you?"

"If you insist."

She did. Damian handed her a plate. Together they walked along the buffet table. Jessica helped herself to potato salad, baked beans and a generous rack of spareribs.

The band started to play a popular tune, and her foot tapping to the beat, Jessica enjoyed the culinary feast. She was content to sit on the sidelines. Evan seemed to have forgotten her, but far from being offended, she felt only a sense of relief.

Damian's invitation to dance came as a surprise. "Why do you want to dance with me?" she asked. She had a sneaking suspicion it somehow involved his brother.

"Do I need a reason?"

Jessica hesitated, then nodded. "If you're thinking it's a way to get Evan to notice me, then I'd rather sit out."

"What if I said it was because I wanted to see how you felt in my arms?"

Her heart gave a flutter. "Then I'd agree." She met his gaze directly. "So, what's it to be, Damian?"

He took a long time deciding, much longer than should have been necessary. Slowly he pushed back his chair and stood. "Why don't we find out together," he suggested, leading her by the hand toward the farthest reaches of the dance area.

The party was in full swing by now, with a good number of couples two-stepping around the area. When several old family friends stopped to chat with Jessica and Damian as they made their way toward the other dancers, Jessica could sense Damian's impatience.

They reached the outskirts of the crowd, and Damian turned Jessica in his arms. They fit together nicely, thigh to thigh, hip to hip. Damian was an excellent dancer, his steps easy to follow, his movements smooth and assured. He held her loosely about the waist and gazed down at her as if they'd been dancing together all their lives.

"You're good at this." Her surprise must have been

obvious, because he threw back his head and laughed. It was the first time she could ever remember hearing Damian really laugh.

"That amazes you, doesn't it?" he said.

"Yes." It was pointless to deny it. She was discovering that Damian was full of surprises. Just then Jessica felt someone brush against her. She turned to see Evan, partnered with the dignitary's daughter.

"Well, well, if it isn't Damian and Jessica." Evan said with a smile, not sounding jealous in the least.

It hadn't taken long to attract Evan's attention, and Jessica groaned inwardly, wondering if Damian had planned it this way.

"You haven't met Romilda, have you?" Evan murmured. Without waiting for a response, he made the introductions.

Jessica could see that the blonde had fallen under Evan's spell, just like most women did when he'd decided to charm them. His magnetism was lethal. Jessica nearly felt sorry for the unsuspecting woman. Evan did have a bit of a reputation as a playboy.

The two couples moved off to get something to drink. They were making small talk and sipping punch when Damian suddenly asked Romilda to dance. The woman glanced anxiously at Evan, obviously reluctant to leave him. Jessica smiled softly to herself, recognizing Damian's ploy. He'd all but thrown her and Evan together.

Damian and Romilda joined the throng of dancers. "It's a wonderful party," Jessica said to Evan. "I've been having a good time."

"Glad to hear it," Evan commented distractedly, his eyes following the other couple. "Shall we?" he asked, holding out his hand to her.

It became apparent as they moved into the dancing area that Evan was more interested in keeping an eye on Romilda than dancing with Jessica. She and Evan made polite conversation, but his attention wandered as often as her own. The dance couldn't end soon enough for either of them.

When it did, she was grateful Damian and Romilda were on the far side of the dance area, because she needed time and space to put order to her thoughts. When the number ended, Evan was coralled by an older couple who wanted to talk to him privately. He cast Jessica an apologetic look and moved away.

She strolled to the far reaches of the property, near the fence that bordered her parents' home. A white footbridge spanned a good-size pond. She stood in the middle of the bridge, dropping small rocks into the still water and watching the ripples radiate to the shore one after another.

Thus absorbed, she didn't hear Damian approach and was startled to hear him speak. "I wondered if I'd find you here," he said.

"I used to come here a lot when I was growing up," Jessica admitted. "I guess you could have charged me with trespassing."

"Not too likely."

"I know, that's why I used to come. It was so peaceful. So safe." A duck glided past, disturbing the water in the pond, and Jessica wished she'd thought to bring some bread crumbs. The ducks had often been beneficiaries of her trips here.

Damian was silent for a moment, then he said, "You're discouraged, aren't you?"

"About what?"

"It's over, you know," Damian assured her softly. "It was over a long time ago—more than six months now. I thought Evan would get over her, but I was wrong."

Oh, dear, Jessica thought. Apparently Damian believed she was here at the pond brooding about Evan, when in fact nothing could have been farther from the truth. She'd been standing on the bridge thinking about her relationship with Damian.

"Who was she?" Jessica was still curious.

"Someone he met on a beach. No name the family had ever heard of before, not that it mattered. Mary Jo Summerhill."

"What happened?"

"I don't think anyone really knows for sure. Whatever it was devastated Evan. He hasn't been the same since. My brother isn't one to burden others with his problems. He's like that duck down there on the pond—everything seems to roll off him like water. He'd been in and out of a dozen relationships, and I assumed he was never going to really fall for any woman, but I was wrong."

"You haven't a clue what happened between him and Mary Jo?"

"No. He changed abruptly after the breakup, started working odd hours. But his heart clearly wasn't in it, so I cut back his work load. That helped for a time, but now I'm not sure it was the right thing to do. I've never seen him more miserable."

"Have you tried to talk to him?"

"A dozen times," Damian admitted, "but it hasn't helped. If anything, he's resented my prying. This broken relationship seems to have cut him more deeply than he's willing to admit."

"He'll get over her," Jessica said reassuringly. "It just takes time."

"I thought so, too." Damian shrugged. "But now I wonder. It's been more than six months." He paused, gazing down at the water. "He needs you, Jessica. You might be the only one able to reach him."

"Me?"

"I knew the minute Dad mentioned you were coming in to apply for a job that you could well be the answer to our prayers." She started to say something, but Damian wouldn't let her. "You're just going to need a lot of patience."

Jessica sighed in frustration. "If I'm going to need patience, it's with *you*. You and your family seem to think I'm still a kid with a crush on Evan."

Damian's eyes darkened. "All right, all right, I didn't mean to offend you. You're old enough to make up your own mind."

"Thank you for that," she said. Turning away from him, she rested her hands on the railing and stared into the serene waters below. "I remember once when I was about six coming to this bridge and crying my eyes out," she murmured.

"What hurt you so badly then?"

"You," she said, turning and jabbing a finger at his chest.

"Me?" Jessica had never seen such an expression of outraged innocence. "What did I do?" Damian demanded.

"Your father was taking you and Evan to the roller coaster at Cannon Beach. My dad was out of town on business, and our mothers were taking the shopping cure. They weren't keen on having to drag me along, and I can't remember who, but one of them suggested I go to the carnival with you and Evan."

"And I didn't want you with us," Damian finished for her.

"Not that I blame you. No fifteen-year-old wants a six-year-old girl tagging along."

Damian chuckled. "Times change, don't they?"

Her mother had said the same thing earlier. *Indeed, times do change.*

To Jessica's astonishment, Damian reached for her hand. He linked their fingers and tugged her off the bridge. "Where are we going?" she protested. He looked at her in surprise, as though she hadn't already guessed. "Where else? The beach. From what I understand the same roller coaster is still running. The party here is starting to wind down, and I don't think we'll be missed, do you?"

She couldn't help but agree.

Chapter 4

Carrying a sticky ball of pink cotton candy in one hand and a purple stuffed elephant under the other, Jessica strolled leisurely with Damian down the long pier. The tinny music of the merry-go-round played behind them, mingling with children's laughter. The scent of the bay and fresh popcorn swirled around them like smoke from a cooling fire. The night was perfect. The sun had set, and clusters of bright stars blinked approvingly down on them.

"I don't think I've ever enjoyed myself more," Jessica said to Damian. She tipped the cotton-candy cone toward him and he helped himself to a handful. Taking another bite herself, she savored the way the sugary sweetness melted on her tongue.

"We still haven't gone on the roller coaster," Damian reminded her.

"That's because you spent all that time trying to win that silly stuffed elephant." She hugged it against her, belying her words.

"Are you game?" Damian asked, looking toward the huge steel structure.

Jessica hedged. "I...I don't know if that's such a good idea after all the junk we've eaten."

"Trust me." He looped his arm through hers and pulled her along, not giving her a chance to protest.

"Great, first you fill me up with popcorn and cotton candy, then you insist on dragging me onto one of the biggest roller coasters in the country. That's not smart, Damian, not smart at all."

The crowds were thicker than ever, and Damian reached for her hand as he led her toward the ride. The line was long, and the wait was sure to be at least thirty minutes. A list of possible arguments crowded Jessica's mind, but she knew it wouldn't do any good. The determined set of Damian's jaw told her that much.

"What am I supposed to do with the elephant?" she asked, clinging to it tightly, as they edged closer.

"Hold it."

"If I'm holding the elephant, who's going to hold me?"

"I will," he assured her calmly. "Stop looking so worried."

"I should tell you, Damian Dryden, the last time I rode on this thing I had a near-death experience. I don't suppose you know when this ride had a safety inspection."

"Thursday."

"You don't *know* that!"

He laughed, seeming to enjoy her unease. "True, but it sounded good. Listen, this roller coaster has been running for twenty years without a single mishap. Well, there was that one time…"

"Damian!"

"I was joking."

"Don't tease," Jessica muttered furiously. She flattened her palm against her stomach and sighed loudly. "My stomach doesn't feel right."

"You won't be sick."

"How can you be sure?"

"Experience. Anticipation's the worst part. The ride itself is fun. The only problem is that it doesn't last long enough. The whole thing is over in no time."

For all her complaining, as the minutes passed, Jessica found herself beginning to anticipate their turn. At last the silver cars came to an abrupt halt right in front of them.

"Just promise me you won't fling your arms up in the air in that bizarre descent ritual," Jessica murmured as the bar fell into place, securing them in the seat.

"I wouldn't dream of it," Damian said, "not when I promised to hold on to you."

Jessica colored slightly, but didn't respond. She dared not look down. Heights were something she generally avoided, which meant she was trapped into closing her eyes. The stuffed elephant was cradled in her arms, much the same way Damian was cradling her.

The cars slowly made their ascent, chugging up the steep incline, making a straining noise as if the weight was too much to bear. The line of cars topped the peak and started its rapid descent. A scream of excitement froze in her throat as they plummeted downward. Damian's arm tightened around her shoulders. Her free hand gripped his, her nails digging into his fingers, but if she was hurting him, he gave no indication. Just when it seemed they were about to break the sound barrier, they started up another steep grade, which slowed the momentum, but once they reached the top they were cast on a crazy twisting, turning journey that left her stomach far behind. Her eyes were closed so tightly her face ached.

When at last they rolled to a halt, Jessica's shoulders surged forward, righted and then sagged with a twinge of disappointment as she realized the ride was over.

"Well?" Damian asked, taking her hand to help her climb out of the cramped car. "Did you or did you not have fun?"

Her legs felt a little shaky once she started walking. "Give me a minute—I don't know what I'm feeling." Confessing he'd been right was too much to ask.

Damian laughed. "Admit it. Don't be shy. It was fun, wasn't it?"

"Yes," Jessica said with ill grace.

Damian laughed again and tucked his arm around

her waist. His action seemed so natural, especially since it was evident that her knees had yet to right themselves. Although his touch was automatic, it had a curious effect on Jessica. She enjoyed being linked with Damian, enjoyed having his body close to hers. She'd experienced it while they were dancing, too.

"You ready to head back?" Damian asked as they neared the brightly lit arched entryway to Cannon Beach.

She agreed with a nod, but in fact she didn't want the night to end. Their time together had been perfect. Perhaps now Damian would understand that it was *his* company she sought and not his brother's. Perhaps now he'd view her as a woman and not the pesky girl next door.

And maybe Evan's obvious attraction to Romilda would blossom into something more, and the Drydens would stop looking to Jessica for solutions. She sincerely hoped that was the case. A man always enjoyed a challenge, and the dignitary's daughter might be just the thing Evan needed.

Damian and Jessica walked along the sawdust-covered ground of the parking lot until they reached his car. The lights from the carnival lit up the night sky, and the sounds droned on behind her.

"I had a marvelous time," she told Damian as he started the engine.

"Me, too," he said. "It's been years since I've been to Cannon Beach. Years since—" He stopped abruptly.

Jessica was reminded of what she'd heard about

Damian's working too hard and not taking time to enjoy life. It felt good to know that Damian had enjoyed her company. The memory of his laughter produced a sudden smile. He didn't laugh often enough, and when he did she felt as if she'd been rewarded with a priceless gift.

Damian drove Jessica to her apartment building. It was after eleven by then, but she was keyed up with excitement. Somehow she felt it would all end when Damian left, and she wasn't ready to let that happen.

"Do you want to come up?" she asked, not really expecting he would, hoping she could change his mind.

He glanced her way as though judging the sincerity of her offer. "All right."

"I'll put on a pot of coffee, and you can gloat over how much I enjoyed the roller coaster."

"I'll gloat, coffee or not." He found a parking spot on the street, got out of the car and then went around to open her door. A true gentleman, she thought not for the first time.

Laughing and joking they strolled toward her building. The doorman held the door for them and smiled at Jessica and the purple elephant.

The laughing and teasing continued as they stepped into the elevator for the ride up to the tenth floor. The doors glided shut and Jessica sagged against the mirrored wall in mock exhaustion.

"You sure you don't want to close your eyes?" he said.

"Why?"

"This elevator is moving at death-defying speeds. Who knows the last time it was checked for safety."

"Thursday," came her glib reply.

Damian laughed delightedly.

"I don't know," she teased. "You might be right." Jokingly she squinted her eyes closed, but when she did, Damian kissed her.

It took Jessica a moment to realize what had happened. Damian had actually kissed her. It was a simple, uncomplicated kiss, the kind a brother gives a sister. One pair of lips touching another.

Only it didn't *feel* simple.

If anything, it left her longing for much, much more. Dumbstruck, she blinked up at him, not knowing how to respond.

"Don't look so shocked," Damian muttered.

"I…" She closed her mouth to stop herself from asking him to kiss her again.

"It was just a kiss."

"I know," she muttered. She realized he regretted the impulse and wished she knew of some way to tell him how thoroughly she'd enjoyed it. But before she could find the words, the elevator stopped.

Jessica led the way to her apartment and unlocked the door. Turning on the light, she moved into the cheery yellow kitchen and, as was her habit, flipped the switch to her answering machine. Cathy Hudson's voice greeted her.

"Jess. Hi, it's me. I haven't heard from you in days, and of course I want to know how the barbecue went with Lover Boy today. Give me a call when you can."

"So your friend knows about Evan?" Damian asked casually, making himself comfortable at her round oak table. He leafed through a newsmagazine she'd been reading that morning.

"I might have mentioned him, but certainly not as Lover Boy, if that's what you're asking."

"That's not what she said."

"She's teasing," Jessica insisted. She hadn't talked to her friend about her new feelings for Damian and was sorry now, because Cathy, like everyone else, it seemed, was intensely curious about the relationship between Jessica and Evan. "I made the mistake of telling her I once had a crush on Evan and she assumed... Well, you just heard." Jessica took out the coffee canister and poured some grounds into the paper filter. The rich coffee aroma filled the room. "This will only take a minute," she promised.

"Listen, don't bother. It's later than I realized."

"You're sure?" Jessica said, disappointed.

"Positive." He set aside the magazine and stood. Pausing in front of her, he drew his hand against the side of her face. "Thank you for a wonderful day, Jessica."

"Thank *you*," she whispered back.

The apartment seemed unnaturally empty when Damian was gone. She'd hoped he'd kiss her again before he left. He'd been tempted, she could see it in his eyes, but he'd resisted, apparently wanting to keep an emotional distance from her.

Jessica wasn't at all tired and, needing to talk, dialed her friend's number.

A groggy Cathy answered on the fourth ring.

"I didn't wake you, did I?" Jessica said with a giggle, delighted to pay back her friend for all the times Cathy had phoned her in the middle of the night.

"From the dead. What are you doing calling so late and sounding so damned cheerful? There should be a law against that. Let me guess. You were with Evan."

"No! Damian and I went to the—"

"Damian? You're dating Evan's brother?" Cathy sounded wide-awake now and interested. Very interested.

"I know in that silly romantic heart of yours you figured once I was working with Evan, all the unrequited love I'd stored up years ago would suddenly blossom."

"Those were my thoughts exactly," Cathy said.

"Cathy, listen to me. Evan Dryden is a terrific guy, but he isn't the man for me."

"How can you be so sure?"

"Because…well, because I just am." Even now it was difficult to talk about her feelings for Damian. She wasn't sure how to describe them. "For one thing, Evan's in no emotional shape to get involved in another romance, which is fine by me."

"What happened?" Cathy demanded. "I thought he asked you to his family's barbecue."

"He did, but only because Damian prompted him. By the time I arrived he'd met a lovely European woman and the two were inseparable."

"How rude!"

If she'd had her heart set on Evan it would have

been devastating, but she didn't, and as a consequence she'd spent a glorious night in Damian's company. She wouldn't have traded the evening for anything. "No, not at all," she said.

"You aren't disappointed?"

Apparently Cathy wasn't as awake as Jessica had believed. "Not in the least. Damian and I drove out to Cannon Beach and rode the roller coaster."

"You? The original wimp on that monster ride? You didn't really, did you?"

"Yes, I did," she announced proudly, "and it was fabulous." She spent the next few minutes relaying the highlights of the evening—Damian's winning the stuffed elephant for her and their walking along the pier and sharing cotton candy. When she finished there was a short silence.

"Hmm," said Cathy thoughtfully. "This could be *very* interesting."

Jessica arrived bright and early at the office Monday morning. Evan had apparently been to work at some point during the weekend, for he'd left her a list of instructions. His notes included a series of laws he needed her to research. Jessica got to the task right away.

Damian found her in the library some time later. "So you *are* here," he said, sounding surprised. "Mrs. Sterling didn't think you'd come in for the day. I phoned your apartment and got the answering machine."

Jessica straightened in her chair and arched her

back, hoping to relieve the tension in her tired muscles. A glance at her watch told her it was nearly eleven. She'd been so involved in her research she hadn't noticed the time.

"I've been in here all morning," she explained, pinching the bridge of her nose. The words were beginning to blur in front of her eyes. Some of the reading was dull, but there were several cases she found intriguing.

Damian left and returned a moment later with a steaming cup of coffee. "Here," he said, handing it to her. "Take a break before you go blind."

"Has Evan shown up yet?" The coffee tasted like ambrosia.

Damian sighed. "Not yet. But Evan comes and goes at will, or at least he has for the past several months."

"Well, he left me some work to do, so he must have been in yesterday." She paused. "What about him and Romilda?" She sincerely hoped those two were enthralled with each other.

"It's too soon to tell, but maybe there's some hope there." Good. Damian sounded as if he really meant it.

"I want Evan to be happy," she said, not exactly sure why it was important Damian know that.

"Exactly." Damian smiled and got up to walk over to the polished bookcase. He pulled down a well-used volume. "Take some advice," he said tucking the book under his arm.

"Sure."

"Don't skip lunch."

"I won't," she promised.

He left then and Jessica smiled and closed her eyes. After a moment she returned to her research. A long time passed before her smile faded.

As promised, Jessica took her lunch hour and returned to find Evan searching for her. He sat down next to her in the library and reviewed her notes, asked a series of intelligent questions and made comments every now and then about her progress. Several times he praised her efforts. He made a few notations himself, and they spent the better part of an hour discussing different aspects of the Earl Kress case.

After Evan left, Jessica was exhilarated. Damian had revealed a keen insight into his brother's personality by assigning Evan to this important case. Representing Earl Kress had given Evan the challenge he needed; had given him a purpose, a cause. Evan was no slouch. He was dynamic, sharp and dedicated to representing this former athlete to the best of his ability and to the full extent of the law.

Several hours of research remained, and although it was late, Jessica decided to trudge on until she was finished.

"It's six o'clock and time for you to go home," Damian said from behind her in the tone she recognized. It was the one he used when he wouldn't listen to a word of argument. The kind that swayed juries.

"I'll be finished in a bit."

"You're finished now."

"Damian."

"Don't argue with me, Jessica. It won't do any good."

She closed the book she was reading and stood up. Every small movement of her lithe body spelled reluctance.

"Did you take time for lunch?"

"You're beginning to sound like my guardian!"

"I see you didn't eat, otherwise you wouldn't be snapping at me."

"I did so—and I'm not snapping!"

"That does it!"

Was he about to fire her for insubordination? Jessica wondered. She stared up at him, wondering what would happen next.

"We're going to dinner," he muttered.

"Dinner! But Damian, you've already—"

"Pizza," he said, "the deep-dish variety. There's a small Italian restaurant around the corner. I swear it's one of the best-kept secrets in Boston."

"Pizza," Jessica repeated slowly and her stomach growled in anticipation. "Well, if you insist, and it seems that you do." She reached for her purse.

They walked to the restaurant, which was nestled in the basement of one of the older buildings. The marble floors were badly worn, and the architecture showed that the structure had been built in the early thirties. Jessica had passed the building a hundred times and barely given it a second's notice.

"How'd you hear about this restaurant?" she asked.

"From the security guard. He eats here regularly

and recommended it to me. I've never tasted better Italian food."

The proprietor greeted Damian as if he were a long-lost cousin, kissing him on both cheeks and speaking in Italian as he looked approvingly at Jessica.

"What did he say?" she asked when they were seated at a table covered with a red-and-white-checked cloth. A candle flickered from inside a small red vase, and shadows danced across the opposite wall.

"I'm not entirely sure. I only know a few words myself."

"In that case you did a good job of faking it."

"All right, if you must know, Antonio assumed we're lovers," Damian said casually, opening the menu.

"You corrected him, didn't you?" she demanded, putting a hand to her chest. She could feel the color rush into her face.

"No."

"Damian, you can't let that man believe you and I..."

"You're probably right, I shouldn't. Especially when it's my brother you're in love with, not me."

Jessica set the menu aside and leaned forward until her stomach pressed against the edge of the table. They needed to get this straight between them once and for all. "I'm not in love with Evan," she whispered heatedly.

"All right, all right."

"You don't sound convinced."

"I'm convinced," he said, without looking at her. Whatever was offered on the menu had apparently captured his full attention.

"Good," she said, reaching for her own menu. She was about to suggest the sausage pizza when a basket of warm bread was brought to their table. The lovely dark-haired woman who'd delivered it caught Damian's face between her hands and kissed him soundly on both cheeks. Jessica must have looked shocked, because the older woman laughed delightedly. "You don't need to worry—I won't steal Damian away from you," she said, then added something in Italian.

Damian seemed to go pale at the woman's words. Jessica's own knowledge of Italian was scant, but she knew what *bambino* meant.

"Damian, tell me what she said."

He was silent while the same woman poured them each a glass of wine and brought a plate of antipasto. Then he sighed. "Nona says you seem good and sturdy."

"*What?* Anyway, she said more than that."

"Jessica, I already explained I only know a few words of Italian."

"You know more than me. She said *bambino.* Doesn't that mean 'baby'?"

Damian sighed again. "Yes. If you must know, Nona said you'll make a good mother to my children."

"Oh." Jessica glanced at the woman, who was standing on the other side of the room, busy ladling minestrone soup into two ceramic bowls, which she then brought.

"I guess we aren't going to get that pizza," Damian muttered after the soup was served.

Antonio returned with the bottle of Italian wine and replenished their glasses with many exclamations of pleasure. Damian thanked him in Italian, then they spoke for a minute or two.

"When did you learn to speak Italian?" Jessica asked.

"I didn't. I picked up a smidgen here and there over the years. I spent a couple of months in Italy before I entered law school and muddled my way through the country. That's about it."

"You're a man of many talents," she said, picking up her spoon and sampling the soup. It was rich and flavorful. In fact, everything was excellent—the meal, the smooth red wine, the cappucino and dessert. Each time she was convinced she couldn't swallow another bite, Nona would bring them something else she insisted they try.

"Either we leave now, or you'll have to roll me out of here," Jessica said.

Damian chuckled, settled the bill, and together they walked back to the office high-rise. The evening was glorious, and Jessica felt wonderful. She wasn't sure if it was the result of the weather, the delicious food and wine or the company—or maybe all of them.

"Thank you," she said in the elevator.

"You're welcome." Damian fell strangely quiet as they walked to the law library. Before she left for the night, Jessica wanted to shelve the volumes she'd been studying. Damian worked silently with her. When they were finished, he preceded her from the room, automatically turning off the light.

The room was suddenly dark and Jessica bumped into a table.

"Jessica."

"I'm fine," she assured him, walking toward the hall light.

"That's the problem," he muttered, reaching for her. She was in his arms before she realized it. "I'm not." With that his mouth came down on hers.

Chapter 5

This kiss wasn't brotherly, nor was it uncomplicated. Damian's mouth fit over hers, warm and coaxing. Jessica sighed and relaxed against him, giving herself up to the sensation. It felt *right* to be in his arms, that was all there was to it.

Her hands gripped the lapels of his jacket, her fingers crushing the soft wool as his mouth moved against hers. Damian's hand curved around the side of her neck, his touch tender as though he feared hurting her.

The kiss was unlike any Jessica had ever experienced. She felt the sensual power of it all the way to her toes, the impact stealing her breath. She moaned and Damian did, too. When they broke apart, neither spoke. Jessica wished he'd say something, anything, to break the silence. She needed him to explain what was happening, because she was lost, taken by surprise, yet delighted to the very depths of her being.

Instead, Damian turned and walked away.

She couldn't believe it. A tear slipped unnoticed down her cheek and dropped onto her silk blouse, the droplet bleeding into a small circle. She raised her hand to her face, surprised by the tear.

Funny that when she couldn't find the words to say what she felt, a tear would speak for her. She'd learned that lesson years earlier. Her mother's tears had fallen onto her grandmother's casket, and they had said far more than a whispered farewell. Tearstains on a letter revealed more than its words.

A tear on her cheek now, after she'd shared a kiss with this man, spelled out volumes. Only to Jessica the language was one she couldn't fully understand.

The sudden need to escape overwhelmed her. Collecting her purse, she stepped out of the library and proceeded down the hallway. She paused outside Damian's open door. She saw him standing in front of his window, looking into the night. His hands were clasped behind his back.

"Good night," she called softly.

He turned and smiled briefly. "Good night, Jessica. See you in the morning."

She wished they could sit down and discuss what had happened, but one look told her Damian was confused and not nearly as delighted as she was. He seemed troubled, burdened somehow. She wondered if he regretted having kissed her.

"Thank you for dinner," she said. "You were right. It's the best Italian food I've ever had." She didn't want to leave, but didn't have an excuse to stay.

"I'm glad you enjoyed it."

Jessica headed for the elevator. Her thoughts remained so muddled that she nearly missed her subway stop on the ride home. The first thing she did when she walked into her apartment was reach for the purple elephant Damian had won for her. She wrapped her arms around it and hugged it tight. It made her feel close to Damian. All she needed to do was shut her eyes and the memories of their night together at Cannon Beach filled her mind. She could almost hear the sound of the carousel, the echo of her own laughter when Damian insisted on winning her the elephant. She could hear the roller coaster as the riders shrieked past and smell the popcorn, candy apples and hot dogs.

Keeping the elephant pressed to her, Jessica slumped into the overstuffed chair and reached for her phone, dialing the number of her best friend. Cathy was far more insightful in these matters than she was. She would help her make sense of Damian's kiss.

"Hi," Jessica murmured when her friend answered.

Her greeting was met with a slight hesitation. "What's wrong?"

It didn't surprise her that her friend knew her so well. "What makes you think anything's wrong?"

"I recognize that tone of voice."

Smiling to herself, Jessica brought up her knees and rested her chin there as she assembled her thoughts. There didn't seem to be an easy way of explaining what had happened. Best just to blurt it out. "Damian kissed me tonight."

"And you liked it, didn't you?"

Cathy sounded gleeful, as though tempted to break into song. Jessica supposed this was what she got for having a theater-arts major for a best friend.

"Yeah—but I'm totally confused," Jessica admitted quietly. This jumble of mixed feelings was the main source of her troubles.

"Surprises you, doesn't it?" Cathy asked, then chuckled softly, again with that note of delight. "I've seen the handwriting on the wall ever since you mentioned Damian Saturday night. The guy sounds perfect for you."

"Don't be ridiculous."

"What's ridiculous about it?"

"I haven't thought of him…that way. Well, I have recently, and frankly, it frightens me to death. I've already made a fool of myself over one Dryden. I'm not anxious to make the same mistake with another one."

"You were a kid the first time. There's a world of difference between what happened then and what's happening now."

"Maybe," was all Jessica was willing to concede.

"Think, woman," Cathy said dramatically. "The man's obviously attracted to you, too. Otherwise he wouldn't be kissing you."

"I don't know that, and you don't, either. We kissed, and then he acted as if it was the worst thing he could have done. He didn't say a word and he just walked away. I don't know what to think. I'm so confused." She pressed a hand to her forehead.

"So you think he regretted it?"

"He must have. Otherwise…otherwise everything would have turned out differently. He looked at me as if I were a stranger, as if he didn't want to see me again."

"What was he supposed to do? Confess undying love? Didn't you tell me you had the whole situation figured out? The only reason Damian hired you in the first place was to bolster his brother's spirits. Think about it, Jess—the man has integrity. He can't very well start dating you himself if he believes you might still have some feeling for his younger brother."

"It drives me crazy that he'd think that!"

"I know, but you've got to look at it from his point of view."

"At the cost of my own sanity?"

"For now," Cathy said sympathetically.

"I don't know what to do!" Jessica cried, amazed at the amount of emotion that spilled into the words.

"There's more," Cathy said, warming to the subject. "If you're interested in Damian, it makes perfect sense that you're going to have to be the one to make the first move. Damian's hands are tied as long as he thinks there's the least chance you're interested in his brother. The guy's in a real bind here."

"Him! This whole thing with Evan's gotten out of hand. The poor guy's suffocating with everyone's concern. I actually feel sorry for him. He got the raw end of a deal in a relationship, and all he needed was some time to work out his pain," Jessica lamented. "Instead, Damian cut his work load until he's bored out of his mind. His parents, especially his mother, are dishing out sympathy by the truckload, and it's all Evan can do to stay afloat."

She paused for breath, then went on, "The only reason Damian hired me was that he thought I'd pull Evan out of the doldrums. I haven't talked to Evan, but I'm sure he resents all this nonsense. And I don't blame him."

"What about you and Damian?"

"I don't know what to think," Jessica admitted. "I wish I did. If he's interested in me, then surely it's his place to say or do something. Regardless of how he thinks I feel about Evan."

"Oh, come on, Jess!"

"I know Damian."

"Huh. You thought you knew Evan, too."

"I do, or rather, I did," she argued. The conversation was frustrating her more by the minute. "Besides, like I said earlier, I'm not interested in making a fool of myself over another Dryden. I learned my lesson the last time. Good grief, that was years ago and my parents and his *still* talk about it. Just this last weekend my own mother mentioned how pleased she'd be if I married Evan!"

"I have an idea," Cathy said slowly as though the scheme was taking shape in her mind as she spoke. "Introduce me to Damian."

"What possible reason do you have to meet him?" Jessica didn't like the sound of this.

"I just want to. Things aren't going well with David...."

"David?" Jessica cried. "Who's David?"

"The director for *Guys and Dolls*. Now listen, I know this sounds crazy, but trust me, it could work."

"What could work?" Jessica was fast losing what remained of her patience.

"Our meeting. I'll turn on the charm, do what I can to enchant him, and—"

"Just a minute, Cath, you're talking about the man *I'm* interested in."

"I know," she replied as if all this were perfectly logical. "But you want to know how serious he is about you, don't you? Also, maybe watching him with another woman will help you sort out *your* feelings for *him*."

"Yes, but—"

"Come on, Jess. You said yourself you weren't willing to make a fool of yourself a second time. This way you'll know."

"This sounds silly to me."

"Not only that," Cathy went on as though Jessica hadn't spoken, "it'll give me a chance to practice some of my best lines. Just introduce us, and I promise I won't do anything to embarrass you."

"All right," she agreed without any real enthusiasm. "How do you propose we do this?"

"I could stop by the office one day soon and suggest lunch. It'd be natural for you to introduce me around, wouldn't it?"

"I...suppose, but doesn't that seem a bit obvious?"

"Perhaps. Do you have a better idea?"

"No." She sighed. "Okay. Do you want me to invite Damian to join us? I'm coming into the office this Saturday to catch up on a few things, before Evan's big court case starts next week. My guess is that Damian will be there, as well."

"All the better, then. I'll see you Saturday around noon."

Jessica hedged. "You're sure about this?"

"Absolutely! I have ways of getting a man to talk."

"That sounds like something out of a movie."

Cathy laughed. "It is."

"That's what I thought," she mumbled.

Precisely at noon Cathy arrived at the office. Jessica envied her petite friend her pixie good looks, short dark hair and big blue eyes. Cathy looked striking in her pants, which were black with huge white dots, and multicolored striped suspenders. Her blouse was white with small black dots and she was wearing black high heels. One thing was certain—no one would miss seeing her walk down the street. If Evan had been in the office, he doubtless would have begged an introduction.

"You must have forgotten about our lunch," Cathy said more loudly than necessary, standing outside Jessica's office. Loudly enough for Damian to hear.

Her friend's ploy worked because a minute later he wandered out of his office.

"Damian, this is my friend Cathy Hudson," Jessica said. "I might have mentioned her in passing."

Damian and Cathy shook hands. "Jessica forgot we were supposed to meet for lunch today." Cathy said.

"It isn't a good idea for Jessica to skip meals," Damian said. His eyes twinkled and the effort to suppress a smile caused the corners of his mouth to quiver.

"So you've seen what happens when Jessica's stomach growls. Wounded bears are easier to reason with than Jess when she's hungry."

"Hey, that's not true!" Jessica flared. They were speaking as if she wasn't there. She braced her hands on her hips and glared at the two of them. She hadn't been keen on this idea of Cathy's from the first and her instincts were proving to be right.

Her former roommate eased closer to Damian and was gazing soulfully into his eyes. He didn't seem to mind in the least; in fact, he seemed to lap it up.

"I'll get my purse," Jessica said stiffly, leaving Cathy and Damian gazing at each other while she went behind her desk and dug in the bottom drawer. The whole charade irritated her, and she was furious she'd allowed herself to be talked into it.

Cathy managed to tear her eyes away from Damian long enough to throw visual spikes at her friend. It took Jessica a moment to realize what was being signaled. Oh, yes—she was supposed to invite him to tag along.

"Would you care to join us for lunch?" she asked Damian, managing to sound polite, if unenthusiastic.

"Please, do," Cathy said, her words like warm honey.

Damian looked at Jessica as if seeking her confirmation, and to her credit, she did produce a smile. She didn't know why she'd ever agreed to this.

"I'll be happy to join you," Damian surprised her by saying. She'd never dreamed he would. The man was *full* of surprises.

"Great, just great," Jessica muttered under her breath.

"Fabulous," came Cathy's melodious response.

Jessica rolled her eyes, and together the three of them headed out of the office. Damian suggested a well-known expensive restaurant, and before Jessica could comment one way or another, Cathy had agreed. Jessica snapped her mouth closed before she said something she'd regret. It irked her that Damian would so easily fall into Cathy's snare. It might be just a charade, but she was left more than a little confused.

Outside the building, Damian waved down a cab, and Cathy managed to have Damian in the backseat with her. Jessica sat in the front while her best friend giggled her way through the streets of Boston. They drove past the Boston Common and the Freedom Trail, the winding yellow path that led history buffs and tourists from one historic monument to another.

She was acting like a jealous fool, Jessica realized with a start. Jealous of Damian and Cathy? The fog that had clouded her thinking for the past several days cleared.

She was falling in love with Damian Dryden. It couldn't have been any more obvious. It was one of the things Cathy had set out to prove, and her friend was right—she'd needed this blunt lesson.

Of course she loved Damian. From the minute she'd walked into his office and asked about the job. From the minute he'd stood on the footbridge that forged the pond on his parents' property and insisted on taking her to Cannon Beach.

From the minute he'd kissed her.

This was what Cathy had been trying to tell her.

When they arrived at the restaurant, Cathy excused herself and Jessica. With her arm wrapped around her friend's, she dragged her to the ladies' room.

Before Jessica could open her mouth, Cathy burst out, "Damian's wonderful!"

"I know."

"I haven't met Evan, but I'm telling you right now if you're not interested in his big brother, I am. He's got a great wit, he's gorgeous, and—"

"I know all that." And a lot more.

"Listen," Cathy said, "I want you to make some excuse and leave."

Jessica was stunned. "You want me to *what?*"

Cathy was refreshing her makeup in front of the mirror, her eyeliner in hand. "You heard me. Remember an urgent appointment, something that will call you away so the two of us can be alone together. Only don't make it sound phony, or Damian will know what we're doing."

"*I* don't know what we're doing," she protested.

"I want you to give me some time alone with him."

"Why?" Jessica demanded. "Listen, you've already

proved your point. I do care about Damian. And I'm
not interested in sharing him with you."

"I know how you feel about him," Cathy said
slowly as if that much had been understood from the
beginning. "But my being alone with him will tell
us both how he feels about *you,* which was the main
purpose of my plan."

"You're sure about this?"

"How many times are you going to ask me? Of
course I'm sure."

"I can't help thinking we're both good candidates
for psychoanalysis!"

Cathy laughed outright at that. "Don't worry,
I'm not going to steal him away from you, although
heaven knows I'm tempted. The guy's a hunk. Why
hasn't he ever married?"

"How am I supposed to know?"

"Have you tried asking?"

Cathy had a way of making everything sound perfectly straightforward. "Don't worry about it. I'll find
that out, along with everything else."

Jessica hesitated. She trusted Cathy—most of the
time. She also knew it wasn't beneath her best friend
to say or do something sneaky. That was what worried Jessica.

"Go back to your apartment," Cathy instructed,
before outlining her lush full mouth with a glossy
shade of lipstick.

"I still don't understand what you're doing."

Cathy patiently closed the tube and shook her head
as though to suggest the answer was obvious. "You

don't need to. When Damian and I've finished lunch I can report my findings to you. Is everything clear now?"

"As mud."

Cathy rolled her eyes. "I'm trying to be a help here. The least you can do is cooperate."

"All right, all right," Jessica muttered, but she didn't like it.

"Let's not keep Prince Charming waiting any longer," Cathy said, taking Jessica's elbow. "Just remember to come up with something brilliant to excuse yourself."

Jessica was feeling anything but brilliant at the moment. "All right," she promised.

Jessica did manage to come up with a plausible excuse. They were seated and given elaborate menus decorated with gold tassels. Jessica set her purse on the floor, and it promptly fell over. When she leaned down to right it, she pulled a small appointment card from the outside pocket. Straightening, she studied the card.

"What's the date today?"

"The twelfth. Why?" Cathy's eyes had never been rounder, or more guileless.

"It says here I've got a dentist's appointment this afternoon." She made a show of looking at her watch. "In half an hour."

"On a Saturday?" Damian asked casually.

"Lots of dentists are keeping Saturday hours," Cathy explained conversationally, spreading the linen napkin across her lap. "I went in for a checkup myself no more than a month ago, and my appointment was on a Saturday."

"It's too late to call and cancel," Jessica said with a defeated air. "It took me months to get this appointment as it was. The Saturday schedule fills up quickly."

"If you made it months ago, it isn't any wonder you forgot." Cathy seemed all too willing to offer Jessica an excuse.

"I'd better see if I can catch a cab," Jessica mumbled. She wouldn't be able to keep up this charade much longer. It'd be a miracle if Damian didn't see through their plot. It had more holes than a golf course.

"I'm so sorry you have to go," Cathy said with enough sincerity to sound believable.

Damian said nothing. If Cathy's theory was true, Damian would reveal some regret at her leaving. Instead, he smiled at her and nodded as if he welcomed the time alone with her friend. Jessica's hands closed tightly around her purse strap as she stood and made her farewells.

Once she was outside, the doorman's whistle hailed her a cab. Jessica climbed into the backseat and gave the man the address of her apartment, thinking this was going to be the longest afternoon of her life.

She was right.

She paced her living room munching on pretzels for a good two hours. Most of the large bag had disappeared before her doorbell chimed. Cathy. In her eagerness to hear what she'd achieved, Jessica nearly jerked the door off its hinges.

Nothing could have surprised her more than to find Damian standing on the other side. She must have looked as dumbstruck as she felt, because he grinned and let himself in without waiting for an invitation.

"How was the dentist's appointment?"

"Ah… I didn't have one."

"I know." He walked over to her bookcase and was examining the titles as if he'd come for that purpose alone.

"You knew?"

"You're not nearly as good an actress as your friend," he said, turning to face her. Jessica tried to read his expression, but found it impossible. She felt rooted to the carpet, unable to move and hardly able to breathe. She wondered if he was angry with her. Perhaps he was amused. She couldn't tell which.

She should have known he'd see through their ploy. "It was a stupid plan," she admitted. Her shoulders sagged with a burden of regrets. She'd allowed Cathy to talk her into this crazy scheme, and she'd followed like a lamb to the slaughter.

"I…we didn't offend you, did we?"

A hint of a smile touched his eyes. "No, it was a very sweet thing to do, but unnecessary."

She blinked, not knowing what to say because she wasn't sure she understood.

Damian walked over to her and reached out a hand to press against her cheek. His touch was gentle, his gray eyes as serious as she'd ever seen them. He spoke as though his words pained him. "I appreciate your efforts, Jessica, but I can find my own dates." Then he bent and gently placed his mouth on hers. The kiss was far too short to satisfy her. Instead, it created a need for more. When he lifted his head, everything within her wanted to beg him not to stop.

"I'll see you Monday morning," he said, turning and heading toward the door.

She opened her mouth to tell him to stay, but by the time she could get the words out he was gone. He actually believed she was setting him up with Cathy. No wonder. That was exactly what it looked like. Why hadn't she thought of this before? Jessica slumped onto her sofa, covered her face with her hands and resisted the urge to cry.

Damian hadn't been gone for more than five minutes when Cathy arrived. Jessica opened her door to find her friend leaning against the doorjamb as if she needed its support. She threw herself down on Jessica's couch and removed her high heels. "That man's a tough nut to crack."

Jessica folded her arms and asked, "What do you mean?"

"I mean he was so closemouthed about you, there's only one sensible conclusion."

"And what's that?"

Cathy stopped rubbing her toes and turned her big blue eyes on Jessica. "You're serious? You mean you really don't know?"

"I wouldn't be asking if I did!"

"He's in love with you."

Jessica didn't believe it. "He can't be."

"Why can't he? Is there a law posted somewhere that says it's a crime to fall in love with Jessica Kellerman?"

"No…"

"He wasn't interested in me, and trust me, I tried."

Jessica stiffened, remembering her reaction to Cathy's attempts to flirt with Damian. She hadn't liked it. None of the crazy stunts her friend had pulled over the years had put their friendship on the line. This one had. Damian was off-limits, and before Cathy left for home, Jessica wanted to make sure she knew it.

"He thought I was trying to set him up with you," Jessica muttered disparagingly.

"What's so tragic about that? That was exactly what I wanted him to think."

"But why?"

Cathy's smile was slow and confident. "This is the reason I'm your best friend. My little performance this afternoon was for both your benefits. You know how you feel about Damian, too. I'm right, aren't I?"

Jessica nodded reluctantly, hating to admit her friend's ploy had worked. But there was a problem. "Damian assumes I was setting him up with you because I'm not interested in him."

"What makes you think that?"

"'Think' nothing. He practically said so."

"When?"

"Just a few minutes ago. He was here. The whole experiment backfired, Cath."

"You straightened him out, didn't you?"

"No... I didn't get the chance." Jessica felt worse and worse. She had no one to blame but herself. She'd allowed Cathy to talk her into this crazy scheme, and now she was suffering the consequences.

Cathy went uncharacteristically quiet. "You'll talk to him, won't you?"

"I...I don't know. I suppose so."

"Good. Explain how you feel, otherwise he'll go right on thinking you're not interested."

Jessica closed here eyes and groaned.

"It won't be hard," Cathy assured her. "He's crazy about you, Jess."

When her former roommate left a few minutes later, Jessica realized what a good friend Cathy had always been—despite her penchant for theatrics.

Jessica considered Cathy's advice for what remained of the weekend and arrived at the office early Monday morning. To her surprise, Evan was sitting at his desk when she walked in. He smiled broadly in greeting. "Good morning, sweet Jessica." He seemed to be in an awfully good mood. His brown eyes were clear and lively, and his smile was warm. "You're just the person I was waiting to see."

She stowed her purse and moved into his office with a pen and pad, fully expecting him to give her another lengthy assignment.

"Sit down," he instructed, motioning her toward a chair on the other side of his desk. He leaned back in his own chair, looking relaxed. "Now tell me something."

"Sure." Her mind was churning with a possible list of requests.

"I've been something of a bad boy around here lately, not pulling my own weight and the like. You know that, don't you?"

"I...I've only been in the office a short time," she said, not wanting to speak out of turn. "It's not for me to say if you have or haven't been doing your share of the work."

"Really, Jess, there's no need to be shy."

"All right," she said, resenting the fact that she'd been put in this position. "I know you were hurt, but we all face disappointments in life. It's time to pull yourself up by your bootstraps."

Evan laughed delightedly, not the least bit offended. "By heaven, I like a woman who can speak her mind."

Jessica relaxed and uncrossed her legs. "Was that all?"

"No." He tipped back in his chair and rubbed the side of his face while studying her carefully. "There was a time when you were rather...keen on me, wasn't there?"

"Yes." She flushed. "Years ago."

"You worshiped me from afar, so to speak."

She lowered her gaze and nodded.

"You're right about my being disappointed," he went on. "I felt the need to prove myself. In looking back, I realize how shallow I've been. I'm not proud of my behavior these past few months, and I'm hoping to make up for it with the Earl Kress trial."

Jessica didn't know how to comment or even if she should.

"My father and I had a good long talk this weekend," Evan added thoughtfully.

"I understand he's considering running for the Senate."

"Yes, and he's decided to give it a shot. Damian and I will be spending a fair amount of time working on his campaign. The gist of our conversation was simple. He wants me to get my life straightened out and start dating again."

"I think he's absolutely right," she agreed readily, assuming Evan was referring to the diplomat's daughter.

"Great." He beamed her a killer smile. "I was hoping you'd feel that way."

Jessica blinked, not grasping what he meant. "Why's that?"

"Because, my dear Jessie, I've decided I'd like to get to know you better. You're very sweet and a hell of a good worker. Dad reminded me that you were keen on me a few years back, and I'm hoping to capitalize on your affection."

"Ah…" Now didn't seem the appropriate moment to bring up her feelings for Damian. Then again, she'd better before matters got out of hand.

"I don't mind telling you," Evan said before she could speak, "my confidence has been badly shaken.

I feel safe and secure with you. Frankly, I don't know how I'd deal with any more rejection."

Ready For Romance

Chapter 6

"Aren't you seeing Romilda?" Jessica asked with a sinking feeling. She *had* to say something, set the record straight, but Evan was studying her with an eager intensity, and coward that she was, Jessica couldn't make herself do it. "You seemed to get along so well with her at the barbecue, and her political connections might help your father's campaign efforts."

"She's already returned to Europe."

"I see."

"Don't get me wrong, Romilda's a sweetheart, but she isn't the one for me," Evan explained. "I want an old-fashioned girl, who values the same things I do. Mom, home, apple pie—that sort of thing. A woman who knows what's really important in life. Someone like you, Jessica."

Jessica didn't doubt for an instant that Evan was echoing his father's words. Maybe the sort of woman he described *was* right for him, but Jessica wasn't the one. She was about to explain diplomatically that there was already someone in her life—without telling him who—when he spoke again.

"I've got a ton of work waiting for me this morning, but my parents asked that we meet later, and I thought the five of us could have lunch together."

"Five?"

"Damian will be there, too. Would noon be convenient?"

"Ah…"

"Great." He returned his attention to the papers on his desk. Jessica waited a moment, then got up and went back to the outer office. She felt the blood drain out of her face as she reached her desk and sat down.

"Is Mr. Dryden here?" Jessica hadn't been aware of Mrs. Sterling's arrival.

Jessica looked up and nodded.

"But it's barely nine."

"I know," she murmured.

"What's come over that man?" the secretary murmured, unable to disguise her amazement. "Never mind, let's not question it. I'd rather count my blessings. I was about to lose heart with him. I was afraid Damian had given Evan too much slack the past few months."

Jessica managed a weak smile. Mrs. Sterling moved about the office with the efficiency that was her trademark. She brewed a pot of coffee and the aroma of the rich Colombian helped revive Jessica. When the coffee was ready, Mrs. Sterling poured Evan a cup and carried it into his office. Jessica couldn't hear what was being said, but apparently Evan was in top form, because his secretary returned grinning broadly.

Jessica sat at her desk, too numb to think clearly. She'd missed her golden opportunity, if indeed there'd been one, to tell Evan she was in love with Damian. Yet it didn't seem fair to make such a confession to his brother when she hadn't said a word to Damian. Nor was she convinced Damian felt the same way about her. All she had to go on was Cathy's faith.

Her theatrical friend had a tendency to exaggerate, to expand the truth and fill it with an enthusiasm that simply might not exist. Damian was fond of her, Jessica didn't doubt that, but as for his being in love with her, Jessica couldn't say.

There was nothing to do but sit by patiently and wait to see how matters developed. Evan was making this effort for his father; it didn't mean he intended their relationship to be anything but show. Certainly he wasn't serious about wooing her. Not when he'd cared so deeply for this unknown Mary Jo.

The morning passed quickly as they prepared for the Earl Kress trial, slated to begin the following day. The attention generated by the local television stations was sure to spark interest in the law firm and in Evan's father's bid for the Senate. In addition, the trial had the potential to affect the outcome of education in school districts across the country.

Close to noon, Evan emerged from his office, and with a warm smile at Jessica, said to his secretary, "I'm going to steal this lovely one away from you for a couple of hours."

Mrs. Sterling nodded approvingly.

Jessica reached for her purse and stood, hoping this lunch would afford her a few minutes alone with Damian so they could talk. She desperately needed to discuss things with him, to explain what had happened and seek his counsel.

To Jessica's disappointment, the opportunity never arose. The three met Evan's parents at the Hilton. The meal was pleasant and cordial, and everyone seemed to be in a good mood—with the exception of Damian, who practically ignored Jessica. She might have been invisible for all the attention he paid her.

She decided to make an effort to let her feelings for the older Dryden son be known, and she waited until there was a lull in the conversation.

"Damian and I were out to Cannon Beach recently," she announced brightly after their salads were served. Evan's parents exchanged meaningful glances.

"From here on out Evan will be the one taking you to the beach, isn't that right?" Damian said to his brother.

"You should have said something earlier, Jess," Evan said, picking up on Damian's cue. "I love Cannon Beach. We'll make a point of going there sometime, all right? As soon as the Earl Kress trial's over."

"All right," Jessica agreed, her heart in her throat.

She looked to Damian, who was busy eating his salad. From all outward appearances, it made no difference to him whom she dated. Apparently the idea of Evan's holding her close while they rode on the roller coaster didn't trouble him. Not at all.

After lunch they made their way into one of the meeting rooms on the second level of the hotel, where a news conference was scheduled. There, Walter Dryden, surrounded by his wife and family, announced his intention to run for the Senate.

Mingling in the audience of newsmen, well-wishers and political-party members, Jessica was able to stand back and view the four Drydens. They were a handsome, wholesome family who believed in the American dream. She admired and loved them, and wished Walter Dryden every success.

Flashbulbs exploded around her as she wandered to the back of the room. She wasn't sure why Evan had insisted she attend this affair, other than to reassure his father he'd taken their father-son talk to heart.

Jessica knew that life was often filled with ironic twists such as this, but why did hers have to be so frustrating? She was pretty sure Evan's father had put the idea of dating her into his son's head. And why not? It was well-known she'd once had a crush on Evan. And their families were so close. She was the logical choice, and the fact that she now worked for Evan made it all the more convenient.

The younger Dryden hoped to enhance his image, assist his father in his campaign efforts and prove he was over a painful relationship. What better way to start than with a woman who'd once had stars in her eyes for him?

Except that those stars were focused in another direction now. On his older brother. A man who seemed determined to do the noble thing and step aside for his brother.

For the first time in months, Evan had revealed a willingness to put the past behind him and get on with his life. And Damian believed she was the reason he had. So he would do nothing to change that—even if he did love her himself.

Every day for the next week the Dryden name turned up in all the media. The television and radio stations followed the trial, and each afternoon the newspaper carried an account of what had happened in the courtroom. Jessica met Earl Kress the first time in the courtroom and was impressed with the young man's sincerity. He wasn't looking to cripple the school system with a huge monetary settlement; instead, he sought changes that would help other athletes. Evan had arranged for a private tutor for the young man. Earl hoped to return to college within a year and work toward a degree in education. His goal was to teach high school students himself.

The more she learned about Evan's generosity to Earl, the more impressed she was with the lawyer's generous heart. Earl had been cheated out of his education, and Evan had made it his mission to make sure this didn't happen to future generations.

At the same time, Walter Dryden was making a

splash across the various media. It seemed there was a social engagement every night of the week having to do with the upcoming primary. Because of his involvement with the trial, Evan wasn't expected to attend these functions. For that Jessica was grateful, although she knew Damian had become actively involved in his father's campaign. She yearned to talk to him, but he seemed to be avoiding her. She rarely saw him, and when she did he was occupied with someone else.

On Friday the jury convened. Jessica returned to the office, preferring not to wait at the courthouse for the outcome of the trial. Evan had built a strong case and she was confident Earl would win his suit, but waiting for the jury's verdict was agony.

The office buzzed with activity, the way it generally did in the afternoons. There was the hum of computers, fax machines and photocopiers, and messengers zigzagged from one room to the next, crowding the hallways. The whole place was filled with an air of expectancy.

Jessica walked over to her desk, removed her shoes and rubbed her sore toes against her calves. Her muscles ached, and she was mentally and emotionally exhausted. This had been an incredibly hectic week. As soon as she got home, she was going to soak in a hot tub and curl up with a good book. Sleeping until noon the next day held irresistible appeal.

Mrs. Sterling had left on an errand and Jessica had just slumped down in her chair when Damian strolled into the office. He stopped abruptly when he saw she was alone.

Jessica froze, her breath trapped in her lungs.

"Hello, Jessica," he said stiffly.

"Hello," she managed.

"Where's Mrs. Sterling?" he asked, recovering first. He was brisk and businesslike, as if he'd never held her in his arms, as if she'd never been more to him than a friend, a casual one at that.

"Off on an errand," she answered, then added, "The jury's still out."

"So I understand." He walked over to Mrs. Sterling's desk and set a stack of papers in the secretary's in-basket.

"Have you been to that Italian restaurant lately?" she asked, desperate to make conversation. Desperate to remind him of the good times they'd shared— and what had happened afterward. She yearned with all her being that he understood her message—that those times had meant the world to her and that she hoped they'd been important to him, too. She prayed he'd realize how much she missed him.

"I haven't dined out lately." Then he turned abruptly and strode from the room.

Hurt and angry, Jessica wanted to shout at him to come back. But it wouldn't have done any good; she knew that. He'd sliced her out of his life without a second thought, and apparently without a single regret.

About an hour later, Evan burst into the office. He paused just inside the doorway, threw back his head and released a yell loud enough to sway the light fixtures.

"We did it!"

Startled, Jessica looked up from her desk. She stood to offer him her congratulations, and Evan rushed to her, lifting her high off the ground and whirling her around. "We won!" he shouted.

"Evan!" She laughed, bracing her hands on his shoulders. He was spinning so fast she was growing dizzy.

His cries of jubilation had attracted the attention of others in the office, but Evan didn't show any signs of releasing her. He set her back down on the ground and, looping his arm around her shoulders, kept her close to his side. Words of congratulations were enthusiastically offered.

"I couldn't have done it without Jessica," he announced to the gathering. "Her research was invaluable. Damian, too," Evan said, holding his free arm out to his brother. "A man couldn't ask for a better brother."

Jessica was looking at Damian, and whether he'd intended it or not—she suspected he hadn't—their eyes met. His guard had lowered, and his expression was one of such emotional intensity that nothing could have pulled her gaze from his. In him she read pride, loyalty and devotion. In him she saw that there was nothing on this earth he would do or say to hurt his brother, even at the sacrifice of his own happiness.

Tears clouded her vision. Gazing into the faces of those around her, she forced herself to smile, forced herself to look as though this was the happiest moment of her life, when on the inside, she'd never felt more miserable.

Evan insisted on taking her to dinner that night to celebrate. A victory gala, he told her. He chose a restaurant well-known for its superb food and service, and Jessica knew when they were seated that she was the envy of every woman there. Evan had never looked more handsome or been more charming.

They were leaving the restaurant, waiting for the valet to bring around Evan's car, when a news photographer stopped them and took their picture. Jessica protested, but Evan told her that this was the price of fame and she might as well smile.

The next morning, Jessica's mother phoned before she'd had a chance to wake, and hours before she'd intended to. She was extremely depressed, and sleep was the perfect escape.

"Jessica, have you seen it?" Joyce demanded, her voice raised with excitement. "I've already called the newspaper and am having them make copies for Lois and me. You both look fabulous."

"Seen what, Mother?" was the groggy reply.

"The newspaper, sweetheart. There's a picture of you and Evan on the society page with a nice little write-up. In case you didn't see it, your name was mentioned in the gossip column, too, on Thursday, linking you with Evan. Oh, honey, I'm so pleased."

"Oh, Lord," Jessica whispered, her mind clouded with exhaustion. "I remember now. A photographer stopped us last night."

"Yes, I know, that's what I've been telling you. The picture's in this morning's paper. I'm thrilled and so is your father, not to mention Lois and Walter."

Jessica was anything but thrilled. "It's only a picture, Mom."

"It's more than that, Jessica. It's a dream come true for you, and for me, too. You've always felt so strongly about Evan and now, after all these years, he feels the same way about you."

"Mother, you don't understand. Evan and I—"

"You don't know how pleased Lois and I are. We realize it's much too soon to be making wedding plans, but it's the sort of thing good friends love to do when their children are dating. You're our only daughter, and I can tell you right now this will be the gala event of the year. Your father and I insist."

She only paused long enough to take a breath, then rushed on, "We'd be so very pleased if you and Evan decided to have an autumn wedding. Lois has been my friend for so many years, and to think that someday we might share grandchildren! It does both our hearts good."

Jessica rubbed a hand over her eyes, repressing the urge to weep. "Mom…"

"I don't mean to pressure you."

"I know you don't."

"Good. I'm sorry I woke you, darling. I should have realized you'd be exhausted after this last week. Go back to sleep. We'll talk later."

Sleep was impossible now. Jessica padded barefoot into the kitchen and made coffee, standing at the counter until the liquid had drained into the glass pot. Then she poured herself a mug, and cradling it in both hands, sat at her kitchen table. Balancing her feet against the edge of the chair, her knees propped up under her chin, she waited until the coffee had cooled enough for a first sip. It did little to revive her sagging spirits, settling unsatisfactorily in the pit of her stomach while she mulled over what she was going to do.

Already it had started, already she could feel the ropes tightening around her heart, binding her. She felt imprisoned by what everyone believed was right for her, what everyone believed she wanted herself, when in reality she loved Damian, not Evan.

The phone startled her, and she swore as she spilled coffee on her hands. "Hello," she snapped, grabbing the receiver.

"What the hell's going on?" Cathy demanded, sounding full of righteous indignation.

"Excuse me!" The last thing she needed was her best friend's accusations.

"I picked up the paper this morning, and there's your bright smiling face to greet me."

"So I understand," she muttered.

"There's something wrong with this picture, though. You're with the wrong brother. Care to explain?"

"No."

"Why not?"

Jessica sighed. "It's a long story."

"Condense it."

She sighed again. "Evan's decided to come out of his doldrums—"

"About time, wouldn't you say?"

"Yes, definitely, but he isn't doing this for himself. His father's running for political office and so Evan's making an effort to smile and put on a happy face."

"By dating you."

"It seems so."

"I know all about his father. Walter Dryden's name's been splashed across the headlines all week, right along with Evan's and Earl Kress's," Cathy said impatiently. "So cut to the chase and tell me why you were out on the town with Evan and not Damian."

A simple explanation was beyond Jessica. This was the most complicated misadventure of her life. "You were wrong, Cath," she said miserably. "Damian isn't nearly as fond of me as you assumed. Otherwise he would have said something long before now."

"Said something about what?" Cathy yelped.

"Caring about me," she whispered miserably. She felt as though she was standing chest deep in quicksand with no chance of getting free.

Cathy groaned. "All right, I can see this tale of woe isn't something you're going to be able to abbreviate. Start at the beginning and be sure you tell me everything."

To her credit, Cathy listened attentively to the events of the week, all that had ensued since Jessica's conversation with Evan on Monday morning. When Jessica finished, Cathy was uncharacteristically silent.

"I see what you mean," she said finally, sounding none too happy herself. "Damian's caught between a rock and a hard place. He's crazy about you, Jess. My instincts told me that the day we had lunch."

"But apparently not crazy enough." Jessica closed her eyes to the sharp pain the thought produced.

"Wrong," Cathy corrected defensively. "Damian's got a sense of family and duty so strong he'd sacrifice his own happiness. That's not loving you too little, my friend, that's loving you—and Evan—too damn much."

"If that's the case, then why do I feel like leaping off a bridge? My mother and Lois Dryden are talking about a wedding and grandchildren."

Cathy let the comment pass. "How often do you see Evan?"

"Every day—we work together, remember?"

"I meant socially."

That wasn't a fair question. Because of the trial they'd been together for the better part of each evening, as well as every day. Lunch and dinner had been haphazard affairs while they discussed different aspects of the case and their strategies. It was business, nothing more. He hadn't so much as held her hand.

"We've been seeing a good deal of each other," Jessica said, and then explained.

"I see, and how do you feel about Evan now?"

"I'm glad he's trying to get his life together. But he isn't attracted to me, and doesn't pretend to be, either."

"Then why haven't you said something to Damian? Why haven't you explained?"

"How could I?" Jessica protested tartly. It wasn't that she hadn't thought of doing so a hundred times. "First off, we were both heavily involved in the Earl Kress case. The timing was wrong. I might have said something over dinner last night if Damian had given me any encouragement, but he didn't. I can't help thinking you're wrong about us."

"We've already been through that," Cathy muttered in frustration.

"I know Evan is dating me for show. I wouldn't be surprised if he'd arranged for that photographer himself. It's the sort of thing he'd do."

"Aren't you afraid he'll fall in love with you?"

"No. His heart is so battered it'll be a good long while before he takes a chance on love again."

Cathy was uncharacteristically quiet. "His family's important to him, the same way yours is to you. So play this hand close to your chest, Jess. Vulnerable as he is just now, Evan might develop a deep…affection for you. That would be a disaster."

This was something Jessica had worried about earlier, and she was greatly relieved that their relationship had turned out to be strictly platonic. "You're certainly filled with happy suggestions."

Cathy ignored that, too. "When are you seeing him again?"

"Tomorrow afternoon. He's picking me up for a fund-raiser for his father. It's a picnic." She dreaded

the entire affair. If it wasn't for the opportunity of seeing Damian, she'd have found an excuse not to attend.

"Have fun."

"Right," Jessica said, knowing fun would be impossible.

After she'd hung up the phone, Jessica took a
shower. She stood under the hard spray, letting the
water hammer at her face. When she'd finished she
felt better—and filled with purpose.

Evan arrived to pick her up early the next day.
He wore a white sweater with a blue braid along the
V-shaped neckline. He looked stylish and debonair,
very Ivy League casual. His eyes lit up when he saw
her in her cheery summer dress with the short white
jacket.

"I can't get over what a beauty you grew up to be."

"You always were a silver-tongued devil," Jessica
teased. He was in a good mood, and he had a right to
be after the success of the previous week.

Evan's sports car was parked right in front of her
building. He held open the door for her and helped
her inside. They chatted amiably on the ride to Whispering Willows, where the fund-raising picnic was
being held. The area was decorated with banners and
American flags, and there was even a small grandstand and a band.

Jessica was determined to find a chance to talk to
Damian, to explain her feelings. He couldn't avoid
her forever.

Jessica's parents were there, handing out small

American flags to the guests. Rows of folding chairs were set up in front of the grandstand for Walter Dryden's speech.

Everyone was busy with one picnic task or another. Jessica helped where she could, keeping her eye out for Damian.

She was busy dishing up potato salad alongside Evan when she first saw Damian. He was talking to an older woman and happened to look in Jessica's direction. Their eyes met for the briefest of seconds before he quickly averted his gaze. Jessica swallowed the pain that constricted her throat.

After the food had been served, Walter Dryden strolled up to Jessica. He was a big man, strong in build and, she knew, equally strong in character. He hugged her and thanked her for all her help.

"You've grown into a beautiful young woman, Jessica." His deep voice echoed what Evan had said to her earlier.

"Thank you. I don't know if I've had a chance to tell you how pleased I am that you've decided to run for senator," she said.

"I wish I'd started my campaign much sooner. I'm going to be stuck playing catch-up the next couple of months, which means a lot of hard work."

"You're exactly what this state needs," Jessica said sincerely.

"Your confidence means a lot to me." They were strolling together side by side. "I've been doing some hard thinking along those lines myself. About how you're exactly what my son needs."

"I'm sorry?"

"You and Evan."

Jessica didn't know what to say. She should have explained then and there that it was Damian she loved, but her throat went dry and her tongue seemed glued to the roof of her mouth.

"He needs you," Walter Dryden repeated.

"He's going to be just fine, Mr. Dryden. I don't think you should worry about him."

Walter Dryden's nod was somber. "Lois and I believe you're responsible for that."

The taste of panic filled her mouth. "I'm sure that's not true."

"Nonsense. You have to learn how to accept a compliment, young lady. It'll serve you well later in life—Evan, too, for that matter." He paused, his look thoughtful. "I believe my son will eventually enter politics himself. He's a natural, but he isn't ready yet and probably won't be for several years. I've had to bite my tongue not to sway that son of mine, but Lois would never forgive me if I pushed him toward something he didn't want."

Jessica hoped he felt the same way about forcing Evan into an unwanted relationship.

"We're getting off the subject," Walter muttered, with a shake of his head. "I wanted to thank you, my dear, for helping Evan."

"But I haven't."

"Nonsense. You've made all the difference in the world to my son these last few weeks. I'd mentioned to Damian that you and I had talked and you'd be coming in for an interview. His decision to hire you was brilliant. I couldn't have thought of anything better for Evan myself."

"I have a lot to thank Damian for," Jessica said, so softly she doubted Walter heard her.

"Ah, here you are," Evan declared, coming up behind them. "Don't tell me my own father is stealing away my favorite girl."

Walter chuckled. "Not likely, son. You two enjoy yourselves now. You've both worked hard all afternoon. Take a break, sneak away and have fun."

"But your speech..." Jessica protested.

"No matter. You can hear me speak any day of the week. Now off with you."

Evan reached for her hand, and they walked along the outskirts of the grandstand area. They were moving toward a stand of weeping willow trees, and Jessica found that Evan's mood had changed subtly. He seemed troubled. She waited for him to broach the problem.

"Do you mind if we take a few minutes to talk?" he said after a moment.

"I'd like that." Her heart swelled with relief. What they needed was a healthy dose of honesty. She stopped and leaned against the trunk of a tree. They were partially hidden from view, and the privacy was welcome.

"I don't feel that you and I are connecting, Jessica."

"I know." She thought about her mother and all her talk about a wedding and grandchildren. Her mind drifted back to the conversation she'd had with Evan's father moments earlier. Everything had gone much too far.

"I've wanted to talk to you all week, but everything was so hectic, what with the trial and Dad announcing his candidacy."

"It was quite a week," Jessica agreed.

"Our names have been linked in the newspaper."

"Your name's often in the paper." He was from one of Boston's most prominent families, after all.

Evan chuckled. "That's true enough." He reached for her hand then, holding it between his own. "I'd like all that speculation about us to change. I'm ready to settle down with one woman."

Jessica's heart stopped beating. If he proposed marriage, she swore she was going to break down and weep. Everything and everyone seemed to be working against her, including her own parents.

"I...I've always been fond of you, Evan, but I think it's only fair for you to know—"

"'Fond' is such a weak word," he interrupted, frowning.

She didn't want to walk over his already bruised ego. "I know, but—"

"Do you realize we haven't even kissed?" He smiled, his eyes twinkling with boyish eagerness. "That's about to be corrected, sweet Jessica." He placed his hands on both sides of her face and, before she could protest, lowered his mouth to hers.

It was a gentle kiss, undemanding and tender. Jessica felt nothing, except an increasing desire to cry.

How could she feel anything for Evan when she cared so deeply for Damian? When she *loved* Damian?

Evan lifted his head from hers and gazed down at her, his eyes now dark and unreadable. He studied her for a moment. "I won't pressure you, Jessica. We'll give this time." He brushed a stray curl from her cheek and kissed her there, his lips warm and moist against her face.

It was then that Jessica saw Damian. He was standing on the edge of the crowd that had gathered to hear Walter's speech. His eyes were on Jessica and Evan. When he realized she'd seen him, he turned and walked away. His steps were brisk and hurried as though he couldn't move fast enough.

For one wild moment, Jessica considered running after him, but Evan had put one arm possessively around her shoulders and was leading her back toward the grandstand.

It was too late.

Chapter 7

"Well?" Cathy demanded without a word of greeting as Jessica opened the apartment door to her friend Sunday evening. Cathy swept her backpack from her shoulder and carelessly tossed it aside. "How'd the picnic go?"

"Politically it was a success. From what I understand, Mr. Dryden raised a lot of money for his campaign." She was avoiding the issue and knew it, but the subject of Evan and Damian had become too painful even to think about.

Cathy knew her well enough to recognize the signs. "Sit down," she instructed, pointing at the overstuffed chair that was Jessica's favorite spot. Her friend became downright dictatorial whenever she felt strongly about something; apparently, she did now.

Jessica followed Cathy's orders simply because she didn't have the force of will to argue. Settling into the chair, she waited while Cathy paced the carpet in front of her. Jessica could almost hear her friend's brain waves crackling.

"I've been giving this matter some thought," Cathy began.

"I can see that," Jessica returned, wondering what Cathy's feverish mind had concocted this time.

"I want you to develop a limp," Cathy said. She sounded as though this was a stroke of pure genius.

Jessica wanted to laugh out loud. "You're joking, right? Because heaven knows I can't take you seriously."

"I'm dead serious, but I only want you to limp when Damian's around, not Evan."

Jessica shook her head, as though that would improve her hearing. For sheer lunacy, this idea ranked right up there with the luncheon invitation. "What possible reason would I have to do something as stupid as fake a limp?"

"Just remember to limp on the same foot," Cathy said, ignoring Jessica's question and looking a bit worried. "This is just the type of thing you'd forget. It might be a good idea if you put a mark on the top of your shoe so you don't goof up."

Jessica held up her hands. "Cathy, have you OD'd on too much sugar or something? This is the craziest thing you've ever suggested!"

"Trust me," Cathy said impatiently. "I'm in theater—I know what I'm doing."

"Your self-confidence doesn't reassure me in the least."

"It should. I know about these things."

"Would it be too much to share the logic of your plan with me?"

"Not at all." Cathy's step was jaunty as she walked over to the sofa, dropped down and crossed her legs. "Sympathy. We want Damian to think you've hurt yourself—a twisted ankle, a trick knee, that sort of thing. If he cares about you half as much as I believe, he won't be able to stand by and do nothing. He'll come to your aid, and the minute he touches you, he won't be able to hide how he feels." She stopped abruptly. "Be warned, though. You should be prepared."

"For what?"

"He might just explode at you. Anger in a man is far more complicated than it is with us women. He'll think you aren't taking care of yourself, and he'll feel responsible for that. Men do that kind of thing, you know. He might even decide to blame Evan, so make sure you take that into account."

"Of course Damian'll get angry!" Jessica cried. "And he'll have every right to be mad once he discovers I'm faking an injury to gain his sympathy."

"Don't let him know that part," Cathy said simply.

"Cathy," Jessica said on the end of a long sigh. "I appreciate your efforts, I really do, but I can't pretend to be hurt. First of all, Damian would know in an instant. I'm not nearly as good an actress as you, and he'd figure out my ploy in no time. You seem to have forgotten Damian's an experienced attorney."

Cathy frowned, chewing on her lower lip as she thought. "Okay," she said after a while. "Forget the limp. The only other thing I can suggest is forthright honesty. You'd be amazed at how well it works sometimes. This might just be one of those times."

"As it happens, I couldn't agree with you more," Jessica said. "This whole situation is preposterous. I'm not any good at charades. I'd like to help Evan, but not at the expense of my emotional well-being."

"Now you're talking." Cathy slid to the edge of the cushion. "What are you going to say to Damian?"

"I...don't know yet." A heaviness settled on her shoulders at the thought. "You know what my biggest fear is? That Damian will smile fondly at me and tell me how flattered and honored he is by my little confession."

"With sadness echoing in his voice," Cathy added, demonstrating her usual flair for the dramatic.

"Right. Then he'll sigh and add that unfortunately he doesn't share my feelings."

"That sounds just like a man," Cathy agreed. "Naturally he'll lie through his teeth, because he's being noble for his brother's sake. Just don't listen to him. Trust me, Jess, this guy loves you."

Jessica wished with all her heart that it was true. She looked over to her friend, realizing how much she treasured Cathy's support, and gave her a thumbs-up. Cathy grinned and returned the gesture.

* * *

Evan was in his office working when Jessica arrived Monday morning. "Good morning," he called out cheerfully. "I was hoping it was you."

"Would you like me to put on a pot of coffee?" she asked. Then she glanced toward the machine and noticed Evan had already done so.

He wandered out of his office, mug in hand, and sat on the corner of her desk, one leg swinging like a pendulum. He smiled down on her, his eyes twinkling. "Are you rested and ready to tackle the world?"

Jessica smiled. That didn't describe her even on her best Monday morning. "Not quite. Give me until Wednesday or Thursday for that."

"Then this should help brighten your day," he said casually, withdrawing two tickets from the inside pocket of his jacket and handing them to her. Jessica read the tickets and gasped. "Two box seats for the Red Sox game this evening!"

"I thought you might enjoy baseball."

"I love the Red Sox."

"So your mother told me. Be prepared, Jessica, my lovely, I'm planning to sweep you off your feet."

Her gaze shot up to his. He was sweeping her off her feet all right, but she didn't like where she was landing. She'd awakened that morning determined to resolve this matter between her and the Dryden brothers once and for all, only to be thwarted at the first turn. As if things weren't bad enough, Evan had been conferring with her mother, learning what he could about her.

"Evan, we need to talk," she said, keeping her gaze lowered. All the way into the office she'd practiced what she intended to say.

"I can't now, Jess. Sorry. I'm going to be in court all day with the Porter case. But don't worry, there'll be plenty of time for talking later. I'll come by for you at six-thirty, all right?"

"All right," she muttered, managing a weak smile.

By the time Evan arrived to pick her up that evening, Jessica was determined to have her say—after the game, she decided, when they were afforded some privacy.

Evan was determined, as well, only his determination was to lay on the charm. Their seats were situated directly behind home plate and their view was excellent.

They downed steaming hot dogs, salty peanuts and a glass of draft beer each. Evan was more relaxed than she'd seen him in a long while, cheering on his team and shouting at the umpire. When the Red Sox scored a home run, he placed his fingers in his mouth and let loose with a piercing whistle. In all the years she'd spied on Evan and his brother, she couldn't remember him once whistling like that.

"My mother would've had my hide," he explained when she asked. "Whistling isn't proper behavior," he said, sounding so much like Lois Dryden that Jessica laughed.

"When did that ever stop you?" she teased.

"I found that my yen to whistle was the one thing

Dad wouldn't tolerate, either," Evan said, as though cheated out of a normal childhood.

Jessica was amazed. She'd assumed that Evan, who'd always been the fair-haired boy, had gotten away with everything.

In the seventh-inning stretch, Evan reached for her hand and squeezed her fingers. She'd always liked Evan and found it impossible to be irritated with him for any length of time. This was his gift, Jessica realized, what his father had referred to during their talk at the fund-raising picnic. Evan was a born leader. People had always been drawn to him. He'd always been accepted, admired and highly regarded. When uncomfortable situations arose, they viewed him as a problem solver.

Suddenly Jessica felt a change in him. He let her hand slip from his grasp. He stiffened and went utterly still. He gasped, and then seemed to stop breathing altogether.

"Evan?"

His smile was decidedly forced. At that moment the crowd roared and fans got to their feet. Jessica hadn't a clue what had happened in the play. Her eyes and mind were on Evan.

"What's wrong?" she asked when the noise died down.

"Nothing." He attempted to convince her with a smile, but failed. Something was very wrong, indeed, and she was determined to find out what.

"Come on," she said, standing and not waiting for him. "We're leaving."

"Jessica, no, it's all right. I'm fine."

"You're not, and don't even try to tell me otherwise, because I know better."

"It's nothing," he said once more, defensively.

She ignored him, gathered her things and left the box. He had no alternative but to follow her.

"Has anyone ever told you what a stubborn woman you are?" he muttered, racing after her. Their steps echoed against the concrete steps as they made their way out of the stadium. Every now and again they could hear shouts and cheers coming from inside. A couple of times Evan glanced regretfully over his shoulder.

"All right, tell me what happened to you in there," Jessica demanded, as they neared the parking lot.

"It was nothing."

"If you say 'nothing' again, I'm going to scream. Now, who'd you see?" But she already knew the answer. Only one person would have evoked such a pain-filled response in Evan, and that was the woman he'd loved and lost.

"What makes you think I saw anyone?" Evan tossed right back at her, irritated now and not bothering to disguise it.

"Was it Mary Jo?"

He stopped so abruptly she'd taken half a dozen steps before she realized he wasn't at her side.

"Who told you about Mary Jo?" His voice was hoarse.

"No one yet, but you're about to."

"Sorry, Jess, but—"

"Now listen here, Evan Dryden, you need to get this off your chest once and for all. You've nursed the pain she caused you long enough. It's time to let it go. Past time!" Jessica tucked her arm in the crook of his elbow as they wove their way toward his car.

He was silent, his mood dark and brooding by the time they arrived at Jessica's apartment. She wasn't sure if she was helping matters by insisting he tell her about this woman he'd once loved. She feared her insistence might well rip open a half-healed wound, but she also knew he couldn't hold this inside any longer.

Jessica led the way into her kitchen, turned on the light and brewed a pot of coffee. Evan sat down, but grew restless almost immediately and stood, prowling about her small apartment.

Soon Jessica was sitting in her favorite chair, watching Evan pace. She didn't pressure him to talk, didn't try to prompt him. When he was ready, he'd tell her what she wanted to know.

"We met by accident," he said, his voice low and intense, "although I've wondered since if it really was."

"You mean you think she arranged it?"

Evan's eyes widened with surprise. "No...not that. I was thinking that there's little in life that really *is* an accident."

"I see," Jessica murmured.

"I was at the beach with a few friends of mine. We'd played volleyball and had a few beers and were enjoying ourselves—taking a real break from the grind of the office. We soaked up sunshine and laughter and got rid of a lot of pent-up energy."

He stopped moving and turned to face her. "Most of my friends had left and I was winding down by taking a walk along the beach, and that's when I met Mary Jo. She was walking her dog and good old Fighto—bad pun, eh?—anyhow, he got loose. She was chasing him down the beach and, being the heroic kind of guy I am, I caught the leash for her. She stopped to thank me and we got to talking. She's small and pretty with big brown eyes that... Well, none of that matters now."

"You liked her right away?"

Evan nodded. "There was a freshness about her, an enthusiasm that bubbled over. I knew immediately that I wanted to know her better, so I asked her out to dinner. It threw me for a loop when she refused."

That must have been something of a novelty, Jessica mused. "Did she give you a reason?"

"Several, as a matter of fact, but I was able to talk her out of her objections. She had the most marvelous laugh, and I found myself saying the most ridiculous things, just so I could hear it. Being with Mary Jo made me want to laugh myself. It was the most exhilarating day I'd had in years."

"She did go out with you, though?"

"Not exactly." Caught in the memories, Evan didn't seem inclined to say anything more for a minute. Jessica watched silently as the emotions crossed his face. First she saw his eyes light up with the recollection, followed by a pain so deep she yearned to reach out and take his hand. The small movements of his mouth were telling, too. It quivered when he first mentioned meeting Mary Jo, as if that first conversation served to amuse him still. But a moment later, the corners sank as his pain took hold. Jessica longed to reassure him, but knew Evan wouldn't have appreciated it.

"As it happened," Evan continued at last, his tone wistful, "I spent the rest of the day and nearly all of the night with Mary Jo. We built a fire on the beach and talked until morning.

"We started dating regularly after that. I found her refreshing and fun. Our lives were so different. Mary Jo was the youngest of a family of six. She's the only girl. I met her family one Sunday, and her mother insisted I stay for dinner. I'd never seen such a spread in all my life. There were kids running all over the place. Several of Mary Jo's sisters-in-law were pregnant at the time, as well. I've never known such a family, the joking and the teasing and fun. Don't get me wrong, I've got a great family myself, but Mary Jo's is different. I really loved being with them."

"I'm sure they felt the same way about you."

He shrugged, his look doubtful. "I'd like to think so."

"What happened next?" Jessica prompted when he didn't immediately continue. She was eager now for the details.

"I knew I was going to fall in love with her that first day on the beach," he said, his voice so low it was a strain to distinguish the words. "Love isn't something I take lightly, but it hit me then—and I knew."

"I know what you mean," Jessica offered. She felt the same way about Damian.

"After I met her parents, I realized how much I wanted to marry her, how much I wanted us to have five or six children of our own. The Summerhills' home was full of love and I wanted that kind of happy free environment for my own children someday."

"Mary Jo sounds like a very special woman," Jessica said quietly.

"She is," Evan whispered softly. "Special enough to marry."

"You asked her to be your wife, didn't you?"

He gave an odd smile, one that was a blend of amusement and pain. "Yes. Afterward I took her to meet my parents. Mary Jo was intimidated by my family's wealth—I realized that from the beginning. Who wouldn't be, seeing Whispering Willows for the first time. My parents had some doubts about our being suited, but once Mom and Dad met Mary Jo, they changed their minds."

"I don't remember hearing about the engagement," Jessica said.

"I wanted to give her a diamond, but she preferred a pearl ring, instead. She'd recently completed her student teaching and been hired as a first-grade teacher. She wanted to delay making a formal announcement until she'd settled into her job, but more important until after her parents' fortieth wedding anniversary celebration that October.

"I wasn't keen on waiting," Evan confessed, "but I agreed, because, well, because I was willing to do whatever Mary Jo wanted." He paused and drew a deep breath, holding it a moment as if he dreaded continuing. "I first suspected something was wrong the first part of October. She kept finding excuses why we couldn't see one another. In the beginning I accepted them—I was busy myself—and although I missed her, I didn't press the issue. I didn't like it, mind you, but I understood how busy she was with school and her family obligations. A couple of times I showed up at her parents' house. They seemed glad to see me, and her mother obviously assumed I was starving and made me stay for dinner." He smiled.

"They sound like wonderful people."

Jessica didn't think Evan heard her. "When Mary Jo mailed me back the ring, I was stunned. I've had some surprises in my life, both pleasant and unpleasant, but none that have shocked me more."

Jessica felt angry at Mary Jo for not having the courage to confront Evan face-to-face. If she wanted to break the engagement, even an informal one, then the least she could have done was have the consideration to tell him in person. Mailing Evan the ring was cowardly and cruel.

"So," Evan continued, "I drove over to her apartment in a fury."

"You had every right to be furious."

He shook his head. "I should have waited until I'd cooled down. I wish with everything in me that I had."

Life was filled with regrets, Jessica thought. She'd

been carrying around a fair share of her own, especially in the past few weeks.

"When I confronted her, Mary Jo told me there was someone else," he whispered. "I didn't believe her at first. I refused to entertain the thought that a woman as fundamentally honest as Mary Jo would see another man behind my back. It didn't tally in my mind—but I was wrong." His voice dwindled to a whisper. "Apparently they met at the school where she teaches. He's a teacher, too. The agony of being engaged to me and in love with someone else must have torn her apart."

Jessica dropped her gaze for fear he would read what was in her eyes. She wasn't engaged to Evan, but she continued to see him when she was in love with Damian. While Evan spoke, Jessica had been casting mental stones at Mary Jo, when she was guilty of essentially the same thing.

"You saw her tonight at the ball game?" Jessica gently prodded.

Evan nodded. "She was with him…at least I assume it was him." The pain was back in his eyes, and Jessica felt the urge to weep. For Evan, yes, but for herself, as well. What a couple they made, each in love with someone else, fighting hard to do the right thing and making themselves miserable in the process.

"Mary Jo's a special woman," Evan whispered. "The man who marries her is a lucky man…" He paused again, and that odd smile, the one of blended joy and pain returned. "She'll be a wonderful wife and mother."

"Under the circumstances, that's a generous thing to say."

"You don't know Mary Jo, or you'd think the same thing yourself. In the months since we parted, I've come to realize that my ego played a substantial role in all this. Mary Jo was the first woman to break off a relationship with me." He smiled as he said it, as though it had served him right after all these years. "I guess I'd gotten a bit cocky."

"We're all guilty of that in one form or another," she offered.

He looked at Jessica then, and his gaze sobered. "I've ruined our evening, haven't I?"

"No," she told him, hoping he heard the sincerity in her voice. She understood how passionately Evan had loved the woman, and how deeply the pain of their parting affected him still.

More than ever, after hearing Evan talk about losing the woman he loved, Jessica knew she couldn't allow the same thing to happen to her. She couldn't continue to mislead Evan by letting him believe their relationship would evolve into something it was never meant to be.

A week passed. Every time she was with Evan he told her more about his relationship with Mary Jo. She soon realized that every invitation to dinner or a show was an excuse to talk. Every outing was followed by coffee and a long heart-to-heart. It was as though a floodgate had opened inside him, and the need to release the pent-up emotion was too strong to ignore.

They were friends, nothing more, and Jessica was comfortable with their relationship. With their frequent talks, she was able to open up to him, as well, in little ways.

"Have you ever been in love, Jessica?" he asked her unexpectedly one night.

"I think so," she said hesitantly as they strolled through Boston Common. "Yes," she amended quickly. "And it isn't what you're thinking."

"Oh?"

"It's not you, so don't get a big head." She didn't realize until she spoke how insulting she sounded, and she immediately sought his pardon.

Evan laughed off her apology.

The night was lovely. The stars were like twinkling rows of sequins that hung so close they seemed draped over the upper limbs of the trees.

"You know when it's love, don't you?" he asked after a few moments.

"Oh, yes," she whispered.

"Does this mystery man feel the same way about you?"

"I...I don't know. I like to think so." Although there were more signs to the contrary.

For Damian continued to avoid her. Other than that brief moment when he'd come into her office, she hadn't talked to him once.

He arrived at the office promptly at eight each morning and left at five. She guessed that his involvement with his father's campaign dictated his hours. That meant if she wanted to see him, it had to be during working hours. With his hectic schedule it was easier getting an audience with the pope. Jessica didn't know how Damian managed to cram all he did into a single workday. She'd tried to talk to him, but hadn't found the opportunity when there weren't other people around.

Jessica was fast losing her patience. And then, just when she was about to throw her hands in the air and scream with frustration, it happened. Quite by accident, and where she'd least expected it.

Whispering Willows. His family's home.

Evan had learned from Jessica's mother that she'd played on her college tennis team; he'd been intrigued, and challenged her to a game. It had sounded like an entertaining way to spend a Saturday afternoon, and she'd agreed. Since he'd neglected to schedule time on the courts at the country club, they drove to his parents' home to play.

They smacked the ball back and forth for a solid hour, and Evan soundly defeated her. Not that his athletic ability surprised her, but in her effort to impress him she strained her knee. It wasn't anything serious, but Evan insisted they stop playing.

They made their way to the house, laughing and in a good mood, her knee long forgotten, to discover Evan's mother anxiously attempting to start her car, without success. She needed to be at campaign headquarters within the hour and was fretting about what she should do.

"Not to worry, Mom," Evan said, affectionately kissing his mother's cheek. "I'll drive you."

"Nonsense," Lois protested when she viewed Evan's two-seater sports car.

"Didn't you tell me you gave Richmond the day off?" Evan said, opening his car door. "No more excuses, Mom."

"But what about Jessica?"

"I'm perfectly capable of entertaining myself," Jessica assured her. She stood in the driveway until the car had disappeared, then wandered back into the house, wiping the perspiration from her brow with the back of her forearm. She walked into the kitchen and, finding a cold soda in the refrigerator, helped herself.

She was humming a show tune when the kitchen door swung open. "Mother, what in blazes are you doing here? You're supposed to be at—" Damian stopped when he saw her. "Jessica," he said, his surprise evident.

"Your mother's car wouldn't start, so Evan drove her over to campaign headquarters," she explained. Her face was red with exertion, and her hair fell in damp tendrils about her face.

"Evan drove her." Already Damian was physically withdrawing from her. "I'd better go see what's wrong with Mom's car."

"Damian…" Cathy's suggestion about faking an injury came into her mind like a stone from a slingshot. She was injured—well, only slightly—but there was no better time than the present to make use of it.

She concentrated her efforts on her right foot and

limped toward him. She hated resorting to such an underhanded method but she was desperate to talk to him. Surely he'd forgive her once he learned the truth.

His gaze went to her knee, his concern immediate. She was wearing a white top and a short tennis skirt. "You hurt yourself," he said, moving toward her. The kitchen door swung in his wake.

"I'm fine," she whispered.

"Sit down," he ordered, his voice none too tender. "Does Evan know about this?"

"Yes, but it's not all that bad," she mumbled. He pulled out a kitchen chair and eased her into it. His hands at her shoulders were gentle but firm. She closed her eyes at his touch. Lord, how she'd missed him! For days she'd waited for the opportunity to be alone with Damian, and she wasn't about to waste it now.

"We need to talk," she said. "Listen, I—"

"We'll talk after I've seen to your knee. What in God's name possessed my brother to leave you like this?"

"Damian, please listen to me."

"Later." He was busy at work packing ice into a bag.

She was irritated now and leapt off the chair. "My knee will be fine. I strained a muscle or something. It's no big deal."

"You'd better have a doctor check it out," he insisted, positioning her back in the chair, raising her leg and resting it against the seat of a second chair, then balancing the ice pack on the knee.

"I need to talk to you about Evan and me," she said, refusing to be put off any longer. "I'm not in love with Evan and he doesn't love me. We're friends, nothing more. He's in love with Mary Jo and I'm in love with—"

"Keep that ice pack on your leg for a good twenty minutes, understand?"

Infuriated, Jessica rose to her feet and tossed the ice pack into the sink. "You're going to listen to me, Damian, if it kills me! I realize I'm making a mess of this. I should never have used my knee to keep you here, but I was desperate."

"Did you or did you not twist your knee?" he demanded.

"Yes, a little, but it's nothing. I want to talk about the two of us. About you and me."

"Jessica," he said with ill-concealed impatience. "You're dating my brother."

"Your brother and I are *friends,* nothing more. How many times do I have to say it?"

"There's a change in Evan," Damian insisted heatedly. "Do you think I haven't noticed? For the first time in months, he's his old self. My brother's back again and it's all due to you."

"Maybe, Damian, but not in the way you think."

"It doesn't matter what I think," Damian said angrily. "You're dating my brother, so there can't be a you and me. Do you understand?"

"No!" she cried. "No, I don't!"

"It has to be this way, Jessica."

"But why?" Hot tears blurred her vision.

He didn't answer her for several time-shattering seconds. "That's just the way it is."

"Is…is that the way you want it?" Swallowing became impossible. She knotted her hands into fists at her sides.

"Yes," he said after a moment, the longest moment of her life. "That's the way I want it."

Jessica turned away from him, grateful to the very depths of her soul that she hadn't declared her undying love for him. This humiliation was bad enough.

"Jessica." Her name was a plea on his lips.

She hung her head, knowing he would abandon her the way he always did—but he didn't. Instead, his arms came around her and turned her to face him. His touch was as if he had to experience holding her, as if the feel of her was the one thread keeping his sanity intact. And then his mouth came down on hers.

This kiss was hungry and hard, unlike the kisses they'd shared previously. Jessica clung to him, mindful only of this man and the sheer joy she experienced in his arms. She caressed his face with wondering fingers as the intensity of their need increased. He angled her head to one side for a series of short nibbling kisses down her cheek, her throat.

"No more," he moaned, then jerked his head away. But she refused to release him, hugging him around the neck and burying her face in his shoulder. "Jessica, please." When he tugged her hands free, she realized he was shaking as badly as she was. His hands closed around hers and his head fell forward.

The sound of the front door closing echoed like

a clap of thunder. Damian moved away from her and had his back to her when Evan strolled into the kitchen, whistling. He stopped when he saw Damian.

"Damian, hello. I'm glad to see you kept my best girl company."

With something less than a curt nod to his brother, Damian strode out of the kitchen, muttering about seeing to his mother's car.

Jessica thought her heart would break.

Chapter 8

"Thank you," Evan said when he dropped Jessica off at her apartment half an hour later. "By the way, there's a formal dinner with three hundred of my father's closest friends Monday night," he said casually. "I'd like you to attend it with me."

Jessica looked up at Evan, realizing she hadn't heard what he'd said. She hurt too much. Damian didn't love her, didn't want her. She'd all but blurted out her love for him, and he'd rejected her, insisted Evan needed her, and then walked away. As he always did.

"Jessica, are you all right?"

"I'm fine." How easily the lie came, even though she was falling apart on the inside.

"I was asking you about the dinner party."

She blinked. Dinner party?

"Monday night," he said slowly, waving a hand in front of her face. "You'd better tell me what's wrong."

"Would it be all right if I go in now?" she asked, instead. She wasn't in the mood to explain anything, least of all what had happened between her and Damian.

"Of course."

Evan insisted on escorting her into her apartment. He placed her tennis racket in the hall closet and stepped into her kitchen to get her a glass of ice water.

Jessica sat at the table and smiled her appreciation. "I'm fine," she said, and this time it was a little less of a lie. Yes, she hurt but it was a clean cut, deep and swift. She knew now what she'd suspected all along. Damian didn't want her, didn't love her.

"Thank you, Jess," Evan said again, and although his words were casual, Jessica sensed a deeper meaning.

"For letting you whop me in tennis?" she asked, knowing it was much more than that.

The smile faded from his eyes. "For that, too, but mostly for listening to me these last few days. Talking about Mary Jo has helped clear my head. It's shown me what went wrong between us and helped me realize how much I still love her." This was issued with a pain-filled sigh.

"That isn't a sin, Evan." Any more than her loving Damian was a sin.

"Talking is what's helped me. Perhaps you should

take note and tell me what's troubling you. You can't fool me—those are tears glistening in your eyes."

Instinctively she lowered her gaze, focusing her attention on the water glass. "I...I'm not ready to talk just yet. Don't be upset with me. I have to sort through my own feelings first."

His hand covered hers. "I understand. You will attend the dinner party with me, won't you?"

Jessica's first inclination was to refuse. Instead, she nodded. "All right." Sitting home feeling sorry for herself would solve nothing. Nor would she give Damian the satisfaction. From here on out, she was going to kick up her heels and enjoy life. Even if it killed her, and that was what it felt like just now.

"Damian will be there," Evan said as if he expected her to comment.

She nodded. After this afternoon it made no difference.

"He'll be bringing someone, too," Evan added. "You won't mind if we share a table, will you?"

"I won't mind in the least," Jessica said brightly. "The more the merrier."

"I thought we'd look through your wardrobe before dinner," Cathy said as she entered Jessica's apartment. Jessica realized her mistake the moment she'd mentioned the dinner party to her friend. From that point on, Cathy had insisted she choose the dress.

"I've managed to dress myself without a problem for several years now," Jessica felt obliged to say.

Cathy was sorting through the dresses in her

closet, shuffling them from one side to another as if this was a mission of great importance. She paused and tapped her foot impatiently. "I can't tell you how disappointed I am in Damian. You're sure you didn't misunderstand him?" She sounded as though the fault was Jessica's.

"There was no misunderstanding," Jessica said firmly, wishing she'd never mentioned the incident to Cathy. She wouldn't have except that her friend had been on virtually every phase of this…this mess. "He doesn't want anything to do with me. He couldn't have made it any plainer."

"I don't believe it. There's something very wrong here, and it's up to you to figure out what it is."

"I know what it is," Jessica protested. It wasn't necessary to dissect the problem when the answer was so simple. If Damian *did* care for her, he would have found a way to make things right. He didn't, and he hadn't.

"You're coming to my opening night, aren't you?" Cathy asked as she continued to examine the contents of Jessica's closet.

"I wouldn't miss it for the world." Jessica was proud of Cathy's big career break. She'd gotten the plum role of Adelaide, after all, in the local production of *Guys and Dolls*. Jessica also thought Cathy was sweet on the director, David Carson. Her friend had mentioned his name several times in passing, and Jessica thought there'd been a small catch in her voice each time.

"I think I'll invite Damian to my opening," Cathy suggested nonchalantly. "After all, I have met him."

Jessica wasn't likely to forget. Cathy's eyes shifted in her direction. "You don't have anything to say."

"Do what you want, Cathy."

Cathy's laugh was short and telling. "You can't fool me, Jess, I know you too well. I don't know what's wrong with Damian, but trust me, he'll soon come around."

"I sincerely doubt it." Jessica hated to be so pessimistic, but she couldn't stop herself.

Cathy took three dresses from the closet and laid them across her friend's bed. Her hands on her hips, she circled the bed, then returned two of the dresses to the closet.

Jessica studied Cathy's selection. It was a full-length black dress, sleek and shiny with silver highlights that sparkled in the overhead light.

"Try it on," Cathy insisted.

Mumbling her discontent, Jessica slipped out of her clothes and into the dress, lifting her hair so Cathy could close the zipper properly. Then she regarded herself in the full-length mirror. Her shoulders drooped as she released a slow, defeated sigh.

"I look like Natasha from the Rocky and Bullwinkle cartoon show," she muttered.

"Nonsense," Cathy said. "The dress is perfect."

"For consorting with spies maybe," Jessica muttered. But then again, maybe it *was* right. If she was destined to sit at the same table as Damian and his date, she wanted to be darn sure he noticed her—and knew what he was missing.

Evan arrived to pick her up for the dinner party five minutes ahead of schedule, just as Jessica was putting the finishing touches to her makeup. "Beautiful," he said, taking both her hands in his. "You're absolutely beautiful."

His appreciation lent Jessica confidence—until they reached the table where Damian and his date were sitting. The woman was tall, regal, blonde and gorgeous. Every woman's basic nightmare. So much for the best-laid plans.

"Nadine Powell," Damian said. "My brother, Evan, and Jessica Kellerman."

Jessica's gaze moved to Damian, and she was gratified to discover he was staring at her the way a child gazes into a store window at Christmastime. Cathy had been right—the dress was perfect. Damian abruptly looked away as if angry with himself for being so obvious.

"Nadine," Evan said, taking the other woman's hand and holding it several moments longer than necessary.

Dinner was a drawn-out affair, with speeches from several long-winded politicians. Jessica lost count of the number of speakers and the number of courses served, but they seemed to be running neck and neck. The speeches made dinner conversation almost impossible, but Jessica did manage to learn that Nadine was a longtime friend of Damian's. Friends and nothing more, Nadine went on to explain, reading the situation with amazing accuracy. As for Damian, well, he pretended she wasn't there. He didn't say one word to her the entire meal.

When the dessert dishes were removed, a ten-piece orchestra began to play on a low stage behind the polished oak dance floor.

"You game?" Evan asked, holding out his hand to Jessica. The music was from the forties, the big-band sound she particularly loved. Evan was tapping his foot and swaying his shoulders.

Jessica declined. She wasn't keen on being one of the first ones on the floor. "I think I'd prefer to sit out a few of the numbers, if you don't mind."

"Nonsense. I won't take no for an answer." Evan all but pulled her out of her chair. He led her onto the dance floor, and although the number was fast, he brought her into his arms and held her close.

"Evan," she hissed, acutely aware of the impression they were creating. It looked as if they were madly in love and couldn't bear to be separated.

"Shh," he whispered close to her ear.

"What's wrong with you?"

"Me?" he asked, then threw back his head and laughed as if she'd said something uproariously funny.

"Nothing. I'm having a good time, that's all."

"At my expense," she told him in an angry whisper. "Soon everyone will be talking about us."

"Let them."

"Something is very wrong," Jessica insisted.

He laughed again. "Not exactly, but soon everything should be just right."

Jessica hadn't a clue what he meant, but she wasn't going to continue with this farce any longer than necessary. As soon as the number finished, she broke away from him and returned to their table.

"Jessica's knee is bothering her," Evan explained, and before she realized what was happening, Evan had asked Nadine to dance and the pair stood and left the table. Damian looked unnerved.

"Well," Jessica said dryly, "I guess you can't keep a good man down."

Damian frowned darkly. "He might have asked someone other than my date." His hand closed around his water glass, and he seemed intent on studying the dancing couples. Intent on not making conversation with her, Jessica thought, which was fine. Just fine. Everything had already been said as far as she could see, and apparently Damian felt the same way.

"How's your knee?" Damian asked unexpectedly.

"It's okay. Evan was using it as an excuse to dance with Nadine."

The music circled them in a warm halo of melody. Soon Jessica was tapping her foot, wishing she hadn't been so quick to insist she leave the dance floor.

"Come on," Damian said with a decided lack of enthusiasm. He stood and offered her his hand.

Stunned, Jessica looked up at him.

"There's nothing worse than sitting with a woman who obviously wants to dance."

"I…" She intended to tell him there was nothing

worse than dancing with someone who obviously didn't want to be her partner. But before she could speak, he'd taken her hand. He was muttering something under his breath, which she couldn't quite make out. She did hear Evan's name, and she guessed he wasn't pleased with his brother.

Jessica wanted to kick Evan for leaving her alone with Damian. The orchestra had been playing fast-paced songs, but when Damian and Jessica moved onto the floor, the band began a slow dreamy number. The lights lowered and Jessica groaned inwardly.

"Let's sit this one out," she suggested.

"Not on your life," Damian said, easing her into his arms. She didn't understand why he felt obliged to dance with her. He held her stiffly in his arms as though afraid to bring her close. His back was rigid and he stared straight ahead.

"Relax," he whispered impatiently. "I won't bite."

"Me?" she said. "I might as well be waltzing with a mannequin."

"Okay, let's both make an effort."

Jessica hadn't realized she was so tense. Determined to do as he suggested, she closed her eyes and released a slow sigh. She felt the tension ease from Damian, and when she opened her eyes he'd brought her closer, close enough for her to rest her temple against the side of his jaw. The solace she found, as their bodies swayed gently to the rhythm, was worth every minute she'd waited to feel his arms around her.

This was where she belonged, Jessica mused sadly, where she'd always belonged. Surely Damian felt it too. Why else would he be holding her as if she was the most precious thing in his world? Why else would his lips be moving against her hair as if he longed to kiss her.

Neither spoke, she realized, because they feared words would destroy the moment. She clung to him even when the music stopped, not wanting this blissful time to end.

"We should get back to the table," Damian said, and the reluctance she heard in his voice gave her hope.

"I don't see Evan or Nadine. Do you want to dance one more number?" she asked.

He didn't answer her for a long moment, and then said gruffly, "Yes."

"I do, too."

"Jessica, listen..."

She chanced raising her face and looking at him, her eyes filled with a longing so great she couldn't hide it. Pressing her finger over his mouth, she smiled. "Please, Damian, not now."

He briefly closed his eyes, sighed and nodded.

Jessica lost track of time. She knew they danced far longer than they should have, for more numbers than she could count. Every once in a while she glanced at their table, but neither Nadine or Evan were in sight.

It wasn't until the music sped up again, that he revealed any signs of regret. She knew something was wrong the minute he eased her from his arms. His face hardened. She looked up at him and blinked, not understanding.

"I'll have my brother's hide for this," Damian muttered.

"For what?" she asked softly.

A muscle in his jaw jerked as he reined in his temper, but that was the only answer she got.

They left the dance floor and sat like strangers at the table. Jessica couldn't bear it any longer. She stood, excused herself and moved from table to table to greet several old family friends. She returned only when she saw that Evan had joined his brother. Nadine was nowhere in sight. The two brothers seemed to be having a rapid intense exchange of words, but when she approached, Damian clamped his mouth closed and looked the other way.

"I've neglected you," Evan said contritely, claiming her hand between both of his. "I'm sorry, Jessica. Can you forgive me?"

"Of course." What else could she do? Demand that he immediately take her home? That would have been silly. Especially as she wasn't interested in him as anything other than a friend. Besides, his neglect had given her all that time with Damian.

A breathless and laughing Nadine returned to the table a few moments later, and the four of them ordered drinks. The waitress had just brought their order when Walter and Lois Dryden approached their table.

"I hope you four are enjoying yourselves."

Evan said that they certainly had been.

Lois smiled benevolently down on Jessica, then gently placed her hands on Jessica's shoulders, leaning forward so that their heads were close together. "We owe you so much," she said, kissing her cheek.

"Nonsense." The words embarrassed her.

"It's true. Tell her, Walter," Lois insisted. "We were about to despair over what was happening with Evan, and that all changed the minute you started working for the firm."

"Mother…" Evan didn't seem to appreciate this, either.

"It's true. You have no idea how pleased Joyce and I are that the two of you are seeing so much of each other," Lois continued.

"I have to agree with your mother," Walter said in his deep, vibrant voice. "You're a good man, Evan, with a bright future. It was a damn shame to watch you waste your life over a woman you couldn't have. It's much better now that you're seeing Jessica."

A stilted uncomfortable silence followed his father's praise. Within a few minutes of the elder Drydens' visit to their table, Damian made an excuse, and he and Nadine got up and left. After that, Evan didn't seem too keen to stay, either. As for Jessica, she was more than happy to get home. Enough was enough.

She lay awake most of the night thinking, and by daybreak, she'd made her decision. With purpose driving her steps, Jessica walked into the office the next morning, her eyes burning from lack of sleep.

"I need to see Mr. Dryden for a moment," she told Damian's secretary.

The woman, doubtless noting the determination in Jessica's voice, reached instantly for the intercom and announced her.

Jessica strode into Damian's office and stood before him. He was sitting behind his desk reading a file. He glanced up, his expression, as always, inscrutable. "What can I do for you, Jessica?"

Her heart pounding, she said flatly, "I'm resigning from my position with this firm, effective immediately." It was an impulsive thing to do, Jessica realized, considering how difficult it was these days to find a job. But her sanity was more important. She'd do temporary work if she had to. Or work in another field.

If Damian was surprised by her announcement, he didn't reveal it. He leaned back in his chair, calm and composed. "This is rather sudden, isn't it?"

"Yes…but it's necessary." She avoided eye contact by studying the painting on the wall behind him. It was a seascape with the ocean crashing against the jagged edge of a protruding rock. A bird was perched on the uppermost point of the rock, undisturbed by the raging sea. Jessica wished she could be more like that bird.

"Does Evan know?"

"Not yet," she replied. "Since you were the one to hire me, I felt obligated to tell you first."

He paused as if gathering his thoughts. "If you could work out your two-week notice, I'd appreciate it."

Jessica wasn't sure what she'd expected. Nothing,

she'd told herself, but she realized now that wasn't true. In the deepest part of her, she was praying Damian would ask her to reconsider, that he'd make at least one attempt to change her mind. Perhaps a raise or some other inducement. Instead, he calmly accepted her resignation as if he was almost pleased to see her go.

That hurt. She held the pain to herself for as long as she could, before turning and walking toward the door.

"Jessica."

She stopped, but didn't turn around.

"You've been a valuable asset to this firm, and we'll miss you."

That was all he was willing to offer. It was damn little.

"Thank you," she whispered, then walked out the door.

She was trembling by the time she sat down at her own desk. After taking a moment to compose herself, she reached for the phone and dialed Cathy's number.

"You did *what?*" her friend cried.

Jessica had never used the office phone for personal calls before, but she made this day the exception. "You heard me. I quit."

"But why?"

"It's a long story," she murmured, "but suffice to say, I'm tired of this whole ridiculous charade."

"Damian loves you."

"No," she whispered, "he doesn't." She'd been swayed by Cathy's comments and her own foolish heart, because she so desperately wanted to believe it was true.

"Jessica, Jessica, Jessica," Cathy said in an impatient singsong, "don't be so hasty."

It was either leave the firm or lose her sanity, Jessica mused. It'd been a mistake to contact Cathy; her friend simply didn't understand.

"What did Evan say?"

"He doesn't know yet," she admitted reluctantly. Not that it would make any difference. No argument Evan offered could convince her to change her mind.

"Keep me informed, will you? Following what's going on in your life is more interesting than my soap operas."

Mrs. Sterling came into the office and stared at Jessica, looking as if she were about to burst into tears. "You're leaving!"

This office had an information network the CIA would envy. Jessica didn't bother to ask where Evan's secretary had heard the news; it didn't matter.

"But you can't go now, not when Mr. Dryden's back to his old self."

"I apologize for leaving you in the lurch."

"You won't reconsider?"

Jessica shook her head.

"Personally," said Mrs. Sterling, "I think it makes for bad politics when men and women from the same office date one another. These things have a way of turning sour."

"What does?" Evan asked, stepping into the room, carrying a leather briefcase and looking very much the professional he was. He paused at his secretary's desk and reached for his mail.

"Jessica's resigned," Mrs. Sterling said baldly.

Evan dropped the mail and turned to stare at Jessica. His mouth fell open with disbelief. "Is it true?"

She nodded. Until she saw the look of dismay on his face, she hadn't believed he held any real affection for her.

"Come into my office," he commanded, leading the way and clearly expecting her to follow. When she was inside, he closed the door.

"What's this all about?" he demanded.

To the best of her memory, Jessica had never seen this side of Evan. He looked and acted like Damian. "It's time I moved on," she said weakly, not knowing exactly how much to say, if anything, about the real reason.

"After less than two months?"

She crossed her arms and shrugged.

"Are the hours too long?"

"No."

"We're not paying you enough?"

"I'm receiving an adequate salary," she returned. She didn't like the way he was putting her on the defensive, and she stiffened her resolve. There was a side of her he hadn't seen, either—her stubborn side.

"There must be a reason you find it so repugnant to work for me."

"I never said I found it repugnant to work for you." She dropped her hands and formed tight fists at her sides. Evan was acting every inch the attorney.

"So it's the firm you don't like. Have we done something to offend you?"

"No!" she cried, hating this interrogation. Evan's reaction was certainly the opposite of Damian's. Evan was clearly upset at the idea of losing her.

"Then why? You owe me an explanation," he insisted.

"I don't feel I do…" She hesitated, her stomach in knots.

"Is it something I've done?" His voice was gentler now, as if he was trying to soothe her, to gain her confidence.

"No," she assured him. "You've been wonderful… a good friend. I'll treasure the times we've had together, Evan, but you don't love me and I don't love you. It seems to me that we should appreciate what we do share and not try to make something of it that isn't there." Or allow their parents to do so, either, she added mentally.

He looked puzzled. "That's no reason to quit working for the firm."

"Perhaps not, but it's the right thing for me. Damian asked me to work out my two-week notice, which I'll gladly do, but I'm not going to change my mind."

"All right," he agreed reluctantly. "In the meantime, you don't mind if we continue to see one another, do you?"

"I'm…not sure it would be wise."

Evan jerked back his head as though her answer amazed him. "You aren't serious, are you?"

"Yes, Evan, I am. I enjoy your company and consider you a friend, but..."

"What about coffee to talk over old times?"

"Perhaps."

Evan grinned then, that devilishly handsome grin guaranteed to stir the heart of any woman. "I'm not letting you back out of our sailing date, though. I've been counting on that. You aren't going to let me down, are you?"

"No, I won't let you down." Nevertheless, Jessica's heart sank as she remembered her promise to go out with Evan on his sailboat in three weeks' time. He'd made the date *before* the formal dinner event. *Before* she'd known she wanted out of the Drydens' sphere.

He beamed her a wide smile.

Jessica stayed late that night, wanting to clear her desk before she headed back to her apartment. Undaunted by her stated reluctance to continue seeing him socially, Evan had asked her to dinner, and Jessica had declined. Besides, she'd been out late the night before, hadn't slept well and was anxious to finish up at the office and head home.

She was leaving just as Damian came out of his office.

"Good night," she said cordially, moving down the corridor to wait for the elevator. Damian joined her there.

The doors opened and they stepped inside together. They stood like strangers while the elevator made its descent. Jessica stared at the numbers above the door as they lighted up one by one. Only a week earlier, she would have been thrilled to have these few seconds alone with Damian, and now she would have given anything to avoid him. Being this close to him physically and so far apart emotionally was agony in its purest form.

The elevator doors silently slid open, and Jessica stepped into the lobby, glad to make her escape. Damian would go about his life, and she would go about hers.

"Jessica." Damian sounded impatient, but she didn't know if it was with her or himself. "Are you taking the subway?"

"Yes, it's right around the corner." She began to move away.

"I'll give you a ride home."

"No, thank you."

"I insist," Damian said in steel tones. "It's time we talked."

If Jessica had thought her heart was beating hard that morning when she entered his office, it didn't compare with the way it thundered against her ribs now.

Silently he led her into the parking garage to his car. He unlocked the passenger-side door and held it open for her, then went around to the driver's side and climbed in. As he inserted the key into the ignition, he asked, "Have you spoken to Evan about your resignation?"

"Yes."

"What did he have to say?"

She gestured weakly with her hands. "He asked me to reconsider."

"Have you?"

"No. I'll work out my two-week notice, since you asked me to, but my decision stands."

Damian's hands tightened around the steering wheel. "Why, Jessica?"

"Why should you care, Damian?" she returned, losing patience with him. "This morning, you couldn't wait to be rid of me."

"That's not true," he said sharply.

"I don't think discussing this will solve anything," she said, reaching for the door handle, intent on letting herself out.

The air was electric. "Jessica, stay for a few minutes. Please." His words were soft, without emotion, and yet filled with it.

Jessica hesitated. "All right." She dropped her hand.

"Did you give your notice because of what happened at the dinner?" he asked.

Confused, Jessica turned to study Damian. "Last night?"

"Evan virtually abandoned you. I know your feelings must have been hurt, but—"

"Just a minute," she said, twisting in her seat to look at him directly. "You don't honestly believe that, do you?"

A puzzled look crowded his features. "Yes. My brother was rude in the extreme to abandon you the way he did."

She was angrier than she could remember being in a long time. When she let things fester inside her this way, her anger took the form of hiccups when she released it.

"Do you think *hic* I'm so shallow I'd quit *hic* my job in a fit of *hic* jealousy? Is that *hic* what you're saying, Damian?"

He blinked when she was finished, as though he expected more.

Jessica threw open the car door, climbed out and slammed it. "I *hic* don't think this *hic* conversation is getting us anywhere."

With that she marched away. She thought she heard Damian's car door close, but she didn't bother to look back.

"Jessica!" he called, storming into the empty lobby.

She hesitated. The hiccups hadn't subsided, and she was having a hard time breathing properly.

"I'm sorry," he said after a tense moment.

She understood then. He was apologizing for much more than their argument. He was telling her how much he regretted not loving her.

Chapter 9

Other than brief glimpses Jessica didn't see Damian at all during the next two weeks. A new legal assistant, Peter McNichols, was hired, and Jessica helped train the conscientious young man.

On her last day, Damian sent word that he wanted to see her in his office. Mrs. Sterling issued the summons. "I hope you'll change your mind," Evan's secretary said wistfully. "You're an excellent worker and I hate to see you go." She cast a speculative eye toward Evan's closed office door. "I'm sure Mr. Dryden's going to miss you, too."

Evan had made several attempts in the past two weeks to bribe her into staying, but Jessica had stood steadfastly by her decision. Although it had been made impulsively, it was the right thing to do.

Jessica reached for her pad and pen before starting toward Damian's office, although she doubted he expected her to take notes. She was promptly shown in by his secretary.

She found Damian standing at the window, his back to her. His hands were clasped behind him, the pose he assumed when he was thinking or when he was troubled about something. She wondered if he found her departure distressing, then decided if that was the case he'd have said so long before now.

"You wanted to see me?" she asked quietly.

He turned around and offered her a reassuring smile. "Yes, please sit down." He motioned toward the chair, then claimed the seat behind his desk. He reached for an envelope on the corner and handed it to Jessica.

"It's your paycheck," he explained. "I took the liberty of adding a small bonus."

"That wasn't necessary," she said, surprised by the gesture.

"Perhaps not, but I wanted you to know how much the firm appreciated the extra time and effort you put into the Earl Kress case."

"I stayed late because I wanted to."

"I realize that. Now," he said, leaning back in his chair, his posture casual, his eyes curious, "have you found another position yet?"

"No." Working every day had made searching for a job almost impossible. There would be time enough for that later, in the days and weeks to follow.

"I see," he said unemotionally. "If you like, I'd be happy to write you a letter of recommendation."

The offer was generous in light of the fact she'd worked for the firm such a short while.

"I'd appreciate that very much." She'd given considerable thought to the consequences of being out of a job. A letter of recommendation would help.

"There are a number of firms I know who might be interested in obtaining a top-notch legal assistant. I could make a few calls on your behalf."

Damian was being more than generous, she thought. "Thank you. I'd be grateful."

He nodded and she got to her feet. Saying goodbye to Damian was much more difficult than she'd ever expected. When she walked out the door she didn't know how long it'd be before she saw him again. Their families might be close, but Jessica and Damian led very separate lives. It could well be months or even years before they ran into each other. But perhaps that would be for the best. She fidgeted with the yellow notepad. "I want you to know how much I've appreciated working for you and Evan," she said, barely managing to keep her voice steady. "You were willing to give me a chance when all I had was classroom experience."

"You've proved yourself in countless ways since then."

She backed away, taking small steps, until her back was against his door. She felt the wood pressing against her shoulder blades. "Thank you, too," she said, and her voice came out a hoarse whisper, "for everything else."

His brow creased with a frown.

"For the dinners and our time at Cannon Beach," she elaborated. The final words stuck in her throat, and she was sure that if she said what was really in her heart, it would embarrass them both.

His eyes revealed his sadness. "Goodbye, Jessica."

She turned then and opened the door, but before she walked out of his life, before she took that first step, she glanced over her shoulder to look once again, to grab hold of this last memory of him.

Damian was standing there, in the same spot he'd been when she first arrived, gazing out the window, his hands clasped behind his back.

"I can't believe you left it like that." Cathy was outraged, pacing Jessica's living room like a caged tiger. She hadn't been able to stand still from the moment Jessica had told her about her last meeting with Damian.

"What did you expect me to say to him?" Jessica demanded in irritation. The romantic part of her had been hoping Damian would come after her, but he hadn't. Even Evan had seemed resigned to her wishes. She'd spent one of the most emotionally draining days of her life, and the last thing she needed was chastisement from her best friend. "If he had a shred of feeling for me, this would have been a golden opportunity for him to say something, don't you think?"

"You don't want to know what I think about that man," Cathy muttered darkly.

"The best he was willing to do was a letter of recommendation. I don't need to be hit over the head, Cathy. Damian Dryden simply doesn't care about me." Kneeling before the coffee table, she jerked a piece of pizza from the box with such force the cheese slid off the top.

"Does he know you're not seeing Evan?"

"Of course he knows."

"How can you be so sure? Did you tell him?"

"No."

Cathy lifted her hands in abject frustration. "Then that's it. He thinks you're still dating his brother."

"Evan's gone out with Nadine Powell twice this week. Damian knows that. Besides, all Evan and I have ever been is friends. I told Damian that. Obviously he's not interested one way or the other, so there's no point in discussing it, is there?"

Cathy dropped onto the carpet and reached for a slice of pizza. "I'm really disappointed."

"So am I." That was a gross understatement, but Jessica had never been one to dwell on past mistakes. It would be a long time before she could consider loving Damian a mistake. She'd learned several lessons about herself, and love, in the process. When all was said and done she was going to miss him dreadfully.

"I thought you told me you and Evan were going sailing this weekend?" Cathy asked curiously.

"Not this weekend. Next."

"Aha!" Her friend slapped the end of the coffee

table with her free hand. "So you *are* continuing to see Evan. Damian must know that, too. No wonder he's—"

"Cathy," Jessica said, cutting her off, "leave it. I probably won't be seeing Damian again, and apparently that's the way he wants it. Heaven knows I couldn't have been any more obvious about how I felt."

Cathy shook her head sadly. "I guess I must be more of a romantic than I realized. I was so sure he was in love with you. I was so confident I was right, I guess, because I wanted to be. I've waited all these years for you to fall in love, and now that you have…" Her voice faded as a frown ruled her features. "I was so very sure," she whispered, the puzzled expression growing more intense as though she didn't understand, even now, what could possibly have gone wrong.

"This is a treat," Jessica said, sitting across the table from her mother in their favorite seafood restaurant. They were given a table that looked out over Back Bay. The waters were green and peaceful, and fishing boats could be seen in the distance, bobbing up and down like corks.

Joyce Kellerman spread the linen napkin on her lap and smiled serenely.

Jessica groaned inwardly. She knew that look well. It was the one that spoke of pained disappointment. Her mother had given her that identical look when she'd learned Jessica had dropped out of piano lessons. The look was there again when Jessica had refused to go to Girl Scout camp when she was twelve; it hadn't helped that her mother had been the group leader. It was her mother's way of saying Jessica's behavior completely baffled her. Jessica didn't pretend not to know what this luncheon engagement was about.

"You think I made a mistake quitting my job, don't you, Mother?"

Joyce looked mildly surprised that Jessica had introduced the subject. "I just don't understand why, that's all. It was the perfect job for you, with old family friends. You and Evan seemed to be getting along so well, and then for no reason I can discern, you resigned."

"It was time for me to move on," Jessica said vaguely.

"But you'd barely worked there two months," Joyce protested. "It doesn't look good on a résumé for you to be hopping from one job to the next. You know what your father has to say about such behavior."

There it was, in black and white, with the emphasis on black. She'd disappointed her father, the man who'd devoted his life to the preservation of her happiness.

"Working for the Drydens had become…uncomfortable, Mom." Jessica didn't explain further. What could she say?

Her mother reached for the menu and focused her attention there. "Lois and I blame ourselves for this, you know. We were both so excited when you and

Evan hit it off that we let our imaginations run away with us. Here we were talking about a wedding and grandchildren, and you two had barely started dating."

"Mom, it wasn't that."

Joyce set the menu aside and clutched the edge of the table, leaning toward Jessica. "I feel so badly about all this. I do hope you'll accept my apology, Jessica."

"Mom, listen to me. Evan and I were never romantically interested in each other. He's in love with someone else. We've had several long talks, and he's simply not ready to become involved in another relationship. That's perfectly understandable."

"Oh, dear, I'm sorry I'm late." A flustered Lois Dryden approached their table, surprising Jessica. This was her first week away from the Dryden law firm, and when her mother had suggested lunch, it had sounded like a great way to kill a couple of hours between job interviews, the very ones Damian had arranged for her. Jessica hadn't realized Damian's mother had been invited to this luncheon, as well.

"With the primary less than three weeks away, I don't think I've ever been busier." Lois Dryden pulled out a chair and sat down next to her friend and neighbor.

"Mom didn't mention you'd be joining us," Jessica said, casting a mild accusatory glance at her mother. The last thing she needed now was another inquisition.

"I hope you don't mind," Lois murmured contritely. "It does look as though we're ganging up on you, doesn't it? We don't mean to, dear. It's just that we can't help being curious about what's going on between you and Evan."

So, her mother wasn't the only one looking for answers. Lois Dryden, too. And the pair *were* ganging up on her.

"We're both far snoopier than we should be," Lois Dryden went on breathlessly, setting her small handbag next to her silverware, "but that's just part of being a mother."

"Jessica was telling me that Evan's still in love with someone else," Joyce explained.

"Oh, dear," Lois said wistfully, "I was afraid of that. Is it that Summerhill girl he was so keen on a few months ago?"

Jessica looked out over the sun-brightened waters of Back Bay and sighed. "Please understand, I don't mean to be rude, but Evan and I are friends, and I don't feel comfortable sharing what he said to me in confidence."

Joyce Kellerman beamed proudly at her friend. "My goodness, she sounds just like an attorney, doesn't she?"

"That's what she gets from hanging around my sons too long," Damian's mother replied. She crossed her arms and leaned on the table, her expression regretful. "I'm afraid I made a terrible mistake when Evan brought Mary Jo out to the house to meet Walter and me."

"I can't imagine your doing anything to offend anyone," Joyce said loyally.

"She was a shy little thing, and it was easy to see that Walter and I made her decidedly uncomfortable. After dinner, I tried to put her at ease, and I'm afraid I made a miserable job of it. You see, it's vital that Evan marry the…right kind of woman."

"Right kind of woman?" Jessica echoed, a little confused. She'd known the Drydens most of her life. They weren't snobs. They were two of the most generous conscientious people she'd ever met.

"Sometime in the future, Evan is destined to enter the political arena," Lois explained. "Being a politician's wife is like being married to a minister. I should know. After the last few weeks, I've been left with the feeling that *I* am the one running for the Senate, not Walter."

Jessica looked puzzled. "To the best of my knowledge Evan's never said anything about being interested in politics."

"Perhaps not recently, but he was keen on it before, and we've talked about it a lot in the past. It's only been in the past year or so that his interest has waned."

"You said all this to Mary Jo?" Joyce asked.

Lois nodded, her eyes betraying her remorse. "I've thought back on our conversation a hundred times, and I see now that I did more harm than good."

"Does Evan know what you said to her?" Jessica questioned.

"I'm fairly certain she didn't repeat it. I've thought

of contacting her since then, thinking if I apologized she might find it in her heart to forgive me for being so terribly presumptuous."

Jessica groaned inwardly. This new information explained much of what had happened between Mary Jo and Evan, but it was too late. Mary Jo was married now, wasn't she? To that other teacher?

"I feel like I'm responsible for ruining things between you and Evan, as well," Lois went on. "I do try to stay out of my sons' lives, honestly I do, but I don't seem to have much success. I do hope you'll forgive Walter and me for pressuring you and Evan."

"Mrs. Dryden, please, you aren't at fault."

"You're such a dear girl, and Walter and I hoped it would work out between you and Evan." She paused to reach for the menu. "You make a handsome couple."

"Thank you."

The waiter came and took their order, and Lois fully relaxed. "Something's bothering Damian," she remarked. "I've tried to ask him about it, but you know Damian. He's as closemouthed as his father. Evan, bless his heart, is more like me. I've always known what Evan's thinking—well, until recently—because he's so open about his feelings. Not so with Damian."

"What about Damian?" Jessica asked, making the question sound as casual as she could.

"You could probably explain more to me than I can to you, dear," Lois said. "You see him far more often than I do, or at least, you did."

"I… Damian didn't make a practice of confiding in me."

Lois sighed noisily. "I figured as much. Mark my words, there's a woman involved in this. Damian may be as tight-lipped as his father, but I know my son. I think he might have fallen in love."

Jessica glanced back at the water, knowing that if Damian's mother was right, the woman was someone else. Not her.

"Once on board, you can go below and unload the groceries," Evan instructed, as they walked along the floating dock at the marina. When they reached the berth where the thirty-foot sailboat was moored, Evan helped Jessica aboard.

While she went below, Evan moved forward and busied himself with the sails, setting the jib and readying the spinnaker.

"It looks to me like you packed enough food for a week," Jessica shouted through the open stairwell that led to the deck above. The day was lovely, the wind perfect for sailing. Despite all his comments about being the captain while she was the crew, Evan seemed eager to do the majority of the work. Putting away a few bags of groceries seemed a paltry task.

"I'll probably set sail while you're below," Evan shouted down to her, "so don't be concerned if you feel the boat move."

Jessica's experience as a sailor was limited. Evan had insisted for weeks that he was going to change all that. Before the end of the day, he claimed she'd be a top-notch mariner. Apparently the lessons started in the galley.

Humming as she worked, Jessica unloaded the three large grocery bags. They were apparently going to eat well this weekend. She was busy cleaning radishes when she heard voices up above, but although she craned her neck to see who Evan was speaking to, she couldn't see anyone. It was probably someone standing on the dock, Jessica decided.

A few moments later came the sound of the sailboat's small outboard motor. The boat dipped slightly as Evan moved ahead and raised the sails. When the motor stopped, she knew they were a safe distance from the marina.

She finished her tasks and, bringing a couple of cans of cold soda with her, climbed up from the galley. It wasn't until she looked away from the helm that she realized someone else had joined them.

Damian.

She cast an accusatory look in Evan's direction, but it was nothing compared to the look Damian sent his way.

"I didn't know Evan had invited you," she said.

"I didn't know he'd invited *you,*" Damian returned, his voice cut by the wind. The boat tilted to one side and sliced through the water.

"Evan?" Jessica glared at the man she'd once considered a friend.

Evan was grinning broadly, clearly pleased with his own cleverness. "Didn't I mention Damian would be coming along?" he asked innocently.

"No," she answered, handing each brother a can of soda and retreating to the galley. Evan was pretending the situation was the result of miscommunication, but she knew he'd purposely set it up.

Damian followed her below a few minutes later. She was sitting at the booth, her back against the side of the boat and her legs stretched out on the upholstered seat. Her arms were crossed over her chest as she tried to take in what was happening.

Damian didn't look any happier with this turn of events than she did. Walking over to the refrigerator, he replaced the can of soda she'd given him as though that had been his sole purpose in coming below.

"I think you should know I didn't arrange this meeting, if that's what you're thinking."

Jessica had nothing to say. She wasn't angry with Damian; he'd been just as manipulated as she had. She didn't know what game Evan was playing, but she wanted no part of it.

"I imagine having me around ruins your day with my brother," Damian said in what sounded strangely like an apology. He investigated the cupboards as if searching for something to eat. He brought out a bag of potato chips. "Have you found another job yet?"

"Not yet, but I've been called in for a second interview." She doubted this was news to Damian. From what she'd gathered at the new firm, he'd made her sound like God's gift to the legal profession, which was going to be one hell of a reputation to maintain.

"Do you mind if I ask you something?" she said.

"Of course not." He slipped into the narrow booth across from her.

"If you thought so highly of me, why'd you accept my resignation?" Not an entirely fair question, she realized, since she'd been the one to quit.

"Did you want me to ask you to stay?"

She smiled and shrugged. "I guess in a way I did, although it's difficult to admit that now."

"Why did you decide to quit?" He opened the bag of potato chips and offered it to her. Jessica took a handful of chips and dumped them on the tabletop, grateful for something to occupy her hands.

"Why did I decide to quit?" she said, repeating his question thoughtfully. He wasn't going to like her answer. "Mainly because of what happened at that dinner party."

Damian's dark eyes glittered with indignation. "Then it did have something to do with the attention Evan paid Nadine."

"No," she flared back. "I quit because of the pressure I felt from both sets of parents. They practically had me and Evan engaged."

"You could do far worse than marrying my brother."

"How can you even suggest such a thing?" she demanded, her voice quavering. She'd never marry a man she didn't love. "What's the matter with you, Damian?"

"With me?"

"Did you or did you not hear me in the kitchen of your parents' home less than three weeks ago?"

He frowned. "Yes." The word was clipped and angry.

"Then how can you ask me something so stupid?"

Damian's eyes were furious. He wasn't the kind of man to take kindly to insults.

Jessica grabbed a potato chip and shoved it into her mouth. Crunching down on something crisp and salty seemed to help vent her frustration.

"But Evan—"

"If you so much as suggest that Evan's in love with me," she interrupted, "I swear I won't be responsible for what I say or do next."

Damian looked taken aback by her angry retort. He closed his mouth and frowned heavily. Reaching for the potato chips, he munched on two or three, and for a moment this was the only sound in the galley.

"You know my problem, don't you?" she said.

"You mean you only have one?" Damian asked with honey-coated sarcasm.

Jessica ignored the comment. "It's that I assumed a man who had passed the bar and was one of the most brilliant minds in corporate law in Boston today, would—"

"How's everything going down there?" Evan called down. "Are you two talking yet?"

Jessica looked up to find that the younger Dryden brother had opened the door to the galley and was sitting almost directly above them, his arm on the helm, steering the sailboat. The wind ruffled his hair and flattened his windbreaker to his chest.

"We're trading insults!" Damian called back.

"That's a good place to start." Evan sounded disgustingly cheerful. "There's something you should know," he added. "I don't have any intention of turning this boat around until you two have reached an agreement."

"About what?" Jessica demanded.

"We'll get to that in a moment. Now, Damian, admit you're in love with Jessica and be done with it. Quit playing these ridiculous games."

"Damian in love with me?" she repeated incredulously. "Not a chance."

"So that's the way it's going to be," Evan called down. "Not to worry, I packed enough food to last us a good three or four days."

"Don't be absurd." Damian was beginning to sound impatient.

"Listen up, big brother," Evan shouted. "You didn't think I saw you the day you kissed Jessica in Mom's kitchen, but I did. You're crazy about her. What I can't figure out is why you insist on hiding it."

"You were the one dating her."

"So?"

"I don't get involved with women you're dating."

"There's always an exception to the rule. Jessica's a free woman. If you're in love with her, like I suspect, then why didn't you say something?"

Damian's mouth thinned. "You wouldn't understand."

"Try me," Evan insisted.

"Listen, you two," Jessica said, interrupting the

exchange. "If you don't mind, I'd rather you didn't discuss me like I wasn't here."

Both men ignored her.

"Jessica's been crazy about you since she was a kid," Damian declared.

"So?" Evan returned. "She grew up and fell in love with you. A woman can change her mind if she wants. They've been known to do that."

"But you love her!" Damian insisted impatiently.

"You're right—like a sister. She'd make a terrific sister-in-law. We get along great."

Damian's eyes, which were now fixed on Jessica, grew dark and intense. "Were you about to tell me you love me?" he asked her in a husky murmur.

"Yes, you imbecile! What do I have to do—hit you over the head?"

"I don't mean to be offering you advice, big brother," Evan shouted down, "but this might be a good time to kiss her."

"I appreciate the help, *little* brother, but I can take it from here," Damian hollered back and slipped out of the booth. He shut the galley door and bolted it, then turned to Jessica.

He was grinning, she noticed, as if he'd just found out he was holding the winning ticket in the state lottery. "You must have thought I was a stubborn fool," he said, grasping her ankles and tugging her across the length of the upholstered bench. Then he gripped her around the waist and brought her upright and into his arms.

"Do you love me, Damian?" she asked.

"Heart and soul," he admitted as his hands framed her face.

"You might have said something sooner, you know," she murmured, thinking there'd been ample opportunity.

"I didn't dare. I assumed Evan loved you and needed you, but I was wrong, Jessica, very wrong. In the past few weeks I've discovered how very much I loved and needed you myself." He stroked her hair as though he couldn't believe even now that she was with him.

His mouth found hers. She wrapped her arms around him and leaned her weight into his. Damian kissed her again and again, until she was breathless with wonder. Until she marveled at how she'd managed to survive this long outside of his arms.

"I can't believe I'm holding you like this," he whispered between kisses. He couldn't seem to get enough of her, which was fine with Jessica, because she couldn't get enough of him, either.

"You're a fool, Damian Dryden."

"I know, but not any longer. I thought I was doing the noble thing by stepping aside for Evan. I was furious with him after the dinner party, but even more furious with myself."

"Why?"

"For being unable to resist holding you." His grip around her tightened. She felt the even rise and fall of his chest and nestled closer.

"You let me walk out of your life," she said, remembering the pain of leaving the law firm.

"I let you walk out of my office," he said, pressing his jaw against her hair, "but not out of my life. Never that. I was waiting, rather impatiently, to see what developed between you and my brother."

A loud knock from above finally separated them. Continuing to hold her, Damian raised one arm to unhook the latch and raise the door. "Yes?" he asked impatiently.

"Can I turn this boat around yet?"

"Not yet!" Jessica shouted.

"Give us a few more minutes," Damian added.

Evan chuckled. "Just promise me one thing," he insisted. "No, make that two."

"All right," Damian said, apparently in a generous mood.

"First, I insist on being best man at the wedding."

"Wedding," Jessica repeated slowly.

Damian nodded insistently. "The sooner the better. I've been waiting for you far too long already."

"Am I going to be best man or not?" Evan demanded.

"There's no one else I'd even consider, little brother."

"And second," Evan said with a hearty sigh, "I want to be there when you tell Mom and Dad Jessica's marrying you, instead of me."

Chapter 10

"I'd feel better if you kissed me first," Jessica murmured, looking up at Damian. They'd called the Drydens from the marina and asked Lois to invite the Kellermans over, as well.

"If you don't kiss her, I will," Evan teased, eyeing his older sibling.

"Not this time, little brother." Damian wrapped his arm around Jessica's shoulders and gently kissed her. It would have been easy to continue had they been elsewhere. Being held and kissed by Damian was the closest Jessica had ever come to paradise, and it was difficult to break away from the tender shelter of his arms.

"I don't know why I'm so nervous," Jessica said as they headed, hand in hand, toward the parking lot.

"I do." Of late, Evan seemed to be the one with all the answers. "Both sets of parents think you're marrying me." He laughed cheerfully. Clearly he was looking forward to this meeting.

Evan had been the one who insisted they talk to all four parents immediately. Damian and Jessica had agreed, but now Jessica wished she'd suggested they return to her apartment first. She needed to change clothes. Her hair was wind-tossed, and her face was red from the sun and wind.

But Damian seemed eager for this meeting, as if he, too, wanted the matter cleared with both sets of parents. He raised Jessica's hand to his mouth and brushed his lips over her knuckles.

"Don't look so worried. Mom and Dad are going to be ecstatic."

She wasn't concerned about his parents' reaction, or hers for that matter. Neither set would object to her marrying Damian. They'd be thrilled. It was just that the idea of Damian's loving her was still so new she was afraid it wasn't real.

Jessica rode with Damian, and Evan followed in his car. They got separated on the freeway, and when they pulled into the long winding drive that led to Whispering Willows, Jessica noticed Evan's car was already parked out front.

"The speed demon," Damian commented with a chuckle. He parked behind his brother, turned off the ignition and reached for Jessica, kissing her soundly. "Are you ready to walk into the dragons' den?"

She smiled and nodded, thinking she'd follow Damian anywhere.

He helped her out of the car, tucking her hand in the bend in his arm, and they walked together into the family home. The elder Drydens and Kellermans stared back at them with a look of anxious interest.

"Hello, everyone," Damian said, leading Jessica to a chair in the massive living room. He seated her and then stood directly behind her, his hands resting on her shoulders. She raised her fingers and placed them over his.

"I imagine you're wondering why we asked you here," Jessica said to her parents. Her mother sat studying Jessica as if trying to figure out what was wrong with this picture.

"Hold on!" Evan shouted from the kitchen. "Don't say another word until I get there."

"Son?" Walter Dryden gave Damian a puzzled look. "What's the meaning of this?"

"Okay, now," Evan instructed breathlessly, carrying in a silver tray with seven crystal flutes and two bottles of champagne.

"I've asked you to be here, Mr. and Mrs. Kellerman," Damian began formally, "to request the honor of marrying your daughter."

Hamilton Kellerman's face wrinkled with confusion as he turned to his wife. "You told me she was marrying Evan."

"She's—I mean, we hoped—" Joyce stammered.

"I'm in love with Damian," Jessica broke in.

Her father scratched his head. "That's not the way

I remember it. You were crazy over Evan for years. Last I heard, you were making a damned nuisance of yourself."

"Daddy, that was years ago."

"She's crazy about *me* now," Damian interjected, lightly squeezing her shoulders. "And I feel the same way about her."

"Oh, Damian." Lois Dryden covered her mouth with her fingers. "We're delighted. Just delighted. Joyce, think of it, we'll be sharing grandchildren, after all."

The two women were hugging each other and dancing around in circles as Evan passed out champagne glasses to the silent, confused fathers.

"You know what this is all about, Walter?"

"Can't say that I do, Ham."

"You object?"

"Hell, no. I haven't seen that much life in Lois in fifteen years. What about you? Would you rather Jessica married someone else?"

"Heavens, no." Hamilton shook his head as if he didn't know what to think. "The wife's been talking about a union between our two families all summer, only she thought it would be between Jessica and Evan. The way I figure it, a union is a union, and the two of them certainly look to be in love."

"Yes, they undoubtedly have the look," Walter said, smiling at them.

The sound of an exploding cork echoed about the room as Evan uncorked a bottle of champagne. "I'd like to propose a toast," he said, walking from person to person filling the flutes. "To Jessica and Damian," he said, setting the bottle aside and holding up his glass. "May their lives always be filled with happy surprises, and may their love endure for all time."

"Evan, how sweet," Lois said, dabbing the corner of her eye.

"For all time," Joyce agreed.

Everyone raised their glasses, then took a sip of champagne.

"Now, let's talk about the wedding," Lois said, prepared then and there to square away the details. She sat on the sofa next to her husband.

"It'll have to be after the November election," Joyce commented thoughtfully.

"We need to make it through the September primary first," Lois said. "I can't see delaying the wedding when we don't know for certain Walter will be in contention for the Senate."

"Nonsense. Of course he'll be on the ballot."

"Does any of this matter to you?" Damian asked Jessica, leaning so that his lips were close to her ear. A warm tingling sensation raced down her arms.

She smiled softly and shook her head. Nothing mattered except Damian and his love. "I'd marry you tomorrow if we could arrange it."

Damian drew in a deep breath. "Don't tempt me, sweetheart."

"Or in six months, if that's necessary. I've waited for you all my life, Damian. A few more weeks isn't going to matter."

Their mothers would have it all arranged within

the hour, Jessica guessed. Their fathers were talking, too, working out schedules and other necessary details. The two families had been friends through all the seasons of their lives. The same way their own love—hers and Damian's—would last, weathering all the ups and downs the years would bring.

Jessica felt as though she'd come to the end of a long journey. She was home now, secure in Damian's love.

Epilogue

As Evan Dryden set aside the brief he was preparing and pinched the bridge of his nose, there was a knock on his door. Glad of the interruption, he called, "Come in."

His brother entered. The changes in Damian in the months since he'd married Jessica were many. Evan remembered a time when practicing law ruled Damian's life. He worked after hours and weekends, rarely taking time away. But now his brother looked younger, happier and so damn much in love Evan couldn't help a twinge of jealousy.

Witnessing the changes in Damian caused him to wonder what his own life would have been like if he'd married Mary Jo. They'd have started a family by now. The glimpse he'd caught of her almost a year ago at the Red Sox game drifted into his mind, and with it came a stab of pain.

Loving her as he did, even now, it was impossible to want anything but the best for her. He tried not to think about Mary Jo, tried to place her firmly in the back of his mind, but every now and again, the memory of her escaped to taunt him with the might-have-beens.

It had been nearly eighteen months since they'd parted, and she still had the power to move him. He'd dated now and again, but there wasn't anyone he'd gotten serious about. He wished he knew what it was about Mary Jo that he couldn't forget.

Evan envied his brother the happiness he'd found and didn't expect to find the same happiness himself. He could see himself thirty years down the road with white hair, dressed in a smoking jacket, sitting in front of a fireplace smoking a pipe. A black Labrador would lie snoozing at his feet....

"You're looking thoughtful," Damian said, helping himself to a chair.

"Just woolgathering."

Damian was more relaxed these days, Evan noted. His brother leaned back in the chair and rested one ankle over the other knee. "Remember last month when Jessica phoned from the doctor's office?"

Evan chuckled. "I'm not likely to forget." Nor would anyone else in the office. Rarely had he seen his brother so excited, so elated. For days he'd walked around grinning like a mad fool. It wasn't every day, he said, a man learned he was going to be a father.

Funny, Evan thought, his brother was wearing a similar grin now. "What's going on now?" he asked. "Did you just learn Jessica's carrying twins?"

"Not quite. I've been approached by the bar about an appointment as a judge."

"Damian!" Evan rose from his chair. This shouldn't come as a surprise; it was Damian's destiny, just as marrying Jessica had been. He walked around his desk. Damian stood and the two brothers embraced.

"You're going to accept." Evan didn't put the words into a question. It went without saying Damian would and should.

"Yes, if Jessica concurs."

"She will." Evan had no doubts about that, either. "Are you going out tonight to celebrate?"

"As a matter of fact we are. Cathy Hudson, Jessica's friend, is starring in a new play that's opening tonight. Did I mention she recently got engaged to some director friend of hers?"

Before Evan could respond, his intercom buzzed and he reached for the button. "The receptionist called," Mrs. Sterling informed him, "and said Earl Kress is here to see you, Mr. Dryden."

"Earl?" Evan said with surprise. He hadn't heard from him in six months or more. "Send him in."

"We'll talk later," Damian said as he walked out of the office. "Give my regards to Earl, will you?"

Evan went with him, meeting Earl in the hallway outside. The two exchanged hearty handshakes. Evan slapped the younger man on the back as he led him into his office and closed the door.

"It's good to see you," Evan said, motioning toward the chair. "Sit down and make yourself comfortable."

"I can't stay long," Earl said, sitting on the edge of the chair. "I probably should have called, but I was in the neighborhood…"

"I'm glad you stopped in. How's school?"

"Good. I got my general equivalency diploma not long ago," he announced proudly.

"Congratulations." Evan experienced a surge of pride at the younger man's progress.

"I have a lot of people to thank for that, but you're the one who started it all. I don't think you ever realized how afraid I was of having the world know I couldn't read or write. It's humiliating to admit something like that."

"I realized at the time how difficult it was for you."

"Without your support, I don't think I could have gone through with the trial."

"I'm sure glad you did."

"Yeah, me, too," Earl said with a hearty laugh. "My life would certainly be different if I hadn't. Listen, I didn't mean to take up your time, but I wanted you to know how grateful I am for all your help."

"No problem, Earl."

"I'm working as a volunteer myself now with grade-school kids, helping out in the slow-reader program. I wouldn't have grown up illiterate if I'd gotten help while I was in the elementary grades."

Evan smiled broadly. "That's great, Earl."

"By the way, I ran across a friend of yours the other day—another volunteer."

"Oh?"

"At least I assume you two know one another. Her name's Mary Jo Summerhill."

"Mary Jo." Evan realized he breathed her name more than spoke it.

"Funny, she reacted the same way when I mentioned you."

"I thought she was married," Evan said.

"Not as far as I know." Earl stood and held out his hand. "Anyway, I won't keep you. I just wanted to stop in and update you about what's been going on in my life."

"I'm happy you did," Evan said, walking his former client to the door. He stood there for a moment, his mind spinning.

A few minutes later Damian strolled into his office again.

"What did Earl have to say?" he asked.

"Mary Jo isn't married." He said it out loud just to hear the sound of it. Damian wouldn't fully understand the significance of those words, but it didn't matter.

"I see," his brother said thoughtfully. "What are you going to do about it?"

Evan thought long and hard, then a slow smile spread across his features.

* * * * *

Dear Reader,

Life is full of surprises! As a writer, I enjoy watching how my characters react to the unexpected. Do they run from change or face it boldly, rising to meet the challenge?

Delia Carlisle does both. A sharp-tongued career woman, Delia didn't have a strong maternal role model and never planned on having kids of her own. Her reaction to learning she's pregnant is to panic and put distance between her and the father of her baby. But with the help of great friends—and the man who believes in her—Delia is about to learn that embracing her softer side isn't a weakness, but a special kind of courage. (You can read more about Delia's friends in the women's fiction ebook *Motherhood Without Parole*.)

It's funny to think that my own children, now on the brink of being teenagers, were just entering elementary school when I first wrote Delia's story. Family and parenting remain key themes in my books, including *Her Cowboy Hero* and *The Texan's Christmas,* both available this year from Harlequin American Romance.

To hear more about my family and my books—or just to say hi and let me know what you're reading—follow @TanyaMichaels on Twitter or AuthorTanyaMichaels on Facebook!

Best wishes,

Tanya

MOTHER TO BE
Tanya Michaels

Motherhood is an exciting journey.

Special thanks to my mom, Toni Spiker, for all she's done to point me in the right direction,

and my husband, Jarrad, for being with me every step of the way.

Chapter 1

*According to your aunt Patti, I'm supposed to
record my feelings, maybe even impart wisdom. I'm
not known for being particularly nurturing or wise,
but...here goes.*
Lesson #1: Life's full of surprises.

Three minutes.

That was the minimum wait time listed in the
pregnancy test's step-by-step directions. Delia Carlisle knew not even a full minute had passed, much
less three, so why bother checking the gold watch
she'd treated herself to after signing new tenants to
a posh Richmond, Virginia, office park? Still, she
glared at the timepiece, mentally urging the hands to

tick faster. No one had ever accused Delia of being patient.

Fifty seconds down, one hundred and thirty to go.

She sat on the edge of the Jacuzzi tub, drumming her well-manicured nails on the deep green tile. Damn, she needed a cigarette. They were in her bedroom nightstand, however, and the last thing she wanted to do was to wake up Alexander—affectionately known as Ringo or, when he annoyed her, less affectionately known as That Man. As in, "That Man is harassing me again to quit smoking."

"I want to keep you around," he'd said last week, frowning at her lighter.

"Worried about outliving me? Don't be." Normally, Delia was in more danger of being called *in*sensitive than hypersensitive, but in the past few weeks she'd become increasingly aware of the six-year age difference between her and her junior lover. "I plan to be stunning in black and looking for a new boy toy the day of your funeral. Poor thing, I'll probably wear you out before you hit forty."

He'd merely grinned in that way of his. "You can try."

A strong sexual appetite was something she and Alexander DiRossi had always had in common. Until recently.

She'd been alarmingly disinterested lately. Was their relationship approaching its inherent expiration date? While Alexander had far outlasted any of her other lovers, Delia didn't believe in forever. It would almost be a relief to blame her flagging libido on familiarity or boredom—a romance coming to its natural conclusion, rather than because her body was aging. When exactly had she stopped feeling like herself, emotionally and physically. What had happened to her energy?

At forty-three, she'd told herself she was in her prime—confident, experienced and successful as an agent for a commercial leasing company. Yet she'd noticed that the last few agents hired by her employers were considerably younger than Delia. She'd seen the way girls who hadn't even hit thirty ogled Ringo.

The nickname dated back to a conversation Delia had had with two of her friends just before Valentine's Day, when Alexander moved into her town house.

"I knew you were getting serious," newlywed Kate St. James had exclaimed, "but cohabitation? *You?*"

"Is it wise to move in with someone you've only been seeing for two and a half months?" Patti Jordan had fretted.

"This is so unlike you!" Kate had said simultaneously.

It *was* unlike Delia. She'd lived with a lover only once before, and none of her relationships had ever made it past the year mark. She preferred short and sweet to messy entanglements and even messier breakups. But the idea to let Alexander stay with her for a while had been her spontaneous suggestion and hadn't given her the itchy, claustrophobic sensation she'd experienced the last time a man had broached the subject.

She'd shrugged off Patti's and Kate's astonishment.

"His lease was up. He didn't want to renew, but hasn't found anything else, so I said he could stay with me. He's at my place most nights anyway. In a couple of months, he'll get restless or I'll feel smothered and he can resume his original plan of looking."

With Alexander officially becoming Delia's Significant Other, Kate and Patti had dubbed him Ringo to go with their husbands, Paul and George. That had been six months ago.

Now, leaning forward on the tub's edge and rubbing the small of her back, Delia took mental inventory of the Beatles' hits and wondered if they'd ever released a song appropriate for her current predicament. *You're overreacting.* No doubt she would start her period in the next day or so and reflect on these three excruciating minutes with amusement.

But if she really believed that, why was she carefully avoiding looking at the white plastic stick lying flat next to her? She had a random memory of her elementary school teacher warning students that they weren't to stare directly at a solar eclipse. Delia turned her head in the other direction, again studying the watch that sat on the half wall surrounding the tub. Three minutes, fifty seconds.

Her time was up.

Taking a deep breath—wishing it included nicotine—she carefully lifted the stick by its plastic thumb grip. Her eyes went wide and uncomprehending for a moment before she blinked the image back into focus. A strangled noise of protest gurgled in her throat. Holy shit, two lines.

Two. Straight. Pink. Lines.

The directions had said one line might be lighter than the other, but these were so dark and vibrant she worried they might somehow be visible through the door. As if Alexander could roll over on one sculpted shoulder, face the bathroom and know she was pregnant on the other side. *Damn him.* She should have known better than to date a virile Italian stud muffin. Though she'd never gotten around to taking time off work and having anything surgical done, she had a long-standing prescription for a hormone-based contraceptive. Apparently it had been no match for That Man.

In all fairness, the warning that came with the birth control did stipulate a 93 percent rate of effectiveness; statistically she'd been pushing her odds. But when she'd emerged from her twenties and thirties unscathed, it had seemed ludicrous that she might conceive in her forties!

Maybe it wasn't the birth control that had failed, she thought suddenly in a mingled moment of hope and hysteria. Maybe something had gone wrong with the test! After all, who knew how long the sealed stick in its long-ago-opened multipack had been lurking under her bathroom sink? Maybe it was expired and unreliable. Maybe the tile around the tub wasn't a completely level surface and had skewed the results. Maybe she was so tired after waking up in the predawn hours of this August morning that her eyesight was blurred.

She pressed the heels of her palms against her

eyes. When she'd managed to relax her heartbeat to a slightly *below* jacked-up-on-illegal-stimulants race-horse level, she took another look. Still two lines. According to the piece of plastic she was tempted to snap in half, forty-three-year-old Delia Carlisle was going to be a mother.

Delia stayed still as Ringo pressed a quick kiss to her forehead, keeping her eyes closed until she heard the front door open, then shut, downstairs. She normally enjoyed sleeping in late on the weekend—her personal reward for high-intensity workweeks—but falling back to sleep hadn't been an option this morning. Then again, neither had been talking to Alexander. So, she'd faked it—something she'd never had to say in the course of their relationship.

Since when are you a coward?

Well, there was a first time for everything. The frickin' pink lines had proved that. Besides, what would she have said? "Have a nice trip to New York. By the way, I'm pregnant." This was *her* uterus, after all; she would tell him when she was damn well ready. Not that she could imagine when that would be.

Antsy with shifting emotions, she kicked off the sheets and comforter. She needed to get out of here for a little while. Maybe she should call Patti or Kate and ask if they wanted to meet for breakfast.

Not Patti, she decided almost immediately.

Richmond housewife Patti Jordan was one of Delia's unlikelier acquaintances, practically Delia's opposite. The two women had become increasingly involved in each other's lives through fellow country club member and mutual friend Kate St. James. Though Patti's and Delia's dissimilar personalities often led to minor clashes, each of them would defend the other to an outsider. Delia was an only child, but she imagined squabbling siblings were much the same way.

Overachiever Kate St. James was closer in outlook and lifestyle to Delia, although forty-two-year-old Kate had married a widower with children. Kate was struggling to find her footing as a stepmother, a situation complicated by her new husband being sentenced to several months in a minimum-security prison due to a perceived corporate crime.

I should visit Kate. With news of a possible pregnancy, Delia might shock Kate into temporarily forgetting her own problems. Both of them *mothers?* It was like a bad cosmic joke.

And Delia had never felt more like a punch line in her life.

Delia was not the "girly" sort. She'd never hosted giggly slumber parties at her house as a teenager—although she had lied once about attending a sleepover to meet a boyfriend—and she hadn't joined a sorority in college. Still, she'd learned enough about business that she made it a point to network with other women at her country club. One club member and fellow unmarried professional was Shauna Adair, an OB-GYN who was as competitive on the tennis courts as Delia. Shauna wasn't her doctor, but Delia hoped their casual friendship would excuse her calling on a Sunday morning. At a red light between her town house and Kate's, Delia scrolled through some saved numbers, hoping she had Shauna's programmed into her cell phone. *Bingo.* The phone rang as Delia accelerated through the intersection.

"Hello?"

"Shauna? It's Delia Carlisle."

"Hey, killer. Haven't seen you on the courts lately."

"Well, I thought I'd give you a break."

Shauna laughed. "Beating Brooke Campbell just isn't as satisfying as winning against you. She doesn't have your serve."

Normally Delia would have rejoined that *nobody* had her serve. She was in a class by herself. "Shauna, if I wanted to talk to you about something medical, would there be doctor-patient confidentiality?"

"Technically you're not one of my patients. But if you have something you need to discuss, you don't have to worry about my gossiping about it over canapés."

Dead air hung between them as Delia found herself unable to voice the situation. She gripped the steering wheel in frustration. *Get some balls.* Of course, if she'd had those, she wouldn't be in this predicament.

"I'm pregnant." Out loud it sounded even more surreal than it had when she'd been alone in her bathroom at oh-dark-thirty. "At least, I think I am, based on two missed periods and two pink lines. In your professional opinion, how reliable are those over-the-counter tests?"

"Pretty accurate. There have been instances of misdiagnosis, but false negatives are more common than false positives. I take it you haven't had the results confirmed?"

"I just found out. Haven't even told Alexander yet. So you can see why this conversation needs to remain confidential," Delia added. "I probably shouldn't have called, only…I have some questions."

"Such as?" Shauna sounded 100 percent like a detached medical professional, not the glib, trash-talking tennis opponent who'd answered the phone.

"Drinking. Even *I* know enough about pregnancy to know alcohol isn't recommended." Delia cast a glance at the bottle of champagne on the passenger seat next to her. It had been the only unopened booze in her apartment, and she'd grabbed it on impulse to give to Kate. The already-opened stuff Delia would either throw out later or drink in a one-woman party if the plastic stick was proven incorrect.

"Don't let any previous drinks bother you," Shauna advised. "Drinking is more harmful as the embryo develops and in repeated doses. Lots of women imbibe before they learn they're pregnant, and most babies are just fine."

In an absent way, Delia was aware her question had been answered, but mention of an *embryo* had distracted her. It was a freaky, sci-fi-sounding word she'd never expected to hear in relation to herself.

"Delia? Was there anything else?"

Yeah. A whole boatload of *elses,* considering she'd never imagined herself in this position. "My age.

Aren't babies born to women over forty more likely to have, I don't know, problems?" She was fuzzy on the specifics. She'd never been around a baby and rarely around pregnant women; her mother had been unsuccessful in conceiving after Delia.

Though Alexander had made some halfhearted noises about a coworker who'd recently become a father and that they should invite the new parents over for a congratulatory dinner, Delia's day-to-day life rarely brought her in contact with youngsters. Kate's stepchildren, Neve and PJ, had been at the wedding, but they'd lived at a private boarding school until Paul's arrest, then spent the bulk of the summer at the beach with their grandparents, only arriving home yesterday. Patti had a son, but Leo was a teenager with a driver's license and an active schedule.

After taking a moment to weigh her response, Shauna answered, "There are some statistical concerns for women who are pregnant after thirty-five, but nothing I'd automatically stress over, not with so many other factors involved. What if you came into my office tomorrow? You could wait to see your regular gynecologist if you're more comfortable, but if you want to swing by early, I'll meet you first thing. We can at least determine for sure whether or not you're actually pregnant."

"Thank you." The sooner she had answers, the better. Then again, that had been her rationale for searching for that lone plastic test stick in the wee hours of the morning, and look how *that* had turned out so far.

By the time Delia disconnected the call, she was

pulling into Kate's driveway. Though competent and intelligent, Kate was no more a domestic goddess than Delia, so it was a surprise when her friend offered, "You can join us for waffles," with a manically bright smile.

Once they reached the usually spotless kitchen, it became clear waffles were not on the immediate menu. Batter slicked the white countertops and a foulsmelling steam rose from the waffle iron. Kate's preteen stepdaughter was attempting damage control.

Kate sighed. "You go talk PJ into cereal," she instructed the girl, "and I'll clean this up."

Delia placed the bottle of champagne on the island. She didn't know why she was so fixated on getting rid of the damn thing. She wasn't such a heavy drinker that she was going to pop the cork and start guzzling. But…the bottle was an uneasy reminder of how suddenly and drastically her life could change. Was the pregnancy why her libido had gone into recent hibernation?

Great. Her love life was on the fritz, she would have to give up drinking, cigarettes and possibly caffeine. Plus, she'd get fat. Force her to knit unending pairs of pastel-colored booties and she'd officially be in hell.

Kate glanced over, catching Delia scowling at the champagne.

Delia pushed it across the counter. "You should put this away for some occasion." Like when Paul got out of prison? "I actually brought it over as a gift. I, um, won't be drinking much for a while."

"Oh?"

It was a perfect opening for Delia to tell her friend what she'd come over to say, but somehow, saying it now, face-to-face... It had been easier to admit the news over the phone, especially to a doctor. Though Delia had never been a superstitious woman, it suddenly seemed as if the more people she told, the more real the pregnancy would become. *Stupid.* She either was or she wasn't.

Delia angled her head toward the living room and the unfamiliar sounds of kids chattering. Kate hadn't expected the children home from their grandparents' until next week, which she'd scheduled to take off of work. "So what are you doing with them tomorrow?"

"With who?" Kate blinked, then smacked herself in the forehead. "Good Lord. It hadn't even crossed my mind." She stared into the distance, probably scrambling for a plan.

Kate faced many changes, child-care challenges that were completely foreign to a woman who'd focused her energies on her career until now. Delia's stomach rolled as she contemplated the upcoming changes in *her* life. Could she raise a kid? While she considered herself stubborn enough to do just about anything she set her mind to, the relationship between Delia and her own mother was...strained, to say the least. At thirteen, Delia had been infuriated when her father walked out on Chelsea Carlisle, mousy but devoted wife, to shack up with a colleague. Yet it had somehow been even *worse* when Chelsea, who'd never made any secret that she was pining for her ex-husband, took him back two and a half years later. How could the woman remarry the bastard who'd humiliated her, acting as if the affair had never happened?

Maybe Chelsea was just really gifted in denial… especially since she'd expected Delia to be *grateful* when Garrett came home to his erstwhile wife and daughter.

A child needs two parents, sweetheart. Instead of being so angry and foul-mouthed all the time, be thankful your family's whole again. Your father made a mistake, but that's in the past.

Chelsea's version of events conveniently made it sound as if he'd repented his ways and left Renee, aka the Home-wrecking Blonde. Why, during divorce proceedings, had Chelsea and her friends always blamed Renee rather than the man who'd actually betrayed his marriage vows and family? But it wasn't belated pangs of conscience that drove Garrett home; it was wounded ego. During an obligatory visit to her father's apartment, Delia had overheard him arguing with his longtime girlfriend. He'd wanted the woman to marry him.

Renee had laughed, genuinely amused. "Why? So you can take me for granted the way you did your poor first wife? Oh, Garrett. I'm not interested in doing your laundry and hostessing Super Bowl Sunday for your friends. I'm interested in being successful, which is why I'm taking that position on the west coast."

In Delia's teenage opinion, the Home-wrecking

Blonde made sense. Renee had wound up with some great job in sunny California, while Chelsea Carlisle settled for emotional leftovers.

Unable to understand or respect her mother's decision, Delia had vowed that *her* life and self-worth would never hinge on a man. She'd worn all black to her parents' second ceremony, a travesty of promises long since broken, then made out with one of the cute waiters at the small reception.

In the last decade, Delia had been back to Kentucky only three times. Up until Delia's graduation in college, Chelsea had seemed manically determined to pretend they were the perfect family. Now, however, Delia's parents seemed almost as relieved as Delia herself when each brief visit ended.

Feeling Kate's gaze on her, Delia shook herself out of the unexpected memories and suppressed emotions. It had been ages since she'd thought about her parents and their dysfunctional relationship. She refused to dwell on them now...even if she was going to become a parent herself.

"You want to talk about it?" Kate pressed.

No. Yes. "It's nothing major. Actually it is. But still not the end of the world, right?" Good God, she wasn't going to be wishy-washy for the next nine months, was she?

"Whatever 'it' is, it's obviously been worrying you." Kate leaned closer to scrutinize her. "Those bags you're sporting aren't exactly Fendi."

Delia peered at her distorted reflection in the microwave door. "Just a little exhaustion some decent eye cream should fix. I've been up for hours." Awake, trying to imagine what life would be like when she had a tiny crying person who needed to be fed every few hours, a person whose health, education and moral code Delia would be responsible for. According to Patti's disapproving remarks, moral codes weren't Delia's specialty.

Katie lobbed her washcloth into the sink and asked point-blank, "What's going on, Dee?"

"Hell, Kate, I'm forty-three years old." Last month she'd thought she was exactly where she wanted to be in life.

"Please don't tell me forty-three's a bad age," Kate teased. "I'm coming up on it fast."

"Forty-three is great for certain things. But pregnancy?"

"Pregnant?" The word boomed out of Kate, nearly making Delia flinch. Within seconds, Kate recovered a measure of her usual aplomb. "When did this happen? Er, I mean, when did you find out?"

"About five o'clock this morning."

Kate sat in one of the two chairs at the small kitchen table and gestured toward the other. "How sure are you?"

"I don't know." Delia explained how, after waking up to pee for the third time, she'd dug out the test just to ease her mind, and how, to buy time, she'd avoided saying goodbye to Ringo before he left on business.

Kate leaned back, processing the news. "You should get a second opinion."

"Oh, *trust* me." Would the visit to Shauna's office

reinstate the status quo Delia had been happily maintaining or confirm that nothing in her life would ever be the same again?

Chapter 2

People will insist change is good. It's always easier to be the one saying that than to be the one actually making changes.

Alexander DiRossi breathed in the oregano-scented chaos that was his mother's kitchen. His job as a software expert who set up systems for companies took him from coast to coast, but his favorite trips were the ones that brought him close to Queens, where his mother and sisters lived. The summer before he'd started high school, he'd lost his father to a stroke; butting heads with strong-willed matriarch Isabella DiRossi during the four years that followed had inspired him to go to an out-of-state college. Alexander didn't regret moving away, but he often missed the opinionated women in his family.

It was a shame Delia hadn't met them, because he rather thought she'd like his loud, hot-tempered sisters.

In fact, Delia had been the frequent topic of conversation ever since his sister Angela picked him up from the airport. The youngest DiRossi sibling, Angie had been married for two years and was the only sister without children. Marie and Blanche were busy chasing their broods around in the next room, while Alexander's brothers-in-law were allowed to watch the evening news in peace. Alexander sat in his mother's kitchen as Angie and Isabella made salad, stirred spaghetti sauce and interrogated him ceaselessly.

"So you didn't even bring a photograph of this woman with whom you are living in sin?" Isabella asked from the stove.

Angela rolled her eyes. "Mama! You know good and well that Dennis and I lived together before we got married."

"Dennis came to my house. Dennis met your family."

"Dennis lives in New York," Alexander pointed out, stretching out his long legs as much as possible in the cramped space. The kitchen was so much smaller than he remembered. "I haven't seen you in ages. Can't we talk about what's going on with the family?"

Isabella leveled a wooden serving spoon at him. "You think you can provoke me into a lecture on how you don't come home often enough and distract me."

He hid a smile, not surprised that his mother had deduced his strategy.

"Isabella DiRossi was not born yesterday," his mother informed him. "What is wrong with this woman you love that we have never met her?"

Love? Alexander scowled. It wasn't a word he and Delia used. Actually, it was a concept he'd heard her mock more than once. They were passionate, and they were monogamous. After dating more than one woman who pressed for discussions about his feelings, it had been a welcome relief to find one who steered clear of those conversations. Especially when she was a sexy, independent, thought-provoking and often outrageously funny woman. Though he valued family, Alexander hadn't been ready for one in his early thirties. He loved the travel and fast pace of his job, but wasn't sure a wife would feel the same way. Luckily he'd found an equally business-oriented woman, who matched him in both wit and temper, made his toes curl in bed and could still surprise him after the better part of a year together.

She'd more than surprised him when she'd said he could move in with her…although her offer and his acceptance might have had something to do with the premium top-shelf margaritas they'd been enjoying that particular evening. Still, they were a good fit.

Angela cleared her throat, making him aware that he'd let too much time pass since his mother's question.

"There's nothing wrong with Delia," he stressed, knowing that it was too little, too late.

Isabella harrumphed. "Yet you don't bring her home for the holidays—"

"We'd only started dating before the holidays," he drawled.

"Now summer has nearly passed, and you still have no plans to make an honest woman of this girl?"

He laughed. "Nobody *makes* anything of Delia. She's her own person. A lot like you, actually."

Isabella pursed her lips. He knew his compliment pleased her, but she couldn't say so without compromising her attempted guilt trip. "You were always my stubborn and arrogant child, Alexander."

"I love you, too, Mama. But if you don't mind, I'm going to excuse myself and spend a little time with my nieces and nephews."

The deceptively cherub-faced rugrats were more than happy to climb all over their uncle, making him the world's only living jungle gym, while he avoided further reprimands from his mother. She wasn't entirely wrong about him being arrogant. He'd always done well in school and equally well with ladies— his good looks and practice dealing with the feminine mindset, thanks to his three sisters, had given him a natural advantage. Maybe another man would have felt insecure about Delia's lack of fawning adoration, but Alexander knew from experience that fawning grew tedious. His current lover could be exasperating, but their dynamite chemistry more than made up for it.

He frowned. Their love life, now that he thought

of it, had waned lately. When was the last time they'd had sex?

As he remembered the past weekend, parts and pieces of their exchanges, he wondered if anything was wrong. It wasn't uncommon for Delia to be emotionally—if not physically—reserved, but in retrospect, she'd been almost withdrawn. Unlike one passive-aggressive—and, consequently, short-lived—girlfriend he'd once had, who resorted to the silent treatment when angry, Delia had no qualms voicing her displeasure. If he'd done something to piss her off, she'd point it out, they'd argue loudly, then eventually have great sex. Come to think of it, Delia hadn't even yelled lately. She'd seemed more vulnerable. *Ha! She'd pummel you just for thinking it.*

Grinning at her imagined reaction, he dismissed the issue. During dinner with his family, everyone was busy enough enjoying food that no one brought up his love life; it probably helped that the children sat at the card table squeezed into the dining room. But as he helped his sister Blanche wash dishes, she took up where their mother had left off.

"Tell me the truth, *fratello.*" His eldest sister stood at the adjoining half of the double sink. "You are happy with this woman?"

"Have you ever known me to tolerate something that made me unhappy?" His sisters affectionately labeled him a brat who always got his way, yet rarely acknowledged that they themselves had spoiled him rotten. He hadn't found many girlfriends in his twenties who'd agreed with his overdeveloped sense of entitlement, but ironically, he'd had little patience with the ones who did. While he knew he'd matured, he also knew he could count on Delia to smack him down when he got too full of himself. Not that it wasn't fun to rile her just to see the fiery glint in her eyes.

"Alexander, do not answer questions with questions." His sister sounded more like their mother with each passing year.

He grinned. "I'm happy, yes."

She paused, staring into his eyes in a way that made him shift his weight as if he were ten again and she'd caught him in a lie. Only this time the lie wasn't what he'd said but what she deemed unsaid. "You love her!"

"What?" Women! It was the second time this evening one had lobbed that particular word at him. Like a grenade. "I'm a man. I act, I feel. I don't analyze."

His sisters wouldn't understand that Delia was perfectly content without those sorts of flowery declarations. Of course, she *hadn't* seemed entirely content lately.

Blanche raised her eyebrows, not impressed with his macho posturing. "Fine. Don't tell me, then. But for yourself, you should answer the question. What does your intuition—what does your *occhio del cuore,* tell you?"

"That I should never have volunteered to help you with the dishes," he said, flicking drops of soapy water at her.

"Brat. Shall we discuss something more to your liking? Monster-truck rallies? Hunting mastodon?"

"Baseball would be a nice compromise."

His sister, a lifelong Yankees fan, obliged him with a discussion of how the season had been going so far. But, whether Blanche knew it or not, she'd accomplished her purpose. Although his mother's house was modest and showing its age, it did indeed feel like a home, full of laughter and family meals and generations of love. Together with Blanche's questions, his surroundings made him wonder if he had reached a point in his life where he wanted more than he'd realized.

When Delia had first given him a copy of her key, they'd both seen it as a temporary arrangement. Was that arrangement turning into a home? As much as he enjoyed his job, he looked forward to coming back to her at the end of the week. And when they were apart, he thought about her more than he'd anticipated. If he told her as much, would she scoff at the sentimentality or admit that her feelings had deepened, as well? They'd often been in sync with their views and desires, so maybe the idea that they'd simultaneously grown to want more wasn't that far-fetched.

One area in which they were vastly different was family, their upbringings. When he'd asked Delia about hers, she'd given him a cursory, disdainful rundown of her parents' divorce. And subsequent remarriage. For all that Delia carried herself as a bold, uninhibited woman, she had guarded—nearly fearful—misgivings about lasting romantic attachments. He knew she'd be uneasy with the idea of loving someone, just as he knew from her passionate nature that she could love deeply if she let herself. Could deeper feelings and her discomfort with them be why she'd been on edge lately? *I can help her overcome that.*

He'd make her see what a great team the two of them were, that they could explore new possibilities and strengthen their undefined relationship without turning into one of those couples she mocked for dysfunctional codependence. It was funny how he was often consulted at work on short-term and long-term business plans, but when it came to his personal life, he tended to live in the moment and put off serious consideration of the future. Experimentally, he pictured himself and Delia five years from now.

Ten.

Twenty? It wasn't nearly as difficult as he'd expected it to be. As he stood gazing out the kitchen window into the golden, almost unreal twilight, Alexander's *occhio del cuore* told him change was in the air.

"Nine weeks?" *I am nine weeks' pregnant.* Delia pressed a hand to her chest, her heart pounding through the thin cotton wrap that tied in the back.

"Approximately." Shauna glanced up from her clipboard. Today, instead of a tennis skirt and sports goggles, the slim redhead wore a long white jacket and gold bifocals. "Keep in mind, with the kind of calendar we use, you're not actually pregnant for the first couple of weeks."

"How can you *not* be pregnant at the beginning of the pregnancy?" Delia snapped irritably. She'd purchased a book on the subject last night, but hadn't been able to focus enough to read much. Hell, she'd barely been able to *buy* it. She would have felt less conspicuous at the cash register with a stack of erotica.

"It's complicated," Shauna said. "For now, the only part that's probably important to you is that you're tentatively due at the end of March. You're still in your first trimester and seem to be doing well. Great blood pressure—we want to make sure you keep those numbers appropriately low. Any nausea?"

"Not until I got the positive results," Delia said. "I've had to pee a lot, although I always figured that part came later, when there was an actual baby sitting on the bladder. And I've been tired. Maybe even, um, testy."

"You?" Shauna grinned, removing her glasses. "Normally you have such a sunny disposition."

Delia arched an eyebrow. "You're just feeling ballsy because you're standing close to the door and don't think I'll chase you with my butt exposed in this 'gown.' Dream on. Modesty is not one of my virtues." Good thing. How would a woman who was shy by nature endure the vaginal ultrasound? While her feet had been in the stirrups, Delia had had the thought that Shauna had chosen one seriously weird-ass career.

The ultrasound confirmed that Delia had an embryo growing inside her; she even had a full-color *photo* now. She'd squinted at the picture, shaded in reds and yellows that were probably significant to people with medical degrees, but no matter how deep she reached to try to dredge up maternal intuition, all she could make out was what looked like a storm front moving in over a lima bean.

"Chasing sarcastic doctors aside," Shauna said, "do try to exercise when you have the energy for it. Not diving for the ball on the tennis courts, but some kind of moderate activity. It's good for you and the baby. As I said, the pregnancy seems completely viable, and you hardly hold the record for oldest mommy. Still, your body might not bounce back the same way a twenty-three-year-old's would."

"So make a concerted effort or end up a fat slug—check. Anything else?"

"I've written out a prescription for prenatal vitamins. Some women with extreme morning sickness have trouble keeping them down, but that doesn't seem to be an issue with you."

"Since I haven't tossed my cookies yet, can we assume I'm home free on that front?"

"Difficult to say. Every woman's pregnancy is slightly different." Shauna nodded toward the book peeking out of Delia's purse. "Guides like that should be helpful if you do start to feel queasy, but if the nausea turns into anything you can't handle on your own, call me."

Delia lifted her chin. "I'm sure I can handle it." A bit of an overstatement, but Delia loathed weakness.

Shauna handed over the prescription, her penmanship so illegible that Delia was impressed more pharmacists didn't send patients home with the completely wrong medicine. "Go ahead and get those medical records transferred to us, and we'll set up an appointment to see you again in about three weeks. Read the brochure I gave you on amnio testing, and then you can ask questions when you come back. You have plenty of time to think about everything and make decisions."

Thinking about the amniocentesis made Delia shudder, but she knew the test wasn't uncommon for women her age whose babies were at a higher statistical risk for certain defects. A significant portion of pregnancies in women over forty didn't make it past the first trimester. Delia's mind rebelled at such a possibility, and she caught herself raising her hand protectively to her abdomen.

Shauna was quick to turn the conversation in a happier direction. "We might do another ultrasound next time for more accurate dating, and we'll see if we can hear the fetal heartbeat. You may want to bring Alexander with you."

To the doctor's office? That seemed bizarrely intimate—an ironic thought given that being intimate with That Man was what had landed her here in the first place. She'd been naked and sweaty with him many times. Yet that was vastly different from being naked in a chilly exam room, where she would be the only one required to drop trou. A shame, that, because Alexander had a spectacular ass.

Delia managed a tight smile. "I'll talk to him."

"I imagine you two have lots to discuss."

He'd left her a message yesterday afternoon to let her know he'd arrived safely in New York, but it wasn't uncommon for them not to talk much when he was away. Even on trips when he wasn't busy with his family, he often worked long hours to get computer systems operating correctly and to answer any client questions before he had to leave. Besides, he knew that when he was gone, Delia herself worked late or took advantage of the free nights to catch up with her girlfriends. She couldn't avoid him forever, though. He'd be home Friday evening.

Her due date at the end of March seemed reassuringly distant—it wasn't even this year! Plenty of time for an assertive go-getter such as herself to figure out how to cope. She just wished she had longer to figure out how to tell Alexander. What would she say? What would *he?* He was a proud and fundamentally decent man; his volunteering financial assistance was a given. Beyond that, she didn't know what to expect. Certainly he came from a closer-knit family than hers, but he'd still opted to move several states away from his relatives. He valued his freedom, but that seemed like the essential sacrifice required for parenthood, far beyond giving up booze or cigarettes. If Alexander heard the news and immediately fled for Canada, it would underscore every cynical suspicion she'd ever had about a man's propensity for walking away.

Then again, since *her* initial reaction had included a good dose of panic, it would be mildly embarrassing for him to respond with calm maturity.

She could imagine dozens of ways that this pregnancy could come between them. Was it possible that it could make their relationship stronger? More importantly, did she even want that?

Chapter 3

Supposedly there's no such thing as a stupid question. And yet, men ask them.

At the unexpected knock on her front door Thursday evening, Delia nearly fell over. She was precariously balanced, standing on one foot as she unbuckled a high heel. These used to be her favorite shoes, but after today, she was considering burning them. She'd had several meetings that required rushing back and forth and had shown office space to some demanding customers. Now all she wanted was to be off her feet.

And possibly a cigarette, though she was ignoring that craving. It sucked that most of the aids produced to help people kick the habit weren't completely safe for pregnant women. No gum, no patch. The substitutes would be better for Baby Lima Bean than cigarettes, of course, but nicotine in any form could further increase the risks— *Rap, rap, rap.*

Oops, the door. Was she actually so exhausted that she'd forgotten she had a visitor in the last ten seconds?

"Who is it?" Fearing that Ringo had come home a day early, Delia froze as shock raced up her spine and straight to her temples, like an ice-cream headache, but rational thinking asserted itself before panic could take hold. Alexander had a key; he didn't knock.

"It's Patti," came the muffled response from outside. "Can I come in?"

Me and my big mouth. If Delia had kept quiet, she could have pretended not to be home.

Truth be told, Patti had been surprisingly supportive ever since hearing about Delia's condition. She'd insisted on buying Delia lunch Monday after her doctor's appointment. But Delia was so brain-numbingly tired that the idea of making small talk…

Conceding that she couldn't just leave poor Patti standing on the front porch, Delia heaved a sigh and wriggled out of her second shoe as she walked. "Hey."

"I wasn't sure you were going to let me in." Patti raised two white bags. "I brought you dinner. I was in the neighborhood, working with Chastity and Brooke on the October fund-raising dinner we're holding at the club."

At the mention of food Delia sniffed gingerly, wondering how her stomach would react. She'd had her first bout of serious nausea after a working lunch when the client had ordered seafood. Right now, however, she felt ravenous.

"Come on in," Delia invited, once she was sure she was in no danger of hurling on her guest.

Patti squeezed past, bustling toward the kitchen. She was more plump than either Delia or Kate, but her fashionable clothes were flattering, and her pretty face was well-framed by a fall of glossy auburn hair.

Soon I'll be double her size.

"There's enough for two," Patti said as she opened cabinets and searched for plates. "I know Alexander's out of town, so if you want company, I'll stay and we can eat together. If you'd rather be alone, I can just put the rest in the fridge and you'll have leftovers for later."

Delia watched from the edge of the kitchen. "You're really being nice to me this week."

Patti paused long enough to flash an uncharacteristically mischievous grin. "I'm *always* nice, you're just too obnoxious to notice."

That surprised a bark of laughter from Delia. "You can definitely stay for dinner."

In the past the two women had held different views on practically everything, including what qualified as obnoxious. Patti tended to think that Delia's outspokenness was selfish at worst, inappropriate at best. Meanwhile, Delia had sometimes found Patti to be judgmental and intrusive, quick to jump into other people's lives and fuss over them. Yet, after a long, hard day and this baby growing inside her, Delia suddenly didn't object so much to having someone fuss over her. It was a foreign feeling, but somehow being around a woman who'd gone through pregnancy herself was vaguely reassuring.

"You okay?" Patti's gaze narrowed. "Your expression got a little odd there for a moment."

"My entire life has turned odd."

"Go put your feet up. I'll bring this out in a sec."

Despite wanting to do exactly as Patti suggested, Delia hesitated. "It's awkward to be waited on, especially at my own place."

"You don't like people to do you favors because you'd rather not owe anyone anything," Patti said matter-of-factly. "Don't worry, there are no strings attached here."

With mixed feelings about her friend's assessment, Delia adjourned to the living room without comment. She was too tired for verbal jousting. Now *there* was a depressing thought.

A few minutes later both women were seated, casually dining on grilled chicken sandwiches and black-bean-and-corn salad. Delia leaned forward to put her decaffeinated tea on the coffee table.

"Should I find you a coaster?" Patti asked, having placed her own drink on a thick section of folded paper towel.

Delia laughed. "I'm not sure I own any." Any resulting water rings just added to the table's character as far as she was concerned. Her mother had been the type to insist on coasters and, in the guest bathroom, decorative soaps that no one was actually supposed to use. What kind of freak scolded someone for condensation on an oak table but blithely forgave her husband for walking out on her?

Glancing around the room, it struck Delia how different this place was from not only where she'd lived as a child but from her friends' residences. Kate and Paul's house was very contemporary—lots of white, ultramodern chairs, the latest in stainless-steel appliances and a flat-surface stove. Patti's furnishings were homier, quality replicas of American antiques, overstuffed throw pillows in earth tones and pictures of her son, Leo, at every possible age covering the walls. Delia's decorating style was…unapologetic.

She bought pieces that caught her eye, from two, framed forties-era black-and-white photographs to the gigantic four-poster upstairs to the deep violet couch Ringo complained was too short for him to truly stretch out on. She rarely purchased items to match deliberately, yet somehow it went together in Delia's eyes. Even the gold-and-black-striped afghan given to her by an ex-lover and colleague who called her Tiger Lady. She'd ditched the guy after a few weeks but kept the blanket. She was possessive about things she considered hers and somewhat territorial.

Ringo's contributions to the town house were limited—he had a lot in storage—but distinctively masculine. His belongings stood out as more leather and mahogany and less "purchased at an upscale flea market and reputed to have once been in the sitting room of a famous brothel." Delia eyed his expensive black recliner. How well did his stuff blend here, among the hodgepodge? Frankly, they'd blended bet-

ter than she could have predicted. She knew damn
well she wasn't the easiest person in the world to
live with, but she and Ringo had managed for more
than half a year not to kill each other.

Of course, it probably helped that the travel his job
required afforded them both space and time alone.
But what would happen when the baby came? Space
and time meant one less pair of hands to help change
diapers or to walk a crying infant up and down the
hall. Conversely, if they agreed that Alexander should
be active in raising their child and he rearranged his
work schedule to be here more often, would she suf-
focate, unused to his constant presence? A crying
baby would no doubt make the two-bedroom place
more claustrophobic.

Delia was fumbling for a lighter in her pocket before she remembered she'd thrown it away.

It occurred to her, not for the first time, that she
didn't *have* to keep this child. Yet the alternatives felt
more unnatural to her than motherhood itself…and
that was saying something. That she hadn't knowingly conceived this baby didn't make it any less hers.
How badly could she screw up, really? Her own parents had made some abysmal choices, yet Delia had
a great salary, cozy town house, handsome and attentive lover and no criminal record. *I can do this.*

Sheer bravado might get her through the next
seven months. The trick was not to think too much
about the eighteen years after that.

"Everything all right?" Patti asked, her tone knowing and concerned.

"Bloody peachy." Delia shoved a hand through her short blond hair.

"It's gotta be difficult, shouldering this yourself with telling Alexander still in front of you."

"Yeah." Delia appreciated the empathy, but doubted Patti really understood. The other woman had married young, and she and George had chosen to start their family immediately. "I'll bet George did cartwheels when you told him you were expecting."

"Hardly."

"I thought you got pregnant on purpose? That it was a mutual decision." One made by two consenting adults and not a whim of fate.

"You're right. Still, we were barely more than kids." Patti sat back in her chair. "In theory, George was giddy with being an adult, holding his first real job and wanting a son to toss the ball with. In reality, there are a lot of stressful years before the ball-tossing part and my husband freaked out over whether or not he could support a family. He was happy eventually, but terror was the predominant emotion there for a while."

Presumably George's version of "terror" was more sedate than most people's, but Delia got the point her friend was trying to make.

"Honestly, I felt it, too," Patti admitted. "There would be days during the pregnancy when I couldn't wait to become a mom and other days when I'd catch myself thinking, holy hell, this thing's gotta come out of me somehow."

Delia winced.

"The trick for me and George was not wigging out at the same time. When I was a wreck, he'd be there to reassure me, and vice versa. I'm sure you and Ringo will be the same way."

"Really?" Delia wasn't sure of any such thing. She'd always assumed sticking by your partner was the exception, not the rule. Hell, *she* hadn't stuck in three-quarters of her relationships. From the students she'd known in college who had divorced parents to club members and colleagues she knew were getting divorces, life had proven time and again that people found excuses to wiggle free of commitment. When the first exciting blush of infatuation started to fade, Delia saw no point in waiting around and pretending otherwise.

But that won't apply to you, she promised her unborn child. Delia remembered too well what it was like to feel unimportant to your own parents. Her father had seemed more interested in chasing a pair of great legs in a power suit, viewing his family as an optional circumstance he could participate in at his convenience. Meanwhile, her mother had been so wrapped up in her own grief and pain during the divorce that she spent more time in a week staring at her wedding photo than talking to her daughter.

Delia would not be repeating her parents' mistakes. She might make hundreds of new ones, but by God, she'd make this kid a priority. All her life she'd set goals and gone after them with gusto—whether the next item on her list was saving up for a pair of great sling backs, clinching a lease or seducing a new neighbor.

Motherhood might not have been a goal she'd *known* she wanted, but now that she found herself on the field with the ball in her hands, she had no intentions of fumbling.

After a long day of standing in airport lines, waiting for takeoff and gritting his teeth during turbulence, Alexander pulled up to the front of the town house with a sigh. *Home.* Maybe not a suburban home with a picket fence and a domestically inclined woman, unless he counted that French maid outfit she'd donned on his birthday— He caught himself grinning at the memory. He was a lucky man.

Was he greedy, wondering throughout the week— after being surrounded by his affectionately married sisters and their spouses—if he and Delia could have even more than what they already shared together?

Maybe.

Then again, he hadn't become successful or won Delia into his bed by sitting back and being a passive spectator. He went after what he wanted. Now he just needed a better idea of what *she* wanted. Sometimes they were eerily on the same page; other times her friend Kate called them oil and water. In the post-coital aftermath of one extremely heated argument, Delia had chuckled that they were more like gas on open flame.

Loosening his tie, he crossed the distance between his car and the front door. Autumn and its cooler temperatures couldn't arrive fast enough. The August heat was oppressive, making his skin prickle and adding to a general sense of restlessness. He opened the door and called out a hello as he stepped inside. Delia's sleek luxury sedan had been parked in its allotted space, but the house was quiet.

He dropped his small suitcase in the entryway, the thud reverberating in the dim silence. The only other sound was the hum of the air-conditioning. The day's heat must have bothered Delia, as well, because she had the thermostat set unusually low. As he progressed toward the stairs, he realized he heard water running.

Upstairs, he knocked outside the master bathroom. "I'm home. You in the shower?" His next question would be whether or not she wanted company.

The water cut off immediately. "I'll be out in a minute. Your mail's in the living room by the television."

He would have preferred joining her to opening bills, but no matter. As he turned to go back down, he stopped, taking a good look at their bedroom. Something was different... She'd changed the curtains. These were much darker than what they'd had before, actually black and made from a thicker material. *From the Goth home collection.* Well, Delia's sense of style did take some getting used to, not that he spent a lot of time formulating opinions on drapery. What red-blooded man would?

He headed downstairs, where hopes for a cold beer drew him toward the refrigerator. Unfortunately there wasn't any. He considered whether making a martini was worth the trouble, but the bottle of vodka was gone. After settling on a glass of iced tea, he went to open his mail. In the living room he had another tingling sense that something was different. His gaze went automatically to the curtains, but nope, as far as he could tell, these were unchanged.

Nothing else jumped out, either. He opened a few envelopes, reading the words with half his attention while his visual memory kept niggling at him. What had been added?

Nothing. Instead a second, closer inspection confirmed that something had been taken away. *No ashtrays.* There were normally one or two lighters on countertops or tables, and cigarettes lying on the arm of the couch, but they were gone, too.

Delia's footsteps on the stairs made him grin in anticipation—damn he'd missed her. Could she possibly have taken his suggestion to quit smoking? If she'd secretly been trying to cut back, that could explain some of her irritability before he'd gone to New York.

"Hey." That was all he managed. Her appearance was even more surprising than the circumstantial evidence that she'd decided to kick the nicotine habit.

Delia owned two robes—the filmy, provocative one in dark pink, and a bulky terry-cloth number that covered her from chin to ankles and was only summoned from the closet when she had PMS or a bad cold. Currently she was huddled into the folds of turquoise terry cloth. Her hair was wet and slicked back from her face; she looked fragile. There were faint smudges beneath her pale blue eyes. Had she lost weight? He'd been gone only a matter of days.

Was she sick? Maybe her quitting smoking wasn't because of his affectionate prodding but because of a doctor's mandate. Delia was such a vital person, practically a force unto herself, that it was difficult to imagine her seriously ill. Protective instincts he'd never felt this strongly for anyone but his mom and sisters kicked in. Nothing was going to happen to this woman; he wouldn't let it.

"Hey, yourself." Delia dropped into the chair closest to her, making no move to come and greet him.

"Are you feeling all right? You don't..." He trailed off, deciding that discretion was the best way to go. She might not take his concerned observations in the intended spirit.

"I've been better." She crossed her arms over her chest, her hands disappearing in the cloth. "Ringo, we need to talk."

At least she hadn't called him Alexander. If the news were dire, she wouldn't use the ridiculous pet name, would she? "I'm listening."

She quirked an eyebrow. "You don't sound surprised. Or even against the idea. I thought guys hated talking?"

If he didn't know her better, he'd say she was stalling. "Just because I'm a man doesn't mean I'm blind. I've noticed that there have been...changes."

She laughed hoarsely, tilting her head back and addressing the ceiling. "Oh, if only he knew."

What the hell was going on? Alexander was beginning to feel as if he'd stumbled into a play and didn't know his lines. Or even the show's title or subject matter. "Whatever it is, you can tell me. I'm here."

"I've been trying to figure out *how* to tell you," she admitted. "All week. I'm a sharp lady, so you'd think I would have decided on something by now."

"Normally you just blurt out the truth, diplomacy be damned."

"Well." She sat a little taller, taking a deep breath. "That was before I got pregnant."

Pregnant?

His jaw dropped, his heart thundering again, but this time without the accompanying dread he'd experienced a few minutes ago when he feared she might be sick. They'd made a baby, he and Delia. Good God, she was carrying his child.

"Ringo?"

Literally speechless, he thought of his little niece Adelina and the trusting way she'd snuggled against him as he read a story. His fearless nephew Jonathan, whose battle cry was "Watch what I can do!"

Silver-haired Isabella, with her gruff exterior and soft heart, was going to be a grandmother again. *I'm going to be a dad.* That thought made him feel closer to his own late father than he had since the man died.

"Alexander? I've blown your mind, haven't I?" Delia asked. "Before you get too freaked, I just want you to know, I'm not asking for anything. I only—"

"Freaked?" He got to his feet, crossing the small room to take her hand in his. "You're amazing. You're strong and audaciously funny and a beautiful woman.

There's no one else I'd rather have as the mother of my child."

Her eyes widened. "Seriously? Because—"

"Marry me, Delia Carlisle." The words were spontaneous, but they felt right. Hadn't people been telling him all week that marriage was the next natural step for a couple who'd been together for nearly a year? A couple who already lived together and knew each other inside and out? *A couple having a baby?*

"What?" Delia's hands slid out of his.

If he'd been involved with a different woman, he might have regretted his impulsive proposal, lacking in roses and diamonds and a string quartet. But Delia wasn't the type who went for those trappings, so he relied on simple, classic words. "Will you do me the honor of becoming my wife?"

Her expression hadn't wavered from its earlier shock, but her eyes glistened. Was she going to cry? He only realized that the gleam he saw was anger a split second before her answer.

"Oh, *hell,* no."

Chapter 4

If you're lucky, you'll find at least one or two people in your life you can always trust for an honest opinion; unfortunately, the honest opinion won't always be the one you want to hear.

Ever since she'd heard Alexander's voice through the bathroom door, above the spray of the shower, conflicting emotions had been rioting inside Delia, each vying for dominance. For the moment anger had emerged the clear victor.

Marry him? What was this, 1955? The two of them had never—not once—discussed making their relationship permanent, yet his immediate reaction to her pregnancy had been proprietary. She heard her mother's voice in her head, telling her that a child needed two parents.

No. She wasn't enduring some pretend marriage for all the wrong reasons; she wasn't as skilled in self-delusion as Chelsea was.

In temper, Delia and Alexander had always been pretty evenly matched, and she could already see hints of annoyance in his dark-chocolate eyes to her reply. Though Delia had been grateful this week for Patti's support and Shauna's knowledge, part of her had unconsciously been spoiling for a fight. Perhaps Alexander would give her one.

"You didn't have to sound so appalled," he said, his words clipped despite his neutral volume. "Or answer that fast."

She shot to her feet. "You mean, I should have put more thought into a serious, lifelong proposition… like the thirteen point two seconds of consideration *you* put into the proposal?"

He cursed in Italian under his breath, then followed it up by swearing in English. "Damn it, Delia, why must you be so antagonistic? Be happy that I got excited by the news." Before she could tell him what she thought of his dictating her emotional state, he added, "There are men who would have turned tail and run, but I'm crazy enough that I'd spend the rest of my life with you."

"Don't do me any favors." If he'd been professing undying love for her, she still would have declined but politely. Right now, she felt no compunction to be cordial. His offer smacked of duty and obligation and legitimizing her child.

My child.

Her emotional world shifted again on its axis. In place of the fury that had been coursing through her veins was a feeling even more potent. Like joy, only fierce and primitive. She interlocked her fingers over her abdomen without thinking about it.

Then she caught herself and felt foolish. "Look, Ring—Alexander. I am grateful you're taking this so well." Even though it had taken *her* a week to adjust to the idea, lying awake at night, uncertain, then waking queasy after a fitful hour or so of sleep. But no-oo, he'd suavely rolled with the punches, never missing a beat. George Clooney meets parenting sitcom.

Though his expression didn't lighten, there was the precursor to a smile in his voice. "Your displays of 'gratitude' are as unique as everything else about you."

Predictable warmth coursed through her, a Pavlovian response to that look in his eyes. The short-lived argument, though not nearly resolved, was winding down and their disagreements had always ended in a pretty specific way. She thought of their bed upstairs and wondered if he'd simply maneuver her to the more conveniently located couch instead.

Just that quickly, her previous irritation boiled up and over like soup forgotten on the stove. "Don't you dare assume you're getting laid, mister. That's how I got into this mess!"

"Is that how you think of it?" He brushed a hand over her cheek. "A mess?"

She sighed, too forthright to indulge the argument-monger inside who wanted to snap that, yes, this was a disaster in the making. "Not really. Maybe at first. I might not have set out to have a baby, but the more I commit to the idea…you know how stubborn I am. Which doesn't bode well. Aren't mothers supposed to be serene and even-tempered?"

He chuckled softly. "You haven't met my mother."

And Delia was in no hurry to do so. From what she gathered, his family was very traditional. She could just imagine how the foul-mouthed, pregnant forty-three-year-old girlfriend would go over. But inevitably, she realized, she would be seeing his family. No matter what the future held for her and Alexander, their lives were permanently entwined now through their child.

"There's…" she swallowed, feeling embarrassingly shy "—a sonogram picture. Not that I have the first clue what I'm looking at, but Shauna—Dr. Adair—assures me it's a baby."

Alexander's eyes went liquid with wonder. "We have a picture of our baby? Already?"

Delia realized that she hadn't clarified yet how far along she was…or that she'd found out about this pregnancy *before* he'd left town. Given the ups and downs of their conversation thus far, it might be best to gloss over that revelation for the time being. "Would you like to see it?"

He was nodding before she even finished the question, so she preceded him into the kitchen. At first, she'd had the picture in her nightstand upstairs. When she couldn't sleep, she'd pulled it out, but the glossy rectangular photo had only magnified her fears. Made them more real. So the photo had gone downstairs, briefly held on the refrigerator with a magnet from the local Chinese delivery place, but she'd felt a little silly displaying the picture so prominently. It was like Patti constantly pulling out her wallet so that everyone could see the latest snapshot of Leo kneeling on a grassy field in the uniform of whichever high school sport was currently in season.

Delia opened a drawer at the kitchen counter and handed Alexander the photo she hadn't shown anyone else. Kate probably wouldn't have known what to make of it, and frankly, Delia was already bonding with Patti more than she preferred. Or maybe sharing the photo with Ringo first was her way of making up for him not being the first person—or even second or third—to know about the baby.

Alexander took the piece of paper from her almost reverently.

"I've been calling the kid Baby Lima Bean," she said.

"This looks about right." He glanced up, meeting her gaze briefly before staring again at the photo mesmerized. Awestruck. "When Marie was pregnant, she e-mailed everyone in the family her sonograms. Wait until later, when you can really make out the face and hands, even the little fingers…"

Delia was caught between fascination with that

prospect and slight unease that said face, hands and fingers would be *growing inside* her. The whole idea still made her light-headed. She was an educated woman who understood the miracle of where babies come from; she'd just never planned on one coming from her.

Gesturing toward the picture, she tried to sound knowledgeable. "Shauna said this dark spot is the heart. I'm supposed to go back in a couple of weeks. If you want to join me, they said we might, um, hear the heartbeat."

Delia had known a lot of men; it was surprising what some of them had found a turn-on—then there were guys for whom being turned on seemed a permanent state that needed no inducement—but she never would have predicted the expression on Alexander's face as he glanced from the photo to her. It was in these moments that he went from being a man attractive enough to draw admiring smiles at a cocktail party to being so inherently sexy that Delia lost her breath. The sensual promise in his eyes sent anticipation quivering through her belly and lower.

He reached one hand around her to set the picture on the counter, while the other braced against a drawer, enclosing her in his arms. In the moment before his lips captured hers, he murmured her name, then he was kissing her hungrily, greedily, as if he would not only take everything she offered but demand things she hadn't known were within her power to give. Perhaps because of the hormones pinballing through her, magnifying her every reaction, or perhaps because it had been weeks since she and Ringo had made love, the pang of longing that shot through Delia was sharp enough to hurt. Her own kiss turned avaricious as she pressed her body to his.

The voluminous terry cloth between them was bulky and awkward, not allowing the intimate closeness she craved. She forcibly pushed away the thought that, in a few months, *she'd* be bulky and awkward—it helped that Alexander distracted her by sucking at her lower lip. He slid the robe's oversize sleeve down to gain better access to the particularly sensitive spot between the base of her neck and shoulder, just exposed by the wide collar of a pajama top. Delia's body nearly melted as his tongue brushed her skin. No other lover had ever discovered the random patch of nerves that had proven to be one of her major erogenous zones. Alexander, however, had taken his time and explored her thoroughly.

He raised his head and she moaned as he caught the back of her earlobe between his teeth; any more thoroughness would probably cause her to spontaneously combust. Unable to find her voice, she moved restlessly against him and began unbuttoning his crisp white shirt. No matter how many times she'd seen him nude, his hard-muscled chest never failed to elicit a wash of feminine appreciation. She tugged at the haphazardly knotted belt that hung low around her hips, knowing that, even through the cotton of her thin shirt, the springy black hair on his chest would cause delicious friction against her breasts.

As if following her unspoken thoughts, Alexander helped her shrug out of the robe, then moved one hand up to cup a breast possessively.

"Ow!" She tried to take a reflexive step backward, couldn't because of the counter, so slapped his fingers away instead.

The passion in his eyes dimmed to confusion beneath a forehead wrinkled in question. "I hurt you?"

She understood why he was perplexed; his touch hadn't been rough. In fact, compared to some of their frenzied lovemaking in the past, he'd been gentle.

"They're sore now," she mumbled, the admission making her self-conscious.

After scanning through a few pages of information on the first trimester, she'd gathered that the breast tenderness that had been annoying her all week was normal at the beginning of a pregnancy. In fact, wanting to shrug off the confines of her bra and change into something comfortable was one of the reasons she'd jumped into the shower immediately after work. It was just that Ringo had temporarily made her forget those aches when he was kissing her.

"Oh." He dropped his gaze to her chest, where her nipples were beaded against the fabric. "I'm sorry."

She'd never been shy about his looking at her. Now, however, she wished that the robe hadn't pooled to the floor because she wanted to tighten it over her.

Alexander leaned back in, toward that deliciously delicate spot above her collarbone, seduction in his eyes. "Any place else that's sore? I'll avoid whatever you want…or kiss it better if you'd like."

No, she wouldn't like. The sizzling anticipation

she'd felt only moments earlier had chilled. "Actually, I was already pretty tired when you got home, so this isn't the best time for…this."

He straightened. Was he irritated that she'd pushed him away or understanding? Was he wondering if her not being in the mood would become the rule rather than the exception? *She* definitely had some concerns along those lines.

But the man was debonair. "Then you should rest. I'll whip us up a special dinner to celebrate."

"Thank you." She sagged in relief, her earlier fatigue rushing back to claim her. Did all pregnant women have this persistent tiredness? Sometimes at work or just now, in Ringo's arms, she was able to forget it for a moment, but the minute she let her guard down, the exhaustion was back so quickly it seemed she could fall asleep where she stood.

She wanted to double-check her book and make sure it was normal, but she was afraid that her age had magnified the effect. If twenty-year-old women bounced through pregnancy invigorated by the whole experience, Delia would just as soon not know.

Alexander's voice was tender when he asked, "You want some help to the living room? I could tuck you in on the couch."

Because she was feeling every inch her forty-three years, she said defensively, "I am quite capable of getting to the sofa under my own steam!"

Once in the living room she felt guilty about having snapped, but she didn't have the energy to turn around or to call out an apology. Instead she sat, blankly staring at a television screen that wasn't turned on. It was Friday night, a night when she normally shook off her workweek with a social evening out or a naughty evening in. Now here she sat, her libido MIA, thinking that it wasn't worth reaching for the remote control on the coffee table.

If expecting a baby was already altering her life, what was Delia in store for when the baby actually *arrived*?

"I just can't believe it." Patti leaned back in a patio chair, regarding Delia with amazement across the umbrella-shaded table. It wouldn't be dark for another couple of hours, but the orange of the setting sun backlit Patti's auburn hair with streaks of fire.

"It's really pretty simple," Delia said. "He asked, I said no, case closed."

Kate had poured all three of them lemonade from the pitcher in the center of the table, but Patti ignored the glass her friend set in front of her in favor of lecturing Delia.

"How can you be so dismissive?" Patti demanded. "A marriage proposal is a huge deal."

"No, *marriage* is a huge deal," Delia rebutted.

"Is he moving out?" Patti asked.

"It's not like they broke up," Kate put in. "Is it?"

"Definitely not. We're not even fighting." There had been weird pauses during dinner conversation last night, as if neither of them entirely knew what to say or think, and they hadn't made love when they'd woken up Saturday morning—partly because her

stomach had been in a state of nauseous rebellion—
but Alexander had held her closely through the night.
"We're just the same as we've always been."

"No, you're *not*." Patti threw her hands in the air.
"You're pregnant. And you could be engaged! Why
would you turn him down?"

"Now that he's had a chance to sleep on it, he's
probably relieved I said no. It was a spur of the moment question he didn't think through."

Patti sighed. "Sounds romantic to me. He was excited about the baby and wanted to sweep you off
your feet."

Some women weren't meant to be swept, even if
she had appreciated the adjectives *amazing, beautiful*
and *funny. Not the point.* "He called me antagonistic.
And implied anyone who married me would have to
be crazy. Not what I call romantic."

"Oh, give over," Kate chided. "You didn't want
romance."

"Exactly! Thank you. I don't want marriage, either."

Until little more than a year ago, neither had Kate.
She and Delia had both been successful and content
over-forty bachelorettes. Yet here they all sat, at Kate
and Paul's house.

The women were on the deck, overlooking a back-
yard that had always been well manicured but was
now shaggy with shin-high grass, untrimmed rose-
bushes and impertinent weeds. Delia suspected Kate
had taken the landscaper off the weekly payroll to
save money after Paul lost his corporate salary. It

was sweltering hot, summer's last blazing hurrah, but Delia and Patti had politely agreed to have their chat outside. None of them was accustomed to speaking in front of Neve and PJ. Delia could understand how she wasn't the ideal model for young children, knocked up as she was by her junior live-in lover. Kate could have banished the kids upstairs while the women talked, asking Neve to take her book to her room and PJ to turn off his video game, but why court the kids' resentment any more than she had to?

Patti fiddled with her glass, the ice cubes clinking against the sides. "I know you didn't think you wanted marriage before, Delia, but you're going to be a mom!"

Yeah, because Delia was likely to forget that little fact without someone pointing it out every five minutes.

"Getting married means having a partner," Patti persisted. "Single parenting—"

"I'd hardly be the first single mother," Delia pointed out. "And getting married means lots of things, not all of them good."

"Well, my hat is off to people who manage to raise a kid with no help," Patti said, "because I can't even imagine. Leo has decent grades and a track record of good health, thank God, but still, I've been glad to have George with me every step of the way. Having a husband makes everything so much easier."

Delia wanted to shake the other woman—Patti sounded too much like Chelsea, not only extolling the virtues of marriage, but making it sound like a necessity. "It's the new millennium, Patti, women can vote and everything. Landing a man is no guarantee of a placid, problem-free life. Look at Kate. She got married, then—"

"Hey." Kate peered over the top of her designer sunglasses. "If you don't want to marry Ringo, don't, but leave me out of this."

Shame rose in Delia, feeling a lot like the morning sickness that had made the room pitch and spin when she first got out of bed today. "I'm sorry. You're doing a hell of a job with everything you've got going on, and I'm a train wreck of a friend."

"This is true," Kate said.

I'd be a wreck of a wife, too. Delia was beyond her initial anger at Ringo's proposal—he meant well, but how long did he think playing house would work out? Too many defunct marriages limped along on staying-together-for-the-kids life support long after even an astute six-year-old, unnerved by the tension at home, could tell it was time to pull the plug.

Patti huffed out a sigh. "Well, I still think she should marry him."

When Delia opened her mouth to respond, Kate interrupted, her lips curved in a teasing grin. "Yes, but then she'd have a mother-in-law to deal with! And how many sisters-in-law?"

"Three."

Kate affected a mock shudder. "Ayiee. I'm having enough trouble with the *one* sister-in-law I have." Although, technically, it was *Paul's* sister-in-law, his first wife's sister and the children's aunt. Delia knew the relationship between deceased wife's sister and second wife had been awkward.

"All right," Patti conceded. "In-laws can sometimes be a drawback to marriage."

"Plus, you're *stuck* with George," Delia pointed out. "I can kick Alexander to the curb anytime I want."

Patti's expression was annoyingly pitying. "You really need that escape clause, don't you?"

So what if she did? Why make an eventual goodbye more complicated than it absolutely had to be? "You and George married young and did a great job of making it work." For all that Delia had been shocked to learn that Patti Jordan had slept with only one man her entire life, it was admirable that Patti and George had been happily married for so long. "Statistically speaking, most people aren't that lucky, and divorce…" Well, living through her parents', which had turned out to be as meaningless and temporary as their marriage, had been enough for her.

"On that chipper note." Kate glanced at her watch. "I told the kids we could go swimming before it gets too late."

The three women carried their glasses inside.

Grudgingly, Delia turned to Patti. "Thank you for suggesting we get together this afternoon."

It had been Patti's idea, but Kate had volunteered her home so the kids could keep themselves entertained. If Delia had stayed alone with Ringo today, she wasn't sure where the conversation would have turned. This way, he'd had some time alone to absorb last night's bombshell…and to see reason about her rejecting his proposal.

"No problem." For a second Patti's smile seemed forced. "Housewives like myself appreciate the opportunity to get out."

Something in Patti's tone struck Delia as discordant. It wasn't as if Patti spent all day sitting around her kitchen. She was an active volunteer with several local charities and one of the football booster moms at Leo's school. With the fall semester starting just next week, Patti would be plenty busy. Although she didn't have a high-powered career like Delia or Kate, she always had plenty of anecdotes to share from her various committees.

The ladies exchanged goodbyes and Kate put an arm around Delia in an uncharacteristic embrace. Until her own marriage, Kate had been a fairly aloof person. Not cold, just someone who didn't intrude on others' privacy or personal space.

"Tell Alexander no if you want to," Kate said softly, "but make sure you know why you're saying it."

"I'm satisfied with my reasons, thanks. And since when do we hug?"

Kate stepped away with a sheepish grin.

On the cobblestone path to where their cars were parked in the driveway, Delia half expected Patti to make one last-ditch recommendation of marriage. Instead the woman was quiet. So Delia took the proactive offensive by keeping the subject off of herself.

"You okay?" she asked Patti. "For a minute in there, you seemed…not perky."

"I'm not always 'perky.'"

This was true; Patti had three other modes: reproachful, cheerfully intrusive and earnestly industrious. But perky was her default setting.

"All right." Delia wasn't one to pry. Besides, she'd almost reached the safety of her car.

"Despite what I may lead people to believe, my marriage isn't *always* perfect," Patti added from left field.

Delia turned, arching an eyebrow and impressed in spite of herself. Admitting an imperfect union was the kind of confession Chelsea had barely been able to make even when her husband was living with another woman.

"N-not that we aren't happy and very much in love," Patti stammered. "It's just, while I do think marrying Alexander would be best for all of you, I'm not naive about the difficulties. Trust me. George and I have our issues."

"Such as?"

Patti hesitated. "You don't want to stand here and listen to a litany of our bumps in the road. Besides, nothing *I'm* going through is nearly as difficult as Kate having to deal with a husband in prison or you turning sixty about the same time your kid gets a driver's license. Don't worry about me." With a final parting smile, she climbed into her car.

So far, Delia had avoided consciously doing the math, but now she winced. Patti was right. By the time her child finished high school, Delia would definitely be in her sixties, easily mistaken for some graduate's grandmother. A shudder rippled through her…reminding her that she hadn't informed her own mother yet that *she* was going to be a grandmother. Lots of women waited until after the first trimester to spread the news, though, right?

Which gave her about a month before she had to call Chelsea and Garrett, break the news to her employers that she would eventually need maternity leave and have to deal with Alexander's family. If that seemed like stalling or denial to anyone else… Well, she hadn't asked anyone else's opinion, had she?

Chapter 5

When it comes to infants, there seem to be two groups of people: those who look at a newborn and automatically react with awwww and those whose instinctive reaction is auuuuugh! Which category I fall in is immaterial; I love you, regardless.

"Hey, Alex, how was New York?"

Alexander leaned back in his chair, glancing up to where Raymond Ness had paused outside Alexander's office. It was possible Ray wanted to discuss business, but it was just as likely he was looking for fresh eyes and someone to ooh and aah over the latest baby pictures. At last year's Christmas party, Ray's wife, Karin, had been wearing a rosy flush on her cheeks and a brand-new maternity dress she hadn't

come close to filling out; now Ray and Karin were
the ecstatic first-time parents of an infant son, Sam.

"New York was great—sharp clients, intelligent
questions, and they were already working well with
the program before I'd arrived." Occasionally, they
helped technologically inept whiners who seemed intent on blaming the software for user errors. "Plus, I
got to visit some family. My sisters' kids are growing like weeds! I guess your son must be…what, four
months now?"

Ray bobbed his head. "Almost. He's rolling over!
He'll be crawling and sitting up before we know it.
Karin had pictures made at three months and we just
got the prints last week."

Obligingly, Alexander held out his hand. Since he
was accustomed to his sisters' long-distance gushing about their kids, he'd never minded Ray's pater-
nal exuberance. But now that Alexander knew he
would be a father himself, he empathized on a whole
new level. He wished he could confide in the man,
ask questions about Karin's pregnancy and newborn
care. Delia had seemed adamant that they not start
telling other people—besides her two closest friends
who were giving her moral support through these
early days of morning sickness—until she reached
her second trimester.

Alexander had never considered himself a superstitious man, yet the idea of crowing his joy did seem
like tempting fate. He was stunned to have been given
this unexpected gift at a time when he'd started thinking he wanted more from his life, and the baby, not

even scientifically designated a "fetus" until eleven weeks, seemed unimaginably fragile right now. There'd be time to talk to Ray and other experienced fathers before Alexander's child was born.

Still, after paying the expected praise over Sam's chubby adorability, Alexander heard himself ask, "Were you and Karin nervous about being parents, or did you know deep down it was the right time?"

"We'd been trying to conceive, so we were excited about the idea even before it happened. Karin was so thrilled about the pregnancy I don't think she truly got nervous until labor. Now she's just so sleep-deprived I doubt she has the energy to question whether she knows what she's doing." Ray colored, looking worried that his doting-dad status might be revoked.

"Don't get me wrong, Sam is starting to sleep for longer stretches, and any walking we do in the middle of the night with him is ultimately worth it, but Karin and I have been tired lately. Cranky with each other. I miss her sometimes, you know? Miss the sparkling wife I used to have, miss just having dinner alone with her. That make me a selfish bastard?"

"Nah." Alexander handed over the wallet-size photo of Sam, shaking his head reassuringly. "My sisters love their children, but I've heard there were days when they barely stopped the car before ditching the kids with my mom. Even the best parents need a break."

Ray's posture relaxed. "Yeah. Unfortunately, neither Karin nor I have family in the area to babysit Sam. We're not about to leave him this young with some teenager who's more likely to tie up our phone line than notice his diaper needs changing."

A seed of an idea took root in Alexander's mind. Even though she hadn't voiced it in such a way, he'd glimpsed the flashes of uncertainty in Delia's eyes. She hadn't planned to be a mother, wasn't close to her own mom and had rarely been around young children in the time Alexander had known her.

"Maybe I could help you out," Alexander said slowly. "You could bring Sam over on Friday evening. Delia and I can watch him, let you and Karin have a couple of hours to yourself."

"You're kidding." Ray eyed him with a wary what's-the-catch expression.

Alexander laughed. "What can I say? Being home for a few days made me realize how much I miss watching my nieces and nephews grow. You caught me at an opportune moment. So you'll talk to Karin and see if she approves?"

"Definitely, but I bet I can guess her answer. She's always liked you, you know."

She'd thanked Alexander profusely for the generous gift certificate he'd included in the congratulations card when Sam was born. And when she'd come to the office to bring Ray some files he'd forgotten at home, she'd watched Alexander make faces at the baby until he laughed, declaring Alexander a natural with kids.

Alexander wasn't an idiot; he knew babies were just as much about stinky diapers as cute smiles. He also knew that Delia rose to every challenge. Maybe an evening with Sam would help her resolve some doubt over being a good mom.

Then, perhaps, Alexander could come up with a plan for overcoming her doubt about the two of them. Though he'd strategically retreated for the time being, he'd only ever asked one woman to marry him and he didn't intend to accept "hell, no" as her final answer.

"Jeez, Delia, still trying to recover from a wild weekend?" Thirty-year-old Terese Reeves held her damp hands under the electric dryer and smirked in "concern."

Delia, dabbing cool water against her face at the sink, didn't bother answering. She was busy trying to keep breakfast down.

"Now that I'm not in my twenties anymore," the rail-thin redhead added, "I don't bounce back from partying as easily as I used to, either."

"Actually," Delia said around a saccharine smile and the lemon hard candy that was supposed to soothe roiling stomachs, "I think I had a touch of the flu. I certainly hope *you* don't catch it."

At that, the other woman wasted no time exiting the ladies' restroom and Delia's supposed germ-ridden perimeter. Delia exchanged a weak but conspiratorial grin with her reflection. For the past three years she'd had the highest success rate of selling and leasing expensive properties. The same week Terese was hired, she'd let it be known that *she* planned to take the number one spot. Their employers were in favor of competition because motivated agents meant more revenue. Honestly, Delia couldn't fault Terese for her ambition—that would be the pot sending the kettle e-mails re: you're black—but she definitely took exception to the woman's veiled but snarky references to Delia's age.

If she thinks I'm going to retire any year soon to level the playing field for her, then all that Twilight Fire hair dye must have soaked into her little brain.

Part of Delia yearned to tell her coworkers that any signs of fatigue they glimpsed or extra hours taken off for doctors' appointments were due to pregnancy and *strictly temporary.* They were not age related and indicative of some long-term decline in her job performance.

Temporary?

Delia paused as she reached for the door, recalling what Patti had said about denial. Nothing about having a baby was temporary. Job performance aside, what the hell was she going to do with the kid while she was at work? Wear the baby in some kind of papoose on her back while she showed properties? Kate was hoping to solve the bulk of her newfound child-care issues by letting Neve stay at home alone after school with her little brother, but Neve was nearly thirteen. Delia didn't have the leave-the-kid-alone option, unless she wanted angry visits from government agencies.

Then again, the nice part about getting knocked up at this age rather than in her twenties was that she made a *much* better living than she had earlier in life. She could afford a private caregiver or placement in a great day-care facility. It might mean the occasional sacrificed shoe purchase or an extra evening home a month instead of an expensive restaurant dinner, but she would manage, especially since Alexander could be counted on for generous and responsible financial contributions.

He made it clear that he wanted to be highly involved in the child's life although, thankfully, he hadn't mentioned marriage since that first disastrous proposal. Obviously he'd come to his senses. Her relief was undeniable—it was good they were back on the same page about their relationship.

By the time she got home that night, Delia had convinced herself that she could have a good week despite its inauspicious beginning. For one thing, Alexander had always been more of a natural in the kitchen than Delia, and he'd fallen into the habit of preparing dinner, barring the nights they ate out, ordered in or she surprised him with something from her limited repertoire. Last week, when he'd been in New York, she'd come home to an empty place and dreaded telling him. Now, not only was spilling the news behind her, she arrived to a place that smelled like lemon chicken. On top of that, on the way out of the office, Delia had found herself getting into the elevator at the same time as Terese, who'd suddenly decided to take the stairs. Once the doors closed, Delia hadn't been able to resist chuckling, and her mood had remained upbeat throughout the drive home.

Stupid optimism, she thought to herself several

hours later, stretched out on the couch with a burgeoning headache.

Coasting on the mellow joys of a wonderful dinner and giggling at Terese's expense, Delia had decided to take a better look at that pregnancy book she'd bought. Now that she'd subjected herself to a few chapters, she had renewed appreciation for the platitude "ignorance is bliss."

According to the book, this week the baby had started "swimming," making movements too slight to feel. Should Delia be having some maternal reaction, experiencing wonder that her child was able to move around? She felt vaguely ill at the thought of little limbs churning inside her—no wonder she'd spent the last few days feeling ill until noon.

But the fun didn't stop there! She apparently could expect a blotchy complexion as well as more veins appearing on her tummy, breasts and legs. How were more veins even possible? Maybe she'd read it wrong and the book simply meant the veins she already had would expand. Either way it didn't sound appealing—a veiny, blotchy forty-three-year-old whose favorite at-home jeans no longer snapped comfortably.

She heard a sniffle and belatedly realized the sound had come from her.

Alexander looked up from his recliner, where he'd been watching a baseball game. Earlier he'd tried to engage her in conversation about what she was reading, but as her answers grew more terse, he'd wisely shut up.

Now he ventured once more into the breach. "Delia? Is everything—"

"I'm fine," she snapped, horrified by her damp, blurred eyesight. "If you'll excuse me, I'm going to take a bath while I can still fit into the tub."

"Not too hot," he cautioned. "I was flipping through the book when I got home and saw that—"

She shot him an incinerating glare. In addition to the other things she'd had to give up, hot bubble baths were controversial, too? Screw that. She'd never been one to play strictly by someone else's rules, and she wasn't going to start now. Since the baby shared her DNA, surely the kid would understand the occasional need for rebellion.

It was like a scab she couldn't keep from picking at, Delia thought ruefully on Thursday afternoon. Though the pregnancy guide was at home, she'd discovered an online site during her lunch break yesterday. Now, here she was, surfing Moms Over Forty message boards at her desk. One woman had cited a statistic that mothers of a certain age were more likely to raise a child who did well in school and went on to be a professional.

Good, Junior will have the necessary salary to support me in my rapidly advancing years.

"Delia?"

She jerked her head up, guiltily minimizing the nonwork-related window even though the computer monitor was turned away from the door. "Hey, Frank. What can I do for you?"

"Nothing. I was on my way out back for the last smoke of the day and thought I'd ask if you wanted to join me. We haven't seen you much this week. Lynette said to tell you we miss your dirty jokes."

Delia had only shared them outside, when they were less likely to be overheard by someone who would judge them as inappropriate. "Actually, I gave up smoking."

"You're kidding." Frank blinked. "How long has it been since your last cigarette?"

"Couple of weeks, give or take." *Eleven days, six hours.*

Although she'd been afraid kicking the habit would be tough, on Tuesday she'd received a little unexpected help in killing the cravings. As she'd walked through the employee parking lot toward the back door, she'd passed someone from human resources stealing a quick smoke. Delia had assumed the familiar scent of cigarette smoke would trigger dark longing; instead it had made her stomach clench, then flip, and she'd held her breath as she hurried inside.

Thinking that the smell and taste of a cigarette might make her hurl was definitely a deterrent to lighting up. She still had occasional withdrawal headaches, but according to the books, she would suffer headaches even if she were smoking, thanks to increased blood volume as the pregnancy progressed.

"Oh, well, I suppose the supportive thing would be to rescind my invitation to join us," Frank said. "Wouldn't want to be responsible for the monkey on your back."

There was an entire forum on that motherhood site about how having a kid altered your social life, but Delia wasn't sure the moderators had parking-lot smoking breaks and dirty jokes in mind.

After Frank disappeared, Delia admitted to herself what she'd known since four o'clock that afternoon. She was done for the day. Her productivity had peaked hours ago, and she was finding it hard to concentrate. Also, she really, really wanted guacamole. She didn't count that as a weird craving since she'd always loved avocados.

She decided to go ahead and duck out a few minutes early, time easily made up by working through lunch tomorrow. There was an upscale farmer's market not too far out of her way home. She'd stop by, grab the makings for some guacamole and maybe even something simple for dinner. She'd surprise Ringo by cooking tonight. He deserved it…and it wasn't healthy the way she'd become so passively dependent on him. Having a man around to wait on you was fun and all, but she needed to reassert that she could take care of herself.

If the cigarette smoke earlier in the week had turned her stomach, the sight of the purplish-brown avocados had the exact opposite effect. For a minute she felt as if she could actually bite through the skin to find the ripe, green fruit inside. She shoved a few into a clear bag, hesitating only when she realized another shopper was staring. Delia stopped and did a quick count. Okay, eight was probably enough. Time to check other aisles for dinner options.

Delia was contemplating a freshly prepared, ready-to-bake vegetarian lasagna when a woman some distance behind her shrieked, "Harrison Tyler, don't you *dare!*"

Turning toward the source of the distress was a reflex. Delia found herself looking down the aisle at a very short, *very* pregnant woman. In profile, she would be nearly as wide as she was tall. Her dark hair was either pulled into a lopsided ponytail or something had died on her head, and her hands were clenched around the handle of a shopping cart wherein a toddler with brunette curls and one fist shoved into her drooling mouth stood babbling in the back. The toddler's frilly pink shorts and the frazzled mother's line of sight confirmed that the kid in the buggy was not Harrison Tyler. Delia peered around a pyramid display of expensive crackers.

Sure enough, only a few feet from her, not tall enough to be visible from the other side of the crackers, was a little boy Delia thought might be about four. The ragamuffin with a shock of unruly dark hair, ketchup smears on his cheeks and a blue T-shirt printed with the unlikely disclaimer I Didn't Do It was undoubtedly Harrison Tyler. He seemed to be reaching for a rectangular box on the bottom of the cardboard pyramid, which explained his mother's hysterical tone.

The mom was suddenly accelerating toward them, which caused the toddler to lose her balance and bump her head on the cart. She responded with outraged wails that could drown out tornado sirens. Harrison had been momentarily frozen, like a rabbit who hoped keeping still would render him invisible to his mother's ire. Now that she was distracted by consoling her other child, Harrison returned his attention to the pyramid of crackers. They appeared stable, but that would change immediately if he removed one of the boxes at the base.

Delia cleared her throat, hoping to distract him. When he glanced curiously at her, she gave him her best hello-youngster smile. Well, truthfully, it was her *only* hello-youngster smile, and it was rusty from disuse. "I'm Delia."

"You're a stranger!" Harrison informed her at the top of his lungs.

Charming kid. Interesting that after having him, his parents had opted to have two more.

"True," she answered, shooting a glance toward his mom and wishing the woman would hurry up. They were separated by yards, not miles. Of course, the poor woman was waddling with the weight of what was either a nine-month fetus or triplets, so it was understandable that she wasn't sprinting through the store to corral her miscreant son.

"If you're not supposed to talk to strangers, just listen. I wanted to warn you that it's not a good idea to play with those crackers. They might fall and hurt you. You wouldn't want a boo-boo, right?"

He stared past her with wide eyes. "Mooo-oooom! This stranger lady said she was going to hurt me!"

"That is not what I said," Delia hissed.

Harrison glared, then turned and swiped one of

the boxes, proving several laws of physics when a dozen or so more tumbled to the ground. Delia had expected worse, but realized now that the display had been built up around a podium base to give the pyramid better height.

"Oh, Harrison." The mother of the dark-haired spawn quickly steered her cart in an evasive maneuver to keep from flattening one of the cracker boxes. The woman's voice seemed more tremulous than angry. "What am I going to do with you?"

In response to that question, Harrison looked down at the mess he'd created and burst into tears. His kid sister harmonized in small, hiccupping sobs. Delia's temples were throbbing in a headache much worse than anything mere nicotine withdrawal could dole out. She couldn't help a glance at the pregnant woman's distended abdomen. Someone should really tell this lady about birth control!

It struck Delia simultaneously that, one, she herself should know better than to think birth control was infallible, and two, it had been a really bitchy thought. If she wasn't careful, God might punish her... with twins.

The other woman forced a smile. "Thanks for trying to help. He's just going through an adjustment because the new baby is coming. I don't think he meant anything by it..." She trailed off as she surveyed the boxes around them.

A stock boy, no doubt responding to all the racket, was already walking to them with a resigned expression.

"Harrison Tyler, you tell this nice lady you're sorry," the woman instructed.

Harrison sobbed harder, but there appeared to be words in there somewhere. Delia gave him the benefit of the doubt that the utterances formed an apology of some sort. His mother then made him apologize to the young man patiently restacking the crackers.

"Now I think it's best if you ride in the cart with Sissy," the pregnant woman said.

Was Sissy the kid's name or sibling shorthand?

"No!" Harrison bellowed. "Don't want to ride in cart! I'm a big boy!" In a move Delia had never actually seen executed outside of movies and television shows, he threw himself facedown to the floor, all limbs flailing. His forehead hit first.

That had to hurt.

Looking sheepish, the woman squatted next to her progeny. Whatever threats or bribes she made, Harrison quieted moments later. Delia hesitated, wondering if the woman would need help standing again. But she stood on her own, making considerable *oof* sounds.

Then she moved her purse from the front of the cart so that the toddler could sit there, leaving the back for Harrison and the groceries. Delia blinked, spotting perhaps the biggest surprise so far. The woman held a designer purse, made by a company Delia herself loved. This was one of their everyday purses, but still costly and fashionable and seeming of a completely different plane of existence than screaming Harrison or his mother's slightly jelly-stained T-shirt.

Delia hurried to the checkout, but couldn't stop

thinking about that purse. She had one nearly identical to it. *Was that woman like me once?* Maybe the purse had been a gift. The thought was irrationally comforting, because it scared Delia to think that she, a woman who enjoyed martinis and tropical weekend getaways, Kate Spade shoes and Coach handbags, could be looking at a future of fast-food kids' meals, thirty-dollar tubes of lipstick being used to graffiti the bathroom wall and yelling her child's first and middle name down the length of a grocery store in a desperate attempt to avoid disaster.

She entered her PIN number on the cashier keypad and accepted her receipt without really seeing it. God, what was she in for? She didn't know the first thing about kids. What would she have done to Harrison if the little monster were hers? Beating the child and abandoning him to customer service weren't possible. Getting into a debate with someone less than a tenth her age was too humiliating to contemplate. She could just scoop the screaming child into the cart and pray that everyone in the immediate vicinity was deaf.

In the welcome solitude of her car, she fumbled for her cell phone, her fingers dialing without conscious direction from her mind. She'd expected Kate to answer, but when that warm, masculine voice came over the line, Delia realized she'd called Alexander without thinking about it.

"Hello?"

She took a deep breath. "Hi."

"Delia? Is everything all right? You sound—"

Like she'd just stared into her future and promptly

gone mad? "I'm at the market. I stopped on the way home because I really need avocados or I'm gonna hurt someone."

There was a pause. "I hope they had avocados."

"This little boy…there was this pregnant mom with kids and, well, she was doing a lousy job. Or at least, it looked that way to an outside observer. The problem is, I don't think I would have done any better." She'd like to believe that her child would be too well behaved to ever pull such a stunt, but Delia was known among friends for her audacious remarks and willingness to live by her own rules. Somehow she doubted those traits would translate well in an ankle-biter.

"Alexander, what the hell are we doing? We can't raise a child. We can barely make it a week without fighting about something stupid."

"Those aren't really fights. We just express ourselves loudly. When have we ever disagreed for long over something serious?"

Did the ill-fated marriage proposal count? Doubtful. He probably felt like he dodged a bullet there. In fact, it was ironic that she'd even commented on them raising a child together. He'd probably be around for weekends and birthdays, but wasn't she ultimately expecting to shoulder the bulk of the parenting by herself? Panic rose in her throat like bile, and she tried to draw deep breaths.

All she succeeded in doing, though, was hyperventilating into the phone.

"Delia? Are you still in the store?"

"My car."

"Will you be all right to drive home?"

"Yes." Eventually.

"Just try to relax. You probably caught this mother on a bad day. My sisters and I could put my mom through merry hell, although she always made us pay for it later. But Blanche, Marie, Angie and I all turned out great. So will our baby. Come home, and I'll fix dinner for you."

"I picked up a pan of lasagna we can heat up."

"All right, then. You just need a nice meal and a chance to put your feet up."

"You're probably right. I only ever feel like myself in the middle of the day anymore. Half the time, I'm queasy in the morning, and by the evening I feel like..." She wasn't even sure what because she'd never been this way before.

"Do you have any plans for tomorrow evening?"

Besides crashing on the couch the minute she walked in the door? That had become her tentative agenda for every evening. "No."

"Good, because I have a surprise for you. I bet it will make you feel a lot better."

She sighed, not wanting to be needy but really looking forward to giving herself over to Ringo's care. He normally came up with great surprises, although she hoped this wasn't a big one. She didn't have the energy for dinner and dancing, but the thought of one of his sensual massages made her melt a little.

"I can't wait," she told him. They hung up seconds later and she felt much more in control of herself.

She rationalized the entire drive home. If she were

this tired and emotionally off balance in just her first trimester, how had that other woman—who looked on the verge of popping into labor—felt? Probably on a normal day, she was a much better mother. Also, Delia planned to stop with one child, which had to be easier than parenting three, no matter how much of a handful her one kid was. She was just overtired from a week of working.

A restful weekend ahead, kicked off by whatever Alexander's thoughtful surprise was, sounded like heaven.

Chapter 6

There will be times when I really will know better than you, and you'll just have to trust me...even if you don't like me. I promise never to use the phrase "Because I said so!" except for extenuating circumstances and when provoked. Look, I'm trying here, okay?

Alexander knew full well that his Machiavellian plan of volunteering both himself and Delia as babysitters would probably land him on the couch tonight, but she'd thank him later. Okay, maybe not *literally* thank him, but he truly believed that this was the best thing for her. Who could hold an adorable baby and not be moved by the experience? Working in his favor were her pregnancy hormones; she was more predisposed to warm, fuzzy feelings than she ever had been before.

Still, despite his certainty that he'd done the right thing, he froze when the doorbell rang promptly at six. He was at the top of the stairs, about to come down after changing out of his work clothes. Delia was in the kitchen, pouring herself a glass of water. He'd hoped to answer the door when Karin and Ray got here—Karin was a protective mom, and if Delia stared at the baby with wide-eyed horror, the woman probably wouldn't feel safe dropping off Sam. Unfortunately nothing short of sprinting would get him to the door before Delia.

Sure enough, he heard her open it, heard voices exchange greetings.

"Ray, Karin." Delia's tone was puzzled but polite. "Are you joining us for dinner?"

Karin giggled in response. "Just Sam here."

After a brief pause, Karin followed up with, "That is okay, right? Alexander talked to you about baby-sitting…"

Alexander hastened down the steps, almost tripping over the last two. Before he could say anything, Delia recovered, improvising.

"Of course he did. Sorry, it's been a long day and I was momentarily confused." Over her shoulder, she sent him a look that clearly said, *Die, you duplicitous bastard.*

He cast an involuntary glance toward the small couch that would clearly be home for the next couple of nights. Or weeks. Maybe he should just sleep in the recliner; at least then he could stretch out his feet.

"Ray, Karin." He conjured a welcoming smile. "You guys are right on time. I take it this is all equipment for the little man?"

The couple had stepped inside the town house, Karin holding Sam in a car seat carrier, and Ray lugging a large diaper bag and several loose items, such as a flop-eared blue rabbit and an activity mat.

Ray was shaking his head in amusement. "Isn't this ridiculous? There are probably A-list Hollywood actors that travel with less of an entourage."

"We wanted to make sure you guys had all the essentials, though," Karin said, setting the car seat on the couch and unbuckling Sam. "If he gets upset for any reason, you have all his favorites to distract him."

"Although his real 'favorite' is just being walked and sung to," Ray said. "'A Hundred Bottles of Beer on the Wall,' only we changed it to bottles of juice. And I start at a thousand instead of a hundred."

"A thousand?" Delia's question came out as a squeak, and they all turned to see her looking pale.

Ray chuckled. "Well, I don't usually get all the way down to zero, but it gives me some leeway on the nights he's really wound up."

"What other things should we know before the two of you go?" Alexander prompted, wondering if Delia would be able to contain her fury until after the Nesses had left. Because he'd had several days to prepare himself, he was confident he wouldn't be goaded into losing his temper. Let her vent—he was man enough to admit he'd been manipulative—but eventually they'd be stronger for this.

"It's almost his suppertime," Karin said. "There's a small plastic bowl of cereal in his bag, with a spoon and instructions. Then there are two bottles of breast milk for later."

Behind the Nesses, Delia convulsed in a full-body shudder.

"Everything you need to diaper him and three changes of clothes are in the bag," Karin continued.

At this, Ray laughed. "We assume three is excessive, but better to leave you extra than not enough. This piece of paper has my cell number and Karin's. And just in case there's any problem with reception, we've also left the number for the restaurant itself. We should be back in two hours, maybe a bit more."

Alexander smiled at a cooing Sam, waiting for Karin to actually hand over the baby. "He'll be fine," he promised the new mother.

She sniffed. "Oh, I know. And it's so nice of you and Delia to do this, really, but…"

Ray took his wife's hand as Alexander gently pulled Sam into his own arms. The baby was a healthy, solid weight, but his wide eyes and the soft spot that hadn't entirely fused on his head were reminders of how innocent and fragile he was.

"You two have fun," Alexander said gently. "And call if you get the urge to check on him."

"Thank you so much." Ray turned to include Delia in his smile. "Both of you. If the two of you ever need a sitter, you know who to call!"

Delia's poisonously sweet smile was aimed at Alexander although, ostensibly, she was speaking to Ray. "Who knows? We may take you up on that someday. Life's just *full* of surprises."

A lesser man would have gulped in fear. Growing up in a household full of women, Alexander had witnessed many variations on the hell-hath-no-fury theory. Still…she wouldn't hit someone holding a baby, would she?

Once the Nesses were gone, silence fell like an anvil. Sam squirmed in Alexander's arms, tilting his head back at an unnatural angle to glance at Delia as if he, too, were curiously awaiting her response. Or perhaps the kid was just looking for his mama, because when he saw no sign of Karin, his face crumpled into the universal baby signal for "I'm about to be loudly unhappy."

Oh, crap. A screaming infant might not be the best way to give Delia warm feelings about motherhood.

"It's all right, Sammy." Alexander kept his tone soothing, adopting the rhythmic bounce he'd seen his sisters and mother use when they had fussy babies on their hips. *Work with me, bud.*

"You might try feeding him," Delia suggested dryly. "They did tell us it was his dinnertime."

"I know that," he said, too embarrassed to admit that the thought of Sam crying had temporarily panicked him into forgetting the rice cereal. In a less defensive tone, he proposed, "One of us can hold Sam while the other gets his dinner ready."

"Well, since you're already holding him, I'll

cook…unless I'm supposed to be doing something else. You haven't made any other plans for me, have you? Like maybe volunteered me to repaint the pool house or offered me as a maid to the Rodrigos up the street?"

Alexander sighed, careful to keep bouncing since Sam seemed to like it. "If I'd asked if you wanted to babysit tonight, you would have said no."

"Damn right." Her voice was admirably calm, but her eyes were tossing so many daggers that she could have joined the circus as a knife-thrower…or a black-ops team as an assassin. "You know *why* I would have refused? I've been exhausted all week, counting the minutes until end of work Friday and forty-eight straight hours of rest. I've been looking forward to recuperating and, ever since you mentioned it on the phone, looking forward to your *surprise*."

He felt ashamed—while he'd known she would be irritated, it hadn't occurred to him that she might be disappointed, too.

"By this time next year," she continued, "I'll have my own child, and there will be Friday nights when I can't do what I want for the evening. But I'm not a mother yet, and you stole tonight from me. You ambushed me with a baby. For the second time!"

In spite of himself, he felt his lips quirk in a smile. "*You* were the one who startled *me* with the baby news, if you remember."

"Yeah, well, it couldn't have come as more of a surprise to you than it did me, pal." She whirled around and headed into the kitchen.

Alexander considered pointing out that she'd left the diaper bag behind, but figured he was living dangerously already. He carried both the bag and Sam into the next room.

A few minutes later Delia peered into the brightly colored plastic bowl and made a face at the prepared cereal. "Are we punishing him for something, or do the Nesses always feed him gruel?"

"Sam likes it, don't you, big boy? He's even saying *mmm*."

Sam, whose upright car seat served as a makeshift high chair in the middle of the table, was in fact gurgling and making mmm sounds.

Delia snorted. "Probably asking for his mother. Or trying to ask for manicotti. You're not fooled by this stuff, are you, kid? You know your parents are holding out on you."

"You want to feed him, and I'll hold the seat steady?"

Alexander was in a chair, one hand on the car seat to keep Sam from suddenly throwing his weight to one side and toppling the thing to the ground. A four-month-old probably didn't have that kind of strength, but why take chances? It had taken Blanche years to forgive her husband, Steve, for the time their son rolled off the changing table while Steve was reaching for baby wipes. She'd fretted for days afterward about possible internal injuries, while Steve had boasted to anyone who would listen about how their gifted child had started rolling weeks before the baby books predicted.

"No." Delia had thought over and rejected his offer. "*You're* the one who promised to take care of this kid. I trust that a big, strong man like you can wield a tiny spoon and keep Sam from plummeting off the table at the same time."

His plan to ease Delia's worries about motherhood by having her interact with a baby might work better if she actually *interacted*. Still, she stood close by, watching over Alexander's shoulder, so that was something. Even if she wasn't reduced to cooing nonsense at Sam, there were traces of grudging affection in her tone whenever she spoke to or about the infant.

Sam made quick work of his cereal, smacking his lips with gusto and leaning toward the spoon as much as his safety harness would allow, all the time murmuring the same enthusiastic *mmm-mmm-mmm* noises.

"I've seen pigs eat with more dignity," Delia remarked, a smile in her voice.

Alexander craned his head to look back at her. "Do we have more? I don't think he's finished."

She picked up the resealable sandwich Baggie from the counter. It contained a small scoop and white flakes. "There's enough here to make another bowl."

"Karin wouldn't have given us enough for two servings if Sam wasn't allowed to have two, would she?"

"So you want me to make another batch?"

"Quickly, please." Alexander was down to the last spoonful, and Sam's babbling had mutated from enthusiastic to agitated.

After checking to make sure the next batch wasn't

too hot, Delia set it between man and baby with a flourish. *"Bon appetit!"*

Sam got down to business, ditching the noises in favor of intense, silent focus. When he was finished, he lolled back with heavy-lidded eyes.

Alexander couldn't believe his luck—was the kid really going to drop off into a contented sleep now that he had a full belly? Sleeping infants were adorable, soft and rosy and warm. *Not to mention quiet.* Surely he'd be able to arrange for Delia to hold the slumbering child.

Turning in his chair, Alexander smiled at her. "I guess compliments are in order to the chef. It—"

A noise that was neither entirely hiccup nor cough was all the warning Alexander got before a wet blast of something warm and lumpy hit him in the shoulder and splattered across his chest. Some of it even dribbled past the collar of his shirt and down his neck. While Alexander had always considered himself a fairly macho guy, unafraid of getting his hands dirty and the sole DiRossi sibling who didn't shriek at the sight of a mouse, he was thoroughly grossed out.

Delia, however, had a completely different reaction. She was laughing so hard an actual snort escaped; when he narrowed his eyes in her direction, she bent at the waist, literally holding her sides.

"So happy to be a source of entertainment," he drawled, reaching for the napkin holder in the center of the table. "I don't suppose you could dampen a few of these for me?" Right, like a few wet napkins could help. He should probably strip down, take a shower, then burn the shirt.

Delia pulled a clean dishrag out of a drawer and ran some water over it. "Do you think he's done, or should we wait to see if his head spins?"

Sam was looking pretty pleased with himself, although he had rice cereal dribbling down his chin.

Alexander should make sure there wasn't any hidden cereal sliming the car seat. "Can you pick him up while I—"

"Hold the exorcist baby? No, thank you. I happen to like this sweater."

He paused, taking a good look at her. All week she'd been coming home and putting on T-shirts and ratty jeans or sweatpants. While she'd changed into something more casual and comfortable after work, the short-sleeved knit top was still nice enough to wear to dinner or a movie. She'd chosen it in anticipation of his "surprise." Had he gone about this all wrong? Instead of forcing her to think even more about motherhood, maybe he should have just taken her out for an evening to take her mind off the stress. Once she was relaxed, she would have been in a better place emotionally to prepare for all the changes in their lives.

"What?" Her tone was laced with suspicion. "You're staring."

"You look beautiful tonight."

"If that's your way of trying to soften me up—"

"It's the truth." And it was. The blue top made her eyes shine like jewels, and her cheeks were flushed from laughter. More than that, there was a new...softness to her that hadn't been there when they'd first met. He'd always admired her bold attitude, but there was something equally appealing about her newfound vulnerability. "Pregnancy suits you, Delia Carlisle."

She looked stunned by this observation, as shocked as when he'd asked her to marry him. Her lips parted and she paused as if trying to find the right response. Her nose scrunched in concentration...no, not concentration. Protest.

Alexander's eyes watered as the smell hit him.

"Oh, Lord, help us." She slapped a hand over her nose and mouth, her voice muffled behind her fingers. "Did *he* do *that?*"

"Either that, or there's been a sewage backup in the pipes." He hoisted the car seat in one hand and the diaper bag in the other, then headed for the living room.

Delia didn't stay in the kitchen, but she didn't exactly follow, either. "Do we really think it's wise to move him around, wafting that...that stench from room to room?"

He unbuckled the now-crying baby from the carrier. "Well, you sure as hell don't want me changing this in the place where we keep our food." Theoretically, the snaps up the legs of Sam's outfit allowed for easy diaper-changing access, but the way the boy was kicking added an extra challenge to the task.

"I need air," Delia said, sounding suddenly rather urgent. "My stomach..."

Glancing over just long enough to concede that she was indeed turning green, he said, "Why don't you go upstairs until I'm finished with this? I can handle one diaper."

She inched toward the door, grabbing her keys from a hook on the wall. "Actually, I think I'm going to go out for a while."

Alexander froze. How long was a while? "You're not really going to leave, are you? I told Ray and Karin—"

"Yes, *you* told them, while conveniently neglecting to even mention this to me beforehand." Her fingers closed over the doorknob. "You wanted to spend your Friday night babysitting? Well, this should be a dream come true."

"Delia." He wasn't sure whether he planned to apologize or to beg her to stay, but her expression softened slightly at the entreaty in his tone.

"I'll be back in around an hour," she told him. "If Karin and Ray show up before then, tell them a friend of mine had an emergency."

Then she was gone.

Alexander didn't know why he was surprised. After all, she'd always made it clear she considered walking out a natural part of relationships.

Some other time, having an hour to kill would have been the perfect opportunity to run inside a convenience store to satisfy a food craving or to buy a decadent to-go dessert from a restaurant. But at the moment, Delia couldn't imagine ever getting her appetite back. Her nose had barely stopped burning when she inhaled.

She hadn't fled her town house merely because of the odor, though, even if it *had* been foul enough to peel paint from the walls. Before Sam had dropped his little bomb, she'd already been squirming. There'd been something in Alexander's eyes when he'd told her she was beautiful...

You're being absurd. Alexander had praised her looks throughout their relationship, sometimes in graphically detailed terms. So what was the big deal about his saying so tonight?

The surreal, cozy atmosphere, for one. They'd cooked together in that kitchen, fought in that kitchen, even made love there once. But they'd never crowded into the room to take care of a child together. Squeezed in with apple-cheeked Sam, laughing at Alexander's efforts to get food into him while the baby was wriggling happily and getting half of it smeared on his face—*that* was what was different about tonight.

If this evening had merely been a favor for one of Alexander's colleagues, it might have been a cute novelty, something she recounted later for Kate's and Patti's amusement. Instead it was a nerve-racking reminder that in the near future, she and Alexander would have a baby that no one was coming to pick up after two hours.

I should kick him out. Not tonight—she wasn't *that* mad about his little stunt—but before the baby came. It wouldn't be fair to the child to become accustomed to his living there, only to lose him later.

Kids had a naive way of assuming that dads would

always be around, but she and Alexander were not a forever kind of couple. Since he'd never broached the topic of their getting married a second time, she assumed he'd come to his senses. She'd miss his company and their chemistry, but passion burned out sooner or later—given how long it had been now since they'd made love, it was likely sooner in their case. Delia's eyes prickled with that singular sensation she would have assumed two months ago indicated something was wrong with her contacts. Now she recognized it as a precursor for tears and swore several imaginative curse words, all strung together to create an überprofanity.

Time alone with her thoughts was obviously not a great idea right now.

She reached for the cell phone in the passenger seat and dialed Kate's number. No answer. Was she doing something with her stepkids? Delia couldn't remember if they'd started school this week or would start next week. Until recently, things like the school-district calendars had been arbitrary, parallel entities that didn't intersect with her reality. Hell, she didn't even know what school district she lived in!

Mentally crossing her fingers, she dialed Patti's number. Would she and George be home on a Friday night?

"Hello?"

"Yes! Patti, I'm so glad to hear your voice."

"Delia?"

"Yeah."

"Are you all right, honey?"

Debatable. "I'm driving around in circles and could use a friendly ear."

"Do you want to come over?" Patti offered.

I take back every ungrateful thing I ever said about her. "You and George wouldn't mind?"

"*George* is on the west coast with his *associate, Marilyn,* and Leo's at a movie. I'd welcome the company."

Delia's eyebrows had shot up at Patti's biting emphasis when mentioning George and his associate. "I'll be there soon, okay?" Maybe Delia wasn't the only one who could use a friend tonight.

Caramel-fudge brownies might not be on the recommended prenatal diet, but they sure did hit the spot. Delia leaned back in the floral-print armchair and exhaled blissfully.

"Patti, you could eliminate smoking in the U.S. Whenever someone craved a cigarette, give them one of these babies and they'd forget all about nicotine."

The other woman chuckled, sitting with her feet tucked up under her on the sofa, her own plate, bare except for crumbs, resting on the end table next to her. "Glad I could help."

Delia had given her the short-story version of how Alexander had suddenly been compelled to play Good Samaritan for the evening without letting Delia know. Delia was surprised Patti hadn't sided more with Alexander, arguing his good intentions or pointing out that Delia could benefit from practice with feedings and changes. Instead she'd hooted with laughter when

Delia got to the part about abandoning Alexander to take care of the toxic diaper himself.

"I swear it was radioactive," Delia had said. "They'll be making horror movies about it in years to come."

"Serves him right!" Patti had said gleefully. "Where's it written that women are the only ones who can take care of kids? Men *should* change their share of diapers."

Then she'd sliced them some brownies and Delia had taken a detour into oral nirvana, so she'd yet to inquire about the man in Patti's life and if there was a specific reason the good-natured woman seemed vindictive tonight.

Delia brushed crumbs from her fingers and started to ask in her typically blunt fashion whether Patti thought her husband was banging his so-called associate. But it occurred to Delia that the question wasn't tactful. *How would Kate approach it?* Their other friend was classy, not bothered by Delia's occasional crassness but not subscribing to it, either.

"So." She cleared her throat. "George is out of town?"

Patti nodded, her earlier smile fading into misery. "They're dangling a vice presidency in front of him, but making him jump through all manner of hoops first, including travel. This is his seventh trip since summer started."

"Is a lot of his traveling with this…Myrna?"

"Marilyn." Patti leaned forward, propped her chin in her hands and said nothing further.

Delia was at a loss. Maybe she wasn't cut out for the Kate approach. "So do you think Marilyn and your husband might be bumping uglies?" If so, Delia planned to counsel her friend to change all the locks and hire a great lawyer. Or maybe she should hire a private investigator to get her all the incriminating evidence she'd need for court.

Surprisingly, Patti giggled. "Lord, no. George is pushing forty-five and balding. Marilyn is twenty-six, cute as a bug and a real up-and-comer in the company. She has a master's degree in business and a fiancé who looks like he could be voted *People*'s Sexiest Man Alive. If Marilyn's even noticed that George is a man, it's strictly in a father-figure sense."

"Then…why did you sound so glum just now?" And pissed off on the phone earlier?

Patti chuckled again, but the sound was hollow. "I wasn't jealous in the sense you think, scared Marilyn might want what's mine. It's more…I want what's hers."

Until recently Patti had always seemed well-satisfied with her life. Still, Delia nodded, her expression deadpan. "Ah, yes. Who *wouldn't* want one of *People*'s sexiest men?"

Patti threw a small decorative pillow at her. "It's not the fiancé I covet. I love my own lunkhead. But the way he talks about her, the look he gets—"

"So even though Marilyn's oblivious, you think George might be having some lustful thoughts?" Typical.

"Why is it always about sex with you? George isn't

lusting. He really admires her, admits that she's already thought of better ideas for the company's website than he's had in the past few years. He laughed, calling himself an old dog who hopes for just enough new tricks to become vice president."

"You have great ideas, too," Delia said loyally. This must be pregnancy bringing out her heretofore unknown gentler side because, truthfully, Patti's lifestyle resembled Chelsea Carlisle's. It was a path Delia could neither understand nor endorse, having seen numerous upper-class housewives have their worlds turned upside down when the male breadwinner of the family decided it was time for spousal upgrade. Yet the praise she found herself giving was entirely true. "You're single-handedly putting together the October fund-raiser at the country club, and it's for a great cause." Proceeds went to an organization dedicated to fighting heart disease.

"I'm chairing a small committee," Patti corrected modestly.

"With committee members like Chastity Dillinger?" Delia rolled her eyes. "That egomaniac is probably more hindrance than help."

"I like the community work I do, honestly. It's just… I got married so young. I've only ever been with one man, I didn't get a college degree, I've never been outside the country. I feel like such a *bumpkin*."

Delia glanced around the carefully decorated living room of the pricey suburban home. "You are no such thing."

"Well, doing Leo's laundry and baking brownies doesn't exactly make me feel worldly." A tiny smile made its way through. "Even if they are kick-ass brownies."

"You could sell them, turn it in to an enterprise. People would love these."

"I want to do something for *me*. Other people can go hang." She stopped, looking horrified. "Oh, no. That sounded so…"

"Much like something I might say?"

"It sounded selfish, which you aren't. At least not all the time."

Talk about your backhanded compliments.

"Like with Kate," Patti said hurriedly. "You've been a great friend to her."

"It's okay. I'm not offended. I make no apology for looking out for number one—who else is going to? How can you possibly be expected to take such good care of George and Leo if you don't first take care of yourself?"

Patti pursed her lips, thinking it over. "That does make some sense."

"Of course it does! If *I* hadn't recognized my own needs tonight, I would have been at home for the past half hour trying not to breathe through my nose instead of here, scarfing down the best damn brownie I've ever tasted." But she had promised Alexander she'd be back soon. Delia might be selfish, but she wasn't a liar. "I should probably return."

Patti stood to see her out. "I'm really glad you stopped by, though. We should do this more often."

It was rare that the two of them got together without Kate, but it had been surprisingly enjoyable. As she drove home, Delia admitted to herself that Patti wasn't the person Delia sometimes painted her to be. At least, she wasn't *wholly* that person. She had unexpected sides to her.

But nothing about the evening so far—and it had been quite a series of events—was as unexpected as the jolt to Delia's heart when she opened the door to her town house and stepped into the living room. She'd been about to call out a hello, but the greeting faded on her lips as she took in the soft duet of snores.

Alexander, who had changed into different jeans and a white undershirt, was stretched across her couch, which really *was* too short for him, with the baby cradled on his chest, secured by one strong arm. Sam's face was turned toward Delia, his bow of a mouth and fanned eyelashes cherubic in the dim lamplight, his butt curved up in the air. Was that really a comfortable position to sleep in? The kid seemed happy enough, snoring in rounds with Ringo, his breathy little snuffles ending just as Alexander's chest rumbled with his next chainsaw imitation.

She felt pulled simultaneously to join them and to flee in the opposite direction, getting as far from man and baby as possible. With her car keys still in her hand, she might even have acted on her emergency flight response if there hadn't been a knock at the door.

Alexander, having enough presence of mind to hold Sam in place, sat almost straight up. The infant didn't so much as twitch. "I'm awake!"

"Liar," Delia said fondly.

He shot her a sleepy grin, the one that had easily convinced her to stay in bed an extra hour on many a morning. "Well, I'm awake *now*."

She was already reaching for the door when the second knock came. Karin Ness, fidgeting and biting her lip, was clearly trying to keep herself from peppering them with questions about Sam's evening.

"We're back," Ray said unnecessarily. "Everything go all right?"

"He's sleeping peacefully," Delia said as she ushered them in.

Alexander handed Sam, whose face bore little creases from Alexander's T-shirt, to his mother. "He made it through the night in one set of clothes. I, however, needed to change."

Karin laughed, looking more relaxed now that her son was in her embrace. "I know how that goes. It's amazing how someone so small can generate so many loads of laundry."

They managed to gather the baby's belongings and to get him buckled into his carrier without waking him up. Delia hoped that the baby stayed peaceful for a few hours and let his parents catch up on their rest…or anything else they might like to catch up on after their rare date. Once she was alone again with Ringo, part of her was tempted to apologize for abandoning him earlier.

Instead she heard herself say, "I'm going up to bed."

After all, she'd told Patti she was glad she'd left

tonight. Wouldn't saying she was sorry be hypocritical? *He shouldn't have sandbagged me with the babysitting.* Trying to nurse her earlier indignation so that it had outpaced her guilt, she reminded herself that it was no sin to do what she wanted rather than let a man dictate her plans.

The only problem was, with each day that passed, Delia seemed to grow more confused about what she truly wanted.

Chapter 7

Unlike most of your friends' parents, I'll probably never say, "Turn that racket down!" because, frankly, I've always preferred to listen to the tunes cranked up loud myself. But as much as I love music, I wasn't prepared for the most amazing sound I've ever heard.

In the pastel waiting room of Dr. Adair's office, Alexander stood out like a tall, dark and handsome thumb. There was one other man wearing wire-rimmed glasses and sitting with his arm around a pregnant lady. Half-full by eight-thirty, the reception area was mostly occupied by women. Women who all glanced up in fleeting and not-so-fleeting admiration when Alexander held the door open for Delia, then followed her inside.

The rush of feminine pride Delia felt knowing he was with *her* was a small but needed boon to her ego; yesterday morning, as she was stepping out of the shower, she'd realized there were jagged white stretch marks running the length of her abdomen. The marks seemed excessive, considering how little she'd actually expanded so far. In fact, she envied some of the women present who looked cheerfully and unmistakably with child, their bellies firm little bumps beneath surprisingly stylish maternity clothes. Delia had improvised this morning with an oversize blouse untucked over relaxed-fitting khaki capris—thank God for casual Fridays. She didn't yet look like an expectant mother; she just looked bloated.

Earlier this week, Terese Reeves had been in line in front of Delia at the coffee shop on the first floor of their building. The woman had asked the barista for a chocolate-chip muffin to go with her latte, then darted a quick but pointed glance over her shoulder before purring, "Make that *just* the latte. With nonfat milk." Delia had zoned out during part of a morning development meeting because she'd been fantasizing about feeding Terese so many of Patti's caramel-fudge brownies that the smug younger agent popped the button on her designer blazer.

"Delia?" Alexander's tone was concerned. "Are you in pain?"

She blinked. "I'm all right."

"But you were growling."

True, but that hardly warranted attention in this room. One woman, probably here for some kind of postpartum checkup, was singing to a tiny baby in a pink cap. On the other side of the room, the couple Delia had noticed when she first walked in were now arguing with increasing volume—about their "birth plan." Delia couldn't help mentally taking sides; it was the woman eventually having to squeeze the kid out, so why should the man get to call the shots on how that happened?

In yet another corner of the spacious area, a curly-haired young woman who looked further along than Delia was crying softly and methodically shredding a tissue. Was everything okay with the girl's baby? Though Delia didn't actually write *X*s on a calendar or say anything out loud, she took notice of each day that brought her closer to her second trimester. While complications could still arise, especially in women her age, she'd feel better, safer, once she and the baby had passed that milestone.

Delia was startled to find herself considering going over to talk to the girl. She quickly talked herself out of it. Until she'd become pregnant, Delia never cried, yet now commercials could catch her off guard and make her weepy. It was entirely possible that the younger expectant mom was having an emotional response to something as simple as one of the black-and-white, mother-with-newborn photos on the wall and would be embarrassed if a stranger approached her. In fact, the way the girl kept tilting her head so that her profusion of curls hid her face, made it seem as if she wanted privacy.

A nurse opened the door that led down the hallway to the exam rooms and every woman looked up, hoping it would be her turn. "Shelly Clark?"

The woman who'd been arguing with her husband stood. The room was a little quieter once they'd left.

Delia stole a peek at Alexander's handsome profile. Did he think about things like birth plans or what they should name the baby? For possibly the first time ever, she wished they were closer geographically to his family. Then she would have seen him with his nieces and nephews, might have a better idea of—

"You're looking at me quite intently," he murmured.

"Sorry."

"Don't be. I'm just afraid that—" he lowered his voice even more "—my reaction isn't entirely appropriate, given our surroundings."

She'd missed that familiar wicked warmth in his tone, and liquid heat flooded her, spiraling to places in her body she'd about written off for dead. Her first real flutters of arousal since the night she'd told him about the baby, and they had to be at the *OB's office?*

"Wow," she teased in a whisper, "doesn't take much to get a rise out of you."

"Not these days. I'm a desperate man, Delia. You got me addicted to being in your bed and then suddenly—"

"You still sleep in my bed," she pointed out, trying not to think about her decision to ask him to find his own place before the baby came.

"*Sleep* being the key word, unfortunately." He cupped her cheek, his large fingers just calloused enough to highlight his masculinity. "You've been so tired and sick to your stomach, and I was unsure… Things have changed between us."

Which was *exactly* what she hadn't wanted, why she'd goggled at any acquaintance who'd asked, "So when are you two getting married?" Even the changes that should be good grated on her. News of her pregnancy brought out a different side of Alexander: he was protective, bordering on nurturing. While she couldn't complain about the meals he'd fixed for her, he'd barely raised his voice since she'd turned down his proposal. Since she knew she'd become no less exasperating, she assumed he saw her as more fragile now that she was a mommy-to-be. That was one part of marriage that had always made her shudder, the way someone else's perception of you could eventually shape who you were. Like the way Patti suddenly worried that she was frumpy because she suspected that was how George viewed her compared to a bright coworker.

Realistically, Delia knew change was inevitable, but she'd enjoyed their passionate and open-ended relationship. She'd wanted to savor it for as long as possible. She'd watched colleagues fall in love and marry, giddy and sleep-deprived during the honeymoon phase, then eventually arguing over the phone in their cubicle about whose turn it had been to put the garbage out for pickup that morning.

Patti had suggested change could be an opportunity for two people to grow closer, but that sounded disturbingly similar to the trite philosophies Chelsea had preferred to reality. *Obviously your father and I have had our troubles, sweetheart, but a marriage that's endured trials and tribulations is twice as strong as one that's never been tested.*

What the hell definition was her mother using for *endure?* Chelsea's marriage hadn't so much endured as ended. Garrett left his wife, who was so incapable of defining who she was without him that she'd taken him back as soon as Garrett's girlfriend poetically left him. That seemed more like weakness than character growth. Which wedding anniversary did they even celebrate?

"Uh-oh," Alexander said idly.

She blinked, glad for the interruption. Just because her second trimester was approaching and she'd have to tell her parents about the baby soon didn't mean she had to waste all her energy thinking about them in the meantime. "Problem?"

"Well, I'd been enjoying the look on your face and the possibility that you've missed making love as much as I have, but then your expression changed. I can see the loving feeling's gone now."

"In the past, you would have tried to seduce me back into the mood." Not that she wanted him to in the doctor's office, but this demonstrated yet again how he was already treating her—and their relationship—differently.

And the baby wasn't even here yet! Delia should officially move their relationship to a platonic level before the birth. Still, she hated to give him up any sooner than she had to. Once the baby was born, who knew how long it would be before Delia was involved with a man again?

"Delia Carlisle?" A nurse in brightly patterned scrubs and holding a clipboard glanced around the waiting room, her gaze locking with Delia's as she and Alexander stood. "This way, please."

The first order of business was a specimen cup and the nurse pointed to the patient restroom. After that, the nurse led her to a scale. As Delia stepped out of a pair of mules, she shot Alexander a glare that suggested he be elsewhere when her weight was read. He took a sudden interest in a poster on proper breast self-examination. Then the nurse took Delia's blood pressure, which remained in a reassuringly healthy range. Finally, Delia and Alexander were shown to a small exam room where she was asked to exchange her shirt for a cotton wrap.

"The doctor will be with you shortly," the nurse promised.

Delia picked up the garment—if it could be called that—and glanced across the exam table at Alexander, hyperaware of the enclosed space and his proximity. It was on the tip of her tongue to ask him to turn around while she changed. *Stupid.* He'd seen her naked thousands of times…just not recently. The changes in her body had made her feel more inhibited.

Whether it was the lack of nausea this morning or the brief flirting with Ringo in the waiting room today, she felt more like herself than she had in weeks. So her body was changing—did she really plan to make love in the dark until the baby was born? Right, and maybe she'd start insisting on only the missionary position and using words like *golly* to replace her saltier vocabulary. Squaring her shoulders, she met Alexander's eyes and let her hands meet at the top button of her blouse, slowly freeing the plastic disc.

By the time she'd reached the third button, Alexander's breathing had grown more pronounced, his gaze locked on the column of skin she'd bared. She hadn't truly realized how much she'd missed this heady sense of feminine power. Of course, if she didn't hurry things up a little, Shauna Adair would walk in mid-impromptu-striptease.

So Delia shrugged out of the partially unbuttoned blouse and reached behind her, deftly releasing the clasp on her bra. Her breasts, heavier with pregnancy and pleasurably tight under Alexander's avid attention, fell free of their confines. After a second passed, she caught herself holding her breath, but he didn't seem to mind the burgeoning swell of her tummy or the jagged marks that gave outward declaration of the changes within.

To her surprise, a fierce possessiveness lit his expression, making him look even more elementally male than he had in the waiting room, surrounded by lavender-cushioned chairs and a dozen women. His eyes dipped to the slight bulge of the child they'd created, then roved upward, appreciating her fuller breasts and darker nipples. The changes to her body were, on the whole, still subtle, but then, he knew her body damn well and in many different ways.

She swallowed, her throat dry. "I—I should put this drape on."

"Funny, I was thinking you should take the pants off."

A sound that was partly a moan of agreement and partly nervous laughter burbled out of her. But by the time Dr. Adair knocked on the other side of the door, Delia had tied the makeshift shirt around her with only slightly shaking fingers and was sitting on the exam table. Alexander sat in the one visitor chair present, not looking at Delia, as if he, too, were trying to regain his composure.

The tall doctor smiled at them. "Glad to see you could join us today, Alexander. And congratulations."

"Thank you." He beamed, and Delia realized that while she'd had Patti and Kate to talk to during the past few weeks, there hadn't been anyone else to reassure or to congratulate Alexander. Even though her parents didn't even know about the baby, she felt a twinge of guilt that she'd asked him not to tell his own family. He deserved to share something so important with others.

He wanted to share it with you, *asked you to marry him and everything.* True, but that had been a sweet, fleeting notion, not a realistic long-term plan.

Delia refocused on the doctor and the exam at hand. When it came time to check for the baby's heartbeat, Shauna rubbed cool gel over Delia's stomach and cautioned, "Don't panic if we don't hear anything. With some patients, we can't make out an audible pulse for another week or two, but it's worth a try. If we have any cause for concern, we can always confirm the heartbeat with an ultrasound."

Delia nodded, but she couldn't resist a smug smile when the doctor immediately picked up a pulse. "That's the baby?"

Shauna glanced down with an expression reminiscent of the look she used when Delia got overcocky on the courts and hit a ball wild. "That's *you.*"

"Oh." Delia darted her gaze toward Alexander to see if he was laughing at her, but he merely winked and squeezed her hand.

They were all quiet as Shauna moved the Doppler around…and then Delia heard it. It was nothing like the stronger *lump dump* she'd known immediately was a pulse. This was a whooshing noise, faster and fainter and indescribably awe-inspiring. Emotion gripped Delia. It felt as if both her heart and womb contracted. Her vision blurred momentarily.

Alexander laced his fingers with hers. His mouth, at first open in shock, broke into a wide grin. "That's our child."

Their child. She knew now that her gut-level reaction about keeping the baby had been the right one. There was no way she could give up this little life inside her, and the reasoning had nothing to do with her being financially solvent or believing she'd make a great mom or even deep-seated moral beliefs. It was simple… This baby was *hers*. On a primitive level that needed neither words nor logic. Delia was willing to share the child with Alexander, but she'd be damned if she could give the kid up to someone else.

When the exam was finished and Shauna stepped outside the room so that her patient could dress, Alexander cradled Delia's face in his big hands and kissed her. It was gentle but deeply thorough. Her body responded with pulses of tingly warmth. She delighted in his familiar taste and touch, in being able to celebrate physically something she wouldn't be able to articulate. Delia had never felt closer to him or to any other person, not even during sex.

And that realization scared the hell out of her.

"It was amazing, Patti!" Delia had been disappointed that Kate was too swamped with work to join them for a late lunch, but she had to admit she would have felt more self-conscious gushing these newfound maternal responses in front of their other friend.

Patti had grinned knowingly throughout lunch as Delia described that morning's OB appointment, which had been the recurring subject of conversation between other topics.

Now, as the two women strolled through the food court, Patti sighed. "I'm jealous of the technological advances since I had Leo. One of the moms I know through PTA is having a baby, and the sonogram video she got to keep was unbelievable. My tiny black-and-white still-shot of Leo is so grainy you could barely tell it was a baby, much less discern the gender."

When it came to the baby's sex, Delia wouldn't have to go by the guess of an ultrasound tech. She had decided, after no small amount of needle trepidation, that when the time came, she would have the amniocentesis. Although she hated to imagine that anything could be wrong with her child—having *her* for a mother seemed like enough of a potential handicap—she'd decided it was better to be prepared. An amnio couldn't tell you everything, but it could rule out, or confirm, certain conditions.

A minor perk of the procedure was finding out for sure whether the baby was a boy or girl.

Delia stopped in front of a dessert vendor. "How about an ice-cream cone before I have to get back to work?"

"I'd better do the low-fat frozen yogurt if I want to fit into the dress I've been eyeing for the fundraiser." The time they hadn't spent discussing pregnancy had largely been spent on the plans for next month's benefit.

They ordered two fro-yo cones and ate them as they strolled through the mall.

"Is it my imagination or have you already dropped a couple of pounds?" Delia asked. She'd noticed earlier, but until Patti mentioned slimming down for her outfit, she'd kept it to herself in case it was merely her pregnancy weight gain altering her perspective and making other people look thinner.

Patti nodded triumphantly. "I've been walking in the subdivision after dinner and having some very healthy salads. George didn't take the new menu well—pointed out that he's a meat-and-potatoes man. I informed him that we keep most of our meats in the fridge and that he could find his pick of potatoes in the pantry."

"Good for you!" These were the kind of small but meaningful steps Delia had always hoped her mother would take in standing up for herself. If Chelsea had, would Delia have respected the woman more? Would they have had a real mother-daughter relationship? As she so often found herself doing these days, Delia glanced in the direction of her navel. *I swear I'll try to do better than she did.*

"So did George start eating the food you made with enough sense not to complain, or did he actually attempt cooking for himself?"

"Neither." Patti's smile faded into resignation. "He ordered a pizza, and he and Leo have been doing takeout most nights since. Which is really hypocritical considering…"

"Considering what?"

Patti sighed. "You know how we talked about my doing something that was just for me? Promise not to laugh—"

"I make no such guarantees."

"You're awful."

"This is not news. But enough about me. You were about to admit something potentially embarrassing?"

Patti licked her yogurt, clearly stalling, then threw

it in a nearby wastebasket. "I was thinking that maybe I could go to school. Enroll at the university for some classes." She lifted her chin defiantly at the end of her statement, in an almost Delia-like gesture, *daring* others to tell her she was too old to hang with the college kids.

"I think that's a great idea."

"You do?" Patti blinked. "George scoffed that the last thing we need is tuition bills for both me and Leo. And my son was horrified to think about running into his mom on campus."

"He's only sixteen and has a couple of years. Technically, you could make it your territory first. Tell him maybe you don't want him ruining *your* cool by acknowledging you as his mom in public."

"That wouldn't be very nice of me." But Patti's eyes twinkled at the idea. "Anyway, I love how the cost of my taking a few courses didn't even merit discussion, but George is adding up delivery charges for Kung Pao chicken. Maybe I'll tell him I'm going to start delivering pizzas to earn my college money."

Delia laughed. "If you do, can I please be there to see his face?"

They were nearing the department store where Delia had parked her car; she needed to discuss some building code information with a client before three.

"I have to run, but seriously, Patti, don't let George get you down. Just because change weirds him out is no reason for you not to take those classes you want." George was a big boy, he could damn well adjust and support his wife the way she supported everyone else.

Patti frowned. "You and Alexander had such a nice morning together, and here I am ruining it by making marriage sound… It's really not so bad, Delia."

Not so bad? Now there was a ringing endorsement. "You haven't ruined anything, Patti."

They said their goodbyes, and Delia fished her car keys from her purse as she tried to remember in exactly which row she'd parked—she hoped she got some of her short-term memory back after the baby was born.

It was funny how Patti and other acquaintances over the years had acted as if Delia didn't have a good enough reason for *not* getting married. Didn't they read current statistics? According to a magazine Delia had been flipping through in the office break room, a higher percentage of women were single than ever before. *Happily* single! In Delia's mind, she didn't need a compelling "excuse" for staying that way instead of falling off the cliff into matrimony like a mindless lemming.

It was like when a couple finally did get married and five minutes later all their acquaintances were asking, "So, when are you guys going to have kids?" as though procreation was a given, not an individual choice. Some people simply didn't want to be parents and shouldn't have to validate that. Although maybe that wasn't the best analogy in her condition.

As genuinely and deeply fond as she was of Ringo and as much as she was anxious to get him alone tonight, ever since adolescence she'd been unable to picture herself shackled to one man until "death do we part."

Really, how bad a policy could it be to eschew a ceremony that mentioned *death* right there in the vows?

The Second Trimester...

Chapter 8

Everyone makes mistakes—some of us frequently and with flair.

Delia came out of the dream slowly, like a diver rising to the warm light of the surface. *Wow.* She'd read how the hormones could not only heighten the senses—chiefly that of smell—but also make dreams more vivid. It was no fun during nightmares, but fantasies were an entirely different story. Women posting on the pregnancy message boards tended to be extremely candid, either because they felt a sisterly bond or because of the anonymity in cyber-nicknames, and one woman had written that while she couldn't remember the actual dreams, she kept waking up from having orgasms in her sleep.

As side effects went, it beat the hell out of morning sickness.

Delia's intermittent nausea had faded more with each passing week. In fact... She rolled onto Alexander's empty-but-still-warm side of the bed. Now that she was awake enough to hear the water running, she realized he was in the shower. Would he want company?

Minutes later she was standing naked outside the shower. "Knock, knock."

The curtain rustled and he peeked out, his smile widening when he saw what she wasn't wearing. "You certainly know how to tell a man good-morning."

She stepped inside the steamy confines of the shower and leaned against him. "Well, I feel like I owe you," she teased. "I kind of passed out on you last night, didn't I?"

He smoothed her hair back, letting the water dampen it. If she was really lucky, he'd offer to wash it for her; he had great hands. "You need your rest. We should have stopped after the first time."

"I didn't want to."

"Me, either." He kissed her then, and her breath caught even though she should be used to the rush of sensation by now, especially after the way they'd spent the previous evening.

As her pregnancy progressed, she'd expected to feel bulky and undesirable. Instead she felt elementally female. Hunger was not the only appetite that increased as the days passed, which was a relief for a woman who'd always had a healthy love life but had nearly lost her libido entirely during the first trimester.

Later, as they worked together to make breakfast—he was in charge of the egg-white omelets while she managed not to burn the toast...much—Alexander joked that he would have to start taking extra vitamins just to keep up with her.

"I've always warned you that I'm going to wear you out," she reminded him with a sly grin.

"All right, but make up a story for my mother, okay?" He reached into a cabinet and pulled out two plates. "Something heroic. I don't want her to know I died in bed."

"You don't think she'll be able to tell from the smile on your face in the casket?"

He smirked at her irreverent tone. "You are a bad woman, Delia Carlisle."

"Isn't that why you love me?" She asked it lightly, unthinkingly, but they both froze.

Shit. A split second ago his dark eyes had glinted with a teasing light; now they were locked on hers with intense sincerity. He was a passionate man, and mostly she found his intensity thrilling. Other times, however, he disconcerted her in a way no one else ever had.

She spun toward the refrigerator. "What did you want on your toast? Jelly, marmalade? Honey? I think we have some—"

"Delia."

She'd fought her normal confrontational instincts and had tried to take the graceful exit for both of them, and this was the thanks she got? "Don't read into it, Ringo."

"I do love you."

She winced. Even if she could say the words back, such a declaration would only complicate the good-bye later. "That's not the kind of relationship we were going to have."

"Your arrogance is showing, babe. Do you really think you can make those decisions beforehand and control other people's emotions indefinitely? Or even your own?"

She'd managed to thus far in her life. Where had things spun off course with him? *Kate and Patti were right months ago. I never should have invited him to move in.*

In the absence of her response, he continued pressing his point. "When we first starting seeing each other, you prided yourself on spontaneity, but the truth is, you're not very flexible. You resist change entirely unless you're the one who instigates it."

"What a load of crap!" She cupped her hands over her stomach. "My life has been a roller coaster of change for more than a month, and there are going to be countless more changes for the next eighteen years! You're lashing out because I don't feel the same way you do."

He took a step toward her, his voice dropping to a silky octave. "Don't you?"

"You don't intimidate me." It was definitely not fear that had her heart thudding against her chest. "And you can't blackmail me with sex."

Reaching out, he traced his index finger over her lips. "This is about so much more than sex, and you know it. It's why you're scared."

"Now who's being arrogant? You've mistaken annoyance with apprehension." She narrowed her eyes in warning. "Don't push me on this."

"All right. But I'm dropping this because it's something I plan to come back to later, not because I ask how high when you say jump." He leaned closer. "You can deny your feelings for now, but we both know you want me."

She considered stalking out of the room, to hell with his omelet, but she was too hungry to willingly abandon good food. Besides, it was *her* kitchen.

They ate in silence, and when he finally spoke at the end of the meal, he'd resumed a neutral pass-the-salt kind of tone. "Speaking of my mother, who, you may remember, I mentioned earlier." He shot her an ironic, challenging glance.

She glared back, waiting for him to get to a point.

"You're in your second trimester now. We agreed we'd tell our families."

The omelet turned to lead in her stomach.

She carried her plate to the sink, commenting over her shoulder, "You're right. I've already told my boss, after all." It had been the proactive thing to do, breaking the news at the office before people figured it out on their own. She supposed the main reason no one had yet was her age…and that she'd never struck anyone as maternal. Her employer had seemed fairly unconcerned when she'd announced that motherhood wasn't going to hurt her job performance.

"We're not worried, Delia," Michael Brower had told her. "You've always demonstrated your ambition quite clearly. In any case, you're hardly the first working mother we've had on staff, and we've discovered that the bills that come with raising and educating kids is as strong a motivator as any incentive plan we could ever offer."

Knowing that Delia had started making announcements, it was surprising that Alexander hadn't mentioned telling his mother and sisters before now. She tried to muster a smile. "Feel free to call your family whenever you want."

"They'll want to talk to you," he said. "You're the mother of my child."

The term rubbed her the wrong way—not difficult to do when her emotions were already rioting and tension practically oozed from her pores. "You've got it backward. You just happened to be the father of *my* child."

He wasn't sidetracked, simply repeating, "They'll want to talk to you."

"Exactly how do you think that conversation will go? I'm a total stranger to them. You don't think 'Hi, I'm pregnant,' will be a little awkward? Or generate expectations?"

"About what?"

"Us, you thick-headed mule!" She tossed her hands in the air. "Your very first response to hearing about the baby was to suggest we get married. When your family hears about this, don't you think your mother's first question will be 'When's the wedding?' It will be easier to explain that there isn't going to be one if you tell them alone."

She softened her tone. "I want you to be a part of our baby's life, Alexander, you know that. As much as you care for your family, I realize *they'll* be part of the child's life, too. But we should start as we mean to go on. Separately."

A muscle in his face twitched as he clenched his jaw. "If that's really how you feel, I should get out of the town house."

"You don't… That wasn't meant to be a breakup."

"That's even worse. I know you didn't expect to get pregnant, I know you have intimacy issues, and I've been trying to give you time. To go against my own nature and be patient instead of giving in to the temptation of shaking some sense into you. Let me see if I can sum up our nonrelationship, according to the Philosophy of Delia. I'm supposed to hang around until it's most convenient for you to kick me out? Make love to you even though you won't let yourself love me? I know how you feel about marriage, and some couples spend their lives together without the formal ceremony, but you don't even…" He looked at her as if he'd truly seen her for the first time—and didn't like what he saw. "I'm not just someone for you to jump in the shower with when you wake up in the mood, Delia."

She steeled herself against his words, and her own wounded reaction, keeping her voice glacially calm.

"You've never complained about my jumping you before."

"Consider this a registered complaint." He pivoted and the front door slammed moments later.

Once he was in his car, Alexander felt regrettably petulant. He was only a few years from forty; wasn't that a little old to be storming out of rooms? His temper had been threatening to get the better of him, however. He wasn't above raising his voice—it was a common DiRossi form of expression—and heaven knew swearing didn't shock Delia, but there was a line of respect he wasn't willing to cross with a woman. Especially the one who carried his child. So he'd walked out rather than cross that line.

Now what, Einstein?

His body wanted a physical outlet for the mounting frustration. God, what was wrong with that woman? He hadn't flinched away from the announcement that they were having a baby, he'd tried to respect her boundaries while still being there for her. He'd been a damn saint!

Did other saints walk around feeling like they wanted to punch a hole in the wall?

He considered playing some golf or heading to the batting cages, but both would be crowded on the weekend, especially on such a pretty September day. Alexander wasn't fit for human company right now. Eventually he found himself at his office.

He loved troubleshooting for the new versions of a program. Bugs in software could be pains in the ass, but they followed certain logic, could be puzzled out and eliminated. Delia followed no logic known to man.

Maybe to women... He sat back at his desk, temporarily abandoning the idea of work. After some thought, he pulled out his cell phone and dialed his mother's number.

"Hello?"

Just hearing Isabella's voice made him feel as if he was sitting at her kitchen table. He smiled into the phone. "Hi, Mama. It's Alexander."

"Do you have another trip scheduled to New York?" she asked, sounding pleased by the prospect. But then her tone turned stern. "Because it's neither my birthday nor a national holiday, and those seem to be the only other times you call."

He laughed. "Do you ever plan to stop scolding your children? We're all grown now."

"I'll scold until my deathbed, then haunt you from the great beyond."

So instead of an angel on his shoulder, he'd have a nagging Italian woman more likely to smack him in the head than play the harp. "I love you, Mama."

She paused. "What is wrong, Alexander?"

"Actually, I have good news. I'm going to be a father. Delia and I are expecting a baby." It hurt more than he'd expected to say it like that—Delia and I. Had there truly been a Delia and him, or had they simply been two people living parallel lives under the same roof?

His mother gasped. At first he feared he'd scandalized her—he couldn't remember a baby in the family born out of wedlock—but then she began thanking the good Lord.

"Oh, I feared never to see the day," she said once she'd offered up a few brief prayers of gratitude. "My son finally having a family of his own and carrying on the DiRossi name! Your father is grinning in heaven. When will the *bambino* be arriving?"

Might be a *bambina,* Alexander thought, smiling to himself at the image of a fair-haired little girl squealing in joy to see him when he got home from work. The smile faded. He no longer had a home. "March. Delia's due date is in March."

"Then you will definitely bring her home for the holidays this year, yes? We should meet the future Mrs. Alexander DiRossi."

Hell. It was galling that Delia had so accurately predicted this reaction. He drew a deep breath and sent up his own little prayer of thanks that he was several states away from Isabella. "We don't have any immediate plans to get married, Mama."

"I don't understand."

"Delia and I talked about it, and we…" It was so tempting to say *she* and shift the blame entirely to her, but even though he was angry with her, he tried to shield her from the brunt of his mother's disapproval. "We decided not to marry." He could go a step further, admit that he was planning to move out, but that would probably send Isabella into convulsions.

"That's ridiculous," she pronounced. "Be a man,

Alexander. Fish or cut bait. You've lived with this woman for how long? You love her, yes?"

"I do." He tried not to think about the caged, frantic expression in Delia's eyes when he'd said as much this morning. Could she really have been that shocked by his declaration? In retrospect, it was bizarre neither of them had said it before.

Or maybe it was only bizarre that *he'd* never said it since she, apparently, didn't feel that way.

"What exactly did she say when you proposed? You *must* have proposed, I didn't raise a son who would walk away from his responsibilities."

Alexander felt disconnected from the conversation; his thoughts seemed to be moving in slow motion and his mother was peppering him with high-speed questions. It was like trying to watch a television show when the sound and picture no longer matched up. "Yes, I asked her to marry me last month, but—"

"You knew she was pregnant *a month ago?*"

Whoops. "It was her decision to wait before we told our families, in case…something went wrong."

Isabella processed this and returned to the more important matter at hand: matrimony. "So you've had weeks to change her mind about your proposal? I myself can occasionally be…difficult to persuade, but your father, God rest his soul, was wise enough to know how to get in my good graces given a few days. How hard can it be to convince the woman pregnant with your child to marry a handsome, virile man who loves her and earns a good living? What's wrong with women today that they're so picky?"

"I think it's the 'man who loves her' part that she objects to, actually." He was thinking out loud as much as he was answering the question. "When I told her this morning that I loved her, she reacted as if—"

"Alexander." His mother's tone was slow, cautious. "You don't mean this was the *first* time you told her?"

He squirmed in his chair. Isabella just didn't understand that modern relationships weren't necessarily spelled out in the same way as courtships when she was young. "It may have been the first time I stated it explicitly, but—"

"You didn't tell her that you loved her *when you asked her to marry you?*"

"I don't remember my exact phrasing, but I was thrilled about the baby. I made sure she knew how happy I was and how much I cared about her."

She muttered something about his intelligence—or lack thereof—in Italian and then entreated the saints to grant her patience. Finally she sighed. "Oh, that your father were alive! He could teach you a thing or two about the proper way to romance a woman."

Alexander wished his father was alive, too. *I could use advice, Pop.* Though Delia rarely mentioned him, Alexander found himself wondering about her father. He knew the man had cheated on his wife and filed for divorce, abandoning his daughter, as well. A father was the earliest and perhaps most crucial male role model in a woman's life. Did Delia not want to trust her heart to anyone because of the mistake her father had made?

It was a sobering thought. Alexander could try to

right his own wrongs, but there wasn't a damn thing he could do to fix something that happened thirty years ago. Worse, he now worried what missteps and misjudgments he'd make in his life that would leave lasting scars on his own children. Parenthood was going to require a measure of courage he'd never really needed before.

Respect and admiration for the job his own mother had done washed through him. "I do love you," he repeated.

"I know. Now convince this woman you love *her*."

Part of him wanted to do just that; the rest of him wondered if he ever had any hope of convincing Delia that *she* loved *him*. And that doing so didn't make her less of a strong, independent woman. Hell, he'd known from their first night together that she wasn't seeking love. Maybe he should cut his losses and save the wealth of emotion he felt for the child they were bringing into the world.

At least the baby wouldn't run from genuine affection or try to control Alexander's feelings with stipulations that were little more than paranoid measures of self-protection.

Delia looked up from the movie she was pretending to watch when the front door opened. Deferred irritation from when he'd walked out earlier and joy to see him again warred within her, and she smothered them both, keeping her expression neutral and her gaze on the television set.

He dropped his car keys on a side table just inside the living room. "Hi."

She nodded, briefly meeting his eyes.

"I called my mother, who has probably already phoned each of my three sisters. They may get in touch with you to express their congratulations."

Normally his family reached him on his cell phone, but there'd been one or two occasions when they'd used the direct number that was in Delia's name. If there was anyone she felt *less* prepared to speak to right now than Alexander, it was his family.

He rocked back on his heels. "You tell your family yet?"

"No." And she didn't appreciate the reproachful downward curve of his lips—her family wasn't any of his business. Thinking of his tendency to be high-handed, she assured herself that she was doing the right thing by putting distance between the two of them. If he thought he had a right to tell her how to live her life now, surely he'd take an even more intolerably patriarchal stance if they ever married. *Never gonna happen.*

When Alexander made no move to sit or to even step fully into the living room, she asked point-blank, "Are you leaving?"

They both knew she meant permanently.

"Maybe that's for the best," he said it challengingly. "Is that what you think?"

"Yes." She forced the word out with no hesitation. The brief but tense time they'd spent apart this afternoon had already given her unpleasant insight into how much she'd miss him, which actually made this the perfect time to wiggle free. As the pregnancy wore on, what if he *was* able to talk her into actually marrying him?

Heaven forbid. Delia had never wanted to be a wife and Alexander had never given any indication of wanting to make things permanent, either. A baby couldn't magically change all of that; it was too much responsibility to put on one poor kid. Despite what Chelsea had once claimed about a child needing both parents, that wouldn't, in Delia's opinion, be a real marriage. And she wouldn't subject her kid to growing up in the kind of uncomfortable and painfully transparent sham her own home had been the last few years she'd lived there.

Seeming unsurprised and even unmoved by her answer, Alexander took a card out of his shirt pocket. "I'm going to stay at these efficiency suites for a few weeks at least, while I look around. Here's the number for my room if you ever need it, but you know you can always reach me on my cell."

He'd already rented a place, just this afternoon? That stung more than she'd expected.

"Thanks." She palmed the card, trying not to think about the brush of his fingers over hers and where those fingers had been last night.

"I'll go by my storage facility, either rearrange the stuff in my unit to make room or rent a bigger one to include my recliner and other things until I've found something of my own." He paused significantly, giving her the chance to say that, instead of going to that trouble or potential expense, he could just leave his stuff here in the interim.

She didn't.

"You know," he began, glancing around. "You might want to think about a new place, too. Something with a yard and more bedroom space, in a good school district."

"I have plenty of time before the baby's old enough for school," she snapped. She didn't need her *ex*-boyfriend to make those decisions for her.

For a second she saw anger flare in his dark eyes and knew they were about to have one of their arguments, but he must have decided it wasn't worth it. "I'm going up to pack."

She stared back at the television, each footstep he made on the stairs a knife-jab beneath her ribs. If she asked him to stay, she was ninety percent sure that he would. But then what? He'd start having a vote on whether or not she gave up her place and moved to the burbs? They'd become that couple in the doctor's office, arguing over which birth plan they'd use. It was best for everyone if she and Alexander went their separate ways, reclaimed the autonomy they'd each agreed was important to them when they'd met.

Even if she hadn't believed that, the ten percent uncertainty that he might leave regardless of a request not to kept her silent when he came down the stairs. She had her pride. People could claim that it didn't keep you warm at night, but she'd had a firsthand look at what could happen to a woman who gave away her pride in a two-for-one deal along with her heart. She wasn't going to be that woman.

Alexander carried a big, black suitcase, the one he rarely used unless it was an international trip or they were going somewhere on vacation and both using it. There'd be no more decadent tropical getaways with him or spontaneous weekends up the coast. She watched as he started to roll the town house key off the ring, and protest welled within her.

"Keep it," she heard herself insist. "In case of emergencies, at least until after the baby's born. Who knows what could happen? Besides, I've been reading these articles about how pregnancy is medically proven to damage your concentration. If I lock myself out or something, it's good to know someone I trust has a spare."

He swallowed. "So you trust me at least. That's something. Not for nothing, but I *do* love you, Delia."

"You know, the only time I ever remember either of my parents say that was during their divorce. My mom would sob it to just about anyone who'd listen, that, no matter what, she still loved my dad. I can't remember either of them saying it to me. Oh, I'm sure they must have when I was younger, before I was a scary teenager, but… The first guy I ever slept with told me he loved me, and I barely remember his last name. It's not that I don't believe you mean it. It's just, love's an abstract concept that's never really applied in my life." Not until she'd heard that heartbeat in Shauna Adair's office. Still, that wasn't romantic love.

He gave no reaction at all to her speech, which at

its core had simply been a variation of "It's not you it's me." "I'll call you soon, make arrangements on when to pick up the rest of my stuff and check on the baby. You let me know what day and time the amnio is scheduled for."

Thank God he still planned to be there. The relief seeped in before she could stop it. While some people might be claustrophobic or agoraphobic, Delia had a sharp-and-pointy-needle phobia. The thought of the procedure always left her in a cold sweat.

Since the man had lived with her for the better part of a year, she decided that the least she could do was walk him to the door. As he reached for the knob, he turned to place one last, fleeting kiss on the top of her head.

"Take care of yourself," he ordered gruffly.

That was the point, wasn't it? She'd always been determined to take care of herself and, now, the baby. It was letting anyone else take care of her that got risky.

Chapter 9

*You'll hear about love at first sight—oh, please—
or meeting a new friend and feeling immediate
kinship. But don't underestimate the number of
people whose special impact on your life you'll
only truly be able to appreciate as time passes.*

"So, the baby's really all right?" It was at least
the third time Delia had repeated the question, and
she was starting to feel extremely foolish for having
called the OB's office from work and insisting on
being seen. The cramping in her abdomen had reminded her too much of menstrual pains and she'd
panicked, thinking that her relief over getting through
the first trimester had been premature.

Shauna nodded reassuringly. "Ligament pain is

common, with all the stretching and jostling going on inside you. However, your blood pressure is much higher than I'd like. You've been doing so well up until now."

Delia bit her lip. "I had a fight with Alexander. He moved out actually, over the weekend." This was the first time she'd admitted it to anyone. With the exception of a pricey recliner, the television in her bedroom and a few other possessions, Alexander was gone.

"Oh. I see. Well, that would probably do it." Shauna paused for a second. "Are you okay?"

"I hate to tell you this, Doc, but the patients are hoping *you'll* tell them whether or not they're okay, not the other way around."

Though she summoned a polite smile in response to the lame joke, Shauna looked perplexed again almost immediately. "The last time I saw the two of you here… I don't want to overstep my bounds, clouding the line between friend and medical professional, but—"

"I'll be fine," Delia said. She didn't want to hear perfectly valid advice that she knew intuitively she wouldn't take.

"All right then. They'll check you out up front and I'll see you for the amnio."

Delia felt the blood drain from her face. It seemed that the closer she got to the procedure, the more apprehensive she got. *Nothing to it,* she tried to convince herself. After all, she'd had a couple of vials of blood drawn for different prenatal tests already, and Delia had made it through those without fainting or punching out the nurse who'd jabbed a needle into her vein. Delia wished she weren't so inordinately relieved that Alexander would be there with her—that was one of her dislikes of relationships: dependency.

She was a successful woman in her forties. Why did she need a man to hold her hand as though she were a child? And since when had she lost the ability to sleep in a bed by herself? For the past three nights, she'd tossed and turned, feeling disoriented when she woke up on his side of the bed.

He doesn't have a side. It's your *bed. It was your bed long before he ever lived there.*

As she handed over the check for her minimal co-pay, she noticed another woman out of the corner of her eye, waiting at the counter for the nurse to find a prescription that had apparently fallen out of her file. Delia turned to study the curly-haired brunette. She was wearing maternity overalls over a long-sleeved pink shirt; she was young enough to make it work. Delia would have looked like a moron.

The woman got her receipt and turned, doing a double take when she realized Delia was studying her.

"Sorry," Delia said. "You seem familiar, and I was just trying to remember…" Now that the younger woman was looking straight at her, Delia could see that her eyes were red and swollen. She'd been crying. It clicked then. This was the mother-to-be who'd been sobbing in the reception area the day Delia and

Al—the last time Delia had been here. "I didn't mean to stare."

"That's all right." The woman spoke with deep twang. Maybe from one of the Carolinas or Alabama? Delia wasn't an expert with accents, but she knew Southern when she heard it. "I can hardly hold on to a thought from one moment to the next now that I'm pregnant…not that I had such a great memory *before*. Bobby always says—" Suddenly her face crumpled and those bloodshot green eyes welled with tears again.

Alarmed by the outpouring of emotion, Delia managed to steer the girl away from the congested appointment desk and toward the exit. "Are you parked out this way?"

The brunette nodded, mumbling something incoherent.

Since Delia had no intention of letting someone in this condition drive a car, she found a pretty wooden-and-iron bench in the shade of an ash tree and sat down, tugging lightly at the younger woman's arm and prompting her to do the same.

Delia opened her purse, looking for tissues, but the best thing she came up with was breath mints. "Want one?"

Strangely, that seemed to mollify the girl somewhat, and she popped a minty disc into her mouth. After a moment she spoke, her words laced with self-disgust but completely understandable. "I'm a mess.

I wish I could blame the pregnancy—not that I don't love the baby!"

"I knew what you meant," Delia hastened to assure her. The girl's eyes had grown so round and horror-stricken, Delia was concerned about further waterworks. "I myself have been considerably more emotional than I used to be."

"I was already prone to being emotional...and prone to making bad decisions thanks to that."

Which was exactly why Delia didn't think a woman should let her feelings navigate.

"Case in point," the other woman continued absently. "Bobby."

"He would be your...?"

"Boyfriend. Ex-boyfriend. On again, off again. The baby's father," she clarified somewhat needlessly.

"You're better off without him." Delia had no relevant information upon which to base this decision, but she'd been telling herself that so often for the past seventy-two hours that repeating it to someone else came automatically. Besides, Delia had seen this kid only twice and both times she'd been alone and crying. Those hardly seemed like points in Bobby's favor.

"Probably," the girl agreed. "I just...miss him so much." And then the crying resumed.

Not exactly progress.

Delia glanced at her watch. "Look, it's almost lunchtime and there's a great Mexican restaurant across the street. You want to go grab a bite to eat?"

The brunette sniffled, looking awed. "You want to have lunch with me? Why?"

Damned if I know. But Delia was having burgeoning feelings of solidarity; this must be how those women who chatted on the message boards felt, a circumstantial sisterly bond even though, for all intents and purposes, they were strangers. "It's only lunch. I'm hungry."

Her new friend offered her a watery smile. "You must have a big heart."

"No, really. I just want fajita salad and a side of guacamole." She stood. "You coming?"

The brunette nodded, brushing a fall of curls out of her eyes. "I'm Joanne. Folks call me Jo."

Of course they did. "Delia."

Seeming steady enough now to at least drive through an intersection, Jo followed in her own car. They waited at the hostess stand for a moment, beneath a string of jalapeno-shaped lights, but the lunch crowd had yet to truly gather steam and they were seated quickly.

Jo unrolled her silverware and promptly blew her nose in the napkin. "I always thought I'd have a big wedding back home, maybe settle down there and raise kids *eventually.* I didn't expect to be pregnant yet! And not even married?"

"If it makes you feel better, I'm single, too."

Jo blinked. "You're alone? But you seem so...so pulled together."

"Thank you. The two conditions aren't mutually exclusive, you know."

Once they'd ordered, Jo shared the story of how, at the tender age of seventeen, she'd fallen for a slightly older "landscape artist" back home—Bobby Calhoun. Apparently the glorified lawn boy had stuck around until Jo graduated high school and was thereby free to come with him without her parents pressing charges—Jo put it more romantically, but Delia had no trouble filling in the blanks. They'd moved to Knoxville for a while, followed by Birmingham, then here less than a year later. His wandering feet had struck again almost immediately; Jo had come home from waitressing a dinner shift a few months ago to a note that bid her farewell, with a postscript that if she didn't pay the cable bill by the fifteenth, it would be shut off.

"I was devastated," Jo said, forlornly dunking a chip into the restaurant's signature green salsa. "And nervous. Bobby takes care of me. We don't have much, but he made more than I did. I've never lived by myself and finding out I was pregnant after he left made me feel *really* alone. I was so excited when he came back!"

Excited? Delia choked on her water. She would have changed the locks on the bastard and thrown his clothes into the streets. What kind of worthless SOB dumped his live-in girlfriend of several years in a note?

"It was a couple of weeks ago," Jo explained. "He

said he wants me back, but…but he doesn't w-want the baby."

"Do *you?*"

"More than anything." The young woman's face momentarily glowed with a madonna-serene light. For the first time there was a wealth of assurance in her expression.

"Then to hell with Bobby!"

"Oh, but—"

"There is no but. As I said earlier, you're better off without him."

"I guess."

Had Delia ever heard a more conspicuous absence of conviction? "The guy dragged you around from place to place, then walked out on you with a cursory note."

"He came back, though."

Oh, well, let's call the Pope and have him canonized. Delia didn't know why she even cared. Jo seemed sweet but terminally naive. Maybe the kid roused some protective, latent maternal instinct, although it was galling to admit that Delia was, just barely, old enough to be Joanne's mother.

"Are you even legally allowed to drink?" she asked suddenly.

"Sure." Jo looked surprised by the question. "But that wouldn't be very good for the baby."

Their food arrived, and eating gave Delia a chance to think about making her point tactfully. Grabbing Jo by the shoulders and rattling her until lingering thoughts of Bobby tumbled out of her head seemed like the wrong way to go. An inner voice that reminded her of Patti insisted Delia be just a tiny bit more compassionate since she knew what it was like to have a hard time eradicating a man from her thoughts.

Yeah, but I'm not bawling about it to total strangers.

In any case, Alexander could hardly be compared to Jo's slimeball ex. Alexander hadn't run from commitment, he'd proposed! While he might storm out temporarily to blow off some steam, he had too much honor to leave a lover without telling her to her face.

Delia gave herself a mental shake. This was not about her. "You say you miss this guy?"

Jo nodded miserably.

"What, precisely, do you miss?" Delia coaxed. The girl seemed young and infatuated, not stupid. If Bobby treated her as callously as Delia suspected, it should be possible to get Jo to see it in hindsight.

"Lots of things," Jo chirped like the steadfast and loyal girlfriend she'd no doubt been. "He has a real nice singing voice. And I really miss how…" She trailed off, blushing.

I hear you on that one. "Besides that," Delia said impatiently.

"He took care of me," Jo said mulishly.

"You can learn to take care of yourself," Delia insisted just as mulishly. "And you will be a better *mother* for it."

"You really think so?"

"Yes."

The younger girl expelled a breath. "You want to know the truth? I think so, too. After he said he didn't want our baby, I found a one-bedroom place of my own. It's hardly the size of a closet, but it's in a cheap building that a lot of off-campus college kids live in. I can afford it as long as I take quick showers and grocery shop with coupons. Even so, I know if Bobby showed up there tomorrow, my willpower... You're obviously a very strong woman. I hope I'm like you when I get older."

Watch it, junior.

"I'm not proud to admit it," Jo said, "but when he told me it was either him or the baby, I, well, for a moment, I...considered it. Considered whether or not I'm cut out to be a single mom. I barely make enough in tips and wages to support me, much less a kid. I only have basic health insurance because I qualified for this special program. I'll bet you have a great job with a decent salary and benefits."

"That's because I focused! Sure, I've enjoyed and cared about men in my life, but I didn't let one slow me down. You can do that, Jo. Focus on the life you want to create for you and your baby, and don't let anyone else get in your way."

"It sounds good now, when I don't have rent due for another week and Bobby's not standing in front of me with those big blue eyes." She fidgeted in her seat. "I worry that I'd take him back. It wouldn't be the first time."

"You mean, other than when he came back and found out you were pregnant? How many times has he left you?"

"Not 'left,' exactly. More like took off with some drinking buddies for a weekend or two without telling me first. Scared me half to death worrying about him. And we had a fight once when I told him he either had to marry me proper or give me the bus fare to go home. He was gone over a week, but he came back real sorry, with flowers and everything. He told me that if he proposed then, we'd both feel like it was just because of the ultimatum and it wouldn't be as special."

Lord, help me. Delia pinched the bridge of her nose. "Trust me, *not* being married to this guy is one of the most positive things you have going for you right now. I'll give you my phone number, and if he darkens your doorstep again, you call me. You can borrow my willpower."

"Seriously?" Jo beamed at her. "You'd do that for me? This is like having my very own fairy godmother."

What this kid needed was a bibbidi-bobbidi reality check. "More like an AA sponsor. I'm trying to help you kick a bad habit, not send you to the ball." Although now that she thought about it... "How far in advance do you know your waitressing schedule? If you're not working the first Saturday in October,

I might—*might*—know of a way you can earn a few extra dollars."

Jo let out a squeal of delight. Thank God there was a table between them. Otherwise Delia suspected she'd be on the receiving end of a hug.

Patti had managed to stop laughing outright, but her shoulders were still shaking with mirth. "Run this by me again. Start with the part where you randomly befriend a sobbing twenty-two-year-old who is now planning to name her child Delia."

"I'm sure that was just a momentary expression of gratitude," Delia said, sure of no such thing. "She's not actually going to name her kid after me. If you get her hooked up for a job at this fund-raiser, she'll probably decide that Patricia is a *much* better name. If she even has a girl."

Patti sat back, looking annoyingly comfortable in Alexander's recliner. He was supposed to pick it up tomorrow, and Delia had avoided sitting in it except for a best-forgotten incident at two in the morning when she'd been unable to sleep and had come downstairs to curl up in the chair, which still smelled faintly like its owner. So much for her willpower of steel.

"I don't get it," Patti said. "Why are we helping this girl? I mean, I'm all in favor of assisting a young single mother, but…"

"You're always doing community service of one sort or another! I can do good, too."

"Your good normally comes in the form of generous donations, not buying strangers lunch and trying to talk me into hiring them as extra waitstaff for the night."

"Never mind, forget it. I warned her it was just a distant possibility, anyway."

"Don't be ridiculous. I'm sure I can swing it. But you have to admit this is out of character for you."

"Nonsense. I've always had strong opinions about women being independent, and I'm putting those feelings into action by helping Jo embrace her own independence. Now, can we please change the subject?"

"All right. How did it go with your parents?" When Delia had called Patti yesterday to ask her to come over tonight, they'd been interrupted when Delia's father had called, returning her message.

"It was fine." Delia forced a shrug. "I told them I was going to have a baby, they said congratulations, that's wonderful. I asked if they're doing well. Apparently they've enjoyed their first real cold snap of the season. All very tidy and civilized."

Her mother had rhapsodized about the special calling of motherhood, making it sound as if Delia had decided to join a sacred sorority instead of the less-glamorous truth—that she'd peed on a stick one morning and been dumbstruck by the results. "You were such a sweet, beautiful baby," Chelsea had said. Then she'd paused, the small silence making it clear that she wondered what the hell had happened.

"You'll love being a mom. But, sweetheart, I don't understand why you're not marrying the father."

"If he's not offering to do the right thing," Garrett Carlisle had put in from another extension, "maybe I should have a man-to-man chat with him."

If Delia owned a voodoo doll in the likeness of her father, she would have chosen that moment to stick a big ol' pin in his butt. How dare Garrett sound so self-righteous, as if he were an exemplary father or shining example of familial responsibility?

"Alexander *is* doing the right thing," she'd argued, struck by her vehement defense of him. "He's assured me that he'll be beside me for whatever I need, including financial assistance and hand-holding for the amnio. But we're not getting married because it wouldn't be for the right reasons."

"What on earth are you talking about?" Chelsea had demanded. "You're going to be a family. What could be a better reason than that?"

After all these years, could Chelsea really still believe that it was a ceremony and signed certificates that made a family?

If Patti noticed the way Delia's lip was curling, she didn't comment on it. "You said Alexander's family already knows? Are they planning to come down and meet you, or just wait until the baby's born?"

"Honestly, I don't know." For the first few days Delia had been too numb to call Patti or Kate and share the news; then she'd decided she would make the announcement that he'd left as casually as she'd told them he was moving in. That seemed fitting. Maybe if she didn't make a big deal of it, neither would they. "I wouldn't be surprised if they come to see Alexander's new place once he's settled."

"His new place? *What?*"

Not a big deal, not a big deal. "We decided a couple of days ago that it was probably best for him to start looking. This was never meant to be a permanent living arrangement. You knew that."

"Yes, but... He left now, in the middle of your pregnancy? And you didn't even tell me?"

"It just happened." More or less. She pointed at the recliner. "He hasn't even come to get his stuff for storage yet. He'll still be involved, of course. He's going with me to the amnio in a few weeks. We parted amicably, like adults." No bitter insult-hurling or tearful arguments over who got to keep what CD, no dragging innocent bystanders into their split. Patti and Kate and all their country club acquaintances could remain on the same friendly basis with Alexander as always with no hard feelings from Delia.

Patti peered at her with the same expression Leo must see whenever he tried to sneak in past curfew. "You sound awfully nonchalant."

"No point in melodrama."

"If it's all so amicable and adult, why did you wait to mention it? You could have told me yesterday on the phone or anytime during the past hour! And why did he have to move out to start looking for a place?

He could have done that here. You're a real estate agent, for crying out loud."

"I specialize in commercial properties, not residential."

"Oh, like you don't know people in the business? Where is he even staying?"

"Some efficiency suites near his office."

"You threw him out, didn't you?" Patti asked.

"No!" Not exactly. "I told you, we mutually concluded—"

"Yeah, yeah. It was all very amicable and adult. Just like the conversation with the parents you barely acknowledge was tidy and civilized. I got it. I'm just not buying it. What did Kate say when you told her?"

"I didn't bother her with this. She sounded pretty harried last time I spoke to her." Now that PJ and Neve were in school, Kate was facing new complications, such as being a soccer mom and having her stepdaughter called into the principal's office. When Paul got out of federal prison camp, he'd be lucky if Kate still wanted to be married to him.

"Ah." For merely a single syllable, it was infuriatingly knowing.

"Ah?" Delia echoed mockingly.

"Your new fairy goddaughter makes more sense now. Parting ways with Alexander becomes a moral lesson, not an act of cowardice."

"Excuse me?" Delia lurched to her feet. "I don't think you know what the hell you're talking about."

"Sure I do," Patti said with a weary smile, not

acknowledging Delia's temper. "Except most of my acts of cowardice are *not* acting at all. I'll go before I irritate you any further. Give me a day to talk to the people at the club, and I'll get Joanne added for the night."

"Thank you," Delia said. Patti obviously didn't approve of Delia's choices—what else was new?—but that wasn't stopping her from being a good friend.

Watching out the window as Patti climbed into her car, Delia had a sudden stroke of inspiration, recalling her friend's tentative interest in going back to school. When Delia called Jo tomorrow with the news, she'd ask the young woman to pick up some course catalogs on the college campus she lived near. Maybe Patti could benefit from an interceding fairy godmother, too.

If Delia couldn't actually send anyone to the ball, she could at least show her fellow women where the glass slippers were kept and encourage them to help themselves.

Chapter 10

*Be proactive, but recognize that some matters—
some people—just can't be changed.*

There'd been a time not too long ago when Delia had
enjoyed late dinners and set reservations for eight
o'clock. This week, however, eight was sounding
more and more like bedtime. Which was why, when
her phone rang at nine-thirty, hours after Patti left,
she had to grope for the receiver with one hand while
prying her eyes open with the other.

"Hello?"

After a hesitant silence, a delicate Southern voice
ventured, "Delia?"

Delia sat up, turning on the lamp. "Hey, Jo. Everything all right?"

"Probably, I'm overreacting. But Alice, the other waitress I work with, thinks I should give Bobby another chance. So she helpfully gave him my phone number at the new apartment, and he called me earlier from some bar he was at with the guys."

"Alice is crazy. Ignore her misbegotten advice and hang up on Bobby next time he calls you."

"I stuck to my guns," Jo said, pride lacing her tremulous words, "and told him it was over."

"Good for you!"

"I'm not sure he was listening, though. It was loud there, and he'd definitely been drinking. The last thing he said before hanging up was that we should talk about it in person."

"Absolutely not!"

"Well, that's what I said, too, more or less, but he'd already hung up. Just once it would be nice if those idiot friends of his would stop him from driving after he's had a few beers."

"Don't let him in!" Delia was already out of bed and wrestling on a pair of sweatpants. She could just envision this sad sack on Jo's welcome mat, whining through the door that if she was going to break his heart, could he at least get a cup of coffee to help him sober up before he drove home? "Tell him to go away, and if he doesn't, call the police."

Jo balked. "I can't do that. He's not a psycho, he's the father of my kid. He's never actually hurt me, not really, but…when he's been drinking, it doesn't take much for him to turn ugly."

Instead of asking for clarification on what exactly

Jo meant by *ugly,* Delia confirmed the location of Jo's small apartment building and riffled through the nightstand drawer for something to jot her unit number on. The first piece of paper she encountered was the business card Alexander had given her with his own suite number on it. She clenched it involuntarily and was rewarded with a paper cut. With effort, she managed not to swear.

"I'm on my way," Delia said. "And I'm bringing reinforcements." She hoped.

"I'm sure I'm overreacting," Jo reiterated, but the relief in her voice was palpable.

After they disconnected, Delia didn't waste time by calling Alexander from her bedroom phone. Once she was in her car, she reached for her cell. Before the pregnancy, Delia would have gone to confront this Bobby fellow with reasonable certainty that she could reduce him to tears with her razor wit. Bullies like him, lulled into a false sense of superiority by accommodating girls like Jo, were no match for Delia.

On the other hand, Delia hadn't made it all the way through her first trimester only to risk some stupid hallway scuffle with a beer-brained Neanderthal. So even though she—to borrow Jo's refrain—was probably overreacting, she dialed Alexander's number.

"Hello?" He sounded alert, so he must not have been sleeping yet.

Her heart did a slow, stupid somersault that she decided to pretend was indigestion. "It's me. I hate to bother you, and I don't have a lot of time to explain, but can you meet me near the university? There's this single mom-to-be, whose ex is having difficulty accepting their breakup. She's scared. I'm going to give her moral support, but it might not hurt to have some muscle on hand. Or at least the threat of it."

"Give me the directions." His willingness to help was immediate. Whatever he felt about Delia right now, he wasn't so petty that he'd refuse to assist a frightened pregnant woman.

"Thank you," Delia said. "I really did hate to bother you."

"Yeah. I know how it galls you to admit you might not be able to handle something on your own, but I can take it from here. Why don't you go home and rest, and I'll call you afterward? There's no reason for you to be out late and adding to your stress level."

"I don't get stressed over losers like this guy." She guiltily pushed away thoughts of her recently elevated blood pressure.

"I've got it covered," Alexander insisted. "You wouldn't have called me for 'muscle' if you didn't think… I don't want you putting our child in danger."

She gritted her teeth. It wasn't as though she were a dim-witted character in a bad horror flick, who was about to take on the chain-saw-wielding bad guy with nothing but an emery board. If she were that stupid, she wouldn't have contacted Alexander in the first place. But what kind of positive, yes-you-*can*-survive-without-a-man message would she be sending to Jo if Delia herself stayed at home and called a man to do the favor for her?

"I'll meet you there," she said decisively.

She hung up, then watched her phone warily. It wouldn't have surprised her if he called back immediately with a bilingual vitriol. When her cell didn't ring, she concluded that Alexander was too busy getting out the door to Jo's.

The apartment building was a three-story block of cement that had a vaguely institutional look about it. In the lot sat a hodgepodge of vehicles ranging from cars that looked older than her, probably held together with duct tape and running on fumes, to modest but roadworthy economic four-doors and hand-me-down luxury sedans that doting parents had likely passed to their college-aged children when it was time to upgrade. Like most of the dorms that were only a few streets over, the building had a main front entrance. Jo had said that the place was too cheap for sophisticated security. After midnight, you needed your resident's key to open the front door, but until then, anyone could enter. Delia did so, wondering if Bobby were already here or if he'd wisely chosen to sleep it off in the comfort of his own home.

The Ballad of Bobby and Jo… Damn, when had her life intersected with a bad country song? Well, Jo's life was about to turn a bit more hip-hop, with her demanding respect and putting the hurt on the man if he didn't leave her alone.

With only three floors, the builder hadn't bothered with elevators, and Delia was chagrined to realize she was breathing heavy by the last set of steps. *Jo couldn't have lived on the ground floor?* The poor kid had to do this every day. Wouldn't that be fun in the last trimester? How did she get groceries up here? And how was she going to unload the car when she had not only bags of food, but a case of diapers and the infant who would be wearing them?

Shame tweaked Delia's gut. It was one thing for her to ceremoniously declare that being a single mother just took determination, but *she* had a good job, a nice town house and a small but reliable support network. If Delia didn't allow herself to get close to dozens of people, at least she knew that Patti and Kate were there for whatever she needed. Even Alexander, if something seriously urgent arose.

If this phone-number-dispensing waitress Alice was any indication of the kinds of friends Jo had made since moving here… From now on Delia would try harder to remember that every single mom faced her own unique situational challenges.

As she pushed open the stairwell door, Delia heard voices. She instinctively turned toward them. Dressed in jeans, a black T-shirt and boots, a young man who would have been quite good-looking if not for his petulant sneer stood outside apartment 302C. Delia couldn't make out all of his words—he seemed to be speaking in more of a growl than a yell—but she knew with dead certainty that this was Bobby.

The door to the apartment was open only as far as the safety chain would allow, and Delia mentally congratulated her young friend on taking at least that precautionary measure.

Also in view was a dark-haired unremarkable man in khaki slacks and an orange polo shirt that made him look jaundiced. He appeared to be a neighbor trying to convince Bobby that now wasn't a good time for Jo to talk, which Delia respected, considering that Bobby looked as if he could pick his teeth with the shorter guy.

"Hey," she called out. "Is there a problem here?"

"Delia!" Jo's voice from the other side of the door was filled with gratitude.

Bobby spun around. "You must be the broad that's been filling her head with weird ideas."

"You mean, crazy stuff like self-respect and equal rights?" Delia drawled. Probably there had been a less incendiary response, but hey, she'd left off the *asshole* at the end of the sentence.

The shorter, dark-haired guy circled wide, nearly putting himself between Bobby and Delia, but still not getting any closer to the obnoxious loudmouth than the dimensions of the corridor absolutely dictated. Behind her, the stairwell door banged open, and Delia saw the short man's eyes go wide. Alexander. She'd bet a year's worth of commissions on it. Gratified by the sudden alarm in Bobby's expression, she smiled grimly.

But the blond man quelled his obvious surprise, looking ready to spit. "Damn, it's like Grand Central up here. Don't you people have lives?"

"They're my friends," Jo said from behind her apartment door. "Don't be mean to them."

He turned back toward her, momentarily swapping the sneer for an earnest, imploring expression.

"I didn't come here to be mean to anyone. You know that, Junebug. I want a second chance."

"Sh-she's already told you t-twice that it's over," the other man stammered. Poor guy. He'd be a more convincing knight-errant if he didn't look ready to throw up from sheer nerves.

Before Bobby could say anything cutting in response, Alexander was there, standing between the two men, his voice so silky-soft Delia had to strain her ears to hear what was being said a mere few feet away.

"Gentlemen, we seem to have a disagreement in need of solving. Let's review the facts and see if we can reach a mutually favorable decision." He met Bobby's gaze. "You live here?"

"My girlfriend does," he said belligerently.

"She's *not* his g-girl," the other man objected.

At the same time Jo called through the door, "It's over, Bobby. That was your decision, remember? You didn't want our baby!"

Delia ground her teeth. It was nice Jo was making the effort, but she shouldn't have given him ownership of the decision, or the chance to try to reverse it by insisting he'd changed his mind about being a father. Glancing back at him, she shuddered at the very idea. This flinty-eyed man with his bloodshot eyes and curled fist at his side would make her own father look like Daddy of the Year twice over.

Delia sidled beyond the men until she was standing directly in front of Jo's door. "Let me in."

With obviously shaking hands, Jo managed to get the safety chain unlatched after two tries. "Thank you so much for coming. I don't know what I would have done—"

"You had it under control. Locked door, telling him to get lost." It was important the girl learned to watch out for herself. "However, as long as we're on the subject, once you've told him that the discussion's over, shut the door. That's the best way to make your point."

Jo nodded, looking so earnest Delia expected her to whip out a legal pad and start taking notes. Delia glanced back out into the hall, where Alexander clearly had the situation under control.

Jo followed her gaze, melting in a sigh. "Nice reinforcement."

"*My* ex." Was that a note of pride she heard? Delia couldn't help it.

"You let *him* go? That sounds like something stupid *I'd* do. Never mind, it's late, and I don't know what I'm saying," Jo said hastily.

Humph. Insulting the fairy godmother was grounds for getting yourself turned into a pumpkin, in Delia's opinion. "Who's the other guy?"

"Len. He lives two doors down and is getting his MBA. Works at a university library part-time and has a second part-time job with some kids' after-school program, too. He heard Bobby making a fuss in the hall. Len's sweet. I almost went out there because I was afraid Bobby would pop him in the nose."

"You let Len take care of Len—he's not pregnant."

With a nod to Alexander, Len turned toward his own apartment. The other two men came to Jo's door.

Alexander nudged Bobby like a cop who was prompting a drug dealer's confession.

"Sorry for the trouble," Bobby mumbled. "But you know I only came by because I—"

"Not interested," Alexander said flatly. "Tell the lady goodbye and that you won't be disturbing her again."

He darted Alexander a murderous look, but the older man had about four inches and thirty well-muscled pounds on him. Not to mention, Alexander's reflexes weren't dulled by pitchers of whatever on-special beer Bobby smelled of.

"Goodbye, Joanne," Bobby said.

"Keep in mind that she has friends," Alexander said congenially. "And witnesses. If you have any future thoughts about reconciliation, I suggest you ignore them."

"She ain't worth it, anyway."

Alexander took a menacing step forward, not laying a hand on Bobby, but certainly giving the appearance that he could throw him out the window at the end of the hallway without much effort or disturbance to his conscience.

In possibly his first smart move of the evening, Bobby took that as his cue to get the hell out of there. If his pace fell short of a run, it was still double the average amble.

"Oh, thank you so much!" Jo stared up at Alexander as though he were the Second Coming. "Thank you, thank you, thank you."

Gone was the menace in his expression; when he

looked at the young mother-to-be, his face shone pure Mediterranean charm. "It was my pleasure to be of assistance. In fact, if you like, I'll give you my direct number. I can be here again in a heartbeat if he bothers you further."

Delia shot him a glare he pretended not to notice. As gallant as his offer sounded, she knew what he'd just done...tried to manipulate it so that Jo went straight to him and Delia would be left safe at home next time.

But Jo surprised them both, squaring her shoulders and settling her hands in a proprietary fashion over her swollen stomach. "That's a generous offer, but it won't be necessary. If he's stupid enough to bother me again, I'm taking Delia's advice and calling the police. I think I have the problem under control."

Hallelujah! Maybe naiveté wasn't terminal, after all.

They all said good-night, Jo continuing her outpouring of gratitude, especially when she told Delia she'd see her at the heart-disease benefit.

"Not that I'll be chatting with you," Jo added. "I know better than to stand around talking instead of doing my job. I won't let you or Mrs. Jordan down!"

Alexander hid his smile until they were safely in the stairwell. "Sweet kid. Where on earth did you find her?"

She'd already tried to make her sudden interest in looking out for someone she barely knew sound totally normal once. She didn't think she could sell it to Alexander, especially at this hour of night.

In a flash, Delia recalled what she was wearing. When she'd received Jo's phone call, she'd jumped out of bed without bothering to brush her hair or slap on lip gloss. It shouldn't matter—he'd seen her look worse—but now that they'd separated… She could go to extra effort tomorrow, before he came to get his stuff, but she'd hate for him to know it was for his sake.

"Thank you," she said when they'd nearly reached the lobby, "for coming over to help."

"Thank you for calling." He sent her a reproving, sidelong glance. "Although I didn't appreciate your hanging up on me."

"I figured."

"And I still don't think there was any reason for you to potentially endanger yourself. But," he added before she could say anything, "you didn't have to call me in the first place, so at least that's something. Never a dull moment with you, is there?"

The ups and downs of the night had exhausted her, and she barely had enough energy to unlock her car door. "Nope."

His words were caught by the breeze as she closed her door, but she thought he'd said, "I'm going to miss that."

Whether the words were true or not, they warmed her the entire ride home.

Chapter 11

Sometimes it seems like the real miracle of life is that a man and woman were able to get along well enough to make a baby in the first place.

Delia had attended dozens of country club events in the past, yet she hadn't fully realized how tedious they could become if you weren't allowed to enjoy the cocktails. *It's not the booze you miss, it's Alexander.* He usually attended these things with her, making droll comments in her ear. Even when they went their separate ways to mingle, they'd occasionally glance up and find each other. He'd made her pulse race with anticipation more than once when she'd looked across the room and seen in his expression exactly what he planned to do with her when they got home.

Her home, she reminded herself. It had always been a temporary stop for him, and she'd come alone to plenty of social functions in her life and had had a wonderful time. She didn't need anyone to entertain her.

"Delia, you're here!" Patti had been off to the side speaking with the caterer when Delia checked in at the registration table to hand over her ticket and get her number for the ongoing silent auction. "You look amazing."

"Thank you." Delia returned her friend's smile. "You look nice yourself. If George has any sense, he'll try to sneak you out on the terrace for a few minutes alone."

Patti wrinkled her nose. "He's running late. His flight from Boston didn't take off on schedule, but he said he'd be here before dinner begins."

First came the mingling portion of the evening in the anterior corridor. The soft lighting provided by candles and dimmed chandeliers accented the elegant decorations, from the flower arrangements to the ice sculptures in the middle of the appetizer table. Cash bars were set up at either end of the hallway, and Delia envied those in line.

"Patti, you've done a fabulous job, honestly, but…I already feel like I've been here for hours. Gretchen Swanson cornered me when I first walked in."

Patti made a sympathetic face. "Her prizewinning shih tzu is expecting a litter."

"Yeah. I now know wa-aay more than I wanted to

about her breeding program. That woman actually asked when I was expecting to birth my 'little pup.'"

A horrified laugh came out of Patti, although she rather unconvincingly tried to make it a cough.

Delia narrowed her eyes at the memory of Gretchen's words. "Was that her way of implying I'm a bitch?"

"Who's a bitch?" Kate asked from behind them. When Delia turned to greet her, the brunette's eyes widened. "Whoa. This is the first time I've seen you look *pregnant*. Honest-to-goodness with child."

"It's the maternity dress," Delia said. She'd splurged on a silk dress she'd probably never wear again, but she didn't regret a penny.

The round neckline enhanced her cleavage without being tacky—thanks to her second trimester, she had the fully firm breasts of a perky twentysomething—and the material fell over her rounded abdomen in a snug but somehow very flattering way. It was an elegant, feminine statement with a silhouette that made it very clear that, yes, she was pregnant without anyone having to ask or speculate. *"Did you notice Delia looked chubby?"* *"Yeah...you think that's why Alexander left her?"*

"Dee?" Kate asked softly. "Are you all right?"

Delia snapped herself out of it, realizing that Patti's expression was pinched with concern, too. "Of course."

The other two women exchanged glances.

"What?" Delia asked. "I just spaced out for a minute."

"All right," Kate said. "But you know we're here if you ever want to talk."

It was then that Delia turned her head a fraction of an inch to the left and realized that her friends had spotted Alexander in the crowd. She hadn't been entirely sure whether he'd come tonight or not.

"I put him at a table close to ours," Patti murmured, "so that he's not so far away it looks like you're avoiding each other, but he won't be sitting with you, either."

Delia couldn't help smiling as she imagined the time and thought Patti had put into the decision. "Thanks, but I really am fine. Kate's going to be my date tonight, right?" The convict's wife and the knocked-up spinster. They'd be the most colorful couple of the evening.

Patti laughed. "I'll see the two of you at dinner, then. There are a couple of auction problems I need to make sure were straightened out, and if I can find a quiet alcove, I want to call Leo. I'm a nervous wreck now that he has a driver's license! He'll roll his eyes when I call, but he was going to a party tonight, and I need to know he got there safe."

As Patti flitted off, Delia turned to Kate. "Where are your rug rats tonight?"

"PJ's with his aunt," Kate said easily, her tone not as strained as it used to be whenever she mentioned her husband's sister-in-law. "And Neve's at one of her friends', watching rented movies. I gotta say, part of me wishes I were there instead."

"I know what you— Oh, Lord. Chastity Dillinger

is coming this way." One of the club's most notorious gossips, Chastity no doubt had questions and sly comments for both of them.

"Our chances are better if we split up," Kate said from the side of her mouth.

Delia would have enjoyed talking to her friend for more than just the few minutes they'd had to say hello, but she agreed with Kate's assessment. As Kate went in one direction, making a beeline for the appetizers, Delia went the other, ducking into the ladies' lounge. When she emerged, she ran into Hazel Watts, a very successful residential real estate agent in her fifties and someone Delia genuinely liked.

Three minutes into their conversation, however, Delia was reevaluating her opinion. As soon as Hazel had ascertained that Delia was pregnant and wished her congratulations, she'd reached out and put a hand on Delia's tummy. Outside of certain sexual situations that did *not* include Hazel, Delia wasn't a particularly touchy-feely person. Yet people didn't seem to notice her subtle hands-off vibe. Tawny Miller patted her stomach, too, and Delia gave Tawny's husband the Glare of Death when he seemed to be considering doing the same.

"Oh," Delia said suddenly, sidestepping the Millers. "I see someone over there I've been meaning to talk to all night." It was a blatant lie, but once she'd walked away, she *did* spot someone she knew replenishing a stack of cocktail napkins on one of the tables.

Jo, wearing a man's white shirt with black pants and an oversize vest, was thrilled to see her. Even her curly ponytail bounced in greeting. "Delia! Isn't this place gorgeous? I helped cater a wedding once, but it was at a fixed-up barn, nothing like this."

Delia could appreciate Jo's nonjaded point of view even if she herself would rather be at home with her feet up right now.

"I saw your…Mr. Alexander," Jo concluded uncomfortably, looking as though she were sorry she'd brought up the subject.

Delia smiled, thinking that the other girl made him sound like a hairdresser. "Yes, I noticed him in the crowd."

"He was real sweet. Said hello and asked if I was having any more trouble with Bobby. Asked how I was doing and listened while I gushed on about what it was like to feel the baby move."

"Speaking of babies." Delia leaned in closer. "Does everyone try to touch your stomach? I'm ready to sock the next person who gropes mine." Really, what the hell was that about? Were people rubbing her for luck?

"Hi." Shauna Adair's voice was friendly but surprised. "I didn't realize the two of you knew each other."

Delia turned and smiled at her doctor. "Met at your office, actually."

"Hi, Dr. Adair. You look pretty tonight. I should get back to work, though," Jo said a touch guiltily.

Delia shook her head as Jo wound her way through the crowd. "She's sweet, but damn, she hardly seems more than a kid herself."

"You wouldn't believe how young some of the expectant mothers I treat are," Shauna said. "I think obstetrics is one of the most joyous medical fields, but some of the stuff I see? Heartbreaking."

Since Delia could well imagine—and didn't particularly want to—she changed the subject. "Can I buy you a drink, Doc?"

"Unfortunately, no. I'm on call tonight." Her eyes crinkled at the corners as she smiled. "I was just telling Alexander the same thing when he offered. I think he was hoping I'd stick around for a few more minutes so he could pump me for information about you."

"He asked about me?" Delia wasn't proud of the giddy rush that news gave her, but there it was.

"Yeah, but I don't talk about my patients. I did, however, point out that you were only a few yards away and that he could come talk to you himself." She paused. "I didn't think the two of you had the kind of breakup where you avoided each other when you were in the same room."

"It's not that we're on hostile terms. This is just the first time we've been together separately, socially." She'd sympathized with Kate earlier, being here without Paul, but at least she wasn't walking around with a polite smile pasted on her face, afraid that she would bump into him the next time she turned around and not know what to say.

Delia blinked. What was she doing *envying* the woman whose husband was in prison? Ridiculous. Delia had broken up with her share of men before and managed to interact with them cordially in public. Of course, she'd never been with a man as long as Alexander, but she had the fanciful thought that he would have left an indelible impression on her even if they'd been together a matter of nights rather than months.

Other acquaintances hailed the doctor, and Delia realized that she needed the ladies' restroom. Again.

As she walked back in that direction, her thoughts returned to Kate. She had been forcibly separated from her husband, with no choice in the matter. Suddenly it seemed selfish somehow that Delia had simply walked away from her own lover instead of trying harder to...to what? Pretend she wanted a life that had never before appealed to her? Honestly, the pregnancy hormones were clouding her brain. If she believed it was poor logic for couples who tried to stay together for "the sake of the child," whether born yet or still in utero, it was far crazier to consider staying with someone on behalf of your married friend.

The closest Delia had come to Alexander all night was when she walked out of the ladies' room and there he was, with Celeste Parker shoving her very expensive, very silicone boobs under his nose. Delia shouldn't have been surprised; Alexander's moviestar looks and generous income had been attractive even when he was with Delia. Now that he was single, they'd swarm him. But even though she hadn't been able to get past the flirting females to say hello, Delia had been aware of him all evening. Suddenly, like an animal scenting something on the wind, he lifted his head and peered directly at her.

She dropped her gaze, but it was too late to pretend she hadn't been watching him. Pivoting, she went the other way and asked herself what in the hell had happened to her. She'd never been the type to retreat. At the very least, she slowed her steps so she wouldn't give the appearance of rushing away.

Maybe if she *had* rushed, his hand wouldn't have closed over the top of her shoulder a moment later.

"Delia." His voice was as thick and sweet as honey. "If I didn't know better, I'd swear you were avoiding me."

"Not at all," she said brightly, turning toward him. "I was just thirsty."

"How fortuitous. I was thinking that I could use a drink. I'll walk with you."

But neither of them moved. His gaze swept over her, unmistakably appreciative. And possessive. Without a word, he reached out and briefly pressed his palm over the smooth silk covering her stomach. The sensation that shot through her was completely different from the urge she'd had to slap away everyone else who'd touched her. If Alexander hadn't moved his hand away, she might have unconsciously arched into it, wanting to share what they'd created.

"You weren't at the town house the other night." He made it sound like a reprimand.

"Didn't you get the voice mail I left you?" She'd worked late. Although her boss was completely understanding about time off for doctors' appointments, Delia tried to take advantage of her occasional bursts of energy during this easier trimester to catch up after feeling sick and sluggish for several months. "I really wasn't avoiding you." Much.

"I did get the message, but I was hoping to see you." On the heels of that endearing admission, he qualified, "I need to ask you a favor."

To cover her disappointment, she teased, "What, bearing your child isn't enough?"

He flashed a cursory grin. "Until now, my mother has managed to summon all her children home for Thanksgiving and Christmas. But apparently some of my sisters' in-laws are beginning to make noises about feeling neglected. This year, Marie and Blanche are going to be with their husbands' families for Thanksgiving. So my mother has decided to come with my youngest sister, Angie, and her husband, Dennis, to visit me—"

"No." Panic rose, tasting like bile in her throat. She knew she'd have to meet them eventually, but something about being together for a holiday... It felt like a cozy lie, a Norman Rockwell painting in which she didn't belong.

"You didn't even let me finish."

"Were you going to ask me to have Thanksgiving dinner with you and your family?"

He nodded.

"Then no."

He stared her down but said nothing. Not reminding her that he'd been there in the middle of the night for a woman he'd never even met simply because Delia had asked, or that he would rearrange his work schedule to be there to hold her hand during the amnio procedure even though Delia refused to love him the way he said he loved her. It was all there in his gaze as he folded his arms across his chest.

Damn it. This was why she hated owing people favors. "I don't even have holiday dinners with *my* family," she reminded him. After college, she'd found excuses to avoid her mother's invitations until the woman got a clue and stopped issuing them.

"Right, you never make big plans for the holidays," Alexander said. "So you should be free to eat with us, then."

"Does this mean you've found a place already, or were you planning on having everyone over in your efficiency suite?" *Please don't ask me to have it at the town house.* That went beyond a mere lie into the Twilight Zone. Her, host the Thanksgiving meal?

"I haven't worked out the logistics yet," he admitted, his expression boyishly sheepish now.

Around them, there was a clamor of activity as the ballroom doors opened and Patti made the informal announcement that dinner would be served.

Delia cast her gaze toward the ballroom as though it were her own personal salvation. "I really need to get off my feet," she said. "Plus, I'm starving. We can…talk about the other thing later."

"And when exactly are you hoping to postpone that conversation until?" Despite his obvious disappointment in her, there was now some humor in his dark eyes. "The thirty-first of never?"

"If that works for your schedule," she said pertly.

"Delia—"

"I know! Just let me think about it, all right?"

"All right." They blended into the throng and he graciously dropped back, falling away from her without the awkwardness of parting words.

She found the round table she'd been assigned to, but so far the only person seated there was George, wearing a tired expression and a crooked tie with his navy blazer.

"Hi," he told her. "I don't suppose you've seen my wife?"

"Several times. She's been busy running the show. She has a gift for organization and leadership, you know." When he nodded absently, she decided to press her point. "Sometimes I think she's cut out to do more, that her talents are wasted as a mere housewife."

That got his attention. "Are you calling the time and effort she's put into managing our home and raising our son a waste?" he asked incredulously.

"Of course not!" Well, she had been actually, but it sounded bad the way he said it. "I just meant... Whatever I meant, it was intended as a compliment."

Unfortunately he wasn't mollified by this and still wore a cranky expression on his face when Patti herself joined them.

"There you are," she said as she neared her husband. "Finally!"

"Yeah." He ran a hand through his thinning hair. "After sitting at the Boston airport, then waiting on the tarmac for longer than the duration of the actual flight, then fighting traffic, I'm *finally* here."

Patti pursed her lips. "Well, I'm sorry to put you to all that trouble."

As two other couples took their seats at the table, Delia caught Patti's eye. "Where's Kate?" Delia had seen her only once after their initial greetings, and that had been just for a few seconds in, naturally, the women's restroom.

Scooting her chair closer to Delia, Patti confided, "There was a problem with her stepdaughter!"

"Neve?" The girl had been at a friend's watching movies. "Did she get sick or something?"

"You know how I called Leo to check in on him? God, I don't know how parents maintained their sanity before cell phones... Anyway, he saw Neve at the party he went to. Leaving with another high school boy!"

Delia blinked. It sounded like something she would have done at Neve's age. Poor Kate. "Was Leo sure? Maybe it just looked like her."

"Well, when Kate called the house where Neve was *supposed* to be, she wasn't there, so..."

"Yikes." Because everything she'd been reading lately was so focused on the care and feeding of babies, Delia had mostly been having minor anxiety attacks over stuff like whether it would be a disadvantage that her child was formula-fed instead of nursed. She tried not to think at all about the stuff that lay beyond that, such as learning to drive and dating.

During the appetizer, Delia realized she was the odd woman out amid three couples. By the time the main course was brought out, she'd concluded that her companions were an unintentional Public Service Announcement for being single. The youngest people at the table were a CPA in his early thirties and his even younger girlfriend, who'd clearly imbibed too much tonight. She tittered at everything that was said, oblivious to her boyfriend's disapproval, and gestured so expansively she nearly stabbed George with her salad fork. Across the table were the Albrights. Mr. Albright was making flirtatious conversation, heavy on the *flirt,* with the drunken woman, and Mrs. Albright looked as if she were considering the benefits of becoming a widow.

Patti clearly sided with Mrs. Albright, shooting the woman's husband a fulminating glare, before mouthing at George, "Do something!"

He mouthed back, looking equally irate, "Like what?"

Delia wondered if it was still considered eavesdropping when you were reading lips.

"So," Patti chirped, "how's your daughter enjoying college, Margaret?"

Margaret Albright could talk about her children even longer than Gretchen Swanson could about her prized pooches, so Delia had high hopes for this conversational gambit.

Mr. Albright, however, snorted derisively. "She'd *better* be enjoying it, considering what we're paying! The tuition costs and living expenses I understand, even if I think what the school charges is robbery, but have you priced a textbook lately?"

George slanted a glance at his wife. Even though

he didn't say or even mouth anything about Patti's pondering a late-life degree, the telepathic *See? I told you* was written all over his face. Delia wanted to throw her chicken Kiev at the man.

But Patti found her own means of retaliation. "You know, with Leo's tuition coming up in just a few years, maybe I should think more about how I could raise a little extra cash to help."

George paused, a forkful of food halfway to his mouth, and flushed a deeply embarrassed red. "You don't need to do that, honey. I've got it covered."

He probably meant that in a reassuring way, that he was doing his job as a good provider and that Patti needn't worry her pretty little head. But *why* did men have such trouble accepting that women had their own separate lives and needs? Patti was more than just Mrs. George Jordan.

Patti ignored him, beaming in Delia's direction. "Sherry Montgomery has become an independent distributor for a company that makes really great kitchen supplies. She had me over for one of her 'parties' and said she's made a tidy part-time salary with it, plus she's up on all the latest baking equipment. And there was another lady in our subdivision who was selling some gorgeous jewelry. The best part of her job sounded like the discount she got! Think of the really gorgeous necklaces I could get at cost."

George now looked equal parts irritated at Patti's persistence and alarmed at the thought of her on a jewelry-buying spree. "Patti, you don't need to start peddling earrings to all of your friends and neighbors. We'll manage Leo's tuition just fine."

"You mean, *you'll* manage it," his usually quiet-natured wife snapped. "You have absolutely no idea, and haven't shown a lot of interest in how I spend my days! I could be having an affair with the club's golf pro, for all you care."

There were collective gasps from around the table.

George looked murderous. "Patricia!"

But Patti had already scrambled to her feet. "I have to… I'll be speaking in a few minutes. I should powder my nose first."

Delia followed, sparing an exasperated glance in George's direction before hurrying toward the women's restroom, the place where she seemed fated to spend the bulk of her evening. "Patti?"

Her friend was sniffling in front of the sinks, fanning her hands in front of her face in some sort of effort to keep from crying. "I don't know what's wrong with me. I've gone completely around the bend. Seriously, Delia, what *is* wrong with me? I know George isn't as good-looking as Alexander or the CEO of a company like Paul is. Was. But George is a good guy. He's never going to cheat on me or humiliate me by flirting with a tipsy tablemate. He's had a long week of business travel. He's exhausted, and I should be more understanding. But tonight is very important to me and he's… Is it wrong that I keep thinking about strangling him with that ugly tie he's wearing?"

Since her friend hadn't thought to do so, Delia peered under the stalls to confirm that they were alone. Then she dropped into the small upholstered bench that sat next to a table of complimentary mints and lotions.

"First of all, I don't know why you'd compare him to anyone else. Alexander and I broke up, so his hotness is irrelevant, and Paul may have been an impressive CEO, but he's also an indicted felon. On the other hand, just because George is definitely a better husband than some of the ones we know doesn't mean you have to settle, without ever questioning him or your marriage. You deserve to be happy. He shouldn't pooh-pooh your wanting to do other things, whether it's college courses, selling jewelry or taking up belly dancing. If you're unsatisfied with your life—"

"Oh, it's not that." Patti frowned. "Actually, it is that, but I don't know why. I love George and Leo and our house and our community. I just suddenly seem to want more. More time focused on me and the stuff I like to do instead of hosting a dinner for his colleagues or sitting in the bleachers on a sweltering afternoon for another one of Leo's baseball games. Not that I resent the dinners and the games!"

"It's all right to have your own interests." It was as if she was talking to Jo all over again, telling her she was allowed to be her own person. Of course, George was many, many steps up the evolutionary chain from Bobby, but the basic principle was the same.

"I'm not even sure what my interests are," Patti said with a sigh. "I feel invisible. Leo's at an age where he's stopped seeking his mother's opinion. And even though the catering manager knows me by name, I've noticed that people keep going up to Chastity tonight to tell her what a great job the committee's done. I'm awful, aren't I? I worked on this because it was a good cause, not because I needed recognition."

"You're not awful. And keep in mind that the reason people tell Chastity what a great job she's done is because she stands there lamenting how much work *she's* put into everything until they finally praise her just to get her to shut up."

Patti giggled, then sobered. "I really feel invisible where George is concerned. In the early days of our marriage, when he'd been out of town, he couldn't wait to get home to me. He'd barely be through the front door before he'd drag me into the bedroom. Now he barely mutters good-night before he drops his suitcase in the laundry room and shuffles off to bed."

"Maybe *you* should drag *him* to the bedroom. I've always been a believer in going after what you want. Screw his brains out, and you won't feel invisible anymore."

"Delia!"

"You're right, ignore me. What do I know about relationships, anyway? Forget jumping George if that's not what you want to do. Find your own hobbies. Join a bowling league. Set up a MySpace page. Start a book club."

"I do like to read." Patti's expression brightened as she considered that. "Would you come? And Kate, if she's not crazy-busy with the kids. You could invite your protégé, too! I like her."

"What are you planning to make us read? I'm not slogging through some of the literature that was required in college."

"I was thinking we could start off with a nice whodunit," Patti said dryly. "Maybe something about a wife whose husband mysteriously dies, and she uses the life-insurance money to fly herself and the pool boy to the Bahamas."

Delia laughed. "In that case, I'm in."

Chapter 12

*Compromise can be difficult, occasionally even
painful, but is often worth it in the long run. Kind
of like getting a shot.*

At first, Delia had suggested she simply meet Alexander at the doctor's office, but he'd pointed out that
it would probably be best if she didn't drive herself
after the procedure, so he offered to pick her up at the
town house instead. She was ready to go when she
opened the door, purse in hand and smile in place. Of
course, the smile was more a grimace, and she had
her fingers clenched in a death grip on the purse's
leather strap.

"You know," Alexander said gently, "you don't

have to do this. We can call and cancel the appointment."

"You're supposed to help me be brave, not encourage me to make a run for it. I could talk myself into that all by myself."

"Okay." Once they were buckled into his car, he said, "I tried to call you last night. You screening callers?" In other words, had she been trying to avoid him and a continuation of their discussion about Thanksgiving?

"I was at book club, and it was so late when I got back that it seemed silly to call you when I knew I'd see you today."

"Book club? You?" He laughed. "If you're dodging me, just say so."

"Hey! I read."

"I know. It's just, you're the only woman I've ever dated who's been bungee jumping. You celebrated your fortieth birthday with target practice at a shooting range. A book club seems so…sedate."

"Well, I doubt Dr. Adair would approve of my bungee jumping in this condition. Patti started a club a couple of weeks ago. I'm being supportive."

So far, Patti, Kate, Delia, Margaret Albright, Jo and Fiona, a single mom of twin toddlers who lived in Patti's cul-de-sac, were the members of the club. Fiona had apologized a couple of times for being so behind in the reading, but seemed just grateful to have something to do for a couple of hours besides work on potty training. And Jo had absolutely sparkled.

Apparently Bobby had made her feel she wasn't

that smart. Initially she'd been shy, limiting her comments to agreeing with whatever Delia or Patti had just said, but when Delia had called her on it, she'd given her own character interpretation and the other women had been impressed. After that, she'd needed no prodding to venture her opinion.

Kate said she might invite Lily, the kids' aunt, to join them when they picked their next book. Neve, who was currently grounded from television or leaving the house, was reading Christopher Paolini's *Eragon* and campaigning for the book club to read the Inheritance trilogy so that she could participate. Kate had told the girl that if she stayed out of trouble long enough, she could start her own book club and Kate would even provide snacks—store-bought, of course. Kate did not possess Patti's skills in the kitchen.

Which reminds me. Delia cleared her throat and glanced at Alexander. "I have something to tell you."

"The last time you said that, it turned out you were pregnant. We aren't having twins, are we?" he joked.

She forced the words out fast, before she could change her mind. "If you're amenable to the idea, I think we've worked out a solution to your Thanksgiving question."

His head whipped toward her. That she'd even broached the subject was probably a shock. "Who's 'we'?"

"Kate and I. Since her husband doesn't come home until January, it puts a bit of a damper on the holiday season for her and the kids. She doesn't want the day to be just the three of them in that huge house. Plus, she's an even worse cook than I am."

At this, Alexander grunted in disbelief.

"They're doing Christmas with Lily's brood," Delia continued. "But she thought that, for Thanksgiving, we could all come over. Patti, George and Leo. Me, you, your mother, sister and brother-in-law." That way, Delia could meet Alexander's family with a home-field advantage.

The expression on his face now was a lot like the one he'd had when they'd heard the fetal heartbeat. "Thank you, Delia."

She squirmed in her seat. "Don't thank me, it's Kate's place. And I told her that we might be able to twist your arm into bringing a side dish. If we all chip in, the meal will be edible."

He gave her a level look. "Thank you."

"You're welcome," she murmured. It was one stupid meal, she'd told herself last night as she'd looked at the blinking light on the answering machine. She hadn't been able to give him the love or commitment he'd asked for—the kind he deserved—but she could give him one Thursday for his family. Family was important to Alexander and even if she didn't understand that, she was grateful for it on their baby's behalf. *He's going to make a wonderful father.*

She could easily imagine him suffering through a tea party with a dark-haired daughter, or teaching a son with a mischievous smile to ride a bike. Once they got the results of today's test, they'd know for sure whether they were having a boy or a girl.

All too soon, they'd reached their destination. Alexander parked the car. Delia shivered with dread. She barely managed not to pace the lobby while waiting for her name to be called.

"You know I'm here for you," Alexander said, sounding helplessly frustrated.

"I know."

As it turned out, it wasn't nearly as bad as she'd expected. Dr. Adair smeared the cool, bluish ultrasound goo over Delia's stomach, using the sonogram picture to navigate where she'd place the needle to extract amniotic fluid.

"This won't poke the baby?" Delia asked repeatedly.

Shauna gave her a reassuring smile. "Don't worry, I'm even better at this than I am at tennis. Now take a deep breath and try to relax."

Was the good doctor insane? Relaxing under these circumstances was impossible. But Delia squeezed Alexander's hand and bit her lip when she felt the prick of the needle. It was more a pinch than actual pain. At least it was over quickly.

Except for the lab work part of it.

"You should have the results in ten to fourteen days," Shauna said. "Maybe less, but don't worry if it takes the full couple of weeks. Take it easy for the next forty-eight hours. Some mild cramping and even spotting aren't uncommon immediately following the procedure, but if you experience anything that seems worrisome, don't hesitate to call me. Meanwhile, start thinking about baby names!"

Shauna had offered to make a gender guess during the sonogram but apparently the baby had been feeling "shy" today and hadn't flashed the necessary bits for observation.

Alexander held the outside door open for Delia, and she tilted her head into the refreshing cool of the breeze. His hand hovered near her arm as though he wanted to help her but wasn't sure she'd welcome the touch just now. "How are you feeling?"

"Queasy. Not so much from the procedure as the thought of the procedure." She seemed to have left-over adrenaline roiling through her with no outlet. "Just thinking about the specifics of what she was doing, where she was putting that huge syringe."

"Yeah, I didn't want to say anything, but it looked fearsome. I don't think I would have let anyone stick that in me. You did great. Really great." He paused. "I took the afternoon off work, and I plan to stay with you at the town house."

She almost laughed at how he deliberately didn't phrase it as a question but a done deal. Having him at home would be bittersweet, and her knee-jerk reaction was to tell him no, thank you, she could take care of herself. But she was supposed to stay off her feet for the remainder of the day. She was finding that, when it came to her baby's well-being, her pride had limits.

Besides, she'd just braved a needle in her uterus. How hard could it be to withstand a handsome, caring man who wanted to wait on her?

Delia was sitting at her desk, having just regret-fully refused Lynette's lunch invitation because she had so much work to do, when the call came. While Delia didn't entirely understand all of the numbers the doctor gave her, two things were abundantly clear: the amnio had not found anything wrong with her baby, and Delia was having a girl.

Tears had already filled her eyes when she hung up the phone. *I'm having a daughter.* She glanced down at her abdomen, trying to remember when babies could start hearing the outside world. "Hey, you! I can't wait to meet you. And find out whose eyes you have, what music you like. Warn you about the wrong sorts of boys, even though they're kind of fun, and introduce you to the joys of shopping. We're going to be a kick-ass mother-daughter team, you and I."

A little girl. Would Alexander be as excited as she was, or had he secretly been hoping for a son? She'd promised to call him as soon as she heard anything, yet she changed her mind impulsively as she reached for the receiver. Maybe she should use the lunch hour to get out of her office, after all.

Twice on the way to Alexander's business park she caught herself speeding and told herself that was no way for a mother to drive. Yet the sun was bright, her radio was loud and she couldn't stop grinning. The car seemed to be zipping a little faster today, in tune with her mood. Surely she could sweet-talk her way out of a ticket if a police officer pulled her over.

Alexander's receptionist did a double-take when she saw Delia. "Hi. We haven't seen much of you lately. Should I just buzz him and let him know you're here?"

"If he's not in a meeting, I'd rather surprise him."

The older blonde hesitated, her finger hovering near the intercom button. "He gave me his change of address. Was the breakup bad? If you're going in there to throw something at him, I need to warn him."

Delia laughed. "The only thing I plan to hit him with is good news, I promise."

"All right, then. You know your way back."

Alexander was on a phone call, pacing in his office and speaking into a headset. He frowned when he saw her and asked the other person if they could talk again later.

"Is everything all right?" he asked Delia as he yanked off the headset. But then he got a better glimpse of her expression and his shoulders relaxed. The way her cheeks hurt from grinning, she didn't imagine she looked like a woman with bad news.

She stopped in front of him. "Mr. DiRossi, you and I are going to have a daughter. A healthy one, as far as Dr. Adair can tell."

His face went blank for a minute, but then he let out a quick whoop that could probably be heard in the neighboring conference room. "A little girl? You're sure?"

She nodded, leaning toward him for the hug he offered. But her body went rigid when he bent his head and brushed his lips over hers.

The hesitation lasted only a second though before hunger roared to life through her body. It was like her inability to control the car and make herself drive slowly; joy was racing through her, rapid and insistent, and she wanted to celebrate with the only other person whose feelings matched hers in magnitude.

When she thrust her tongue against his, he dropped his hands to cup her butt, dragging her against him. Her moan was a sound of both pleasure and urgency. She missed this, needed it more than she ever had. And she might have had her way with him if Alexander's timid receptionist hadn't been worried about protocol.

The intercom on his phone beeped. "Sir? I imagine she's already in your office, but I just wanted to say that Delia's here to see you. I hope it was all right, my just letting her in."

Alexander broke away, breathing heavy, his gaze not leaving Delia's as he angled back to press a button. "It's quite all right. She had some news she wanted to give me in person."

As he disconnected, Delia smirked. "Definitely in person. That wouldn't have been quite the same over the phone."

"I should apologize for kissing you," he said, "but I'm not sorry."

"Me, either. I'm only sorry we were interrupted." She took a step closer, trailing her index finger along his jaw. "What if…you came over for dinner tonight?"

His sigh told her what his answer would be before he gave it. "I love you, Delia, but that doesn't mean putting myself at your beck and call. If you want to be in a relationship with me, be *in* the relationship. All the time. Not just when you feel like it."

Frustration, both sexual and emotional, gnawed at her. "Those aren't demands I can live with. The baby's schedule will have to come before my convenience, and that's a big enough change for now. I'm forty-three years old and unmotivated to revise my entire lifestyle, always running every decision past another person. I make up my own mind and have my moods, good and bad, without having to factor in another person's.

"You mention 'all' the time," she said softly. "I can't do that. Not even for you."

He nodded. "That's what I thought. So, no to dinner tonight."

Dinner wasn't what he was turning down, and they both knew it. She stood there, reeling in the unfamiliar shock of rejection. She swallowed. "See you at Thanksgiving?"

"See you at Thanksgiving."

At least there she could count on the presence of his family to keep her hormones in check. It was humiliating to proposition a man and have him inadvertently make you feel like a heartless slut because you just wanted the sex. She made a mental note never to put herself in that position again.

"Patti, make her stop," Kate ordered. "She's driving me crazy, and I'm already stressed about cooking for this many people."

Instead of pointing out that the cooking was a

group effort and not Kate's sole responsibility, Patti asked in a fake whisper, "What do you expect me to do? She didn't want to watch the parade with George and the kids, so we're stuck with her."

"She's wearing a hole in the tile!"

"She's pregnant. It's not like I can club her over the head with one of your cast-iron skillets."

Kate paused, looking bemused and comically out of place in her own kitchen. "Do I actually have a cast-iron skillet?"

Meanwhile, Delia continued pacing. If her friends were going to talk about her as if she weren't there, she didn't feel obligated to join the conversation. She could barely concentrate on what they were saying, anyway. Within the next two hours, Alexander would be here...with his mother and sister in tow. And also some guy named Dennis, but Delia wasn't worried about him; she tended to make a good first impression on men.

It was the DiRossi women, the ones who loved Alexander and wanted what was best for him, that concerned her. On the one hand, they may decide that Delia wasn't good enough for him, for raising his child, which would be irritating and awkward. If, on the other hand, they liked her, they might push even harder for Alexander to marry her, which—as he swore he'd explained to them—wasn't going to happen.

Patti put down the mixer she'd been using and laughed, not unkindly. "For a woman who keeps telling me I should do what I want, other people's opinions be damned, you seem awfully worried about what these people are going to think of you."

"Only because I want what's best for my daughter. It could be uncomfortable for my daughter if her mother and grandmother hated each other." Delia barely remembered her own grandparents, who had been deceased by the time her parents had divorced. Was that one reason Chelsea had been pathetically eager to overlook the affair and two lost years and reclaim her marriage? She'd been an only child herself and with her parents gone, Delia and Garrett had been her main family.

Maybe if she'd stopped trying to talk me out of my anger and wallowing in her own misery, we could have been closer.

When Delia's daughter was grown, Delia didn't want them to avoid each other on national holidays. Of course, that didn't mean they had to bow to convention, either. Maybe they could take a Thanksgiving cruise or go to Vegas for Christmas.

Patti grinned over the word *daughter*. "I'm just so excited you're having a baby girl! I mean, my Leo is great, but have you seen the adorable little baby dresses in stores? And Alexander will be such a great daddy. He'll scare off any boys with impure intentions."

"Can I borrow him?" Kate interjected dryly. Even though Neve was barely thirteen, there had already been teen-crush drama in the house.

"And you'll be a great mom," Patti told Delia.

"Yeah, I'm sure that's what you thought when you

first met me!" She was teasing, but it was nice to hear someone thought she'd do a good job.

"Just look how much you've helped Jo," Patti added proudly.

"Can we *not* hold her up as my adopted daughter?" Delia pleaded. "It makes me feel old."

"I wasn't necessarily calling you the mother figure in her life. How about experienced and wiser big sister? I just meant that you went out of your own comfort zone to befriend her, that you're something of a role model. You care about her well-being. These are all good signs."

Kate nodded. "As a mom, you'll have to kiss your comfort zone goodbye. I'm learning that the hard way, you know, the kids are actually worth it. And I like Jo. I'm glad she's joining us today."

From what Delia could glean, Jo had been more or less disowned by her family for running off with Bobby. Delia couldn't fault Joanne's parents for objecting to her taste in men, but didn't they see that cutting her off from their emotional support had only made her more dependent on the jerk?

Patti nudged Kate. "You're just relieved Jo offered to bring food today."

"That, too. Did you try her lemon bars at the last book club meeting? It's a shame none of us know of any bakeries that are hiring."

Jo was growing increasingly concerned about her job situation, doubting that she would be able to waitress right up until the baby was born. Already she was growing fatigued midway through her shifts, yet she was trying to sock away as much money now as possible to brace herself for the income-free weeks after the baby was born.

"That's one plus of breast-feeding," she'd said, after debating the pros and cons of different infant formulas with Fiona. "At least the kid eats free for a while."

Patti and Fiona had both agreed to keep their eyes open for anyone who might be hiring, but waddling into an interview six months pregnant didn't win a lot of offers. Delia couldn't imagine Jo in some of the competitive corporate environments *she'd* witnessed. Women like Terese Reeves, clawing their way to the top-of-career ladder, would eat Jo alive.

Delia paused. Interesting that she didn't lump herself in with Terese because, the truth was, until recently, they hadn't been all that different. They were both ambitious and, on occasion, snarky. *I've softened.* Did that mean she'd lost her edge? Would bragging to everyone at the office that her daughter had been picked to be an ear of corn in the school nutrition play someday be more important than accepting congratulations from everyone on her latest big-dollar lease?

Honestly, she didn't know. After all, she'd worked hard to get where she was. Was it selfish that she didn't want to give up all the parts of her life she enjoyed to make room for her little girl? She took hope in the admirable job Kate was doing, balancing career, parenting and a modest social life.

Then again, Kate wasn't getting up twice a night

for feedings and didn't have forty-three years' worth of generational differences between her and Neve.

When the doorbell rang, Delia nearly jumped out of her skin and immediately chastised herself. Alexander wasn't due to arrive with his family yet. This was probably Jo, who'd agreed to come early to help with the cooking. Delia suspected she was equally motivated by not wanting to be alone. Jo didn't seem entirely comfortable with her own company, on a holiday or any other day of the year.

A suspicion that Jo inadvertently confirmed when she unpacked her food processor. As she carried shopping bags inside, she said that since they were preparing a meal for such a large group, it would be helpful to have extra cooking supplies. "I think you guys are really going to like the sweet potato casserole I made. I did a test batch when Len came over for dinner, and he—"

"Len?" Patti asked as she shoved the turkey she'd been basting back into the oven. "And who is he?" Her tone was full of friendly curiosity and feminine teasing.

Delia groaned inwardly, knowing that Patti was the romantic in their group. It was odd, given her flashes of malcontent in her own marriage, that she was still so quick to pair off everyone else. Delia hoped her friend wouldn't encourage Jo to get back out there and start dating, especially since Jo was in her third trimester and on the rebound, to boot. By her own admission, she'd rarely lived alone, having gone straight from her parents' home into a nomadic lifestyle with

Bobby. Before she got involved with someone else and promptly leaned on him, she needed to prove to herself that she could stand on her own two feet.

But neither Patti nor Jo noticed Delia's silent misgivings. They were chattering on about Jo's kind neighbor as they assembled various chopping and mixing apparatuses that, from Delia's perspective, might as well have been props from sci-fi movies. No wonder she never cooked; there were apparently a zillion requisite gadgets she didn't own.

"He's so smart," Jo gushed. "Bobby never even earned one degree. Len will have two by the end of next year."

"Is he cute?" Patti asked with an impish grin.

Damn it, Patricia, you're not helping.

Jo paused, then answered honestly. "Not exactly. He's about my height and has no sense of color-coordination. Crooked teeth. But his eyes are really kind. He has lots of attractive qualities beyond his looks."

"Absolutely," Delia chimed in, seizing the opportunity. "Qualities like intelligence and determination and self-reliance are what truly defines a person. The ability to set goals for yourself and succeed."

Kate and Patti were both staring at her, as if she should perhaps dial back the I Am Woman roar a notch. Jo, however, was nodding thoughtfully…and missing the point entirely.

"That's Len to a T. You saw that crummy little building I live in, Delia. He could be staying somewhere else, but he's studying hard and saving up every penny so that when he gets his MBA and finds just the right job, he'll be able to move into a great place. You can tell from the questions he asked me about the baby that he's going to have a family someday. He'll be a wonderful provider."

Neve came into the kitchen then, claiming that she and Leo and PJ were *starving* and couldn't they have a snack of some kind since dinner wouldn't be for another hour? Kate rooted through the refrigerator for something healthy to give them, and Patti, having had two glasses of wine, excused herself to use the restroom. Delia found herself at loose ends with Jo. Was there a way to inquire gently whether this Len guy from her building was just a friend, or whether Jo had ignored all the sane advice she'd been given and was rushing into another relationship under the misguided notion that a man would "complete" her?

"Delia, can I ask you a question?"

Oh, thank heavens! If Jo sought her advice, Delia could give an opinion without being guilty of the same type of meddling disapproval she used to accuse Patti of. "Absolutely, ask away."

"Well, you know I have only a couple of months left before the baby arrives. I signed up for birth classes that start immediately after Christmas, one hour a week for the duration of the course. And I was wondering…" Jo sighed. "I can't believe I'm going to ask you *another* favor after everything you've already done for me, but I need a partner. Everyone in the class is supposed to have a 'birth coach.' I suppose I could ask Alice or maybe even Len, but I

figured you'll probably want the information eventually any—"

"I'll do it."

Jo beamed. "Really?"

"Like you said, I probably would have needed to
look into one of those classes myself. Why not? It'll
be…fun."

Delia saw the value in arming herself with knowledge, so a Lamaze class made some sense. Still,
despite Jo's already stated preference for natural
childbirth in her case, Delia planned to ask for drugs
when the time came. Lots and lots of quality drugs.

The next time the doorbell rang, Delia didn't
jump—she was too paralyzed. This was it. After having accepted decades ago that she and her own parents weren't really wired for the family connection
that seemed to come naturally to everyone else, she
was about to meet the family of the only man she'd
ever…well, the man she'd come closer to loving than
anyone else.

Kate's gaze locked with hers over the kitchen island. "Do you want me to answer the door, or would
you like the honors?"

Delia's throat felt dust-dry, which made sense because all the moisture in her body seemed to have
fled to her now-sweaty palms. But she raised her chin.
"If you don't mind, Kate, I'll greet them, thanks."
Moving with what she hoped was some semblance
of graceful bravado, despite her increasing girth, she
crossed through the living room, then opened the
front door.

Was it a hormone-induced illusion, or did Alexander actually get better looking every time she saw him? This was the first time they'd seen each other face-to-face since that undisciplined kiss, and she had to force herself not to look away shyly. Delia Carlisle was not shy.

He wore a black leather jacket over a white button-down shirt and jeans, radiating such potent masculinity it was surprising women didn't get pregnant just by *looking* at him. Next to him, at a comparative disadvantage, was a stockier man with a goatee and pleasant smile; he held hands with a petite dark-haired woman who had every bit of her older brother's good looks. On the other side of Alexander was, unquestionably, Isabella DiRossi.

Tall for a woman, she came up to her son's shoulders. She'd aged well into handsome features and silvery bobbed hair with only glimpses of the black it had once been. Both of the women carried casserole dishes.

Isabella's eagle-eyed gaze went to Delia's stomach, then back to her face. "So you must be Delia, then."

"Yes. And you are Isabella."

The woman's salt-and-pepper brows beetled together. Should Delia have gone with the more formal *Mrs. DiRossi?* "It's a lovely name," Delia added, even if it seemed oddly lyrical for the militant woman standing in front of her.

Isabella grunted. "Are you going to invite us in, or will we be eating on the lawn?"

"Mama!" Angela snapped. "I'm Alexander's sister Angie. This is my husband, Dennis."

Since he was the only one with a free hand, Delia shook it. "Pleased to meet you all."

Alexander was noticeably quiet as they all came inside, as though his self-preservation instincts wouldn't allow him to interfere between the women in his life. Both Alexander and Dennis brightened visibly at the sight of George watching some pre-game football highlights now that the parade broadcast had concluded. Delia sighed inwardly. *Men.*

Before she disappeared into the kitchen with the other womenfolk, Alexander caught her hand for the barest of seconds. "You look nice."

She glanced down at the slate-blue maternity dress she'd chosen after more deliberation than she would ever admit to anyone. "I wanted to wear my Rolling Stones T-shirt, but since it doesn't fit anymore, I made do with this."

"And how's our daughter today?"

"Fine, as far as I can tell. But hungry. At least, that's the excuse I'm giving for wanting to scarf down every edible substance in sight. Which rules out anything Kate or I helped prepare. The Food Network could give us our own show, *What Not to Eat.*"

Delia glanced over her shoulder, where her friends were introducing themselves to her non-in-laws. "Even though I'm not a lot of help in the kitchen, I should get back in there. It was nice of Kate to suggest this."

"It was good of you to agree to it," Alexander said

somberly. "I know it wouldn't have been your first choice."

Maybe it would have been, once. She tried to remember back to her early childhood. Had she dreamed of big family holidays with lots of teasing and even bickering and enough food to feed a village? As an adult, she'd been comfortable with small numbers and temporary people—spending a holiday weekend not at home in cozy sweaters but with a current lover in San Tropez. Perhaps that's why Alexander's family made her feel so itchy and claustrophobic. They represented the kind of permanence she wasn't accustomed to in any aspect of her life. She'd never owned a home, had always leased something she liked until she'd decided she wanted something different. Even in her job, where she'd been happily employed for years, she'd always accepted business cards from people who threatened to steal her away from her current position.

She liked to have her options open, but the DiRossis, through the bond of her child, would be a part of her life *forever,* whether on the periphery or directly. It was odd to feel that Alexander's mother could be more of a presence in her life than her own. It made Isabella important. To say nothing of the added pressure of knowing how much Alexander's family—this day—meant to him.

In the kitchen, Angie was fussing over Jo, giving her all kinds of advice she'd picked up during her two sisters' pregnancies. And Isabella was helping Patti at the oven. Kate and the kids were upstairs, expecting their prearranged holiday call from Paul any second now. Delia was glad for her friend that Paul would be home in less than two months; they'd made it past the halfway mark and were counting down the weeks now.

Delia sat on a stool that had been pushed to the island, hoping she was able to keep her balance now that her center of gravity was shifted.

Angie turned to her with a conspiratorial smile. "My sisters will be *so* jealous that I've met you. I knew you were special the first time I heard Alexander talk about you, but none of us expected news like this! He's going to make a wonderful, wonderful father. You should see him with the kids…"

"He really is wonderful," Jo put in with a dreamy sigh. "Movie-star good looks *and* he likes children? Men like him must be nearly impossible to find."

This was an uncomfortable line of conversation. Delia had no grounds to disagree with them, but if she did agree, she made herself sound crazy for letting him go. "Jo, did I hear you telling Angie you found some more cute baby stuff?"

"Yeah, my apartment's too small for a true nursery, but I'm turning most of the living room into a play area. By the time the baby's outgrown the bassinet next to my bed, hopefully I'll have found a different job and can look for a two-bedroom place. What about you, Delia? Are you going to move into something bigger?"

"Oh, I—"

"You'll need more room than you think," Angie

said. "You wouldn't believe how much room the baby's things take up. Blanche had a swing and two play mats and a crib and a playpen and a high chair and a bouncy seat... They added a ten-pound person to the household and ten tons of stuff. You should definitely get a bigger place if you can afford it."

In the midst of their conversation, Alexander strolled through the room toward the cooler of drinks George had brought over. Alexander paused when he caught what his sister was saying, ruffling her hair the way he'd probably been doing all her life. "Ange, you haven't even known Delia a day, and you're telling her what changes she should make? I'd expect it from Blanche, but you don't even have your own babies yet."

"It was just a little friendly advice," Angie said. "Delia doesn't mind." As she spoke, she cast Delia a sidelong glance as if checking to see if this were true. Delia managed a smile.

"Still." He angled his body almost imperceptibly so that his words encompassed Isabella even though he wasn't addressing her. "Delia's a smart woman who's going to be a great mother. She doesn't need anyone, no matter how well-meaning, trying to railroad her into any decisions."

Delia was amused by the irony. Not long ago, Alexander himself had suggested she move, yet now he was cautioning Angie against it. Except Delia didn't think the warning was really for his sister. She thought it was a reminder to Isabella that if Delia didn't want to get married, then his mother should leave the subject alone.

The protective gesture was heartwarming. If Alexander were a different kind of man, he could use his family to outnumber her, but he was better than that.

She'd say this for herself—whatever other flaws she might have, she had incomparable taste in men.

The interrogation she'd been half expecting from Isabella didn't come until the two women were assigned the task of polishing the rarely used silver for each place setting. For a few minutes, Angie was with them in the dining room, but then she vanished. Was this prearranged, or had Isabella given some signal Delia missed?

Isabella didn't waste time with subtlety, which Delia had to respect. "You've hurt my son."

Delia stiffened at the accusation. "That wasn't my intention. I...care a great deal about him."

"Not enough to marry him, though."

"That's not personal." *And none of your business.*

Isabella laughed, gesturing toward Delia's stomach. "Looks like the two of you got plenty personal. It's hard work to be a mother. You seem strong-willed, and Alexander obviously sees many qualities in you, so you'll do well. But it's difficult when you have no partner to help, to worry with you when the little one has a high fever in the middle of the night. To stand behind you when a teacher screws up and you have to go down to the school to tear someone a new one."

Delia choked on her laughter at Isabella's unexpected terminology. "You're not what I expected."

Isabella set down a fork, then met Delia's gaze. "You are exactly what I expected. Alexander needed someone who challenged him, and he finally found her. Keeping the man you love on his toes is good. I approve. Pushing him away, however... My children would have given anything to have their father back when he died."

"I'm not denying my daughter her father. Alexander will be part of our life."

"It will be complicated," Isabella predicted, adding with deceptive casualness, "Especially when he finds a woman who *is* willing to marry him."

Delia swallowed. If she couldn't give him her heart, she had no right to ask for his celibacy. Of course he'd eventually find someone who was good enough for him. She forced herself to sound nonchalant. "Blended families aren't uncommon. We'll work it out when he falls in love with someone. I do want him to be happy."

For a long time Isabella peered at her. Then she gave an almost affectionate smile. "You know, I believe you. Just as I believe you'll be as fiercely protective of your child as I am of each of mine."

"Anything I can do to help, ladies?" Alexander's voice from the doorway was a bit breathless, as if he'd sprinted to this end of the house as soon as someone warned him that Delia and Isabella were alone together.

Delia smiled, but she couldn't quite keep the melancholy out of her voice. "Your mom and I have everything under control. She's been giving tips on how to be a good mother." If circumstances had been radically different, would Isabella have come to accept Delia as a daughter of sorts? Just from first impressions, Delia thought she might have more in common with Mrs. DiRossi than her own mother.

Later, as they placed the centerpiece on the table, Delia couldn't keep herself from asking, "Isabella, what would you have done if Alexander's father had ever cheated on you?"

The woman's face went blank. "He never would have done that. What kind of question is this?"

"Probably a rude one. I'm not trying to insult you or his memory. I just…needed to know."

Isabella pondered the matter. "Well, I couldn't have let any of the men in my family know about it or they would have killed him. If it came to wanting him dead, I'd take care of it myself. I'd probably bring home a butcher knife from my uncle Sal's shop and make it clear that he'd lose a valuable piece of his anatomy if he ever touched another woman again, but that, perhaps with enough groveling, he could work his way into my bed again someday. Maybe."

Delia wasn't sure she could ever forgive a man who betrayed her like that, yet she still found Isabella's answer satisfactory. She patted her stomach contentedly and smiled to herself, glad her daughter's gene pool included strong, passionate women. *May you get all our strengths and minimal fear or self-doubt.*

That would be something for which Delia could truly be thankful.

The Third Trimester...

Chapter 13

While it's not productive to dwell on the negative, there's no point in sugarcoating the truth, either: sometimes, life sucks.

"So are you two, like, life partners?"

"What?" Delia followed the man's gaze to where Jo was getting a bottle of water at the back of the classroom, his meaning belatedly registering. "No!"

A strawberry-blonde woman waddled up to the man and smacked him on the arm. "Justin! Tell me you did not ask her if they were a couple."

"So? It's politically correct to talk about stuff like that now, right?"

The strawberry-blonde forced a smile in Delia's direction. "I apologize for him." But any goodwill

Delia felt toward the woman dimmed when she over-heard her tell Justin as they walked off, "I told you, there's too big an age difference for them to be a cou-ple. What if she's her mom or something and you just totally grossed her out?"

I am not *her mom!*

Jo, doing a fair amount of waddling herself these days, joined Delia in one of the chairs that had been arranged in a semicircle. "I got you a water, too, in case you changed your mind about wanting some-thing to drink. You know how important it is to stay hydrated, especially at this point in the pregnancy."

Delia smirked. "Yeah, I get the same lectures from Dr. Adair that you do."

"One of the ladies at the back table was saying that she goes to Dr. Adair, too. All of the people I've talked to here have been so nice! I saw you chatting. Making friends?" Jo asked brightly.

"Something like that."

"If you'll all take your seats," the instructor at the front of the room said. "We'll get started."

Their teacher, a lady with a reedy voice, horn-rimmed glasses and bright purple broomstick skirt had come as something of a shock to Delia. Not to be ageist, but she'd expected the birthing class teacher to be in her child-bearing years. Instead, Harmony had introduced herself as a sixty-four-year-old mother and grandmother. She was definitely familiar with the course material, having given birth five times herself.

"Now then," Harmony said. "I had custodial put the chairs out so we could get to know each other, become comfortable before doing any exercises, but we'll be working most of the time on the floor. Feel free to bring a beach towel or small pillow. Let's go around and give our names. Tell me a little about yourself and what you hope to get out of the birthing experience."

Other than a healthy baby? Delia wasn't sure she understood the question.

They started on the far left, with couples introducing themselves and Harmony interjecting comments like "Lovely!" and "I quite agree!" But when she got to Delia and Jo, she frowned.

"And which one of you is the mother-to-be?"

"Well, obviously we both are," Delia said. "But she's here as the student, and I'm her coach."

"I see. I'm going to give you all some forms, including information on our other classes, such as the one on breastfeeding, which I highly recommend. And some of these are actually hospital registration forms. Rather than fill them out when you're admitted in labor, you can have them ready beforehand and leave them on file at the nursing station to speed up the process on your big day."

Delia glanced through one of the form's disclaimers, her eyes widening at one of the hospital's boilerplate you-won't-sue-us clauses in the case of accidental death or dismemberment. She squeaked involuntarily. *"Dismemberment?* Has there been a woman who came into this hospital to have her baby who left without limbs?"

Panicked whispers and the sound of people flipping quickly through their papers surrounded her, and Harmony shot Delia a look that completely belied her peace-and-love name. The teacher tried to regain everyone's attention by mentioning that each week, they'd be seeing videos that demonstrated different types of births, some of which could be chosen on a patient's birth plan, and others that became medically mandated, such as a cesarean section.

"According to the current statistics," Harmony said somberly, "at least two of you will probably end up needing a C-section."

Delia knew that the odds of having one were even greater for someone of her age…and after being forced to watch a video that reminded her of those cautionary films they used to make kids see in driver's ed classes, she was thinking maybe a C-section was just fine with her. Good Lord. Sure the ending was happier, but the amount of blood seemed roughly the same. Jo, however, had seemed so transfixed by the miracle of life playing out on-screen that Delia expected her friend to announce that she, too, had decided to give birth in a pool.

As they left the classroom, Delia sighed in relief. "Well, that was interesting. Let's never do it again."

As Alexander stared unseeingly at the tarmac, the plane taxied toward the runway. He'd spent more time looking out these little windows lately than the windows of his own home. Not that he had one, exactly.

January was always a busy month. There were often clients who needed help, but postponed scheduling the training sessions until after the irregular hours and vacation requests brought on by the holidays. Then there were those soon-to-be clients who'd been interested in purchasing the program, but wanted to wait until the next financial quarter to do so. Between going to New York for Christmas and the two trips he'd already taken in the new year, including this latest to Philadelphia, Alexander had barely been in Richmond to house hunt.

He planned to change that immediately, weariness seeping into his bones. It just wasn't that refreshing or satisfying to come home to an impersonal efficiency apartment. And it *definitely* wasn't the same as coming home to Delia. She wasn't domestic like her friend Patti or his mother, but even if Delia didn't color-coordinate and set out potpourri, she gave a room life just by being in it. She made it warmer and more interesting.

He missed her.

He'd called her several times since Thanksgiving to wish her a merry Christmas and to check to make sure her gestational-diabetes test results were good. At least, those were the reasons he gave; saying he'd wanted to hear her voice seemed like the wrong admission for a man who was supposed to be moving on with his life.

Delia gave no hint of pining for him. If she sounded tired, he attributed it to her having reached her last trimester, which Blanche and Marie agreed was the most draining, when the expectant mother was just ready for it to *end* already! Other than the usual complaints, such as heartburn, everything seemed to be going smoothly. The last time they were on the phone, Delia's biggest gripe had been not being able to settle on a name, although she'd asked his opinion on three that both of them had liked but neither loved.

"I'm starting to feel a little stupid about it," she'd admitted. "I talk to the baby—mostly to ask her to please quit kicking me in major internal organs while I'm trying to sleep. I can't keep addressing my daughter as Hey You in There!"

My daughter, she'd said, although he doubted she'd meant to slight him that way. When he'd moved out, he hadn't truly realized how much it would pain him not to be lying there with her at night, getting to feel the baby kick and turn in her belly. Months ago, before he'd even known there would be a baby, Blanche had asked him if he loved Delia. His sister had told him that even if he didn't want to talk about it, he should have an answer for himself.

He loved Delia, all right. Would it have made a difference if he'd shared that with her *before* she got pregnant? When she couldn't argue that his feelings were influenced solely by the baby? Or would she have pushed him away, no matter the timing of his declaration?

Knowing her as he did, he'd have to say the latter.

"Excuse me, sir?" A pleasantly husky, feminine voice cut through his thoughts.

He turned, expecting to see a flight attendant. But rather than the East-West Air uniform, the blonde was wearing a red sweater and held a purse in her hand, with her ticket sticking out of the leather side pocket. "Hello there."

"I was just wondering…if this seat's empty, would you mind my taking it? I was sitting farther back, and the person next to me fell asleep the minute he sat down. He's already dropped onto my shoulder twice, and his snores are so loud and grating I thought the engine was having trouble with takeoff."

Alexander was moved by her plight, or at least her pretty face and the pleading expression in her glass-green eyes. "Feel free to join me."

"Thank you!" She sat, then extended a hand after she'd fastened her seat belt. "I'm Grace."

Without meaning to, he immediately evaluated her name; he'd been doing that with every female moniker he'd heard in the past few weeks. *Grace* was elegant, popular without being trendy…of course, if his daughter turned out to be at all clumsy, the name would just be a cruel irony. And perhaps it was too feminine and elegant for the child he and Delia had created. After all, the baby's mother was a spitfire and…

He realized that he hadn't released his companion's hand and that he was grinning. Grace smiled in return, now peering up through her lashes at him. Uh-oh.

An hour later, though, he admitted to himself that even if she'd mistaken his interest as more personal than he'd intended, her cheerful conversation was making the flight go a lot faster. She seemed friendly and optimistic without being so perky his head hurt, and she was obviously a bright woman, discussing some of the topics that had been in the news recently and asking intelligent technology questions after he'd told her a little bit about the software his company designed. Grace worked in the human resources department of a mid-size law firm and was coming back from visiting her mother. She had one sister and a brother, so they shared sibling anecdotes up until the time the plane touched down.

Should he ask her for her phone number, or would that seem presumptuous? This was a plane, not a singles' bar. Which was absolutely ridiculous—if he'd really wanted her number, their location wouldn't have stopped him. No, he knew the real reason he wasn't telling her that he'd enjoyed their chat and would love to do it again some time.

Delia.

You idiot. They'd already been broken up for several months. How long was he planning to postpone his own life?

The opportunity to ask Grace for her number had passed, and he ground his teeth in annoyance. He'd thought he had wanted a permanent partner when he popped the question to Delia, but there'd been little premeditated thought then. At Christmas, he'd watched his sisters content in their marriages, and now that he'd had time to consider it he realized he desired that soul-deep commitment when you wake up in the morning knowing that, despite any fights or flaws, that person will still be there for you at the end of the day.

What chance did he have of finding that if he continued to live like a monk cloistered in an ugly efficiency suite?

Standing at the luggage carousel and waiting on his garment bag—the laptop and projector he used for training classes ate up his carry-on allowance—he saw Grace standing a few feet away. Not one to waste a second chance, he put himself in her line of vision.

She smiled immediately. "Hello again."

"I don't know about you," he said, "but I could go for dinner right about now. I'll understand if you just want to get home after traveling, but I know a place not far—"

"I'd love to!"

Well that had been relatively painless. They both got their luggage and agreed to meet at the restaurant shortly. Alexander gave her directions and his cell number. It was a place he and Delia had eaten at frequently, and the host smiled in recognition when he saw Alexander.

"Mr. DiRossi! It's been too long."

"Yes, it has," Alexander agreed, kicking himself for the pinprick of guilt he experienced as he stood there waiting for his date. *I have nothing to feel guilty for!*

Cold air gusted around him as the door behind him opened again and the host smiled in greeting. "And, Ms. Carlisle. I have a table ready now if the two of you would like to follow me."

Alexander froze. *You have got to be kidding me!* The first date he'd had since— To be fair, Delia was

the person who'd introduced him to this restaurant
and it was close to her work. But still… He turned
slowly.

Her eyes were wide with surprise, but they quickly
turned appreciative as she took in the sight of him.
Delia might not want the white picket fence, but she'd
wanted *him* since the moment she saw him. He knew
this because she'd unabashedly purred it into his ear
a few days after they'd met.

"Ringo." The word came out as more of a sigh, and
he couldn't help grinning at the absurd nickname.

"Hi." He did his own once-over, wanting to pull
her into his arms, wanting to put his hand on her
stomach and greet his child. "You've gotten bigger!"

"How nice of you to notice." Her tone could cut
glass.

He laughed self-consciously. "I just meant—"

"I know what you meant, trust me. I see it in the
mirror every day." But her hand had dropped to her
abdomen, and she didn't sound as dissatisfied with
her changing physical appearance as he would have
once expected.

Realizing that the host was still patiently waiting,
two menus in his hand, Alexander glanced between
the man to Delia and back again. "We're not actually together."

"No?" The man raised an eyebrow.

Delia shook her head. "I drove by to pick up an
order, but well…" She shifted her weight and glanced
past the bar.

Alexander bit the inside of his cheek to keep from

laughing. She'd intended to grab dinner on the way home from work, but she hadn't been able to make it that far without using the bathroom. "I won't keep you, then. But it's nice to see—"

The door opened again, and the cold that hit him this time wasn't from the breeze but from the shiver of dread that went up his spine. Even in his peripheral vision, he saw enough red sweater and gold hair to know it was Grace. Not that there was any reason to hide his having dinner with her, but the evening might be less awkward if it didn't start with this particular introduction.

"Hey," she told him brightly. "I found the place with no problem, just like you said. I pass by here all the time and can't believe I've never been in here."

The restaurant was tucked behind some stores and office complexes and netted most of its business by word of mouth, not advertising. "It's one of the city's hidden treasures," Alexander said before he could catch himself. That's how Delia described it whenever she recommended the place to someone.

Delia somehow studied Grace without breaking eye contact with him.

He swallowed. "Grace, this is Delia Carlisle. Delia, meet Grace." Whose last name he didn't know.

"How nice to meet you." Delia's tone was pleasant enough, yet the glare she shot Alexander was lethal.

The host, looking thoroughly confused, cleared his throat. "And are the *two of you* together?" he asked. At Alexander's terse nod, the man said, "Right this way, please."

They were seated, and Alexander managed to smile at his dinner companion, recommending one of the house wines. But he couldn't help tracking Delia with his eyes, and he noticed immediately when she'd returned from the restroom and was headed toward the front door.

Let her go.

Despite the arguably wiser inner voice, he heard himself ask, "Grace, would you please excuse me for just one second?" Delia was already on the sidewalk when he caught up with her.

"Delia, wait."

"I'd rather not," she snapped, hefting the white plastic bag that bore the restaurant's understated logo. "My food will get cold."

"I felt like I should explain." Would it matter that Grace was someone he'd just met? Somehow it bothered him that Delia might think he was already in another relationship.

"You're having dinner at a nice restaurant with an attractive woman. How much clarification could that require? It's a free country, Alexander. More to the point, *you* are a free man. Go. Eat."

Was he more pissed off because the twinge of guilt he'd experienced earlier had now swelled to the point that there was no possible way he could enjoy his evening, or because he was here in the first place only because Delia had rejected what he'd had to offer? He hadn't *asked* to be a free man, damn it. At least, not in a long time. He'd been wrong when he thought he'd never want strings tying him to one person, and she'd been naive to think she could go through life forever avoiding ties to others.

"I *should* go eat," he retorted, the wash of temper as familiar as his earlier reaction of wanting to take her in his arms. No one pushed his buttons quite the way Delia did. "I should get to know this nice girl, who, just maybe, will turn out *not* to be emotionally stunted, and see where this leads."

Delia paled so quickly he grew concerned for her health. What the hell was he doing out here yelling at a pregnant woman? His mother would kill him. "I—"

"Don't you dare apologize," Delia snarled, "because we both know you meant it."

He had. Just as he'd meant it when he'd told her he loved her.

And look how well *that* had turned out.

By the following week, Delia's mood had not improved. On the plus side, in the middle of one of Terese's snarky comments about maternity leave being "just around the corner," Delia's face had contorted into such an expression that the skinny redhead had actually taken a step back. That, Delia admitted as she buckled herself into the driver's seat, had been kind of fun.

Everything else, though, had pretty much sucked.

While she was excited about the baby, she felt crowded in this last trimester, as if her little bundle of joy were making it impossible to breathe. Could that help explain the suffocating despair she'd experienced when a petite blonde sauntered into *her* favorite restaurant and smiled up at Alexander as though she planned to have him for dessert? Delia was even starting to feel claustrophobic in her own town house. She hadn't been sleeping well at night—ironic, since any time she sat at her desk for more than ten minutes, she felt like she could easily slip into a coma—and all her nocturnal pacing had given her a chance to wonder just where she planned to put all the baby stuff.

It was odd how Alexander's moving out hadn't actually created that much space. His recliner and a small desk upstairs had been the biggest pieces of furniture.

Several of the baby books suggested that women having trouble sleeping in their third trimester try to do so upright, making it easier to breathe and helping manage heartburn; Delia missed the recliner.

She missed Alexander more. He was a great guy, and he deserved to be with someone who would fully appreciate him in a way that Delia couldn't. She sighed, not realizing until someone jabbed their horn that the light she'd stopped at was now green.

Obligingly pressing the accelerator, she flirted with the notion of skipping Patti's book club tonight. Spending another sleepless evening in her town house held no appeal, though. More importantly, tonight they were throwing Jo a surprise book-themed baby shower. Delia had to be there. She was the one who'd introduced Jo to her new friends in the first place; she was Jo's Lamaze coach, for crying out loud!

Trying to convince herself that she'd have fun once she was out of traffic, Delia navigated the roads to

Patti's house. Kate and Lily were already there, hanging streamers and tying balloons to doorknobs and the backs of chairs. The entire place smelled like sin dipped in chocolate and sprinkled with coconut, which meant Patti had been baking.

Patti appeared in the living room, looking both comfortable and rosy-cheeked in a two-piece pink-velour set over a designer T-shirt and holding a spoon. "Fiona called. She said it took her and her mom longer than normal to settle down the twins, but she'll be here in a few minutes. I hope she and Margaret get here before Jo so that we can surprise her together."

The corner of Delia's mouth lifted. "Are we absolutely certain that it's a good idea to surprise a woman eight months' pregnant? I mean, you don't really want this baby born in your living room, do you?"

Patti laughed. "Maybe we should have asked Dr. Adair to join the book club, just in case. Speaking of baby showers, Delia, I don't suppose you've bothered to register for any baby stuff?"

"Nah, I'm not the registry type. Surprise me. You know more about what babies need than I do, anyway." Delia could tell Patti that gifts weren't necessary, but she knew her friend better than that. At Christmas, Patti had given her a large pink gift bag filled with tiny pink clothes, a pink bath set and even a pink velvet-bound book with blank pages. Patti had said it was a Mommy journal, meant for Delia to fill with observations and special moments for her daughter to read when she was old enough. Delia had actually opened it one night when she couldn't sleep, pen poised, but no motherly wisdom had come to her.

Lily cleared her throat and Delia turned to the mother of four, still sometimes surprised that she and Kate had turned out to be such good friends. Delia imagined both women were excited that Paul would be home in less than two weeks.

"I know you didn't ask my opinion," Lily said with a self-deprecating smile that made it clear she was going to give one anyway. "But I've heard you talk about Alexander's family."

Delia flinched, the memory of running into him on his date still raw, but not a wound she was willing to examine in front of others. "Yeah?"

"Well, they're going to want to contribute in some way, which will be harder given the distance they live from here and given that…"

"Alexander and I are no longer together?"

Lily nodded. "If you have a registry, they can pick something off of it and feel good about giving to the baby, being part of her life right from the start, *and* know that they've selected something you'll like. It's not always easy to read your in-laws," she added with a cheeky grin and sideways glance at Kate.

"I hadn't thought about that," Delia admitted. She didn't know when she would get used to thinking of the DiRossis in terms of family, but for her daughter's sake, she needed to practice.

Headlights flashed through the window and they all froze in anticipation. Kate peered out the window for a closer look and announced that the car was Margaret's. Fiona was pulling into the driveway before Margaret even got to the door, and the two women walked in together, both carrying wrapped gifts with big bows, which were added to the stack on Patti's coffee table.

When Jo rang the doorbell, Fiona actually giggled; Delia repeated a prayer that this shower didn't constitute a big enough surprise to send her young friend into early labor.

Luckily it didn't. However, it *was* enough to make Jo cry.

"Ohmigosh, this is the absolute best day ever!" Jo said as she tearfully hugged Patti, then Kate. "First, the news about the *job*—Fiona, how can I ever thank you?"

"You mean, you heard back?" Delia asked.

Fiona knew of an upscale day care that had been looking for some help; Patti and Margaret, who had considerable standing in the community, had written letters of recommendation about Jo's unflagging energy and cheerful disposition. The salary she'd bring in would barely match what she earned waitressing, but it came with benefits and the advantage of nearly free child care.

Jo had interviewed last week, taking along the names and numbers of several families whose children she'd babysat over the past few years.

Jo pulled out of a hug with Fiona. "The director didn't even seem to mind that I'm practically going to need time off before I start. She said she hopes I'll recommend the place to other new mothers I meet."

Then Jo tried to hug Delia, but their protruding stomachs made it difficult.

"How about some cake to celebrate?" Patti offered.

After they were all buzzing on sugar, they opened gifts and Jo got weepy over each and every children's book she received. Margaret had also bought her a baby blanket that matched the one the little boy in the accompanying story dragged around in the illustrations. Patti had bought a set of Winnie-the-Pooh books and a Pooh Bear nursery lamp. Delia had wanted to get Jo a Cinderella book, but figured that her son would prefer something a bit more macho. So she'd gone with a book on construction equipment and a play mat shaped like a little red truck that featured different baby-friendly activities and sounds.

Jo glowed with happiness. "With all the stuff in my apartment, I'm really beginning to feel like the baby is coming, you know? The bassinet is ready and waiting in my living room, and the other waitresses all chipped in and got me this really fantastic baby swing. It can swing either back and forth or from side to side, depending on the baby's preference, and it has this adorable musical mobile that hooks on to it. It took Len a couple of hours to get everything assembled right. Thank goodness he lives only a few doors down, or I never would have been able to put it together."

Those were the kinds of comments Delia would love to see eradicated from Jo's vocabulary. "I'm sure you would have managed just fine if you had to."

"Maybe," Jo said with a skeptical expression. "But

it's nice that I didn't have to. Not that long ago, I was wondering if I could make it here without any family in Virginia, but I've just met the most amazing friends. Delia, thank you so much for everything. And, Fiona, for helping me get that job!"

Fiona shook her head. "We may have pointed you in the right direction and put in a good word for your character, but they hired you because they see how great you'll be with the kids."

They toasted their mutual friendships with a ginger-ale punch Patti had made and then talked about this week's book selection: *The Girlfriend's Guide to Pregnancy.* They didn't normally choose nonfiction, but not only was the pick an homage to Jo and Delia, it spurred conversation about how female friends sometimes reach a point of being able to discuss truths they wouldn't be comfortable sharing with family or husbands. In some cases, *especially* with husbands.

Delia caught Patti's eye, wondering how relations were with George these days. Around Christmas, Patti had decided that maybe Delia was right—if Patti wanted a little something extra in her marriage, she should just go for it. She had planned a night of surprise seduction for last weekend, when Leo was away on a ski trip with their church's youth group. Delia had meant to call this week, but she'd avoided talking to Patti because Delia suspected she'd wind up venting about Alexander and his date. She didn't want to have that conversation since Patti would, very reasonably, point out that it was Delia who'd let go of Alexander.

The party began breaking up when Lily stood, saying she still had some sewing to do on costumes for her son's elementary school play. Fiona walked out with her, and Margaret followed soon after. Kate stayed to help Patti clean up; Delia felt that she should assist, but honestly, she was so exhausted that the idea of leaving her comfy position on the couch was overwhelming. She missed the energy bursts of her second trimester; earlier this week, she'd dozed off for a moment in the shower and awakened trying to remember whether or not she'd washed her hair.

Jo sat in Patti's living room, looking around as if trying to memorize every detail of tonight, her smile almost shy. "I really can't thank you enough."

"You can and have! Don't be so quick to attribute your successes to other people. *You* were the one who followed up on Fiona's lead and called the children's center about the job opening. *You* were the one who charmed them during the interview."

"It's more than the job that I'm grateful for," Jo protested. "Have you ever felt like God or fate put someone into your life for a reason? If I hadn't run into you that day at Dr. Adair's and met you, been inspired by your strength, I probably would have taken Bobby back when he showed up—I'd done it before. Recognizing a bad habit is far easier than breaking it."

Delia, thinking about the frustrating first months after she'd given up smoking, agreed. Right now, the baby's health gave her extra incentive; she liked to think she wouldn't backslide once her daughter was born, but there were still times when she got annoyed or restless and thoughts of a cigarette popped into her mind.

"You just have to stay vigilant, strong-willed. Remember why you made the change in the first place and remove yourself from temptation." It's why she'd thrown away all her cigarettes, lighters and ashtrays immediately.

And while he had been a healthier habit, it was why she'd wanted Alexander to go. The longer he was at the town house, the harder it would have been to see him leave later.

Jo stood, gathering her gifts and making her good-byes. "Patti, thank you so much for hostessing this! You really surprised me. And, Delia, I'll see you at birth class, although…"

Delia waited for the rest of the sentence, trying to look upbeat at the reminder of another class. Thank goodness they'd be over soon—the weekly videos were not filling her with expectant joy over her own impending miracle.

"Didn't you see how *happy* the mother was when she held her baby at the end?" Jo had challenged, wiping tears of joy away from her own face.

"Didn't you see everything that happened *before* that part?" Delia had asked.

Now Jo smiled. "I realize birth class isn't the highlight of your week." She turned to Patti and Kate. "I'm not sure Harmony and Delia clicked. But good news, Delia. You might be able to skip out of a couple of sessions. Len suggested that maybe he could go with me."

What? Attending birth class was not something you did with a neighbor and casual friend. In fact, every other couple in the class included both the mother and father of the baby. "You're kidding. Didn't you warn him about the films?" She remembered the short grad student was easily flustered; he'd probably lose consciousness at a camera shot of a baby being squeezed into the world.

"He's from a big family," Jo said with a shrug. "Says he thinks the miracle of life is a beautiful thing."

Then he'd probably never been in the room when it happened...although it did sound as though he and Harmony would get along. The cranky, irrational part of Delia—which was considerable, given that she was very pregnant and very tired—wondered why she'd never realized before how replaceable she was. First Alexander, with that blonde in their restaurant. Now Jo, replacing her with Len. Hell, while Delia was away on maternity leave, her boss would probably just give Terese Delia's office.

She made an effort to keep her jaw from clenching. "Well, if you really want Len to be your birth coach—"

"No, that's still you! He was just thinking maybe it would be good to have a backup. Especially since you're pregnant yourself. What if you went into early labor, or got put on bed rest? That's not uncommon late in pregnancy for women over... Anyway, it's not uncommon," Jo said as Kate smothered a laugh.

Delia darted the other woman a quick look, and

Kate busied herself taking down streamers and pretending to give them privacy. Turning her attention back to Jo, Delia wondered whether this was a case for diplomacy or straight shooting. "I think you've been spending too much time with Len."

"What?" Jo sounded as surprised as Kate looked—she'd glanced over her shoulder and given up any pretense that she wasn't following the conversation. "He's a great guy."

"Which isn't the point. You just got out of a long and unhealthy relationship, and soon you're going to have a baby to think about! It seems like Len's over there a lot, making himself indispensable. You're always insisting that you can't do things by yourself. You owe it to yourself to try."

Jo was frowning at her. "You make it sound like I'm using him."

"That's not what I meant! It's just...you're used to being taken care of. First your parents, then Bobby. Now here's this nice guy willing to stand up for you, willing to assemble baby furniture, willing to go into the delivery room with you! You said yourself that bad habits were hard to break." And dependency, whether on nicotine or on other people, was among the hardest.

Jo's eyes were blazing now with a combination of tears and anger, and she grabbed her gift bags close to her like armor. "Len is not a bad habit. He's a friend! Like I thought *you* were."

Delia got to her feet, not sure how to make this

right. Giving advice came more naturally than apologizing. "Wait, I—"

But Jo was in no mood to be placated. She nodded a final goodbye to everyone and was driving away a few minutes later.

"Boy, that was fun," Patti said, obviously wanting to say more but censoring herself in light of Delia's expression and Kate's quick shake of the head.

After that, Delia decided that it was time she take herself home, too—hadn't she told herself she wasn't good company tonight? She felt deeply wounded to have the young woman who'd darn near idolized her turn on her like that. Was this how Kate felt during arguments with her stepdaughter?

Of course, the biggest difference was that Neve was a preteen; Jo, despite her and Delia's difference in age, was a grown woman. As Delia had said more than once, she was not the woman's mother!

You should respect her ability to make her own decisions. You tell her to be more independent, but then criticize her choices. Sometimes friends did that, though. Witness Patti's protestations that Delia and Alexander should have stayed together and worked out their relationship.

Was it better to stand by your friends and let them make their own mistakes, or to fulfill your obligation as someone who cared by objectively pointing out mistakes they themselves were too close to see? Delia had no idea. But as she unlocked the door to her lonely town house, Jo's hurt and angry expression slashed through her mind.

If I suck at being a mother as much as I suck at being a fairy godmother, my daughter is doomed.

Chapter 14

All of us, at one time or another, hurt people we love. Thank God forgiveness is part of loving.

"So I was just calling…again…to say how sorry I am," Delia said into the phone on Saturday. Her first message to Jo had simply said she wanted to talk. When that call hadn't been returned, she'd tried again, saying she wanted to "apologize for hurting Jo's feelings." A true sentiment, without negating any of the points Delia had tried to make at the book club meeting. Now Delia just wanted to make sure things were all right between her and Jo. The young woman's unexpected friendship had come to be surprisingly important to Delia, and she didn't want it to end because they were both hormonal and annoyed with each other. So this latest message was a flat-out apology, without the implied disclaimer.

At the knock on her door Delia jerked her head around. Was it possible Jo had decided they should work it out in person?

But it was Patti who stood on the other side of the door, wearing a we-need-to-talk expression along with blue jeans and a long-sleeved polo shirt. "Hi."

"Hey, this is a nice surprise. I wasn't expecting you this morning."

"That's because sneak attacks are rarely announced in advance," Patti said with a teasing smile that didn't meet her eyes.

"And this is a sneak attack?"

"We can call it an intervention, if you like."

That didn't sound good. Delia didn't ask any more questions as they each took a seat. She wasn't sure she'd like the answers.

"I left you a voice mail the other day," Patti said. "After the shower."

"It was a busy week at work." Delia defended herself. "I was planning to call you this weekend."

Patti arched an eyebrow, saying nothing.

"I was!" Delia sighed. "And before you hassle me about it, I've called Jo. Multiple times. I was leaving her another message when you knocked. I was in a bad mood this week, and my tone when I spoke to her may have been—"

"So you're not deliberately trying to push her away?" Patti looked genuinely shocked.

"Of course not! What kind of idiot deliberately sabotages their friendships?"

"The same kind who deliberately kicks out the man she loves, then stops talking much to her other friends." For the first time, Patti let some of the hurt in her own gaze show. "I feel like you've been avoiding me. Then I hear you give this lecture about being self-sufficient..."

"It's not a new lecture," Delia pointed out. "It's the same philosophy I've had since I met you, and we've managed to stay friends. As I said, it's just been a bad week."

"You want to talk about it?" Anticipating Delia's shake of the head, Patti followed up with, "Talking is what friends do."

Delia sighed, both recognizing the point as valid and feeling she needed to do penance for the way she'd behaved at Patti's house, ruining the end of what had been a truly enjoyable evening. "Ringo's dating." She shouldn't call him that now, it had been a personal endearment, a stupid one at that, and he wasn't hers to endear anymore.

"Ah." Patti sat back in her chair, looking both surprised by the information and enlightened. "I wondered if there was something more to your harsh tone the other night. You're right about your philosophy not being new, but I didn't think Len's assembling a baby swing was enough of a reason for you to get your big ol' maternity panties in a bunch."

Big ol' maternity panties? "I was just trying to

look out for her." This late in her pregnancy, Jo was in an emotionally delicate state.

"Ironic," Patti said, "since you keep admonishing *her* to look out for herself. Surely you see the paradox there?"

"Aren't I allowed to be irrational in the third trimester?"

"Sure. It's plenty irrational but understandable to push Alexander away, then be upset that he's seeing someone else." She paused before asking in a gentler tone, "It's not serious, is it?"

How would Delia know? She'd have to talk to Alexander to find out, and that kind of communication hadn't been strong even when they *were* together. "No idea. But she's cute, I can tell you that."

"Oh, it's someone you know?" Sympathy laced Patti's voice.

"No. Total stranger, not anyone from our social circle." She ruthlessly quashed her curiosity over how and when Alexander had met her and what they might mean to each other. "I ran into them on their date." At the beginning of it, thankfully. If she'd had to watch them leave, hand in hand, imagining Alexander kissing the woman good-night or even—

Delia slammed her mind closed on that particular image, having just discovered something that would be even more horrible to watch than those birth films.

"I doubt it's serious," Patti said, answering her own earlier question. "I saw how he watched you all night at the fund-raiser."

"That was October. This is January. A lot can change in four months."

"Maybe, but it's hard to believe those emotions would have completely disappeared."

Delia laughed dryly. "Emotion is susceptible to all sorts of changes, and I don't think time limits apply. I have a picture somewhere of my parents' wedding. The first one. They looked deliriously in love." Even before the affair came to light, she had memories of her mother trying too hard, needy in her attempts to be the perfect wife and goad a more emotional response from her husband.

"And they're why you never wanted to get married?"

"I've never understood having to defend *not* wanting to get married. When you do something that life changing, you'd better have a whole heap of reasons. It shouldn't be something two people do just because they can't come up with an eloquent excuse not to. Although, as long as we're on the subject of spouses… Why don't you tell me what happened with you and George? I have no love life of my own these days, so spill all the salacious details."

"That implies that there are salacious details to share."

Delia was confused; Patti's dry tone seemed at odds with her grin. "The seduction didn't go as planned?"

"Hardly. But then, seduction was a stupid idea," Patti said firmly.

"Hey! If I remember correctly, it was *my* idea." She

was batting a thousand these days. Maybe Delia could work at home writing her own relationship column; as long as people did the direct opposite of whatever she advised, they'd have great success.

"For you, seduction might not have been a bad idea. You take to it more naturally than I do. I'm a suburban housewife and soccer mom who bakes brownies."

"You're more than just that! You can be anyone you want, Patti."

"I know. And it turns out, I like being a suburban housewife. I guess I forgot that. Hearing you and Kate talk over our lunches about everything you were doing on the job, your busy work schedules and wearing suits, then George waxing rhapsodic about Marilyn, I felt dull in comparison, and because our love life isn't the same as it was in our twenties, I convinced myself George saw me as dowdy. It was a mistake to try to capture that former glory instead of celebrate what we have now. A big mistake," she added with resigned amusement.

"How big?"

"I think I put the lingerie on wrong, satin sheets are more slippery than romantic and, at a certain point in your life, you shouldn't attempt particular activities or your husband will throw his back out."

"He threw his back out? Patti, you animal."

"The thing is, when you get down to it, the sex was no better than it's been the rest of the time. What makes it good is how we feel about each other, not the setting or position or even the technique."

"A good technique helps," Delia intoned.

"While I was taking care of him after he hurt himself, I told him I was just tired of feeling like a second-class citizen in the house, feeling either invisible, or asking permission, the way I did when I brought up college courses. I think putting together the book club was the first thing I've done in years that I haven't sought his opinion on before doing. When I asked him about my taking on the October fund-raiser, he shrugged and pointed out that I did fund-raisers every year and it made no difference to him. In retrospect, I don't think he meant to sound as if it didn't care about what I do with my time, even if it did seem insensitive."

Considering what she herself had sounded like the last time she spoke to Jo, Delia figured she was the last one to throw stones at George's lack of sensitivity.

"One of the things George told me when he first hired Marilyn was that he respected her initiative. Maybe that's all I needed. Not a major life change, but some initiative. I started the book club, signed up for a Wednesday art course on campus and volunteered over at the hospital."

"For what?"

"Helping with classes for moms who plan to breastfeed—don't you dare laugh. Jo said the instructor she had meant well but sounded so dry and mechanical that all the mothers-to-be felt like dairy cows. She said that I answered all her questions *and* made her laugh. I have to do a brief training class, but then I'll be all set."

"Look at you go." Far from laughing, Delia was impressed.

"You're not disappointed that I didn't make bigger changes? Enroll in a degree program or e-mail George dirty pictures of myself at work?"

"Not at all. I'm in favor of drastic steps when they're necessary, but as long as you're happy…"

"The drastic Delia approach was definitely not for me. And, after careful thought, I doubt the Patti Jordan approach would be right for you."

"You mean, the whole suburban soccer mom thing?"

"I mean marrying Alexander. If it was something you strongly didn't want, then I was wrong to badger you about it. But just because you don't want the wedding ring and white picket fence doesn't mean you can't have happiness. There are couples who've been together for decades who haven't signed marriage certificates. Is it really Alexander you don't want, or just the ritual trappings?"

Wouldn't they go hand in hand? Alexander came from a fairly traditional family. It was moot now, though. He'd moved on.

"I should move on," she said out loud, surveying her apartment with a critical eye. The space no longer fit her— Of course, being that she was the size of a killer whale, *nothing* fit her these days. "I think it's time I call Hazel Watts to see if she could help me find a better house."

Patti seemed surprised by the change in subject but excited nonetheless. "If you get a new place, can

I help you decorate the nursery? See, this is the kind of offer I made before and feared that it was a pathetic attempt to fill empty spaces in my life. Turns out I just really like this stuff. So will you let me butt in and give my opinion?"

"Absolutely."

But there was someone else whose opinion was even more important; it was time Delia sought him out instead of making all the decisions on her own.

Alexander was surprised to see Delia's number on his cell phone readout. They hadn't spoken since he'd run into her on his ill-fated date with Grace. He'd been a poor conversationalist, wondering how much he should explain about who Delia was to him—not that he had a clear grasp on that himself. Once he'd volunteered that the pregnant woman they'd seen was in fact carrying his child, the date had quietly imploded. He'd paid the check without first asking if she cared for dessert, then forgot to thank her for her company. She'd even angled away from the quick kiss on the cheek he'd intended.

"Hello. Delia?"

"Hey, Alex. Did I call at a bad time?"

"No, not at all." Had she ever called him Alex before? He couldn't remember. Usually it was his full name or the silly nickname, nothing in between.

"I have some news and wanted you to be the first— well, one of the first—to know. I'm moving. At least, I hope to move if Hazel can find me a suitable house. She's going to line up a few prospects and I thought…

Don't feel obligated to come, but since I'll be picking the place where your daughter is raised, you're welcome to join me while I look around. You might think of questions I forget to ask or have a different take on the pros and cons of each home."

"You want me to help you pick a house?"

"Only if you want to," Delia said, sounding nervous. "Along those same lines, Patti is after me to register for things for the baby, pick a nursery theme, all that. If you're free one night this week, maybe we could, ah, look together. You've spent more time around babies than I have."

Which was nothing more than the truth, but Delia rarely admitted anything if it sounded like other people had more expertise or better ideas.

"I'd love to," he told her quickly, before she could take it back. Even if he had to accept that a romantic relationship with Delia was over, he was going to be a daddy. Since he planned to be involved in his daughter's life, it was a good sign that Delia was welcoming his involvement now.

"Thank you for calling me."

"Thank you for being there," she said simply. "Just let me know what night works best for you."

"Tonight is open. In fact, the whole afternoon—" He cut himself off, deciding his eagerness verged into desperation.

She didn't seem to notice. "Really? I wasn't sure you'd be free on the weekend."

"Delia, when it comes to being there for my kid, I swear I will always make time."

For a long moment she said nothing. Then, finally, very softly, "You're a wonderful man. I probably didn't deserve you."

Actually he didn't think he'd been quite so "wonderful" as recently as a year ago. It had taken the months with Delia, the repeated trips to see his family, the announcement of her pregnancy, to gradually help him figure out what he wanted from his life. "How soon do you want to meet?"

"You sure you don't want a theme?" Alexander asked, standing in front of a row of fake windows on the back wall of the store, all adorned in different nursery curtains.

"I'm sure. When have you ever known me to be that coordinated? Besides, I like the idea of picking out individual pieces even if they weren't intended to go together." Delia hoped her daughter wouldn't mind that the furnishings didn't match; if she did, she could help redecorate. Of course, she'd have to learn to talk first.

"These are cute curtains." Alexander indicated pale lavender fabric covered in pairs of pudgy animals and a small ark with Noah waving from the deck.

"No." She winced inwardly, then tried to soften her quick rejection. Although she'd been serious about getting his input, there was little disguising the fact that she had strong opinions of her own. "I mean, yes, they are very cute curtains, but Noah? I'm not super-religious. It feels blasphemous to decorate with Bible stories, considering how rarely I show up in church.

What kind of message does Noah's ark send to the kid anyway? That humanity sucked so much even God wanted to drown us all out?"

Alexander stared at her in fascinated horror. "You have one twisted perspective. What about the teddy bears and rainbows? Very cheerful!"

"She grows up in a room like that, she'll rebel as soon as she's old enough, paint everything black and start dating a guy who insists on being called Viper."

Alexander ducked his head, his shoulders moving a little. Was he amused? Exasperated? Alarmed that half of his child's DNA would be coming from Delia?

"I'm not sleeping much these days," she offered. He could take it either as a statement that she had a lot of time on her hands to analyze the possible ramifications of nursery decor, or as a reason for why she'd partially lost her mind.

"I haven't been sleeping well myself." His gaze darkened, any traces of humor disappearing. "The efficiency suites are no substitute for your bed."

Trying to ignore the hot tingles that shivered through her, she said, "It's probably not fair to Grace for you to make comments like that."

"Considering that I haven't spoken to Grace since our one and only dinner date, I don't actually think she'd care."

Oh.

"Which is a little ironic, if you think about it," he continued. "She was sweet and intelligent, the kind of woman I could take home to my family. Only, instead of celebrating, I think they'd be disappointed. Blanche and Marie hate that they didn't meet you, and Angie loves to gloat about having spent Thanksgiving with you. She and Mama really liked you."

Delia couldn't keep herself from asking. "What did Isabella say about me?"

"That you were hardheaded and stubborn, even a little abrupt. When Marie pointed out that these were some of our mother's qualities, too, Mama said that yes, they are…which is why she knows you'll make an excellent mother."

Delia grinned. "I liked your mother, too."

"Wait until you meet Blanche and Marie. All of you together is enough to terrify me."

Her grin widened. Poor Ringo. Three sisters and now a daughter. The number of women who could gang up on him was growing—not that he'd ever had much difficulty handling females. He— The chords of a Ramones song muffled but still audible, blared from her purse.

She fished her cell phone from the debris of keys and credit card receipts and packets of gum. "Hello?"

"H-hi. Is this Delia Carlisle?"

"Sure is." Was the call work-related? She didn't recognize the man's voice, although his shaky tone gave her a sense of déjà vu.

"This is Len—"

"Jo's neighbor?" Momentary surprise that he even had Delia's number gave way to realization and panic. "Oh, my God. Did something happen with Jo and the baby?"

* * *

Even though Delia and Alexander had met in two separate cars, he insisted on driving her to the hospital. "You shouldn't have to negotiate traffic on top of worrying about Jo," he'd said. Which sounded kinder than pointing out that she was too upset to drive safely.

Jo's water had broken and the baby was in distress. She was only thirty-five weeks pregnant! Most pregnancies went forty weeks; Jo was still two weeks shy of being considered full-term. Since Len hadn't mentioned any specific complications and nothing unusual had happened during her friend's pregnancy, Delia couldn't help reflecting that stress was bad for a mother-to-be. The fight they'd had days earlier…

Don't be so egotistical, she tried to bully herself. *The world isn't about you. For all you know, she's decided you're a pain in the ass and not worth stressing over.* But Delia knew better than that. Jo's parents had turned their backs on her, and the girl had come to look at Delia and her friends as a replacement family of sorts.

Delia blinked. Until that moment she hadn't thought about it in those specific terms, but weren't Patti and Kate her replacement family, as well? They'd been the first two people to hear her news that Ringo was moving in, and later, that he was moving out. They'd also been the first two to hear about the pregnancy. Though Delia was an only child who'd unofficially shut out her parents and their dysfunctional marriage, she was hardly alone in the world.

And neither was Jo! Delia wondered if she should call the book club girls to let them know about their friend's premature labor. Len wouldn't have all those numbers; he'd been able to get in touch with Delia because she was on the paperwork Jo had already turned in to the hospital. After a second's consideration, Delia decided to wait on contacting anyone else. She should get to the hospital, so that she had an update on Jo and the baby and could better answer questions later.

Alexander pulled through the hospital's circular driveway. "You go in and find out what's up. I'll meet you in the maternity wing after I park."

She nodded her brief but heartfelt thanks and hurried inside, guilt-stricken that she and Jo hadn't been on the best of terms. When Jo hadn't called her back earlier, Delia should have just marched over to the girl's apartment to apologize in person. Maybe she would have noticed something wrong, maybe she could have been with Jo when she was admitted to the hospital—living up to her job as birth coach!

Knowing these were nonsensical thoughts didn't stop her from having them, and Delia never would have guessed that she could be so happy to see Len. Hopefully he could allay the worst of her fears. He was smiling.

"I got here as soon as I could," she said by way of greeting.

"Just in time to hear the good news," he said in a goofy tone. "They just finished the operation. She didn't want a C-section, but the doctors said that the cord was around the baby's neck and that Jo wasn't progressing fast enough to deliver yet. She has a healthy baby boy!"

Eyes wide and unseeing, Delia dropped into one of the waiting room chairs. Amazing. This morning Jo had probably been thinking she had almost another month; now she was a mommy. In only minutes, she saw Alexander sprinting toward them—he was able to travel at a much faster pace than she was, which made catching up easier. He stopped a foot in front of them, black eyebrows raised in questions he didn't want to voice.

Delia stood, hugging him out of joy and the need to hold on to someone at that moment. "She has a healthy little boy!"

Alexander hugged her back, letting her decide when it was time to pull away. But, before he let go, he pressed a hard kiss to her lips. The move was quick, but substantial—more claim than peck.

Delia felt her knees tremble and was patently glad that the row of orange chairs was directly behind her. It had been too long since Alexander's mouth was on hers. How had she thought that it would be all right for him never to kiss her again? Did she really want to see him year after year, as their child grew older, and know that every kiss and caress was behind them? She'd been so relieved to hear that Grace hadn't meant anything more serious to him, which was stupid since, if he didn't end up with the blonde, he'd simply end up with someone else eventually.

When a nurse came to let them know that Jo was

in recovery, groggy but holding her son, Delia pushed all thoughts of her fractured love life out of her mind.

"Is one of you Delia?" the nurse inquired. "She's asking for you."

Delia shot to her feet. "That's me! I was her birth coach, not that she needed me." Which Delia had tried telling the girl all along. It was funny because, in retrospect, Delia had needed Jo. Her friendship with the woman, giving her advice on everything from what to wear to the job interview to what model of high chair was getting the best consumer ratings, had helped fill what could have been a bleak and impatient time. It was tough being the only one to feel the baby kick and to look through baby names alone, instead of curled up with your lover on the couch laughing over the more outlandish possibilities. The prospect of being a single mother had become a lot more companionable because of the time Delia had spent with another single-mom-to-be.

"Right this way," the nurse instructed.

The sight of Jo in her hospital gown, a blue-wrapped burrito baby in her arms, created a lump the size of Rhode Island in Delia's throat.

"Hi," Jo said dreamily. She was either really moved by the circumstances or still coasting on the drugs.

"He's beautiful," Delia said immediately, peering down into the wizened little face. "How are you?"

"Fantastic. Except I'm wanting my money back from the birth class. Turns out that when you go into sudden labor and they have to perform a C, none of that information about pacing the hospital halls or bearing down is actually helpful." Jo's smile faded. "I just want you to know, I didn't not call you because I was mad. It happened so fast, and Len was right there…"

"Oh, honey, don't give that a second thought. This is your big day! I'm just glad that you're all right. Do the doctors…did they say why they think this happened?"

"No. They say that sometimes it's just spontaneous and no one knows why. Although it's apparently more common with women who spend too much time on their feet, and since I was reluctant to give up the waitressing tips as soon as I probably should have… I don't care why it happened. I'm just happy he's okay."

"Have you picked a name yet?" Delia asked. She was surprised by how much she wanted to hold the baby, but it seemed too soon to make the request. Jo was clearly reveling in her new role as mother.

"No. I have it narrowed down to a few, and I had this whimsical idea about looking at him and seeing which one fit best. Except, well…"

At the moment he was wrinkled and reddish. "Spend a few hours with him," Delia advised. "Then you can decide when you know him better."

"I have made one decision, though," Jo said. "Would you… I've joked that you're something of a godmother for me. Would you, officially, be godmother to my son?"

Delia Carlisle promptly burst into tears. It took five minutes and eight tissues for her to regain composure. "Oh, Joanne. I'm flattered, but… Are you sure? I know I project confidence and success, but the truth is, I'm a train wreck."

"You're not that bad," Jo protested with a laugh. "Most of the time anyway. You care, more than you like people to know. My parents may have been right about Bobby, but I still think they were dead wrong to just give up on me the way they did. You might be opinionated, but you wouldn't just walk away from someone you cared about."

Alexander's face flashed in her mind, the taste of his kiss still on her lips, and shame filled her. Even though he'd technically been the one to move out, everyone knew it had been her doing.

"I know you and your mother aren't close," Jo said. She'd asked one day whether Delia's family was planning to be here for the birth, which had prompted a summary explanation of how rarely Delia saw her parents. "But I think that just means you'll try harder because you want to do better than she did."

"Well, I am competitive." She thought it over. "Jo, I'd be honored to be his godmother. And since I never did get the chance to say this, except on your machine, I'm sorry about what I said at Patti's. If you're interested in Len, you have my blessing. Not that you need it! But I may have misjudged him. The way he's always there for you is inspiring."

"He *is* a great guy, but, Delia, the only man I'm going to have time for in my life for the next year or so is this little guy right here! I spent years with Bobby and now I'm a mommy. Why on earth would

I rebound with a neighbor I hardly know? This is the wrong time for me to get into a relationship."

Delia grinned weakly. "You have a good head on your shoulders."

"Don't sound so surprised," Jo said kiddingly. "But as long as we're talking about men who are there for you…"

"Is this where you subtly imply that I should give Alexander another chance?"

"If you don't, can *I* ask him out? I know what I just said about not having time for relationships, but some guys are worth the extra effort and emotional risk."

For someone so young, Jo was wise beyond her years.

When Delia and Alexander finally left the hospital that night, he offered to drive her home. "You have to be pooped," he said. "We can always work out something for picking up your car later."

She spent the entire ride thinking and stealing glances at his profile. He only got better looking with time, which seemed unfair since she'd recently stopped being able to see her own feet. The people she cared about and trusted thought Delia should be with this man. Did she deserve to be? Normally she insisted that she deserved the best—and Alexander was definitely that—but her track record for lasting relationships sucked. She hadn't even kept up a real relationship with her parents, which came so naturally to most people it was taken for granted.

She knew she could be a real pain in the ass. What

reason did she have for assuming her relationship with Alexander wouldn't fall apart?

It already has. They had broken up, yet still he was available for middle-of-the-night calls, weekend crises, following her around a baby supplies warehouse and listening to her inane commentary on nursery drapes.

Alexander parked in front of her town house, a flicker of emotion passing over his features. Nostalgia? Regret?

"Want to come in?" She invited him impulsively.

He was quiet for an eternity. "I'd better not."

She unfastened her seat belt and decided to take this as a sign. Then she called herself a chickenshit and added, "It would mean a lot to me if you could. I…think we need to talk."

His eyebrows went up. "All right."

Now *that* was a sign. Once again, he was there for her. She only had to ask. Which didn't come naturally, but she was a quick learner and strongly motivated.

Inside, she asked if he wanted to have a seat. They both looked to the empty square of carpet where his recliner had been, then Alexander joined her on the sofa, sitting close enough that the scent of his cologne tantalized her nerve endings.

"You kissed me at the hospital," she blurted. "And I…liked it." Stupid, tepid words, but she had no idea what to say. Admitting she was wrong came even less naturally than asking for someone's assistance.

"Delia." Her name was like a groan, a plea, an invitation for her to end both of their suffering.

"I miss you," she said. "I even... I..."

His eyes crinkled at the corners. "You can't say it?"

"But I feel it," she admitted, rushing to get at least those words out before she choked on them. "You have to understand, I didn't grow up in a family like yours. I spent most of my teenage years convinced I didn't even want a family, but I've been building my own. Kate, Patti, Jo. You. You're more than my family. You're my home. Since you left, this place feels barren. I think that prompted my wanting to move as much as the baby."

He looked stunned, speechless, a wary hope in his gaze as if these were the words he'd wanted to hear but had never expected. Why would he? She'd given him every indication that they'd never come.

"I don't think love comes easily to me," she admitted, feeling like a failure. Wasn't love a basic element of humanity? Something so ingrained it didn't have to be taught?

"That's crazy," Alexander said firmly. "Whenever you talk about our daughter, you unconsciously rub your stomach, loving her even though you've never met her. And you spent hours looking at nursery accessories, as if assessing what the emotional ramifications of a specific night-light might have on her! You know how to love, Delia, even if you're not comfortable with the knowledge."

Her voice was a bare whisper. "Thank you."

When he kissed her, joy bubbled through her, fizzy and golden, like a champagne fountain. She couldn't believe what an idiot she'd been! At work, when there was a great deal on the table, she usually advised clients to snatch up a hot property before it was taken by someone else and off the market. So why hadn't she realized sooner that she should pull Alexander close to her and never even let him think about being available again?

"I hear," she said between kisses, "that you're looking for a house. It just so happens, I am, too."

"Really?" His tongue traced the shell of her ear, sending little spasms of pleasure through her.

"Maybe we could find a place together, a place for all our stuff—yours, mine and the baby's. In fact—" She broke off, not because the idea was so overwhelming, but because he'd found that secret spot above her collarbone and rendered her incapable of speech.

He pulled away for a moment. "I don't want to rush you. Don't say this because you feel you have something to prove."

She laughed. "Rush me? How long have we known each other? And you might have noticed how I'm *extremely pregnant* with *your* daughter?"

"Our daughter." He placed a hand on her belly.

"Our daughter," she agreed before his mouth captured hers again. Delia wanted to think that, eventually, she and Alexander would have found their way to a more permanent connection even without the impetus of a baby. But the what-if game was always precarious. Maybe they simply would have parted after a few more months, the way she'd first predicted. Luckily, life rarely went as predicted.

Perhaps someday she'd thank her daughter for giving Delia the precious gift of family and love. A gift Delia intended to return as often as possible.

Epilogue

*Your nonna told me the day I married your father
that every family has its own traditions, its own
stories. This is ours.*

It took twenty-six hours of labor. The first few were
fairly easy before the pain really kicked in and Delia
started swearing in words Alexander said even he
hadn't heard before. The anesthesiologist's name
was Steve, and Delia informed everyone she came
into contact with that Steve was her new best friend,
even if he did wield a needle. At one point she offered to leave Alexander and run away with Steve,
which the doctor laughingly assured Alexander was
just the drugs talking.

After twenty-six hours and cursing in three languages—she'd had that semester of German in college, in addition to picking up some creative Italian expressions from her new husband—Delia DiRossi gave birth to their seven-and-a-half pound daughter, Elena. The baby's indignant howls after being delivered proved that she'd inherited her parents' combined temper; the way she wound all her subsequent visitors around her tiny, tiny finger proved that she'd also inherited a healthy dose of charm.

Patti got teary-eyed holding the baby the next day. "Elena, huh? It's a lovely name."

Delia smiled and leaned back against her pillow, more exhausted than she'd ever imagined she could be, but also more content. "We discussed calling her Patricia Katherine Isabella Joanne, but the nurse said that bordered on child abuse, unless she was a princess."

"Well, of course she's a princess," Patti cooed. "You're royalty, aren't you, darling? She's not even a day old yet and we're all her loyal subjects. Neve's already begging to babysit as soon as you think she's old enough."

When Kate and Neve had come by, Delia had been just waking up and wanted some alone time with her daughter, so they'd taken Alexander to the hospital cafeteria for an early lunch. It felt like the first time the man had left her side in two days. He had to be ready to drop on his feet, but he showed no signs of being anything other than deliriously happy.

About the time Patti was saying that she had to run—she had a test in her art history class today, but planned to come back that evening—Alexander returned with Kate and Neve. In one hand, he held a pink teddy bear for his daughter; in the other, gorgeous roses for his wife.

"I can't believe how tiny she is," Neve whispered, her voice full of reverential awe one normally hears in church. "I don't think I was ever that small."

Kate squeezed her stepdaughter's shoulder. "We should ask your dad if he knows where all the old albums are tonight. I'd love to see baby pictures of you and PJ."

Patti shrugged into her jacket. "I know it's insane now that I'm practically an empty nester, but seeing that beautiful baby almost makes me wish… Nah. I can always borrow yours for the afternoon without going through the labor."

"The *twenty-six hours* of labor," Patti, Kate and Alexander chorused.

All right, so Delia had been a bit repetitive last night in her complaints about the actual process. But, God, the reward!

She took Elena from her husband and cradled her daughter close. Her tiny, delicate features were so unbelievably perfect. It boggled her mind that she and Alexander had created this new life. *I swear we're going to do everything we can to be the parents you deserve.* Hopefully her daughter would turn out to be patient by nature, because heaven knew Delia and Ringo were bound to mess up a lot along the way.

After her friends had filed out of the room, Delia

cleared her throat, swallowing away the lump of emotion that had gathered there.

"Are you doing all right?" Alexander asked. Considering some of the things she'd screamed at him around hour fourteen, she was lucky he was speaking to her at all.

"Never better." With Elena nestled into one shoulder, Delia extended her free hand toward him. "But I owe you an apology."

"That's okay. The doctors did a quick X-ray of my hand and say that I may one day regain use of my fingers."

She smirked. "Whiner. How hard could I possibly have squeezed? Besides, that's not what I was sorry for. It's about us, about my being so slow to realize—"

"You don't have to apologize for that."

"You'd better take advantage of the sentiment while you can," she told him. "'Cause when the last of these pregnancy hormones fade away, I'll be back to being stone-hearted, ballsy Delia Carlisle."

His gaze was soft with love as he watched her with their baby daughter. "I don't believe that for a second, Delia DiRossi."

"I don't know why I was so scared of this," she admitted. "But thank you for being patient with me. I love you."

He squeezed onto the hospital bed as much as possible, encompassing his wife and infant daughter with one arm, their entire family in that shared embrace. Happiness like nothing she'd ever known surged through her, making her wonder what other joys were in store for them in the years to come.

Alexander kissed the top of her head. "Trust me, you were worth the wait."

* * * * *

We hope you enjoyed reading
READY FOR ROMANCE
by #1 *New York Times* bestselling author
DEBBIE MACOMBER and
MOTHER TO BE
by reader-favorite author
TANYA MICHAELS

Both were originally Harlequin® series stories!

Discover more heartwarming contemporary tales
of everyday women finding love and becoming
part of a family or community from the
Harlequin® American Romance® series.
Featuring small-town settings and irresistible
cowboys, **Harlequin® American Romance®**
stories are must-reads.

SPECIAL EXCERPT FROM

HARLEQUIN®

American Romance®

Read on for a sneak peek of
THE TEXAN'S TWINS
by Pamela Britton, part of American Romance's
TEXAS RODEO BARONS *miniseries!*

"You going to take off your dress now? Or later?"

The woman's eyes widened. *"Excuse me?"*

"Don't worry. My friends didn't know I was meeting a man. A project engineer, actually, and you don't exactly look the part. Nice try, though."

"Let me guess—Jet Baron."

"One and the same." He gave her a welcoming smile, his gaze slowly sliding over her body.

"Why am I *not* surprised?" she asked.

Her sarcasm startled him, as did the way she eyed him up and down. So direct. So appraising. So…disappointed.

He straightened. "If you're going to start stripping, you better do it now. I'm expecting the engineer at any moment."

"You think I'm some kind of prank. An actress hired to, what? Pretend to have a meeting with you? Then strip out of my clothes?"

He was starting to get a funny feeling. "Well, yeah."

She took a step toward him, and he would be lying if he didn't feel as if, somehow, the joke was on him.

"Tell me something, what makes you think the engineer in question is a man?"

"I was told that."

"By whom?"

"I don't know who told me, I just know he's a man. All engineers in the oil industry are men."

She took another step toward him. "There are actually quite a few women in the business. I graduated from Berkley with a degree in geology." She took yet another step closer. "I interned for the USGS out of Menlo Park then moved back to Texas to get my master's in engineering. My father was a wildcatter, and it was from him that I learned the business—so let me reassure you, Mr. Baron, I can tell the difference between an injection hose and a drill pipe. But if you still insist only men can be engineers, perhaps we should call your sister, Lizzie, who hired me."

Jet couldn't speak for a moment. "Oh, crap."

Her extraordinary blue eyes scanned him, her derision clearly evident. "Still want me to strip?"

He almost said yes, but he could tell that he was in enough trouble as it is. "I take it you're J.C.?"

"I am."

"I should apologize."

"You think?"

*Look for THE TEXAN'S TWINS
by Pamela Britton next month from
Harlequin® American Romance®.*

HAREXP0914

HARLEQUIN®

American Romance®

Save $1.00 on the purchase of

THE TEXAN'S TWINS

by Pamela Britton,

available September 2, 2014, or on any other
Harlequin® American Romance book.

Available wherever books are sold, including most bookstores,
supermarkets, drugstores and discount stores.

- ✂

Save $1.00

on the purchase of
THE TEXAN'S TWINS
by **Pamela Britton**
available September 2, 2014, or on any other
Harlequin® American Romance book.

Coupon valid until November 5, 2014. Redeemable at participating retail outlets in the
U.S. and Canada only. Limit one coupon per customer.

52611751

Canadian Retailers: Harlequin Enterprises Limited will pay the face value of this coupon plus 10.25¢ if submitted by customer for this product only. Any other use constitutes fraud. Coupon is nonassignable. Void if taxed, prohibited or restricted by law. Consumer must pay any government taxes. Void if copied. Millennium Promotional Services ("M1P") customers submit coupons and proof of sales to Harlequin Enterprises Limited, P.O. Box 3000, Saint John, NB E2L 4L3, Canada. Non-M1P retailer—for reimbursement submit coupons and proof of sales directly to Harlequin Enterprises Limited, Retail Marketing Department, 225 Duncan Mill Rd., Don Mills, ON M3B 3K9, Canada.

U.S. Retailers: Harlequin Enterprises Limited will pay the face value of this coupon plus 8¢ if submitted by customer for this product only. Any other use constitutes fraud. Coupon is nonassignable. Void if taxed, prohibited or restricted by law. Consumer must pay any government taxes. Void if copied. For reimbursement submit coupons and proof of sales directly to Harlequin Enterprises Limited, P.O. Box 880478, El Paso, TX 88588-0478, U.S.A. Cash value 1/100 cents.

5 65373 00076 2   (8100)0 11955

® and TM are trademarks owned and used by the trademark owner and/or its licensee.
© 2014 Harlequin Enterprises Limited

NYTCOUP08